Be

MW01717417

COLD DREAD

Bernadette Calonego

COLD DREAD

Translated by Gerald Chapple

dK darkKanada

Previously published as *Schrei im Eis,* by Calonego Media Inc. in Canada in 2023. Translated from the German by Gerald Chapple.

Published by Calonego Media Inc., Gibsons, B.C., Canada
bernadettecalonego.com

Cover design by Vila Design, viladesign.net (Photo by biletskiy_e/Depositphotos, eve134lin@gmail.com/Depositphotos)

Interior design by Inca Vogt, inca-vogt-autorin.com

Editing by Lindsey Alexander of Reading List Editorial: readinglisteditorial.com

Paperback ISBN: 978-1-7380648-2-3

For all the kind women in Noddy Bay and area who, after a hiking accident, helped me with food and errands and comforting words.

1

As he creeps through the dark toward the house, it starts to rain. He pulls his hood farther down over his face. A heavy, drumming summer rain. Luckily no thunder to wake the neighbors, and the moon isn't bright. He's not wearing a black ski mask. She's got to recognize him, to know he's the one inflicting horrible things on her.

She doesn't have an alarm system. She won't spend any money on it. He found that out by some clever questioning. How good is that? She feels so safe. He can't understand where women get this feeling of security from.

An outdoor light goes on. A motion sensor.

Not to worry; he'd counted on it. She told him raccoons roamed around the place, turning the light on constantly.

He'd listened carefully while she nattered on. Any information is important. She hasn't got a dog or a cat. Or a garrulous bird. He's got it all in his head. He stowed his bicycle behind some bushes a block away and then walked across the dark field behind the single-family homes. There's going to be construction there soon; the ground has already been staked out. Lucky he's still got time.

She's so naïve. Maybe she's never had anything awful

happen to her. Nothing ever knocked her life off the rails. Nothing shattered her belief in order, justice, and the regular course of events. No death from cancer in the family, not one serious car accident, nothing valuable ever stolen. There are people like that.

He's not one of them. He's about to destroy this idyllic life once and for all.

He puts on his gloves and tests the sliding glass door from the yard into the living room. It's locked. He could open it with a tool, but he feels too exposed. The neighbor's windows are looking right at him. He turns the doorknob on the back kitchen door. Locked. She's not so careless as to leave her doors unlocked. After all, she lives alone. She got the house in the divorce.

For a second he visualizes himself living with her here. He could persuade her to do it; he's convinced. He knows the rules of seduction, knows what not to say to ensnare women. She's met him three times for a drink and seems to be attracted to him. She's a good flirt. She's never invited him into her bed, though. She's rather reserved in this respect. She wants something serious. The divorce didn't frighten her off. It was an amicable one, uncontested; she confided that much to him. Even then, she suffered no harm.

He sneaks around to the side of the house, shines his flashlight on the cellar windows. Here's his way in. He takes the tools out of his jacket pocket, where the knife is, too, and gets to work. Not child's play, as he'd hoped, but not impossible either. Nothing's moving in the house. Sure enough, no alarm system.

It takes him ten minutes. He slips through the low window into the house.

He listens for any sounds, but nothing's stirring. He silently feels his way up the cellar stairs. A door. He turns the knob. It opens with a soft squeak.

He stops. Listens some more. Squeaky hinges are always

shit. Typical woman. He'd have fixed it with a drop of oil long ago.

The rain is hammering the house, swallowing up any sounds. That's fine. His hoodie is wet. He can't wait to see the terror on her face when she recognizes him. She won't be able to turn him in. The dead tell no tales.

The stairs are carpeted. A stroke of luck. Softly he climbs up to the second floor where her bedroom is. He's observed her there in the evenings. He has a knife in one hand and a flashlight in the other. The bedroom door is ajar. He shines his light down at the floor and slips into the room. He doesn't want any more squeaks until he's got his victim well in hand.

He sees an outline under the bedcovers. A sweetish aroma hangs in the air. Adrenaline's racing through his body. The blinds are down. He feels for the switch on the wall. Finally finds it. A soft light comes from a floor lamp.

In a single bound he's beside the bed and rips back the covers. The knife in his hand stops in midair. He can't believe what's in front of him.

He stares at the body for several seconds.

Naked and bloody.

A man.

His brain registers much too slowly what it all means.

Then he hears a soft squeak.

Somebody pushes the door wide open.

2

Detective Sergeant Calista Gates
Port Brendan, Labrador
Saturday, February 10

The snowstorm suddenly explodes with full force. I only see Gerald's snowmobile in vague silhouette. He's moving slowly so that I won't lose sight of him. The storm was predicted for tonight. It's eleven in the morning. You can't rely on weather predictions in Labrador all that often. Fortunately, we don't have far to go to Port Brendan.

Snowflakes stick to the visor of my helmet. I can see less now than before, but stopping isn't an option. It's only going to get worse.

The biting cold penetrates my face mask and helmet. I must buy one that's heated, like the handles on my snowmobile. What a difference from British Columbia, where just five weeks ago I was hunting a murderer out in the wilds on a snowmobile. Even there I found it cold, but it wasn't as bad as here.

Gerald keeps turning his head to see if I'm still following. As if he could see anything in this drifting snow. How quickly you can get lost in a storm like this! While I was in British Columbia,

Gerald was stranded on pack ice in Labrador. His snowmobile had run out of gas and he'd gotten lost in a whiteout. He spent two nights on the pack ice in life-threatening cold until a Search and Rescue helicopter found him. Lance Peyton, who was traveling with him, wasn't so lucky. He disappeared in the fog and froze to death. Gerald only had to have two toes amputated.

He sticks out his arm and comes to a stop. We've made it to the road.

I wipe a glove over my visor. Now I can see the nearest houses in Port Brendan. Relief winds me down. I didn't really have to venture out in this cold, but I wanted to stay active in the hard winter climate in Newfoundland and Labrador. I'm steeling myself—I'm the police chief in St. Anthony, after all—and they won't be transferring me back to warm Vancouver so quickly. I've come to realize this in the last few weeks. I won't be getting my job back as a profiler in the Major Crime Homicide Unit any time soon. I'm an undesirable in Vancouver. Three Royal Canadian Mounted Police officers there will be charged at some point if things go the way they should. I exposed their dreadful crimes but have yet to get a single word of praise from RCMP headquarters. On the contrary, I'm treated like a traitor.

We cross the road and head for Gerald's house. It's one of the largest in Port Brendan, bigger than the fishermen's homes, not ostentatious but appropriate for a contractor. Gerald surely had a large family in mind when he built it. But then he and his former girlfriend split, and he got to know me when I was still stationed in Port Brendan.

In spite of my thirty-six years, I'm definitely not thinking of having children. I'm wedded to my profession.

I take off my snowmobile gear in the basement of Gerald's home. My arms and legs are stiff and clumsy.

Gerald's gaze is on me. He grins when our eyes meet.

"Well, was that adventurous enough for you?"

"That's my quota for today," I reply. He hugs me, and I don't resist.

Almost nine thousand kilometers lay between us. Now it's not even millimeters.

Afterward we have gnocchi and pork tenderloin wrapped in bacon and pastry—I need a break from moose meat and salted fish. We'll drop in on Gerald's parents after lunch and bring a coffee cake. Until then, we want togetherness because we've had to do without it for so long.

Right after the first bite, Gerald bursts out with some news: "I've landed a major project."

I look at him expectantly. Something in his tone of voice makes me antsy.

"A tourist lodge on Crater Lake."

I stop eating. "Crater Lake, way up north?"

"Yes, the Ilungilak Crater."

"I thought it was protected and with no access."

"The lodge will belong to the Inuit. They'll supervise what goes on there."

Gerald's grandmother was an Inuk. He has connections to the Inuit regional government. I understand why he can get a construction job like that.

But there's something I don't understand at all.

"Outsiders aren't allowed in the Crater Lake area," I say. "Because it's cursed or whatever."

Gerald laughs.

"Not cursed, darling, sacred. It's a very special lake for the Inuit because it symbolizes their spiritual bond with nature."

"I believe you, but I've heard that bad things happen to people if they climb up to the lake."

He shakes his head.

"Things only happen to trespassers, to someone with wicked things up their sleeve."

He cuts himself a slice of tenderloin and drops it on his plate.

I'm having hot tea because I'm still freezing inside.

"But the Inuit have always defended themselves against intruders, if memory serves."

"That's right, because it wasn't clear until now who has sovereignty over the Crater Lake area. Now it's going to be a protected national park, Ilungilak Park, to be administered by the Inuit. But you're not to tell anyone because it won't be officially announced for a few days."

"So, will tourists be permitted there? How will they get to the lodge?"

"There's a landing strip for bush planes nearby."

I can imagine that Crater Lake will be a desirable destination. It's an especially attractive lake because it's evenly round, an almost perfect circle. You can even see its outline from space.

Gerald leaves the kitchen for a minute and comes back with some papers. He lays a page beside my plate. I glance at it. There are facts about the Ilungilak Crater. I browse through the text. The crater was created when a meteorite crashed to earth. Fishing or swimming in the lake is not allowed, but you can circle the lake on foot in about seven hours. The Inuit consider it a privilege to drink the water because hardly any other lake in the world has water that pure. The crater is solely fed by snow and rain. Experts estimate that it takes roughly 330 years for the lake water to renew itself completely. Ilungilak Lake is four hundred meters deep, and its water is so clear that you can see thirty-five meters down.

That's enough for me right now. I go back to my meal. The construction project is a great honor for Gerald, I don't want to dampen his enthusiasm.

Nevertheless, I must mention the four missing persons.

"When word gets out about the national park, the missing women will be all over the news."

Gerald obviously expected my objection. He nods.

"It's unavoidable. The women died because there was no supervision. They didn't have a trekking guide. They didn't have a clue. They were inexperienced and unprepared. It will all be different with the park."

Inexperienced and unprepared. Lost their way and died in the wild. That's what the media reported eight years ago. I was twenty-eight at the time and can recall the headlines. The locals expressed similar opinions. But nobody actually knows how and why the four women vanished without a trace. I was fascinated by this, naturally, as a young policewoman. My interest is aroused all over again.

"Maybe they were close to Crater Lake without authorization?"

The question doesn't please Gerald; he makes a crude gesture.

"Nobody saw them there. That's a stupid rumor."

"You've got to follow up rumors," I respond.

He frowns.

"There seem to be some people who have a good idea of what happened to the women. You mustn't underestimate the wilderness. It's not hard to die there."

"Those people should tell the police what they know. Are you one of them?"

His face grows hard to read.

"Tourists who take insane risks and underestimate danger give a place a bad name—unjustifiably. Even the police can't do anything about it."

I feel he's provoking me.

"Won't the Inuit resist if a sacred place like Crater Lake is suddenly thrown open to everybody? Airstrips and tourist hotels and who the heck knows what else?"

Gerald says nothing. I'm a killjoy during our first weekend together in the new year. He's otherwise never so reticent, especially with me. Something about the whole business must be making him jumpy. His silence tells me that I'm largely in the right. Surely not everybody agrees with the Nunatsiavut regional government's plans.

I don't say out loud that people disappear without a trace time and again in that inhospitable subarctic region. The four women weren't the first; they just caused more of a sensation.

Gerald's cutlery comes down on his plate with a loud clatter.

"I'm going to Crater Lake in three days to have a look around."

3

Fred van Heisen, RCMP Constable
St. Anthony, Newfoundland
Sunday, February 11

The polar bear tracks are clearly visible in the snow. A full-grown animal. Fred follows the trail until it disappears over the hill behind Goose Cove. Hopefully the bear will stay on the tundra, away from the houses. Somebody in Goose Cove raises ducks, and there's a chicken coop farther along.

Fred called the wildlife officer, but he's laid up with COVID. His cover is on her way to Goose Cove. She was baking bread when Fred contacted her.

"A polar bear at the beginning of February? Are you sure, constable?"

He can understand her amazement. Normally, polar bears don't show up before March on the northern tip of the island of Newfoundland, when the predators head back to Labrador after they've stuffed their bellies with seal meat. The Wilsons told him that polar bears were seen around homes in April, May, and last year, even at the beginning of June. Eleven or twelve years ago, a polar bear broke into the kitchen of a house in Goose Cove, terrifying the family. It killed another family's sheep and ducks but didn't eat them. The animal was obviously not hungry but very aggressive. The wildlife officer had to shoot it.

Fred has organized everything so it won't go that far this time. The bear will be anesthetized and returned by helicopter to the uninhabited north of Labrador in a net. Calista would not be happy if a polar bear were killed in the area that she's responsible for as chief of police. She's in Labrador this weekend with Gerald Hynes, and Fred's filling in for her. He's been doing this for some time. He returned to St. Anthony from Vancouver before Calista did. She stayed in her hometown for six weeks to undergo medical tests while he's been in northern Newfoundland for three weeks.

He shares station duties with Heidy and Dustin Wilson, to whom he had to deliver a precise report of all that went on in British Columbia. They also quizzed him about his fiancée. Presumably they can't fathom why he and Lucinda aren't married yet. And how could they? The Wilsons have been married for twenty-two years; both are in the RCMP and work together every day. It's completely different in his case. Lucinda lives with her family in the province of Saskatchewan, and he's happy with that. There's a lot he must think hard about, and the geographical distance between him and Lucinda—and Calista—helps make it possible. Calista was far too close to him in Vancouver. In every respect.

A snowmobile's approaching. And another. Fred makes them stop. They are young people; he can see that despite their helmets. They're not wearing face masks for the cold because that wouldn't look cool.

"Leave the polar bear alone," he shouts. "It doesn't fool around."

"We're just going to our cabin," the teen answers.

"You'll have to put it off until tomorrow. It's too dangerous."

"We gotta work tomorrow. We won't hurt the animal."

Fred knows the kid. He also knows he lives off unemployment insurance during the winter and there's no chance he'll be working tomorrow.

"If you don't want to get into trouble, then you'll head for St. Anthony right now," he threatens.

That's a language they understand. He can afford to be unpopular. He's going to a new posting in Saskatchewan at the beginning of June. As deputy chief investigator, he won't have to bother with polar bears.

"We've got rights, we're Newfoundlanders," a teenaged girl protests, but then they take off.

Fred watches the snowmobiles make the curve by the harbor. He hopes they won't try to cross the ice in the bay. A favorite test for show-offs. The layer of ice isn't thick enough anymore. A snowmobile nearly broke through two days ago. But many people think you can avoid that by going over the ice at high speed.

Then he notices that one of the snowmobiles turns and races back through the village, and on the road to boot, which is prohibited. He goes and stands on the road with a hand raised. The snowmobile comes to a stop just in front of him. It's the young man from a few minutes ago. He's shouting something.

Fred doesn't get it at first. He often has trouble with the Newfoundland accent.

The young man is yelling at the top of his lungs: "She's lying in the snow! Blood everywhere!"

Is this a joke? Are these kids trying to put one over on him? Do they want to distract him, so they can go on hunting for the bear? The snowmobile driver points to the end of the bay and to a solitary house with an unpaved road up to it.

Fred must respond; there's nothing else he can do.

"I'll follow you," he shouts and gets into his pickup.

The snowmobile turns and goes ahead, driving on the road once again. Fred suspects that the guy wouldn't do it if it weren't an emergency. The kids aren't all that brazen.

At the harbor he stops behind the snowmobile. The long road to the remote house isn't plowed. He sees the second snowmobile farther up. There's no time to get his Ski-Doo off the back. He gets out of the pickup, jams on his helmet, and climbs onto the seat behind the young man, who roars off at once. After about two hundred meters, Fred sees something lying in the snow. He can't make it out very well because two people are bending over it.

He slides off the snowmobile and tromps toward the scene. A woman's lying in the snow with her eyes closed. A down jacket is folded under her head. It is the yellow jacket he saw on one of the girls earlier. It's already red with blood, as is the snow. He takes the woman's pulse. Checks her eyes, wets a finger, and holds it under her nose. Feels some breath.

She's still alive.

He pulls out his phone.

"Have you called an ambulance?" he asks routinely.

At that moment he notes that the injured woman's hood has been placed under her shoulders.

"Yes," the girl says, who's now wearing the jacket of the other young man, whose arms are crossed over his chest to keep from freezing.

"Well done," Fred praises her.

He calls the St. Anthony station.

Dustin Wilson, who's on duty, picks up immediately.

"A woman in Goose Cove's badly hurt," Fred tells him without taking his eyes off the shape in the snow. "The ambulance has been called; please make sure that it's on its way."

"Hurt by a polar bear?" Wilson asks.

"No, by a person unknown."

He looks at the unconscious woman and thinks: By a person who did worse than a wild animal would.

"Where are you? I'm coming right now."

Fred gives him directions.

Then he turns to the others.

"This is a crime scene. I must secure the evidence and take your statements."

4

Tiffany Staid, Musher
Tulliq, Labrador
Sunday, February 11

She takes a quick glance at her dogs in the kennel. All there.

She's relieved. Somebody's been stealing sled dogs in Tulliq. The thief is either plain stupid or unscrupulous and smart. Another musher has had two dogs stolen. Where does the thief take them? It's not easy to hide sled dogs in Tulliq. Unless he takes them somewhere else right away. But how? And where to?

She won't let it come to that. She's even installed a surveillance camera. She can see the kennel and a part of the driveway. Sometimes she gets up at night and looks at the images on her laptop.

The dogs are her whole world. Her children. They're her lifesaver above all. She would never have gotten a handle on her life without those dogs.

Mom moved away from Tulliq. She left Tiffany's father, who beat her. She took Tiffany with her, when she was just four. It was a giant step for Mom, not only because she's Inuk. She found a job in a chicken factory in St. John's. Piecework. She earned enough for them to live in an old house with a yard. But Mom was rootless, without her culture, without family. She switched out her men as quickly as the color of her fingernails. Tiffany understands today the void her mom tried to fill.

The same void she used to feel in the past.

The dogs make an earsplitting noise. They want out, want to run till they drop. Today's a good one. No snowstorm. Dry. Excellent visibility.

She opens the kennel door. The dogs howl frantically. She got used to it long ago. The more excited the dogs are, the calmer she gets. Her calm is the counterbalance to the tumult; it's the only way she can control the situation. The dogs are each in a separate compartment so that there's no fighting, no bites if she's unable to supervise them.

She goes first to Pretor. He's hurt his left forepaw. She grabs him by the scruff of his neck and commands him to sit. Then she examines his paw. She's the doctor who disinfected the wound and sewed it up. There's no vet in Tulliq. The paw looks much better already. Pretor can run again with a leather shoe on.

She owns eight dogs. A fantastic team. She's worked with the animals for a long time. She's a musher, a dogsled driver. They didn't take her seriously in Tulliq at first. But now she has a reputation that nobody can take from her. And if anyone should try anything, she'd stop at nothing. That's what she learned on the streets of St. John's.

She harnesses the dogs in sequence to the front of the sled that's secured by a snow anchor. The dogs bark, jump up, pull at the lines, barge into one another. She puts on the pulling harness first. A strenuous effort that she has learned to tackle on her own. Two leaders are up front, her strongest dogs. The wheelers are closest to the sled, the swingers and team dogs in the middle.

Pretor is her lead dog. She wants to see if he can keep it up when they're at Crater Lake in a few days. She absolutely wants to have him there; he finds a trail with infallible dependability.

She's calmer when he's leading. Everything must go off without a hitch at Crater Lake. As hitch-free as possible, at least, up there in winter.

Her throat goes dry when she thinks about it. Nerves. But also joyful anticipation.

Anything's possible up there. A dangerous region if you don't know what you're doing. The terrain's unpredictable, Irvin told her. She learned the art of mushing from him. He helped her select her dogs. Pretor's the only one she bought without his advice. It was love at first sight.

She used to work at Remote Point Lodge. Mainly in the kitchen, but she also did some cleaning—a girl Friday. Later on, she led hiking tours through the tundra. That was before mushing. She'd saved every dollar for the dogs. For her dream.

The people who flew up to the lodge had money. They were mostly hobby fishermen. Solo travelers or with male friends. Most of them tipped generously when they returned with a good catch. The men's faces faded over the years; they were interchangeable.

On the other hand, the four women stood out. Tiffany will never forget them, although the group of four was only at the lodge for three days. She discovered in the news afterward that they were older than she'd thought; one of them was forty-two. Women like that keep their youthful looks; they can afford to. All but one wore makeup. They appeared in expensive outdoor wear. Brands that Tiffany can't afford.

She didn't find it surprising. Anyone coming to Remote Point Lodge had to have deep pockets. Not that the lodge was luxurious, but everything had to be flown in.

What baffled her back then was something else: the women didn't want a guide.

Tiffany feels her disappointment to this day. The guide—that would have been her. The long-awaited initiation with a trekking tour. She'd been so looking forward to it. And then it all turned out differently.

She squeezes Anaisha's flanks between her legs and pulls her harness on. Anaisha's just a year old, but Tiffany thinks she has a great future. She's still a team dog in the middle, but she's going to be a lead dog one day. Dogs never disappoint her.

The team is good to go. At the beginning of a dog-team race, volunteers must hold the dogs back at the starting line. Otherwise, they'd shoot ahead like a rocket before the starting signal. But her dogs don't run races. Tiffany has trained them for recreational tours. She's about to pull the snow anchor out of the ground, which has kept the sled in place, when she hears a snowmobile approaching.

Now, of all times.

She doesn't recognize the driver until he takes his helmet off.

Bud Abel. Since when does he own a snowmobile? He's never had that kind of money.

"Are you going out?" he asks.

As if it isn't obvious.

"Who'd you steal the machine from, Bud?"

"Not stolen, just borrowed."

He grins. He should finally get his teeth fixed. He's probably too lazy. The government provides free dental care for Inuit like him and her. Bud's her age, but his broken teeth make him look years older.

"So what's up? You're making the dogs jumpy."

"Heard you're flying to Ilungilak. With your team."

She doesn't mind everybody talking about it. She's proud to have been asked.

"Anything else?"

Pretor growls at a dog behind him. She doesn't need to have the lines get all tangled up.

"I wouldn't go there," Bud warns. "They're planning something."

She shakes her head impatiently.

"Of course they've got plans. Or they wouldn't need any dogs."

She picks up the lines on the sled again.

"Will you please get lost? I want to get going."

Bud keeps sitting on his snowmobile, helmet in hand. He doesn't make a move to leave.

"Make sure you take a gun along," he recommends.

As if she didn't know. Too many polar bears stalking around.

She loses patience. The dogs as well.

She rips out the snow anchor and jumps on the rear of the sled.

"All right!" she shouts.

The dogs race off, pulling the sled after them.

5

Fred van Heisen, RCMP Constable
St. Anthony, Newfoundland
Sunday, February 11

The stretcher with the injured woman is just being pushed into the ambulance as Dustin Wilson drives up. Fred is relieved, because he's had his hands full keeping curious bystanders away from the crime scene.

Dustin takes a quick look at the victim.

"I know her," he says, visibly shocked.

Fred found out her name in the meantime and made note of it. Nielle Helfrey. Nielle is short for Danielle.

"She cares for seniors in their homes. She's well-liked." Dustin watches the ambulance as it accelerates on the highway. A snowplow had cleared the road that morning. "This isn't an accident?"

"Highly unlikely." Fred looks over at the young people waiting at the harbor building. He can't stop them from talking to onlookers. Good that Calista can't see this.

As if reading his thoughts, Dustin asks: "Has the sarge been informed?"

"I haven't been able to get to it," Fred says.

He would like to turn that call over to his teammate. Who knows what Calista's doing in Port Brendan right at that minute? At Gerald Hynes's place. But he's her deputy and can't shy away from these things. He touches her name on his cell phone.

It's not long before he hears her voice.

"Fred?"

"Sarge, we've got a potential assault on a caregiver from St. Anthony, crime scene Goose Cove. Name of Nielle Helfrey."

She doesn't interrupt; no cry of surprise—she's too professional for that.

He goes on: "Beaten on the head, probably with a hard object. She was unconscious but had a pulse and pupil movement. Couldn't talk to her. She has a large head wound. Lost quite a bit of blood. She's on the way to the hospital. Dustin's with me. I've secured the crime scene, but four young people on two snowmobiles were here before me and pretty well trampled everything down. They discovered the victim."

"I'll leave immediately but probably won't get a flight today. Is it life-threatening?"

"Hard to say. I must speak to the doctor."

"What are you going to do now?"

"We're documenting the scene carefully; I've already taken photos on my phone. Then we'll question the four witnesses individually."

"Witnesses? Aren't they potential perpetrators?"

"Very unlikely, as I see it. But you never know."

"Do you have anything on the victim's background?"

"No, just that she cared for old people in their homes."

"Good. You lead the investigation, then we'll know more when I'm back. What's with Heidy?"

"She's still in Corner Brook."

"She must come back immediately."

"'kay. Have you got a theory, Sarge?"

Might be that she's already figured out some connections. Her ingenuity impresses him every time.

A brief pause. Then she says: "People around me are constantly getting bashed on the head."

She must be very conscious of that, of course, because she herself was brutally attacked the same way in Vancouver over two years ago. Which she barely survived.

But he must put the situation in perspective right away.

"We've also had cases of gunshot wounds and knifings, sarge," he counters. "Not only broken skulls."

"Right," she concedes. "Give it your best, Fred."

She knows he will. He always does his best. But some things are impossible. He can't protect Calista from herself. From the risks she takes, for instance, with no thought of her personal safety. Or from the dark thoughts simmering inside her. She usually doesn't mention them, but he can guess what they are.

You can't sidetrack a highly gifted investigator like her in Newfoundland forever. Canada's highest-ranking police officer, RCMP commissioner Jill Perrier, knows that, too. She's publicly promised to advance women in the federal police. But often even her hands are tied. As Fred sees it, the old conservative guard in the RCMP is like a parasitic wasp that lays its eggs in living animals so that its larvae eat their victims from the inside out. He doesn't tell a soul, of course.

For the moment he's very motivated and anything but dejected. Calista has no doubts that he'd do everything correctly. She believes in him. She could have instantly organized the forensics people from Corner Brook. Until she makes that decision, he, Fred, is responsible for inspecting the crime scene.

He watches more and more people gathering in the harbor square. Dustin Wilson is talking with a gesticulating woman.

Fred speaks into the phone: "It looks like an interesting case, sarge." An inappropriate choice of words, given the tragedy.

They end their conversation.

Fred goes over to Dustin, who's at the harbor guarding the

driveway to the remote house. He's already put up crime-scene tape.

"Well done," Fred says in praise.

"What does the sarge say?" Dustin inquires.

"Heidy must come back."

"I've already sent her a text. She's leaving right away."

Fred resists making a comment. Heidy Wilson is in Corner Brook for police-dog training. The Wilsons recently acquired a German shepherd. Dustin's not enthusiastic that his wife has a new hobby and is often away training to be a search-dog handler.

Fred nods.

"First the crime scene, before it gets dark, then the witnesses."

"On foot?"

"Yes." They walk up to the site.

Fred hadn't noticed any footprints leading to the victim but had seen a snowmobile track instead, running not far from the house to over a hilltop. It doesn't belong to the young people who found the victim. They came from the opposite side and intended to go back along the coast.

"It's possible the victim came by snowmobile from this direction." He points east.

"And where's Nielle's snowmobile now? And where's her helmet?"

"Maybe she was on the rear seat."

"So, she knew the perpetrator?"

"I haven't seen any signs of a struggle."

The house at the end of the snowed-in driveway is not directly on the shore but somewhat above it. A modest frame house. No neighbors, and with a view of the village and the harbor. A wonderful view of a pretty little bayside community and the hills beyond it. A large white church stands on the edge of the community; in summer, hiking paths lead from it to the cliffs and the tundra.

"The house is uninhabited right now," Dustin informs him. "The owner's daughter has just told me her father's been living with her for several days. Her husband normally plows the driveway, but he's in St. John's at the moment. The father's eighty-three, but otherwise lives alone in the house. That's the way he wants it."

"So why did the caregiver come when he isn't even here?"

"And why was she lying in a spot where she can be seen from everywhere?" Dustin asks in return.

Fred wonders, too. There must be someone who saw something. Some bored locals sit at the window with their binoculars almost the whole day. Probably dozens of eyes are following Dustin and him right now.

They come to the spot with blood on the snow. Fred describes the crime scene verbally, recording it on his phone the way Calista always does.

There are far too many tracks; everything trampled by boots before he could prevent it.

And then Dustin grabs his arm and points to the snow.

6

Gerald Hynes, Building Contractor
Port Brendan, Labrador
Sunday, February 11

Dad always wants Calista to sit in the armchair beside the woodstove. He thinks she's still not used to the Labrador cold. Of course, it's too warm for her so near the fire, but it can't be too warm for Dad.

Gerald sees Calista slide her chair away from the heat.

Dad says: "Vancouver only gets two or three days of snow in the winter." He got that from the TV. It's inconceivable for him. "They don't have real weather there," he pronounces.

Gerald grins. No snow, no ice, no whiteouts, no storms—for Dad that's not "real weather."

"What do people in Vancouver talk about?" he wonders.

"The rain," Calista says.

Dad laughs, Gerald and Calista along with him.

Mom wants to know what's so funny. She doesn't hear well anymore but won't always wear her hearing aids. Now, since Calista's visiting, she's got them in.

Gerald's happy about that. The TV's in the background, as always. He's turned it down a bit. Outside, beyond the little windows, the storm's hurtling over the coast. Daylight's fading. Mom's seventy-six, Dad three years older. She was always the driving force in the household, but now he notices her energy slackening more and more.

Calista tries to engage the two of them in conversation. Gerald realizes that her Greek appearance must make her seem exotic to Mom and Dad. Those big, dark eyes with heavy eyelids. The striking mouth. She practically never wears lipstick, as it would make her mouth even more striking. Her slim, long fingers, like he's seen on Greek alabaster statues. She asks questions cautiously and responds to answers enthusiastically.

He marvels at this, because her thoughts must be in St. Anthony, where a caregiver apparently is in the hospital with serious injuries. Before they left for his parents', she talked to her colleague, van Heisen. Gerald knows it was van Heisen; he guessed it from the few words he overheard.

Calista spends too much time with her deputy for Gerald's liking. During her stay in Vancouver, the RCMP bosses had van Heisen act as her bodyguard because she had to be protected from an unknown assailant. The perpetrator has been caught in the meantime, but Gerald's under the impression that Calista's still in danger. Three Vancouver police officers were arrested thanks to her investigating and charged with manslaughter in the death of a young man. But they were freed on bail. Calista has clearly made many enemies in the police force because she uncovered the crime.

It's never good to make enemies—he knows that from his own experience. But he wonders whether that's exactly what's going to happen to him if he takes on the Crater Lake project.

Mom asks him what they had for lunch. She could ask Calista directly, but she's probably afraid of choosing the wrong words. Or fears that Calista wouldn't understand her accent. Mom's never lost her shyness in front of strangers. And yet she used to be a teacher and is not uneducated. She gave him his love of classical music. He played the violin as a child.

"Pork tenderloin in pastry," he answers.

Calista explains to her how she prepared it. She makes an effort to speak clearly and distinctly.

He's brought more firewood inside to dry out. He couldn't persuade Mom and Dad to come live with him; his house is big enough for everybody. But he didn't expect anything different. They want to be independent, although they aren't anymore.

He looks in on them regularly, as do his brothers and sister-in-law. They've considered hiring a caregiver to take over certain chores. That's why the assault in Goose Cove shocked him so. Who would ever beat up a woman who helps the elderly?

Calista didn't give him any details; it's a criminal case, and an investigation is underway. She's handed the assignment over to van Heisen for the time being because she can't be in St. Anthony until tomorrow. There are no more flights out of Blanc Sablon today.

Dad's turned up the TV again. "Did it snow in Vancouver while you were there?" he asks Calista. His favorite topic.

Calista smiles. Gerald sweats. She's so beautiful when she smiles. She's put up her dark hair for the visit, but when she's at his place she lets it fall down her back. He's aware that earlier he reacted to her questions somewhat testily. He's jumpy, which makes him feel uncomfortable, but he can't tell Calista the reason why.

"No, not in Vancouver," she explains, "but I was near Kamloops in the British Columbia interior, and there was a lot of snow there."

Gerald's only half-listening to her describe the region, the ski slopes of Sun Peaks, the hilly landscape, the mountains, the snowmobile rides. He's preoccupied with the crater project. If only everything works out. Calista's right: as soon as the Ilungilak Crater is proclaimed a protected national park, and as soon as the plans for the tourist lodge are announced, the fate of the four women will resurface. Their unexplained disappearance. He's not convinced it was an accident. But he's careful not to say so in public.

"What did you bring to eat?"

Mom's on firm footing again, now that the topic is food.

Gerald stands up. "A lemon roll." His parents' favorite.

He tries to catch Calista's eye. But she's looking at the TV. It suddenly goes totally quiet in the room; their eyes are all fixed on the screen. There's a report on the incident in Goose Cove.

"The injured woman is thirty-nine-year-old Nielle Helfrey," the announcer says. "She has been employed for eight years as a caregiver for the elderly in St. Anthony and the surrounding area. Her life is not in danger. Doctors expect a full recovery. The St. Anthony RCMP have opened an investigation into the attack but didn't give any details."

"Is she dead?" Mom asks, who didn't catch everything.

But Dad did, and Gerald sweats even more when Dad shouts: "Nielle Helfrey? We know her. She's from here."

Mom finally gets it.

"Nielle? *Your* Nielle?" She looks at Gerald.

As does Calista.

He's got to come out with it.

"Nielle's an old girlfriend of mine. She used to live in Port Brendan."

"Are you still in touch with her?" Calista fires back.

He's never discussed his former lovers with her. Why should he? It's enough that she knows about Melissa. A delicate situation. The man Melissa left Gerald for was found dead.

It is clear to him that Calista asked her question because Nielle's attack is under investigation. He might have information that's important.

"No," he begins, then stops short.

She studies his face. Intelligent as she is, she concludes from his hesitating that he can't say more with his parents present.

She gets up.

"Come on, we'll cut up the cake, and I'll set the table. You two"—she smiles at Mom and Dad—"can watch TV until we're ready."

She makes an extra loud racket with the cutlery in the kitchen. Music from TV commercials invades the room.

"What can you tell me?" Calista whispers.

"Nielle called me recently. She wanted to know when you'd be back from Vancouver."

"Did she say why she wanted to know?"

"She said she needed some information. But I had the impression that was an excuse. She could have got what she wanted from the Wilsons. She certainly knows them."

"You've never mentioned this."

He turns on the kettle for the tea to gain some time.

"I assumed she wanted to find out if you were going to stay in Vancouver forever."

"Nielle wanted to get back together with you?"

Under normal circumstances, he'd have been flattered. But these weren't normal circumstances.

"I really can't imagine that."

Dad comes in. As if he'd heard Calista's question, he says: "Nielle and Morris Tye are an item."

Gerald drops the tea bag.

"How do you know?"

"My dear spouse found out."

"Who's Morris Tye?" Calista asks.

Good heavens, Morris Tye. That can't be true. He looks back at her.

"Morris Tye is a member of the provincial parliament in St. John's, the House of Assembly. He got me the project at the Ilungilak Crater."

Calista waits for him to explain.

"What's the problem?"

He shakes his head.

"It's only a stupid rumor about them being an item. Morris is married to another woman."

"Maybe not for long," Dad says dryly. "If word gets out."

"Let's all sit around the table," Calista suggests.

Now she'll start to drill down, Gerald thinks.

That kills his appetite for lemon roll.

7

Ava Zittner, Criminology Student
Toronto, Ontario
Fourteen Months Earlier

The woman hesitates at the entrance to the restaurant, and Ava raises her hand to attract her attention.

She's chosen a corner table so they can talk in peace and quiet. The topic is too explosive for nearby customers to overhear.

"Ava Zittner?" the woman inquires as she comes to her table.

Ava described herself over the phone: a shocking green sweater and a silver newsboy cap. Fashion is something she's never bothered with. She always dresses however she wants. Anything else is a waste of her time, which she needs for more important things. Like her criminology studies.

"Hello, Mrs. Calambaro . . ."

"Martha to you. May I call you Ava?" She sits down with the alacrity of someone always on the go.

"Sure. Thank you for taking the time . . ."

"Tell me again what university you're at."

"Windsor. I'm in my third year."

"So, you've been looking into the Joe Salomon case?"

Ava doesn't fail to notice that Martha hasn't taken her coat off yet. So she must make good use of her meeting.

"Yes, I chose it for a seminar paper because the murder happened not far from my parents' place. I was nine at the time, but I remember how shocked everybody in Amherstburg was. We've actually had very few violent crimes for a city of twenty thousand. The Joe Salomon case was weird. But you covered that for the *KMP Evening News*."

Martha Calambaro was a young reporter back then; Ava figures she'd been around twenty-two, the same age Ava is now.

Martha gives her a quick smile.

"Yes, it was my first big crime case, and I wanted to do it really well. I would only go home to sleep."

A waiter appears at their table.

Martha orders mineral water.

"I've got to get right back to the office."

Ava's hungry but restricts herself to an orange juice.

"As I mentioned, an article of yours struck me. That is, one passage in particular caught my interest. You wrote that there were gaps in the criminal investigation. Things that didn't make sense to you. My feelings exactly."

Now she's got the journalist's full attention; she doesn't take her eyes off Ava.

"What stuck out to you?" Martha asks.

"The surveillance cameras around the house were turned on and off that night. Just Joe Salomon is caught on film. The cameras weren't running shortly before he broke into the house, and they didn't start recording again until he was coming in through the basement window. And they stopped shortly afterward. The police said the camera controls were defective and only worked sporadically. I simply don't believe it."

"I think you're right; that's how I see it, too. Somebody manipulated the cameras so you couldn't see what else was going on around the house. Anything else?"

"The knife that was found on Salomon. He was supposed to have a knife and a revolver on him. Why both? Wouldn't that be overkill? Another thing: the revolver used to shoot Colin Hatterbush was stolen, but the police couldn't prove Salomon stole it."

"What's your bottom line?"

Martha's listening. Ava feels she's being taken seriously. She's in her element and continues: "The court adopted the police's theory that Joe Salomon shot his victim—Colin Hatterbush—and that Fiona Gelp shot Salomon afterward in self-defense because she witnessed the murder and also believed that Salomon was really out to get her. What I can't understand is: Fiona was separated from Mr. Hatterbush. So what was he doing in her bed?"

"She said in her statement that they were working on a reconciliation. However, she was apparently afraid of him and hated him, which she told some people."

"That's really very strange. But where I'm going with this: somebody could have put the gun in Salomon's hand after Fiona Gelp killed him. Many people confirmed that Salomon was left-handed. But the weapon was by his right hand when he was found dead on the floor. And there were no traces of firearm discharge residue on his hand." She looks at Martha's face for signs that her words are having some effect. She doubles down: "Why were Fiona's fingerprints not on the Colt she shot Salomon with? Did Fiona clean off the Colt afterward? Or did she wear gloves? If so, why?"

The waiter brings Martha's water, and she drinks half a glass at once.

Then she says: "I remember there were two guns. The revolver that Hatterbush was shot with was lying next to Joe's hand. The police did not find the second firearm, the Colt, in the bedroom but in the living room on an end table. I've always thought that odd. So, did Fiona go down to the ground floor, gun in hand? That scenario bugs me somehow."

Ava nods vigorously.

"It's also odd that Fiona first called her sister, Ann, and only afterward the police and an ambulance."

Martha adds another thought: "Not only that. The experts disagreed as to the time of death for both men. To my mind that was never satisfactorily resolved. The investigators didn't try to investigate properly at all. They wanted Salomon as the culprit right from the start. He had a record of sexual assault. Second, he'd come on to Fiona previously; Fiona and he were seen in a bar together two or three times. Third, more than once her neighbors saw a man on a bicycle in the area behaving suspiciously. Fourth, the cops needed a win after they'd completely botched the pizza murderer case."

Ava's amazed at how vivid the investigation still is in Martha's mind. That encourages her to emphasize: "The missing firearm discharge residue didn't prove anything conclusively."

Martha nods.

"That's also suspicious. Shots were fired with the weapon lying beside Salomon, but forensics couldn't find any gun powder residue from the shooting. Really weird."

Ava glances at the list of points she wants to discuss with Martha.

"The crime scene was pretty well contaminated because Fiona let the neighbors in, and they stomped all over the bedroom before she called the police. And her sister got there even before the neighbors did. Was that really only by chance?"

Martha chews her lower lip as she reflects.

"Fiona evidently began a new life abroad under an assumed name after her acquittal."

"How did you find that out, Martha?"

"I heard it from police sources."

"Do you know where she's living now?"

Martha shakes her head.

"I got tied up with other things and didn't really bother with the case anymore."

Ava's disappointed. She'd tried all sorts of ways to find Fiona, without success.

"Martha, maybe you should review the case. Maybe experts could go over the sequence of events again. Wouldn't that be something for you? Was the blame pinned on someone for a murder he didn't commit?"

Martha shakes her head again.

"Nobody's interested anymore. Fiona was found not guilty. Salomon was unsympathetic, a sex offender—who knows what he was doing in Fiona's house. Certainly up to no good. And he's dead."

"But if he didn't murder Hatterbush, then the murderer's still on the loose. He might kill again."

"Or *she* might."

"Exactly."

Martha finishes her mineral water.

"You know what, Ava, keep doing your research. If something really exciting comes out—if you find Fiona, for instance—then there'll be something there for me, too, for sure."

8

Tiffany Staid, Musher
Outside Tulliq, Labrador
Sunday, February 11

The dogs are flying over the plain. Here's where they reach their top speed because the ground's flat. Irvin says they hit twenty kilometers an hour. He measured their speed. His dogs are faster than hers. He runs them in races. Her dogs are better behaved; that's why she's popular with tour operators.

Irvin's rough on his dogs. She saw him once whack an aggressive dog on the head with a shovel.

"You're too soft, Tiff," he's often told her.

Not true. She can grab a dog by the scruff of the neck, flip it on its back, and kneel on its ribs. She can show the dog that she's the master; she just does it differently from Irvin.

The snow's good. Not too soft and not too hard. She hopes it will be like that at the crater. She's proud that the Inuit administration asked for her. There are mushers who've been in the business longer. But it's *her* dog team that will be up there in three days.

At the same time, nobody has really explained to her what to expect in Ilungilak. She's heading for Remote Point Lodge to find out more.

The dogs dash ahead like a mighty river. Unstoppable, powerful, in unison.

Pretor shows once again that he's completely bounced back. It's great that his wound has healed. A blissful feeling flows through her body. She's at one with the dogs and the terrain and the mountains on the horizon. The snow's glittering in the sun that's broken through the cloud cover. The sled's bumping to the rhythm of the galloping paws over the ground beneath, and Tiffany's bouncing along with it.

The lodge is relatively easy to access in winter. The ground is swampy or stony in summer. You must go along the coast by boat, and then it's a hard trek through the tundra. Unless you hire a seaplane.

She doesn't like to admit it, but Bud Abel *did* frighten her. She was not scared for herself: all her worries are focused on the dogs. Everything depends on them: her well-being, her pride, her identity. And her winter income.

Nobody knows where the money for the dogs came from. She had no qualms about it. Many people have too much money, many too little. She found the cash by chance in one of the guest rooms in the log cabin the four women had booked. While she was dusting off the moose antlers on the wall, she caught sight of something in the space between the board the antlers were fastened to and the indentation between the logs. Who carries that much cash around these days and then forgets about it? Somebody who's up to no good. She knew instinctively the women wouldn't be coming back. She kept the money. Enough there for five dogs. She didn't buy them until two years later so nobody would get suspicious.

She hears snowmobiles. She can see them on the horizon, very small. Probably hunters. Irvin knows her plans and where she's going in case something happens to her. She also called the lodge to be sure that she and the dogs were expected.

Three snowmobiles cross her path twenty minutes later. The drivers wave but don't stop. Tiffany recognizes them from the village. They know it's not as easy to bring sled dogs to a stop as it is with a machine.

Not far to go now. She goes round a line of hills and the lodge comes into view. The frozen lake is covered in snow. It's all familiar: the six log cabin chalets, the low forest stretching out behind them, and the long, broad hill above.

Smoke rises from the chimney of the main building, which is larger than the chalets. Kellyann and Noshi never let the stove go out.

"Whoa!" she shouts, stepping on the brake. Its metal claws burrow into the snow, bringing the dogs to a halt. She immediately rams the snow anchor into the ground so that the animals don't run off with the sled. She takes the harnesses off the dogs, one after the other, and ties them to the building's railing, at some distance apart from one another. Then she gives them a snack and water from a container in the lodge mudroom that's kept warm.

Noshi sticks his head into the room as she's taking off her ski suit and boots.

"Need some help?" he asks. "You've come at the right time. I've made soup."

"Be right there," Tiffany says as she gets rid of her heavy clothes.

Minutes later she finds Noshi in the warm dining room with the big windows, a space that's normally reserved for guests, but there are none there at this time. He points to a plate across from him. He's grown a full beard since she last saw him.

"Where's Kellyann?" she asks.

"She's got a doctor's appointment, won't be back until the day after tomorrow."

Tiffany hadn't expected that. She's never been with Noshi in the lodge all by herself.

"Nothing serious, I hope."

"No, she just needs some tests."

Tiffany doesn't want to ask why tests are necessary. Noshi doesn't look concerned, so why should she be?

She sits down at the table; Noshi fills her bowl.

It's odd, without Kellyann. So empty.

Kellyann fills any room she comes into. She always looks like she's freshly showered—one of those irrepressible women who's always in a good mood. She wears a baseball cap and a ponytail in summer, braids and colorful woolen hats in winter. She stayed in Labrador because of Noshi. She's not only athletic but a good businesswoman. Tiffany's learned a lot from her.

Noshi's not all that smart about money, but he's an excellent fishing guide. Sport fishermen are basically the lodge's lifeblood. If it hadn't been for the incident with the missing women, there would be more hikers in the lodge these days. Kellyann won't hear of unguided tours, although guided hikes are too expensive for many people. This is what Tiffany has heard from tourists. By contrast, visitors always seem to have money for angling. The lodge website has lots of photos of men beaming with pride as they hold a big fish up to the camera. Many more pictures of men than of women, of the magnificent landscape, and of wild animals.

Tiffany notices how hungry she is. She can see the dogs out the window from where she's sitting.

"Kellyann recommended you to the tourism people."

Noshi never talks much except when he's praising his wife. But now he has to, because Kellyann isn't there. Otherwise, she takes over for him.

"What's going on at Crater Lake?" Tiffany feigns ignorance.

"Some government announcement or other."

"The Nunatsiavut government or Ottawa?"

"Both."

"I'll bet you know more about it."

"They want to build something for tourists."

"At the crater? Can't imagine."

"Oh yeah, but the Nunatsiavut government will control it all."

Tiffany stops eating and stares at Noshi.

"That's a no-go-zone. We don't let anybody in there."

Noshi breaks off a piece of bread and starts to chew.

"Not anymore. The Inuit just want total control over who goes in," he says with his mouth full.

"Tourists?"

"For sure. I've always thought Crater Lake would attract people."

"Fishermen?"

"No, they don't fish there but in another lake nearby. What's its name?"

"Cloud Lake. We've been fishing there for thousands of years."

"Don't exaggerate. Your ancestors didn't come to our part of the country until around 1000."

"There were a number of different Inuit groups here long before that."

"Yes, but *your* direct ancestors are the ancestors of all Labrador Inuit living here today; they derive from prehistoric Thule and didn't come here until 1,300 years ago."

Typical Noshi. He can be terribly didactic at times. Better change the subject. She asks: "What does Kellyann think of it?"

"Of what?"

"That they're going to build something at Crater Lake."

"That it's fabulous. They'll come to our lodge either before or after. And we'll fly people in."

"Won't they fly direct?"

"They'll have to spend the night with us if they don't stay at the hotel in Tulliq."

Why is Noshi so positive about it? Tiffany is skeptical.

"When the media find out, they'll bring up the affair from eight years ago."

The affair.

Noshi dismisses her objection with a sweep of his hand.

"People disappear in Yellowstone and other national parks. They're overrun with tourists regardless."

She'd like to say: But in those cases, four women didn't disappear all at once. She catches herself in time.

Maybe somebody will get the idea to investigate the incident again. Maybe somebody will make a Netflix documentary about it. Maybe the women's families will create a lot of angry noise about the matter.

Maybe then it will come out who's really to blame for their disappearance.

But Noshi says: "There were rumors at the time that the four of them tried to go to Crater Lake. Maybe they'll finally discover some bones or other clues if more people are running around up there."

Tiffany can't believe Noshi's just said that. Kellyann must have worked on him. It all looks like an advertising stunt. But Kellyann wasn't managing the lodge when the incident happened, of course. That was Noshi's ex. And she was shattered by the catastrophe. Exactly the way her relationship with Noshi was shattered by it. His ex lives in St. Anthony, working as a caregiver for seniors. Tiffany won't dare bring her name to mind when she's at the lodge, or else it might slip out. Noshi wouldn't like that.

No, they won't find any bones at Crater Lake, she thinks to herself, dipping her spoon in the soup once more. Because one of the women was smarter than the rest.

9

Detective Sergeant Calista Gates
St. Anthony, Newfoundland
Monday, February 12

Fred holds the evidence bag up high.

"Can we make any sense of this?" He lays the bag down before me.

He'd told me about it over the phone, but I could hardly believe it.

I stare at the object.

A little piece of dark blue material. A patch. A crown and three parallel stripes, applied in the shape of a gold *V*.

The insignia of an RCMP sergeant.

Like the one on the upper arm of my official uniform. But it's not mine—I checked immediately.

Dustin Wilson found the patch near where Nielle was lying. It was dusted with snow that the young people's snowmobiles had stirred up, but Dustin's eagle eye spotted a small irregularity in the white surface and investigated it. I am impressed.

"Can you buy a thing like that on the Internet?" Heidy Wilson asks. She came back from Corner Brook early, which I was glad about. The future search dog is lying asleep in the corner of our conference room. He's the sixth teammate in St. Anthony, along with the Wilsons, Fred, Rex at the reception, and me. Heidy takes her job as a dog handler very seriously. Since her son Adam began university in St. John's, she's needed a new task. I think it's all very good, but I would have chosen a different name for the dog. What German shepherd wants to be called Woolly? Really nothing woolly about him.

"I've only found buttons and metal pins on the internet," Dustin says. "But maybe there's an illegal trade in RCMP insignia."

The Wilsons seem to have switched roles. Heidy made her mark researching on the internet all summer and fall. She spent a lot of time on the computer, while Dustin was patrolling the streets on his e-bike. But now he seems to have discovered the World Wide Web for himself.

I can tell by the look on Heidy's face that he hasn't told her everything about his research. Suddenly there's an invisible boundary between the two.

"That mass murderer in Nova Scotia even owned a genuine RCMP uniform," Fred says.

We all know what he's referring to. In April 2020, a violent man in the province of Nova Scotia ran amok and shot and killed more than twenty people, a seventeen-year-old teenager and a policewoman named Heidi among them. He wore an authentic RCMP uniform and had a car that looked like a police car, with all the bells and whistles: police markings, siren, blue light on the roof, radar gun, and a metal grille between the front and rear seats. He used the car to travel around the province killing innocent people. It took a long time to discover he was the murderer because of the fake police car.

"He had the police markings made in a print shop where he knew an employee," Fred continues, "and he bought a lot of things online. He got some through friends or had goods shipped to a Maine address and picked them up there."

Heidy raises her eyebrows. She had her short hair touched up with bleach in Corner Brook. I take note of such things.

"Does that mean there's a mass murderer going around *here*?" she asks.

"No," Fred answers. And falls silent.

An eloquent silence. I find it better if we call the elephant in the room by name.

"Does this have anything to do with my rank? With me?" I scan the group.

Nobody says anything at first, then Fred utters a single word: "Perhaps."

That encourages Dustin: "You've probably made enemies, sarge."

Heidy immediately pounces.

"In Vancouver, but not here. That's simply absurd."

Heidy's on a collision course with her husband for whatever reason.

I defuse the situation.

"We'll keep that in mind in any case. Not in public, but among ourselves." I say it with some emphasis. Rumors spread like weeds in remote areas. "How's the patient doing?" I avoid the word *victim*; I want Nielle Helfrey to survive.

"She's in stable condition," Fred replies. "They took her to St. John's by helicopter. The doctors are confident."

I don't like it that the patient is so far away. Now we can't question her as soon as we could otherwise.

High time to give my team some more news.

"I found out in Port Brendan Nielle tried to reach me when I was in Vancouver. As far as I know at this point, she's told nobody what she wanted from me."

Fred shoots me a quick glance. He definitely suspects I got my news from Gerald. Can't do anything about it.

"I talked with her mother in Port Brendan," I go on. "She was beside herself with worry and couldn't really help. She said Nielle didn't have any enemies and she doesn't understand who would assault her daughter like that. She said something interesting, that Nielle wasn't supposed to work yesterday. But another caregiver was ill and canceled, so she filled in for her."

Heidy comes out with what everybody's thinking.

"Then Nielle wasn't the target of the attack at all?"

Dustin picks up the ball: "The elderly gentleman living in that house wasn't even there at the time. His daughter took him to her place because his driveway couldn't be plowed."

"The question is, did Nielle know that?" Fred says.

He's in his element as an investigator; I can see that. I like the way he gets to the bottom of assumptions.

I spread out Fred's photos of the crime site on the conference table.

"I can't imagine that Nielle was attacked at this site. The blood patterns wouldn't look like this. I think she was driven to Goose Cove from the actual scene of the crime."

"But there was a lot of blood at the site," Dustin objects.

"Blood on the snow always looks dramatic, but look here: it's all in one spot. No splatter around."

My argument seems to make sense to the team.

"I must mention another important fact," I explain. "Nielle Helfrey is apparently in a relationship with Morris Tye. So I heard in Port Brendan."

"What? That's a game changer!" Heidy exclaims. "Did Nielle's mother tell you that?"

"No, she denied knowing anything about it when I asked her. We should pursue it."

"That will be a disaster. He's a married man. And a politician. He won't say a word about it." Dustin sometimes verbalizes what's obvious but draws the wrong conclusions.

We must question Morris Tye, of course, whether he's a member of the House of Assembly in St. John's or not. We've got a crime to solve. Maybe Dustin doesn't like our discussion shifting away from the sergeant's patch and his discovery.

Fred makes no comment on Dustin's remark. I already told

Fred about Nielle's relationship with Tye; he's my deputy, after all.

Dustin's nevertheless right on one point I worry about that I won't keep from my team: "I hope that nobody will influence the patient while she's in St. John's. Meanwhile, we'll talk to some people here. For instance, with the caregiver who swapped her assignment with Nielle."

Fred pipes up: "We've already questioned the four people who found the victim. They were near the harbor when they noticed something dark lying in the snow. They supposedly didn't have a clue what to expect. I find that credible enough. But it's too bad they trampled all over potential evidence."

"There must be other witnesses," Dustin says. "In this neck of the woods, everybody sees everything. I'll be keeping my ears open around town."

"Excellent. We'll send out an appeal on all channels." I turn to Heidy. "Could you . . . ?"

Suddenly Rex calls on the internal telephone. He's discreet and never simply breaks in when we're discussing ongoing investigations.

"Sarge, the polar bear's been trapped," he announces. "The wildlife officer wants the police to be there when it's put into the net. Too many curious onlookers standing around. She's waiting on the road to Goose Cove."

10

Fred van Heisen, RCMP Constable
St. Anthony, Newfoundland
Monday, February 12

It seems like old times to him: he and Calista chatting while riding in a police car. They don't have much time. Goose Cove's only a short hop away. But he feels that Calista is trying to avoid the thornier issues. She sticks to talking about polar bears and how they're better off in Newfoundland and Labrador compared to other places. And how fascinating it is that there are polar bears in this world, and how she greatly admires the way the locals accept these unusual visitors so calmly.

However, she doesn't reveal that Nielle Helfrey used to be Gerald Hynes's girlfriend. Does Calista think he won't find out? He was stationed in Port Brendan for four years and knows a lot of people there. Is she protecting Hynes from something?

Fred has the impression she wants to keep her boyfriend out of their conversations.

Just as he doesn't mention Lucinda to her.

They go up a steep rise on the road that's a challenge in winter, even though it's been salted. Past the hilltop, the road goes just as steeply downhill; he mustn't get distracted by the panoramic view of the still, white landscape. Practically no wind, a blue sky—he almost can't believe it. The winter can be so beautiful in Newfoundland some days.

Does Calista think so, too? Or does she still long for Vancouver? She doesn't talk about her hometown. Nor about the blue rank insignia patch Dustin found in the snow. Is it a warning to her? If so, who in heaven's name smuggled it to where Nielle was found? He doesn't believe for a minute that Calista's absolutely safe in St. Anthony. Newfoundland is not far enough from Vancouver. Things are bubbling over inside the RCMP. A power struggle is playing out that affects her directly because she plans to be a witness in a court case against her corrupt colleagues. She's behaving like a woman who has nothing more to lose. That makes her dangerous. To others and to herself. And to him.

They pull up to where the wildlife officer is waiting. They find a large gathering of people already there. A captured polar bear is a welcome diversion when winter rolls around. The spectators hold up their smartphones despite the cold. Polar bear photos regularly go viral on social media. A man in St. Anthony made a video of a neighbor when she opened her front door and came face-to-face with a polar bear; it went all over the world.

Fred stops, climbs out, and shoos the curious onlookers away from the anesthetized bear. Calista goes over to the wildlife officer standing beside the trap. It's a primitive one: a wide metal tube with a grille on the front and a trap door at the back. It's mounted on a metal platform with two wheels that can be attached to a vehicle.

Fred leans down. The bear is slumped over in the tube, knocked out by an injection. The simple contraption functioned properly again this time. A large, sturdy net is spread out next to the trap.

The helicopter will be here in twenty minutes, the wildlife officer says.

Calista nods. She must be as relieved as he is. The polar bear will be set free in the habitat he came from.

The animal in his prison is oblivious. Fred can smell its scent. He's fascinated, but he wouldn't like to meet this guy in the wild without a gun. Polar bears have no natural enemies; they're the number one Arctic predator. When Fred's little nephews asked him about polar bears at Christmas, that's exactly what he told them.

"We can go ahead now," the wildlife officer says. She opens the trap door.

Fred helps push the trap upward so that the tube slopes down. The bear slides slowly onto the net on the snow.

The warden and Calista offer some assistance until the bear's fully on the ground. They wrap the net around the animal so it can be lifted by rope.

They all stand there looking at it, impressed. Fred studies the teeth and claws.

"The pelt is not really white," Calista comments. "Kind of yellowish."

"Right. The outer coat is not white; the hairs are hollow and transparent," the wildlife officer explains. "The coat absorbs the sun's rays. The skin underneath is black."

"How much do you think it weighs?"

"Three hundred and fifty kilos is my guess. But I could be wrong, of course."

A roar is heard, getting louder. The helicopter. In a few seconds it's hovering above them. A thick rope with a hook is lowered. The wildlife officer grabs it. Fred helps her fasten the massive carabiner to the net. She inspects it carefully before she gives the pilot the sign to take off.

The chopper gains altitude, the bulging net swaying above them. Fred sees the bear lying with its head up and its hind legs underneath. He can see the dark underside of its paws. Then the load vanishes in the direction of the ocean.

Calista thanks the wildlife officer for her successful effort.

They hook the trap to her pickup. The bystanders slowly disperse.

"Do you know who assaulted the woman in Goose Cove yet?" the warden inquires.

"We're still investigating," Calista replies. "Have you heard anything?"

The wildlife officer takes off her gloves and flexes her fingers.

"I was on the way to Goose Cove yesterday, and a snowmobile crossed the road from the right. I had to hit the brakes because it suddenly appeared out of nowhere."

She puts her gloves back on. A cold day.

"I saw something shiny and red," she went on. "It happened so fast. But I remember thinking, Has the polar bear struck? Which is completely absurd, of course." She shakes her head at herself. "But when an animal like that is running around people's houses, you're on high alert."

"You're saying the clothing was red?"

"I don't know now. It was like a flash. Red color. I watched the snowmobile drive off because I was mad at the person's thoughtlessness. But I didn't notice anything else."

"When was that, exactly?"

"The time? Let me think. When did you phone me, constable?" She looks Fred's way.

"I'd estimate about one thirty."

"Then it was probably going on two."

Fred takes out a notepad and writes it down. He doesn't take his gloves off. He'd learned in Saskatchewan how to write with them on.

"What was the color of the person's clothing?" Calista asks.

The wildlife officer hesitates before answering: "The jacket rather light, I think. Certainly not black or blue. Pants were dark."

"And the snowmobile?"

"Gray or silver."

"What was your impression? A young or old person? Man or woman?"

"On the young side. But it was hard to know with the helmet."

"Good," Calista says. "If anything else occurs to you, please let us know."

The wildlife officer promises, climbs into her pickup, and drives off, the beartrap in tow.

A few people are still chatting on the shoulder of the road.

Calista doesn't move off. She's frowning.

"Have we got a clue here?" he asks.

She presses her lips together.

He knows this reaction. It makes her full mouth redder than before.

He turns his head away.

"I think she didn't see any blood," she says. "You must always be very cautious in interpreting witness testimony. Particularly a day later. Your brain sometimes plays tricks on you. It puts things together that didn't happen like that. It all went very fast. In a flash, she said. The snowmobile might have been partly red. Maybe with red stripes. When she heard about the assault, she linked it to the color of blood. But what struck *you*, Fred?"

"The light-colored jacket she mentioned. Men around here hardly ever wear light-colored ski jackets."

"That could be a useful clue. If the attacker—male or female—was smeared with blood, he or she would have taken the jacket off. You can't go riding around looking like that."

"The snowmobile driver apparently drove very fast. Was he or she leaving the crime scene?"

"Or was the driver a witness and didn't want to get involved?"

Fred feels more alive. They are discussing a case and coming up with theories. He finds it exciting every time.

He won't be able to do this with her for long. Beginning in

June, he'll be the deputy chief investigator in Saskatoon. He still can't believe it.

It's better this way. Calista's taking up too much space in his life. Sometimes he feels like he's on an icy track with her, in the same sled racing into the depths. It might end well or it might not, but it's going down, and Calista's driving too fast.

He'd like to save her from the abyss. Save her from taking the fight to a very powerful opponent, a fight she can only lose.

Calista adjusts her hat.

"Let's go. We're going to pay a visit to Nielle Helfrey's colleague."

11

Bud Abel, Cook on a Food Truck
Tulliq, Labrador
Monday, February 12

Smoke rises from the mobile home's chimney. Bud parks his snowmobile beside the front door. The machine and mobile home belong to his friend. They're two possessions Bud would love to have, too. If he helps his friend, it might be possible. He never calls him by his given name; he's Iqaluk to everybody. The Fish. Nobody can remember how Iqaluk got that nickname; Bud's heard various versions. It's a sure thing that his friend has never been a fisherman; he's a wheeler-dealer.

As in: "You scratch my back, and I'll scratch yours."

No drugs. Iqaluk is too smart for that. Bud's in his debt. When he came out of prison, Iqaluk gave him a job as a cook on the food truck. But now it's winter, and the truck's in the harbor only in summer.

Nevertheless, Iqaluk has plans for him. If Bud's a good boy, he could really earn some money.

He opens the front door and slips inside. Heat from an oil

stove envelops him. He almost trips over the dog lying in the entrance.

Iqaluk's slouching on a battered bench and barely looks up from his tablet. The dog has put his head back down on his paws.

Bud throws his ski jacket on the floor.

"She's gone to the lodge."

"Did you follow her?"

Dumb question, Bud thinks.

"No, that might have made her suspicious."

"How do you know she's at the lodge?"

"I met some people on snowmobiles. They saw her in the vicinity."

"You could have ridden on the sled with her." The Fish says it as if commenting on the weather.

Bud knows he's joking. Iqaluk makes jokes like that. You've gotta watch him in case he really does mean it.

"Yeah, Noshi would have been real happy if I'd showed up there." He can crack jokes, too, when he wants.

"Kellyann's worse than Noshi. It's Kellyann you've got to look out for." The Fish lifts a cup off the table. "Make us some tea, Bud. I'd like another full bladder."

Bud plugs in the kettle and looks around for the package of tea bags.

"Over there, on the radio," the Fish says, pointing to it. Things in his place are found in the most unlikely locations.

"So, she'll fly to Crater Lake, if we don't shoot her dogs."

Bud doesn't bat an eyelash. Iqaluk would never shoot an Inuk's sled dogs. Not even if dogs were about to eat his grandmother. Iqaluk wants to prevent Tiff Staid and her dog team from flying to Crater Lake because he believes she'll be heading into a trap.

The Fish has a finger in every pie, but Tiff's bullheaded. She does what she wants.

Bud puts two steaming cups on the little built-in table and sits down.

"Somebody has to watch what's happening up there," he says. "Somebody has to smuggle himself in." He knows what the Fish wants to hear.

"We've got our plans, all right." Iqaluk dunks a hard biscuit in his tea.

Bud does the same.

"With all those security people, it won't be easy."

"It's Inuit country, goddammit!" Iqaluk shouts so loudly that his dog lifts its head to see if he must defend his owner.

"Will that cop from St. Anthony be there?" Bud asks.

"Haven't been able to find out yet." The Fish bites into the wet biscuit. Chews. Ponders. Finally speaks: "The truth mustn't get out. Not for anything."

Bud knows when he's got to keep his mouth shut. He's sweating. The Fish knows what he's doing, he tells himself.

He's just reaching for another biscuit when Iqaluk grabs his outstretched arm and says: "We gotta throw the pack some red meat."

12

Detective Sergeant Calista Gates
St. Anthony, Newfoundland
Monday, February 12

"I'll just be a minute," Trina Modeste assures me, carrying the dirty dishes to the sink. She comes back to the table with a damp cloth and wipes it clean.

I watch her from the chair she's offered me.

Her movements are calm and focused. She smiles at the old lady at the table.

"That was tasty, Mrs. Eddison, wasn't it?"

The woman smiles back but doesn't answer. She regards us with curiosity.

Trina dries her hands on a colorful towel.

"We can talk here. Mrs. Eddison doesn't have her hearing aids in; she always refuses to wear them. I'll clean up the kitchen afterward."

Fred folds his arms and leans back on the kitchen counter. He wants to survey the situation and leave the talking to me.

Trina sits down.

"How's Nielle? How bad is it?" she asks. Her hands are red

from the water, but her fingernails are flawless: a blue varnish, with glitter. How does she do it? I quit painting my nails long ago.

"The doctors in St. John's are doing their very best. They're confident."

Trina sighs.

"Do I have to be more careful after what's happened to her?"

"That's what we're trying to find out. Did she ever say she felt under threat?"

Trina shakes her head.

"No."

She's probably a little younger than me, maybe thirty-two or -three. She has two barrettes in her ash-blond hair, bright-colored leggings, and a sassy sweatshirt with squirrels on it, sticking out their tongues. I'd like to have them on my socks; I bought some in Vancouver with chess pieces on them. It seems to me that Trina wants to show off her sense of style. Nothing indicates that she was sick yesterday.

That's the first thing that interests me.

"You swapped assignments with Nielle Helfrey yesterday?"

"Me? No, I went to work as usual. Who said I didn't?"

I ignore the question.

"And Nielle? Did she go to work as well?"

"No, it was her day off."

"So why was she in Goose Cove?"

Trina shrugs.

"I'd like to know, too. Her client wasn't even home."

"Can you imagine how Nielle got there?"

"She must have walked. Wasn't her car down at the harbor?"

"What does she drive?"

"A blue Chevrolet Trax."

"When were you last in touch with her?"

Trina Modeste thinks for a second.

"Two or three days ago. She wanted to swap a day with me, but not Sunday."

"Do you do that off and on, switch assignments?"

"Yes, it does happen."

"How well do you know Nielle?"

"Not that well. We don't have the same friends. But I find her friendly and willing to help."

"Has anything been worrying her?"

"We worry about our clients. If their condition gets worse, we tell each other what to keep an eye on."

Mrs. Eddison pushes her chair back.

"May I watch television?"

Trina puts a hand on her arm.

"Yes, but first we must put in our hearing aids." She points to her ear.

Mrs. Eddison imitates her motion and giggles.

Trina rubs her arm.

"Is Nielle in a relationship?" I ask quickly.

Trina takes her hand off Mrs. Eddison's arm.

"We don't talk about such things. You'd have to ask Nielle's family." She glances at Fred, an inscrutable look.

"Why do you think she was in Goose Cove?" I've got the impression that Trina knows more than she's saying.

"Maybe she forgot something at her client's place. It's happened to me."

"Has she got a key to the house?"

"Doesn't need one. The houses aren't locked."

"Even with polar bears wandering around the village?" I can't resist asking.

Trina knits her perfectly lined eyebrows together. Her reaction surprises me.

"Yes, I've been asking myself, why did Nielle go there alone and on foot despite the polar bear alert?"

"I want to watch television," Mrs. Eddison repeats.

Trina stands up.

"Excuse me, I must see to her." She takes the old lady's arm, and they slowly go into the living room together.

Fred doesn't open his mouth until we're in the car.

"Why does she think Nielle was walking? We haven't wondered publicly how she got there."

"Maybe she simply assumed as much. She apparently thinks Nielle drove to the harbor and then walked to the house."

"But she didn't."

"True, but we haven't made that public."

We drive across the snow-covered tundra on the road from Goose Cove to St. Anthony. Fred swerves to avoid a flying cardboard box that somehow got on the highway.

"Someone told me that Nielle and Trina are friends."

"They probably think that because they're both caregivers for seniors and sometimes swap assignments. Which is convenient for them both."

We pass the place where the drugged polar bear began his homeward journey that morning. Nobody there now.

"I thought she seemed rather distanced, as far as Nielle goes," Fred remarks.

"Trina was in Goose Cove yesterday," I say. "She had to care for a client. And she didn't know that Nielle was also there."

Fred keeps looking straight ahead. He's probably organizing his thoughts. He seldom speaks impulsively, unlike me.

"Do you know what stood out for me, Fred? When I asked Trina if Nielle was in a relationship, she said they never talked about things like that."

"What's your conclusion?"

"If Trina often fills in for Nielle at work, then she would know when Nielle isn't feeling well. She *must* have some thoughts on that."

"Could be, yes."

"Does this get us anywhere?"

"Trina says Nielle has other friends. We must find them."

"I've got the name of another caregiver. Vyann Kippen. She and her husband used to run the Remote Point Lodge in Labrador."

"Okay, she's next."

The sun has vanished. A light mist has spread over the landscape; everything looks flatter than it is. Small lakes and low rises break up the vastness. When I drive along this stretch, I always feel like stopping and running free. There's a hiking trail that Fred and I explored together before Lucinda joined him in St. Anthony. The trail snakes over stony ground and past several bogs. Now it all looks black and white. My eyes glide over this expanse, my thoughts glide with them. I wish they'd get stuck on something. I need clear direction.

Trina probably knows better than to discuss Nielle's affair with anyone else—above all with the police. Maybe she's afraid of Morris Tye's influence. Or his anger if she makes him look bad. I've only been working in Newfoundland and Labrador for a year, Fred for approximately four.

"How powerful is Morris Tye?" I ask.

Fred answers surprisingly fast: "The guy has a finger in every pie. He's very ambitious."

"Aren't we as well?"

Fred turns off the heater. It's so loud.

"There's a rumor making the rounds in Labrador that he wants to get out of the province and have a career in national politics."

"How much could his extramarital relationship hurt him?"

"His wife's the daughter of a big-time player in real estate. I don't think Tye wants to jeopardize that connection . . ." Fred accelerates to make it up the steep hill outside St. Anthony. "Men sometimes risk too much where women are concerned."

"Is Nielle a femme fatale?"

"You don't have to be a femme fatale to wrap a man around your little finger."

In a different situation, I'd have razzed Fred about his comment. Or maybe not. That kind of teasing could take us into a tight spot, and I don't need that. So I say, quite objectively: "What have you found out about that?"

"Nielle's well-known for being popular with seniors and their families. She gets along well with people. She's patient and even-tempered."

We come into St. Anthony. He turns onto the main street that goes to the post office. The streets look dirty, with grimy snow on both sides.

I wonder how we can get to Morris Tye.

If I start tracking him, then I'll have powerful enemies *here*, not only in Vancouver.

13

Vernon Lindental, Bush Pilot
Tulliq Airport, Labrador
Monday, February 12

The hangar's heated, but Vernon still isn't warm. He doesn't fail to miss the irony: it's really the politicians' plans he can't warm up to. They all want to fly to Crater Lake in two days and announce the new national park with great song and dance. In the middle of February! Hard to believe. The weather's stable for the moment, but what does that mean? February's the worst month for snowstorms.

He usually never flies in that month except for emergencies. The Ilungilak park is no emergency; it's a marketing ploy by the politicians. Can't they wait until summer?

He's warned them: if it's dangerous, he's not going up.

If something happened, he'd hang for it, they wouldn't.

Like eight years ago with the four trekkers. Those women didn't stick to the prearranged route, or he would have seen them. He searched for hours on end. For days. Used up tons of fuel. Nobody ever paid him for it. All the thanks he got were attacks in the media.

No, he's not going to get sucked into that again.

He walks over to his eight-seater Cessna. A mechanic's fiddling with it.

"Well, everything okay?"

The mechanic nods.

"Tires and brakes are perfect. The prop, too. You've got a good crate here, buddy. Checked for moisture as well." He pats the Cessna's metal side as if it were a horse. "When do you have to take off?"

"They want me to take up supplies tomorrow." Vernon shakes his head. "Everything in boxes will be frozen by the time the politicians get there."

"Not your problem, man. I've heard they're heating the cabins."

"Who?"

"Inuit, I suppose. The Nunatsiavut government's organizing it."

"They're making a big deal out of it. They're even having a dog team flown in."

"Really? Who's the musher?"

"Tiffany Staid from Tulliq."

"Wow." The mechanic leaves it at that, says no more.

Vernon doesn't say anything either. He won't hear a word against Tiffany. She should have led those women as a guide on their hike eight years ago. She was barely twenty at the time. Noshi had trained her. Tiffany's a smart, tough girl. If she'd been their guide, there would have been no catastrophe. But the women canceled on her at the last minute. Did they think she couldn't do it because she was so young?

"They wanted to go it alone," Vyann said at the time. "I believe that was the point of the trek. That they could do it without any help."

Though Vyann was peeved, she wasn't the kind of person to lay down the law with her guests unless danger threatened. Experienced trekkers didn't need a guide for the hike along the ridge high above the river. Any number of groups and solo hikers had managed that route successfully. There had never been a problem. Vyann thought that genuine adventures should still be possible. After all, that's what Remote Point Lodge was offering their guests. An unforgettable experience. Not constant restrictions and rules upon rules. People had their fill of those in their everyday lives.

Tourists had to sign a waiver. Vyann and Noshi disclaimed any liability for their guests' activities unless a lodge guide was with them.

The four women signed the waiver. Three of their families tried to sue the lodge later for damages but had no success in court.

The mechanic's voice jolts Vernon out of his thoughts.

"Hope the dogs don't shit all over your plane," he jokes.

"It's not as bad as when the passengers puke all over the plane," Vernon says. He'd been through a lot in his twenty years as a bush pilot.

He had a smaller plane back then, eight years ago. Only six seats. The women were cheerful as they boarded his Cessna. Nevertheless, he could discern some tension in their conversation.

"Carla!" one of them shouted as they were loading their backpacks onto the plane. "Where's the backup cooker?"

"I'm Yellow. Have you already forgotten that?" the woman shouted in return. "Anyway, Blue's responsible for the backup cooker."

He quickly found out the women called themselves by the color of their jackets and not by name: Red, Blue, Yellow, and Orange.

That wasn't the only thing he found odd.

The mechanic wipes his hands on a rag.

"So who all's going to be at Crater Lake?"

"Dunno. They're making a huge secret out of it."

The mechanic grins.

"Well, it's not hard to guess. Morris Tye, for sure. He shows up everywhere when they're dishing out the credit. And a few reporters."

"The Mounties have run a check on me. As if I were a threat."

"Morris had better watch it," the mechanic says. "Somebody almost whacked his mistress in St. Anthony."

"He's got a mistress?"

"But of course! They all do. Hush-hush, naturally. Maybe she thought about spilling the beans, and he tried to get rid of her."

"Man, are you a gossip columnist or an airplane mechanic?"

At that moment the hangar door opens, and a young man walks in.

"Mr. Lindental?" he calls.

"Right here." Vernon goes over to him.

"Mick Hudson from the *Labrador Tribune*. I want to write something about flying in Arctic conditions. Can I talk to you about it?"

Vernon frowns. Mick Hudson. Never heard of him. Must be new. Looks like a rookie too. Arctic conditions! Exaggerating right away. Subarctic would be more precise.

Vernon shakes his head.

"Sorry, Mick. I'm too busy. Maybe another time."

"Just fifteen minutes. I don't need more than that. It'll be good advertising for you. I won't beat up on you, if that's what you're afraid of. I don't want to lose my job."

What a smooth talker. Vernon can't believe his ears.

"Like I said, maybe in a week. It can wait, eh?"

"My boss wants it in the paper day after tomorrow."

In two days. That can only mean the *Labrador Tribune* will feature the plans for Crater Lake.

Vernon wants nothing to do with it.

"Go ask somebody in Happy Valley-Goose Bay. You'll certainly find another bush pilot there."

"But you're the most interesting one of them all, Mr. Lindental. Your reputation is legendary. Everyone knows your name."

Vernon's heard enough. He was right to be suspicious. This kid wants to rehash the disappearance of those four women. *Everyone knows your name.*

"I've already said, in a week, maybe. Give me a call." He spins around on his heel and turns his back on the reporter.

But the guy keeps talking: "Someone told me you'd found a backpack belonging to one of the women. Is that true?"

Vernon has the sensation his legs are buckling beneath him.

He slowly turns around,

"Let's go to my office," he says.

14

Vyann Kippen, Caregiver for Seniors
St. Anthony, Newfoundland
Monday, February 12

She watches a police car pull up. Trina warned her. They'd already talked to her at Mrs. Eddison's place.

Vyann slams the door to the garage. She's sick and tired of police investigators making her feel she was to blame for other people's misfortune. And yet it was other people who caused *her* misfortune. Eight years ago, the Mounties had harassed her and Noshi for months. The lodge had barely survived as a result. And it wasn't even their fault. The four women who disappeared went off at their own risk. They could have taken Tiffany as their guide, but they refused. Although she's happy today that Tiff wasn't with them. Maybe something would have happened to her too. Maybe she wouldn't have come back either.

Those women had something up their sleeve. She's convinced of it to this day. She actually had closer contact with only one of them. The others called her Red because she wore a red jacket. Her name in the lodge's guest registry was Paige

Warner. Paige was in charge of logistics. She was probably super-efficient in her job. She talked about "island rationality" and "cascading."

When Vyann informed her that she ought to postpone their flight for a day because of bad weather, Paige declared she had to discuss it with the group: "We are not a pyramidal alpha organization."

Vyann never forgot that crazy sentence. And yet it wouldn't have been such a bad idea to have had an alpha person on that trekking venture. Someone to make the ultimate decision. Because you must constantly make decisions out in the wild. Should you stop for the night or keep going for another hour? Where's the best spot for the tent? Should you keep walking in the rain or wait until it stops? How much sugar for each person? Are those berries poisonous or not? Is the GPS indicating the right direction? How fresh is the bear dung you've found? How do we divvy up the food? Do we have to call off the trek? Who's carrying the gun? Who has the emergency transmitter?

Vyann spies through the curtain.

Nobody gets out of the police car for a while. Then the doors open, and a man and a woman appear. She recognizes Police Chief Calista Gates. Trina alerted Vyann to be on her guard with her. She asks something, and right away you can sense an ulterior motive.

Why are the officers just standing there? Vyann feels queasy. She's got something to hide, although she's not the only one. Everybody's got something to hide. Like Noshi, who carried on with that tourist. She'd been too preoccupied with the missing trekkers and the consequences of the calamity to pick up on it when the affair began. It was too late afterward. Noshi had already fallen in love with Kellyann. All the bad things began with that damn gang of females.

Tiff happened to overhear the four of them talking while sitting in the Adirondack chairs by the lake. Tiff never admitted it, but Vyann's convinced she'd hidden in the bushes to spy on the women.

Tiff told her about the conversation later, and she's never forgotten it.

"They're in for a big surprise," one of them said.

"So you've all kept mum?" asked another.

"Of course. Why do you even ask? That's what we agreed."

"I'm asking because otherwise it will all go up in flames."

"Don't you trust us?"

"Do you think I'd go along with it if I didn't trust all of you?"

"Then don't act as if we hadn't agreed on it."

There's a knock at the door. Vyann lifts her chin. She can keep mum, too, if she must. She's ready.

She goes to the door in her stocking feet and opens it. Her eyes fall immediately on the package lying in front of the door because the policewoman is pointing to it.

"Are you expecting a parcel?" she asks.

Vyann's about to bend over and pick up the box.

"Wait," the policewoman says, stopping her with a hand gesture. "Do you know what's in the package?"

"No. Perhaps someone brought it, and I wasn't home."

"But you *are* home."

Vyann doesn't get where the woman is going as she takes latex gloves out of her pocket.

"If you're in agreement, we will open the package," the policewoman says. She lifts the cover off the box, which isn't tied or taped.

Vyann emits a scream.

The two Mounties stare at the exotic bird lying in the box. Its wings are cut off.

"Oh, my God!" Vyann puts a hand to her mouth. "It's

Simmi. My sulphur-crested cockatoo!" The exact name is important to her; she's had to explain to people so often. She doesn't know anybody else on the Northern Peninsula who has a pet sulphur-crested cockatoo. Thanks to Simmi, she never feels lonely, especially when Marcus isn't with her. He helps his father at the lodge in summer; the rest of the year he's at community college in Corner Brook. He's learning to be an outdoor guide. One day, when Noshi and she are old, he'll run the lodge. She has seen to it that Kellyann will not take over the business. She and Noshi were agreed on that point.

She's about to bend down again to pick up the box, but the policewoman stops her for the second time.

"We don't want your fingerprints on it, Mrs. Kippen."

Fingerprints. Of course. No way she would think of that.

"Who did this?" She can't tear her eyes off Simmi's head and its crest feathers.

"May we come in?" the policewoman asks.

She takes them to the living room, where she collapses on the sofa.

The policewoman sits down on an armchair. Her colleague stays near the wall with the television, directly across from the empty birdcage.

"I am Detective Sergeant Calista Gates. This is Constable Fred van Heisen. So, the cockatoo was your pet?"

Vyann nods, then bursts into tears.

Calista Gates gets up, sits down beside her, and squeezes her arm.

"I know it's terrible to lose a pet. You must be so sad."

Her condolence relaxes Vyann.

"I've had Simmi for six years. I bought him because I felt so lonely after . . ." After Noshi left her for another woman, and she moved out of Remote Point Lodge.

"I can empathize, Mrs. Kippen. That's painful."

Vyann heard that Calista Gates is divorced. Her ex left her

when she was in the hospital with a severe head injury. He got himself another woman right away.

Dustin Wilson told her that in the RagnaRöck pub after two large glasses of beer.

"It's no secret now. The media covered it because her ex was done away with," the constable said that night to explain himself. "And everybody around here knows it too."

That wasn't correct: *she* did not know. She tries to keep away from gossip. Didn't she suffer from it long enough herself?

"When did you notice Simmi was missing, Mrs. Kippen?"

"Today. I gave him his food first thing this morning. Then I had to go to a client. I see him Mondays. When I came home . . ." More tears.

Calista Gates hands her a tissue.

Vyann finds her voice again after some sobbing.

"Simmi wasn't in his cage. I thought I must have forgotten to put him in. I often let him fly around the house. But . . . I did *not* forget. I know that for certain."

She looks at Sergeant Gates as if the whole awful truth hadn't hit her until then.

"Somebody stole Simmi."

"Who has access to your house?"

"I don't always lock the door. I often forget to." The policewoman must think she's careless, so she adds: "Many people in St. Anthony don't lock their homes. Nothing ever happens."

"I must ask you, Mrs. Kippen. Might it have been an act of revenge?"

"Revenge for what?" She looks at Calista Gates in astonishment. What does this woman know? Why does she think somebody would want to take revenge on her? Because of Nielle? Does she think the attack on her was an act of revenge?

The policewoman says nothing, waits for her answer.

Is she suggesting that Noshi might have something to do with her dead pet? But that was so long ago. It was a messy divorce, that's true. She didn't let Noshi off so easily. She wanted to make him pay for being unfaithful. But despite all that, Noshi has no reason to want revenge. He kept the lodge. He's got Kellyann. And he has a son who will take over the business. He's got everything he needs. The lodge is the most important thing for him and for her.

Or does Calista Gates think somebody's looking to take revenge for the disappearance of the four women? But why now, after eight years? She doesn't want to dredge up that story again.

When she acquired Simmi, some people made fun of her, calling her a birdbrain. Who's ever had an exotic cockatoo in a cold place like St. Anthony? But Simmi meant the world to her. She taught it to speak. It brightened her day, made her laugh. Particularly when there was nothing to laugh about.

"Does it have to do with Nielle's attack?" She must ask the question, to be clear about it. The police would certainly expect her to ask something like that.

Sergeant Gates's eyes stay on her. Vyann can't see any distrust in them.

"We're investigating," she says. "We're looking at all options. Maybe you can help us."

The constable near the wall clears his throat.

"Are you and Nielle close friends?"

She hesitates. Although mindful of Trina's warning, she responds anyway: "Yes, we're good friends."

"Has she told you that she's worried about anything?"

Vyann hesitates again.

"Will you keep this confidential?"

"We make nothing public concerning ongoing investigations."

She takes a deep breath. She must come out with it.

"Nielle has received anonymous threats. She believes Morris Tye's wife or her relatives are behind them."

15

Paige Warner, Entrepreneur
Toronto, Ontario
Eight Years Ago

She locks herself in the bathroom. She's riled up but doesn't want to show it.

How dare he! How can he leave her out in the cold like this? Three months before they were to leave. So close to their trip! They'd planned it all so carefully for two years. A trek through the jungle in Papua New Guinea. She and Howard and two married animal researchers, along with some native bearers for the supplies.

What an adventure! It would have fit beautifully on her résumé. Company bosses must be surrounded with an aura of daring, fearlessness, and stamina. She'd achieved so much in her professional life. Her company isn't large, but it's well-known. She's a showpiece for the success, for the vision that an ambitious, creative, assertive female entrepreneur can realize. She's made it all the way to the top, she, the daughter of a struggling pig farmer.

Her breathing is shallow. She opens the window. A huge

balloon fills her stomach. Howard had just a moment ago asked her to come into the living room and given her the bad news: the Papua New Guinea team has decided not to take her with them, saying that she posed too big a risk for the expedition. That she wasn't enough of a team player and made demands that were incompatible with a research trip such as theirs.

"Not a team player?"

She'd stared at Howard, uncomprehending. What did he say? Has he gone mad?

He remained unshakeable despite her protests.

So, she mobilized her calm but gritty negotiating mode. No screaming, even if his words were absurd. Stay relaxed, even if you're trying to force a person to his knees. But she hadn't expected this from Howard. She wouldn't have chosen him as her life partner if he didn't respect her.

"Teamwork is my strong suit," she declared, "nobody knows that better than you. Everyone works as part of a team in my company. That's how we've accomplished so much."

Howard looked as if he wanted to get this behind him as quickly as possible. At the same time, *she* was the one who hunted up the animal researchers, not him. She needed popular models for her products—hats that are lightweight and protect you in any weather. That didn't look stodgy but cool. Water- and dirt-resistant. That didn't make you sweat. You can crunch them up into a ball and they don't lose their shape. She markets her hats with a promise of adventure. It's like with SUVs. Most people drive them on regular streets and think they're so daring.

It's important to Paige that her advertising reaches younger people, not only retirees who work in their garden. The animal researchers are in their early thirties.

"It's a scientific expedition, not a marketing gimmick, which is how it comes across to the researchers." Howard talked like a robot. Had somebody indoctrinated him?

Stay calm. Businesslike, decisive. *Let money talk, Paige*, she said to herself.

"My company is financing part of the expedition."

"Nowhere in the contract does it say you're guaranteed to be part of the expedition."

That's correct. But it says that Howard will film the trip.

She felt as if she were lying on the floor and someone were pressing a foot on her throat. How foolish of her! She assumed that she, as a sponsor, would be welcomed with open arms. The renowned Paige Warner, spotlighting the couple's research project! Who wouldn't want that? A few damn scientists don't, obviously. They don't play by business-world rules.

"I'll talk to them." She was about to get up, but he gently pushed her back on the couch.

"Paige, it's been decided. I'm sorry, but it's a project with a lot of risks, and we can't endanger more people than there normally are."

"We? So you're going without me?"

"Yes, I'm on it. We're adding a student too."

A student! She's being pushed out by a student. She's shocked.

The cool evening air enters through the open window. She paces up and down the large, elegant bathroom she'd designed herself. Emerald green, silver, bamboo. She hears not a peep from Howard. He certainly knows it's pointless to try to calm her down. She's seething inside.

What are her options? She can't wreck the expedition for the researchers. They're wearing her products. That would hurt the company's reputation.

Her eyes fall on the black bathrobe on the wall. His bathrobe.

Howard's going without me.

That thought hurts her the most.

She'd so hoped he would propose to her in the Papua New Guinea jungle. At last, after seven years of living together. They're a photogenic pair. She's astounded that it's so important to her that the man ask *her* and not the other way around.

She's usually the one who's always wooing: customers, models, coworkers, the public, people on social media. All of a sudden, *she* wants to be the person courted.

She's already visualized it, the scene in the dank, semidark jungle. Apes screaming in the background. Tropical plants as décor. Howard taking something out of his pocket. He's carefully prepared. Looked forward to it. The love of his life. What other woman can say she was given a sparkling engagement ring in such an unspoiled, exotic wilderness?

It would have been a triumph.

And now, nothing.

The disenchantment burns like a hot brand.

She feels like hammering on the glass shower door.

Stay calm, Paige. Don't show weakness. That has always worked well so far.

Don't get mad. Get even.

Don't act like a sorehead. Act like an avenging goddess instead.

She opens a drawer, picks out a pillbox. Turns on the faucet. Swallows the tranquillizer.

Then she goes to her home office. She sits at her laptop and surfs the internet.

It takes her an hour to find something that fits the bill.

A crater lake in Canada.

A place sacred to the Inuit.

Now that *does* sound at least as exotic as Papua New Guinea.

No white people have ever been there except for scientists.

A lodge not too far away offers trekking tours. And bush plane flights. Remote Point Lodge.

Paige writes down the name. Looks for the account on Instagram. Her own company's on Instagram, too, but she herself is active on it under a pseudonym. Even Howard doesn't know about it.

Remote Point Lodge.

The pictures are spectacular. So is the wild landscape.

Driven by inner turmoil, she composes two sentences in the "Comments" section below the most recent photograph: *Wouldn't this be something for a small group of adventurous women? I'm all for it. Who wants to come with me?*

She gets her first answer the next day: *This looks absolutely fantastic. Am very interested in group trekking.*

Posted by *wonder_wick_it_woman.*

16

Vernon Lindental, Bush Pilot
Tulliq Airport, Labrador
Monday, February 12

Vernon takes a box off the one chair in his office and throws it onto a stack of them behind his old desk. The boxes he's got to fly to Crater Lake. The old building is an office and storeroom in one; he's the only person able to survey the freight and the piles of paperwork on the table.

The journalist doesn't want to sit in the vacant chair. It's probably too dirty for him. Mick Hudson. He must remember that name; his type could mean trouble.

"What's with the backpack?" he asks, wondering whether he should offer Hudson a coffee. No, the guy shouldn't feel too comfortable in his office; they're not there for a coffee klatch.

The reporter comes straight to the point.

"Rumors are going around Tulliq that an Inuk saw a backpack after the disappearance of the women. And that you also saw it because you landed nearby on a lake."

Vernon sits down on his chair and leans back.

"I thought you said *I* had found a backpack. And all you're going on are *rumors*."

Hudson sticks his hands in his jacket pockets.

"If somebody saw it, then it's the same as finding it. And the rumors are rather specific."

"Do tell."

"The backpack's rain cover was orange. And a yellow police whistle was attached to it."

The tremor in Vernon's jugular eases off. Not exactly earth-shattering news. This reporter's just fishing in murky waters and hoping that something comes up.

"Mick, you know the police described the backpacks in detail. The women all had the same model, only the colors of the rain covers were different. Anybody could know that, even the gossips in Tulliq."

"The police didn't say that something was stuck to the covers."

"And what might that be, pray tell?"

He won't say, Vernon thinks. He's saving his scoop for the article. But he's fooling himself.

"A sticker with the words *Sweet Revenge* on it."

Sweet Revenge. Vernon sees the sticker before his eyes. He sees his hand reaching for the backpack and tossing it into the Cessna. The sticker wasn't big, and he mightn't have seen it if he hadn't turned the backpack around.

"Revenge on whom?" he asked the women waiting on the shore beside the Cessna.

They just laughed. One of them said: "You'd really like to know, eh?"

He told the investigators back then about the sticker, but the police never made public what it said. And now this reporter knows about it anyway.

So, an Inuk saw the backpack with the orange rain cover, unless Mick is just making it up. And the man watched him land nearby on the lake. He was probably one of those caribou hunters. The man had left the backpack lying there. The thing was too inconvenient to take on a hunt. Maybe he went back to it later. But the backpack wasn't there anymore.

Vernon is absolutely sure about that because he had picked up the backpack and thrown it in the Cessna. Then he flew over a lake and dumped it, never to be seen again. And told nobody about it.

"When was that?" he asked Hudson.

"What?"

"When did the guy see the backpack?"

"Some years ago."

Vernon leans forward so he could intimidate the reporter.

"Some years ago? And you believe that the backpack lay there for years, and some animal didn't find it? That the wind didn't blow it away? That nobody else saw it?"

The reporter raises his eyebrows like an indulgent schoolteacher.

"That's very likely. Some years ago, a young German tourist froze to death in the Yukon while trekking over the tundra. His backpack was found two years afterward. Completely intact. There was even food still in it. Not one bear, nor a wolverine, nor an eagle, nor a moose had touched it. Even though animals had scattered the trekker's bones around when they ate the corpse." Hudson's smile was triumphant.

Vernon could have hit him in the jaw. Instead, he said sternly: "If you have important information, you must go to the police."

"The Mounties, you mean, who gave almost zero information to the press eight years ago? The guys who kept reporters away and only spoke to the press when it was useful to *them*?"

It had been a nightmare for Vernon. For him and the lodge, for Noshi and Vyann. And certainly for Tiff. For everybody working there. The stampede. The police. The media. The women's families. It seemed unstoppable. It almost broke

Vyann, strong woman though she was. Noshi escaped by finding another lady.

For him, Vernon, there wasn't any woman. He clenched his teeth and rode out the storm.

The four trekkers probably did, too, when that completely unpredicted storm came upon them. The storm's power caught everyone by surprise. They'd never experienced anything like it at the end of July, and with no warning. Noshi and Vyann were under fire in the media. They were attacked for not holding the women back. But they had been waiting for two days, and then the weather report had said the conditions were stable. Besides, the women had emergency transmitters and a satellite telephone with them.

That's what everyone believed.

Until one day he found the backpack with the orange rain cover. With a satellite phone inside. And on top of that . . . He doesn't even want to think about it.

He is *not* to blame.

He could have rescued the women if they hadn't left the trail. If they hadn't sought out dangerous terrain. And all that just to get revenge on somebody. Who? What for? With a trek over the tundra? Ridiculous.

He was vehemently criticized by the public. Some people felt he could have kept circling over the group because he should have known how inexperienced they were. No way the women would have wanted that. And who would have paid for the fuel? When he took another charter flight along the river three days later, there was no sign of them.

He found out shortly afterward they'd made off with the rubber dinghies that were reserved for the tourists. He discovered the unmanned boats farther downstream. Noshi and Vyann were so furious. The aggravation. The complications.

They had those damn bitches to thank for it because they didn't stick to the route. They were frivolous, cocky, and thirsting for fame.

He'd riffled through the backpack before throwing it away. That was his personal revenge on the four of them, whose actions almost destroyed his means of existence. *Sweet revenge.*

What he found in the backpack besides the satellite telephone haunted his dreams. Four emergency transmitters. Why all in one single backpack? Why did the other three women have nothing to call for help with? That little piece of news would be a scoop for this smartass rookie here. But nobody's ever going to know about it. Nobody.

At that moment he realized that Mick Hudson would not want to write about the Inuk, the backpack, and the rumors. Because if he wrongfully accused an Inuk, that young idiot could kiss his Labrador reporting career good-bye. The *Labrador Tribune* can't afford to infuriate certain people.

His cell phone rings.

He says hello. A voice says: "Gerald Hynes here. When do we take off?"

17

Detective Sergeant Calista Gates
St. Anthony, Newfoundland
Monday, February 12

I come home in the dark, and suddenly the area around the house is illuminated. It's the motion sensor I had installed, along with two surveillance cameras and an alarm system. I realize that I'm no safer in St. Anthony than I was in Vancouver.

My attacker from back then is behind bars, of course, but there are still plenty of people around who'd like to have me out of the way. I open the door—the handle feels ice-cold—and punch in the code to turn off the alarm. My house is a source of joy for me. It's part of a large property with trees and bushes that was formerly a campground. The sites for tents and RVs are still there, but the owner shuttered the business and moved to Alberta. I love this little piece of wilderness and the paths winding through it. Maybe I should see if Fred wants to join me jogging through the woods after the snow's gone. He'll probably do it, since Lucinda's still in Saskatchewan, and he has nobody to go jogging with.

I walk through the quiet house; only the fridge is humming.

I miss my parents and siblings in Vancouver. What good is it having six brothers and sisters if you can't see them? Maria, the youngest, lives in Costa Rica, and Frank is in the US, so I'd miss them anyway. I understand how Lucinda feels. She certainly loves Fred but wants to have her family around her and for that reason hasn't come back to St. Anthony.

I open the fridge to get one of the meals Warsame has prepared for me. A Somalian dish. Warsame's a refugee from the chaos of war there, but he sticks to his country's cuisine. To my great good fortune. He's become my indispensable household help. Although he works for security at the hospital, he still finds time to take care of my place and my meals. He writes the ingredients on all the containers. Today it's *cambuulo iyo maraq*. Rice, adzuki beans, diced tomatoes, tomato sauce, and onions. I've had it before, and it tastes great. My mouth's watering already.

Suddenly an image pops into my head. The dead, mutilated cockatoo. I squeeze my eyes shut to get rid of it and warm up my meal in the microwave. Mom always wondered how I can still eat when I'm so involved with violence and death. I think it's the urge for survival. Mine must be very strong, or I wouldn't have pulled through some tough times I've gone through.

I sit at the table and eat. My thoughts pester me during the meal, naturally.

How did that patch with the RCMP insignia happen to be in the same spot where Nielle Helfrey was discovered?

"Under no circumstances should we make it public," Fred warned at the team meeting in the station.

"No way," Dustin Wilson agreed. "Or it will look like some people want to get back at the sarge because she puts innocent people in danger."

They all stared at him.

Heidy exclaimed: "What are you talking about? That's crap! The sarge doesn't put anybody in danger."

"I mean . . . ," Dustin stammered. "But all of you surely think the same way."

"No, not me. It's absurd," Heidy contradicted him indignantly.

I didn't want the Wilsons quarreling, so I tried to calm them down: "I think there are more direct ways to hurt me, if somebody really wants to."

Now, in the silence of my kitchen, I'm wondering whether what Dustin said is really all that absurd. As an investigator, I rarely exclude something in advance, even if it looks grotesque at first blush.

I stick my spoon into the mound of rice on my plate. Is it possible that one of the locals is trying to create the impression that I'm a risk factor for the area? That I'm a threat to the people here because of my position and my enemies? Is somebody taunting me? Or is it intimidation?

I fill a glass with tap water and add a few lemon slices. And then there's that dead cockatoo. Fred and I analyzed the incident in the car.

He thought it was weird that the package appeared at the door precisely when we went to see Vyann Kippen. We found it before she did.

"Is it a symbol of something?" he asked.

"What? The bird?"

"Yes. And the cut-off wings."

"A symbol of what and for whom? For Vyann?"

"For you, Calista."

"You believe the package was meant for *me*?"

I looked at him dumbfounded. Fred sees threats coming at me from all sides. But maybe it isn't so farfetched.

Nonetheless, there's a difference between brutally attacking a woman and butchering a bird. I shipped the cockatoo and the box off to the forensics lab in Corner Brook for analysis. They probably think I'm off my rocker, but I can live with it.

I put the empty plate in the dishwasher and take my glass to the big window in the living room. I have a view of my little lake from there. It looks particularly pretty by moonlight, but it's pitch-black tonight.

The remoteness of my house stands in stark contrast to my time in Vancouver. The six weeks there went by too quickly, though I made the best of it. I spent a lot of my free time with my parents and siblings, above all with Daphne and her three kids. Jeremy's my godson. I would also pay visits to Nikos, his life partner Maxwell, and my two little nieces. Their youngest is named after me. Little Calista's still a baby, but she'll be growing fast. My sister Aretha sometimes came with me. It's nice having so many brothers and sisters.

I had some FaceTime with Jeremy three days ago. He's still sad that his godmother has gone away again. He's too little, at six, to understand certain situations. I found it so hard to say good-bye to him.

When Fred leaves St. Anthony in the middle of May, I'll be even more alone. How am I going to cope? I can't conceive of our station without him. RCMP headquarters hasn't announced his replacement yet. They probably think I could manage the work single-handedly, along with the Wilsons. I'd have to put some pressure on HQ, but that seems to me like a betrayal of Fred. I don't want a replacement; I want him to stay.

But at least I've still got Gerald. A ray of light. I feel warm all over.

He sent me a text. I stretch out on the sofa and punch in his number.

"Darling, at last." Hearing his voice is comforting.

"I know. It's been frantic all day."

"I'm flying to Crater Lake tomorrow."

"Tomorrow? So soon?"

"Yes, I want to go and scout out the property before things get going with the political bigwigs and the press."

"That means you'll be there on Wednesday?"

"Officially, I mustn't say a word."

"Where will you spend the night?"

"In one of the hunting cabins. There'll be three of us. And a pack of sled dogs."

"And a musher?"

"Yes."

That's reassuring. The Inuit know their way around up there. Gerald's in good hands. Ever since he got lost on the pack ice on his snowmobile in January, I worry whenever he takes off for somewhere.

"How's the weather up at the crater? I haven't checked . . ."

"So good that it hasn't been called off. Main thing is it looks doable on Wednesday."

So, the official event is on Wednesday. I'd love to be there, but some colleagues from Happy Valley-Goose Bay are sure to fly in. The Mounties like to make an appearance on these occasions. Good for our image.

"Have you caught the guy who beat up Nielle?" Gerald asks.

Nice try. He knows I can never say a word about ongoing investigations.

So, in return, I ask him about something he's not supposed to tell *me*.

"Who's the politician who'll be in Ilungilak?" He knows who I mean, of course.

"Well, someone who never passes up an opportunity like this," Gerald says. He's understood exactly.

Wow! Morris Tye isn't at his lover's bedside in a St. John's hospital. He wants to be in the spotlight, just not the wrong one.

But Gerald tells me something after all: "They say his wife called the police because of some domestic violence. But then she denied it when the patrol car showed up."

I don't think I'm hearing right.

"Where'd you get that from?"

"Their teenage daughter apparently told a friend, and the friend passed it on to her mother."

The whole business must have been plenty scary for their daughter. I'm so glad it never happened in my home growing up.

"And her friend's mother told you?"

"Yes, she's my cousin. A miracle that the media never caught wind of it."

Maybe there's no miracle behind it, but influence instead. Of course, we will discreetly ask our colleagues in Happy Valley-Goose Bay the next morning if they know of anything connected to Nielle Helfrey that we should take a closer look at.

"Take care of yourself, darling," I say, but my thoughts are already in a different place.

18

Fred van Heisen, RCMP Constable
St. Anthony, Newfoundland
Monday, February 12

The bitter-cold air burns his lungs. Jogging is no fun. He's in danger of slipping on icy spots in the dark. Really the stupidest time to break a bone. But he needs outdoor exercise to keep his head clear. That's why he drove to St. Anthony Bight, a sparsely populated bay he sees from his house every day.

He's jogging in the plowed lane in the middle of the road. His legs move as if on their own. He can see the asphalt because of his headlamp. Four kilometers out and four back; he can make it in fifty minutes if he keeps up the pace.

He's supposed to be working on the Nielle Helfrey case, but Lucinda's words are haunting his thoughts.

"Mom and Dad think we should move near them. That would be more practical for everybody."

She phoned him an hour ago just as he was changing for his jog. He misses having her around the house, the warmth and coziness she radiates. He misses the closeness of her body in bed.

But then there are her expectations, spoken or unstated, that hem him in.

He still hasn't bought a house in Saskatoon; he hasn't even sold the one in Regina that he grew up in. Decisions that give him a headache. He doesn't want to live too far away from the RCMP station in Saskatoon; that would be practical for him, but not for Lucinda. Her parents' house is in the opposite direction.

He's afraid of being co-opted by Lucinda's family. It's a big enough commitment for him to get married. A deadline that's sure to come soon when he gets to Saskatoon.

It all seems surreal to him on the dark road outside of St. Anthony Bight. Something crosses the pavement a few meters in front of him. A fox. There are lynxes in the area too. Coyotes and moose. Black bears and polar bears.

The polar bear from yesterday's gone, but he has no idea if more of its species are wandering around there. A local advisory is warning people not to go out on the street at night alone. It's best not to go outside in the dark at all. And here he is, running on a lonely road where he's only met one single car.

His cell phone plays a tune. He sees Calista's name on the display.

"Are you alone?" she asks.

"Yes, I'm out jogging."

"Where?"

"On the road to St. Anthony Bight."

"Can you come over?"

He doesn't need to be asked twice. He wheels around and jogs back to his car. Fifteen minutes later, he's inside her house, which feels so inviting on this cold night. She meets him with a hot chocolate, whipped cream floating on it. Just what he loves.

He's never been to her house after Lucinda left. She'd never had him and Lucinda over for dinner. Calista's his superior. She's wearing a bulky sweatshirt and sweatpants. Her hair's in a ponytail. He's only seen her once with her hair loose. It was a few weeks ago in a hotel room in Kamloops, British Columbia, when her bosses assigned him to be her bodyguard. Her transformed appearance almost bowled him over.

He takes a seat at the big kitchen table, and she opens fire.

"There are rumors that the Labrador RCMP got a domestic violence report from Morris Tye's wife. But she took it all back when the police got there."

He lets the whipped cream melt on his tongue.

"A rumor? And the source?" he asks.

"Their daughter is said to have told a friend, who passed it on to her mother."

"Dustin heard nothing about it when he called Happy Valley-Goose Bay today."

"Dustin probably didn't ask the right questions. He seems to be distracted lately. I should have given the job to Heidy."

Fred's of a different opinion. Dustin has a good rapport with the Mounties in Happy Valley-Goose Bay. Sure, Heidy's smarter than her husband, but she often moves in too fast and makes people sense how impatient she is. Heidy ought to be promoted; she's got potential. He knows Calista sees it the same way. Training to be a search-dog handler is a fitting outlet for her skill.

"It's tricky," he responds. "Dustin's also working on the list of red Ski-Doos, if indeed the wildlife officer actually did see a red Ski-Doo. That could get us somewhere." He clears his throat because he must bring up a delicate subject.

"Dustin feels neglected right now. Heidy's several lengths ahead of him. He complained recently that the dog is more important to her than he is."

"Woolly. That little ball of wool," Calista says.

She makes them both laugh. They haven't shared too many moments like that. She's too serious. He discovered her lighter side in Vancouver when she was with family. Their joking and teasing. He now knows where her quick wit comes from.

"Dustin has to grow with Heidy," she says. "That will be so good for him."

Fred senses it's more likely that Dustin will resist. Perhaps it's related to the fact they've been in St. Anthony for so long. When will the bosses send them to a new place, as the RCMP normally do? They don't seem to be in any hurry.

He changes the subject.

"Morris Tye has an alibi for the day in question. He wasn't in St. Anthony or Goose Cove."

Calista licks the whipped cream from her lips, and he lowers his eyes.

"Tye's flying to Crater Lake with his entourage tomorrow," she tells him, "to announce the creation of the new national park."

Aha! She probably got the rumor about Tye's domestic violence from Gerald Hynes. Why is Hynes skating on thin ice, sharing information about such a powerful politician? He bagged the contract for the lodge thanks to Tye, so Dustin Wilson told him. Dustin heard it from their colleagues in Happy Valley-Goose Bay. He got some more info from them, but not what Calista really wants to know.

"So, if Morris Tye can't be connected with Nielle's attack . . ."

"Maybe he wasn't there in person, but that doesn't rule him out."

Fred wishes he had the notes he left at home. But he can still recall one thing clearly.

"Vyann Kippen did mention that Nielle received anonymous warnings and that Nielle believes Tye's wife or her relatives are behind it."

Calista shrugs.

"Doesn't prove a thing. It's in Nielle's interest to think poorly of Tye's wife. Or her family."

"Tye's father-in-law is quite influential."

"Fred, do you really think they could have been sending her

a warning? That would draw a lot more attention to the sexual relationship everyone wants to cover up."

"Morris will try to keep it hush-hush, naturally, but maybe his wife won't."

Calista looks at him, then stares at the table.

He's simply unable to persuade her today.

"His wife will probably not want to jeopardize her husband's career either," she objects. "He might be a cabinet minister in Ottawa someday. At least in her dreams. What a promotion that would be. Tye would be more interested than she would be in ditching an inconvenient lover. That's my gut reaction."

Fred says nothing. He tries not to think about where Calista's gut is.

They're fumbling around in the dark. They might as well be walking through the shut-down campground in the snow, stumbling over roots.

She abruptly slaps the table. Not loudly, rather in disbelief.

"How come not one person has reported they witnessed the attack on Nielle? That just can't be! In broad daylight. Somebody must have seen *some*thing."

She stands up.

"Fred, we're off to Goose Cove tomorrow. We're going to go door-to-door and question the same people again. *Every one of them.*"

19

Tiffany Staid, Musher
Tulliq, Labrador
Tuesday, February 13

The pilot and his assistant keep loading boxes onto the Cessna. There's dog food in one of them. Tiffany wonders if there'll be enough room for her team and the sled. It's a collapsible sled, one she borrowed from Irvin. He often takes it to international races. Her dogs sense that something new is awaiting them. They tremble with joy, they want to get going and not sit still.

The aircraft mechanic watches it all from the hangar. They'd chatted briefly. He told her they're waiting for one more passenger. A contractor from Port Brendan. Hopefully he'll be here soon.

She'll be responsible for taking him from the plane to the hunting cabin by dogsled. Some Inuit from Alliarkuk will meet them before the VIPs arrive the next day. The police are already up there, so she's heard, but many rumors are making the rounds.

A snowmobile quickly approaches; is it the man from Port Brendan?

No, Bud Abel. Why does Bud show up wherever she is? He should leave her in peace for once. He takes his helmet off and comes over to her.

The dogs strain at their leashes, which are tied to snow anchors.

Bud stops two meters away from her.

"Hey, Tiff, does nothing scare you?"

"What's there to be scared of? The only thing that scares me is you. You're getting my dogs worked up."

"What did Noshi and Kellyann promise you?"

"What? Are you nuts? What are they supposed to have promised me?"

"Something so you don't spill the beans."

"Bud, bugger off. You're nuts."

"If you go up there, you'll be sorry. Weather's gonna be bad."

"You always think of something, but you don't scare me."

"I mean well by you."

"Okay, then please get lost."

"Think of the dogs. You don't want to lose them, eh?"

"Is that a threat? Are you the guy stealing dogs around here?"

"Do you even know who all's going to be in Ilungilak?"

"What's it to you?"

"Who's gonna help you there if something happens?"

She'd already given that some thought. She doesn't know the people from Alliarkuk but Inuit always help one another. The event's organized by the government, for heaven's sake. Nothing can happen to her.

Another snowmobile drives up, towing a sled. A man gets off the rear seat.

As he takes a large backpack off the sled, Bud says: "Another idiot running to his doom."

"What doom do you mean, eh? If you know so much, then out with it, now. Once and for all!"

Bud says nothing.

She gives a gloating laugh.

"Well, now we see it again. Big mouth, nothing behind it."

But she's more concerned than she lets on. Noshi told her some Inuit wanted to stop Crater Lake from being turned into a national park.

"Why?" she asked him. "If it's to be managed by our people?"

"The caribou herd crosses that area. The folks from Alliarkuk are especially afraid that their caribou hunt will be disrupted."

"There won't be that many tourists to bother them. You can keep them away from the caribou."

"That's not the point," Noshi explained. "Most of the tourists don't want to have any hunting near where they are on holiday. They can turn public sentiment against it. That's how it happened with the seal hunt."

But the caribou in Ilungilak are protected, Tiff was about to argue. There's a hunting ban because the herd could be exterminated. She bit her tongue instead. Many people respect the ban, but some go hunting anyway. It's a hot-potato issue among the Indigenous people. A simmering, constant conflict among hunters. Some want to wait until herd numbers have recovered; others want to keep hunting. Tiffany steers clear of this tricky issue.

Besides . . . she has the feeling it's not only about the caribou. So, what *is* it about?

The man with the backpack goes to the Cessna. He has a few words with the pilot. Then they both look at her. The pilot waves her over.

It's time to load the dogs onto the plane. One after another, because they must be tied down inside. Nobody wants to have a dog running around loose in the plane.

"I'll keep an eye on the dogs," Bud assures her, watching the team.

She doesn't refuse his help. Bud knows his way around sled dogs, knows how to earn their respect. He finds it harder with people.

She unties Pretor's leash from the snow anchor and takes him to the Cessna. The pilot helps her lift him onto the plane. She climbs aboard and secures Pretor in the open space at the rear. Fifteen minutes later all the dogs are loaded on and secured.

Bud helps her fold up the sled and heave it onto the Cessna. Then he helps lift her backpack.

"Thanks," she says.

The contractor from Port Brendan comes over and introduces himself.

"I'm Gerald Hynes."

"Tiffany Staid."

He's a customer, a guest. It's her job to see that he feels safe with her and the dog team.

"Have you ever been to Crater Lake?" he asks.

"No," she says. But she was in the vicinity during the search for the women. She doesn't tell him that. The women are taboo.

"Well, then it's an adventure for both of us." He gives a friendly smile and is about to let her board the plane first.

But Bud shouts: "Tiff, there's something I've got to tell you."

She follows him reluctantly to a spot several steps away from the plane.

"You know who that is?" he whispers.

"Yes, he just introduced himself."

"He and that policewoman are an item. The RCMP chief in St. Anthony. Be careful what you say. It will get passed on to the cops."

This is news to her. She had indeed heard about the police chief who's said to be more dangerous than a polar bear. For once she's happy to take Bud's advice.

Nevertheless, she says: "I don't need a babysitter. I can take care of myself."

She doesn't sit next to Hynes in the plane but in the back with the dogs.

This guy will get nothing out of her. Nothing at all.

The pilot gets in, shuts the door.

The engine kicks in. The roar drowns out the dogs' whimpering.

She sees Bud standing beside the hangar.

Maybe he's right. Maybe it's no accident that they assigned the police chief's boyfriend to her.

Do the cops want to find out at last what happened to the women?

She suddenly feels uneasy.

20

Paige Warner, Entrepreneur
Toronto, Ontario
Eight Years Ago

Has she blundered? The three women at the table look taken aback.

Paige feels all of a sudden like she's walking on thin ice, although she prepared everything to a T. She carefully selected these three women from the eleven who'd responded to her on Instagram. She's well versed in choosing coworkers. She has an infallible instinct for who would be a fit for her company. She always tells applicants right off what she expects of them. She was just as direct with these three women she wants for the trekking tour.

And now this. She'd just finished laying her cards on the table.

"I'm sponsoring this trip," she said, "if you agree to wear my hats and allow me to publish photographs of you wearing them in my advertising."

Admittedly, she hadn't told this to the women right at the

start. She wanted to be sure first that she liked all three applicants at the first meeting.

She'd invited them to a restaurant where the tables were spaced far apart. It was off to a good start. The meet-and-greet part was successful. The women seemed to get along with each other right off the bat. They all looked fit and athletic, went jogging, or were regulars at the gym. Their faces were attractive. They had another thing in common: they'd all been greatly disenchanted by a relationship with a man. Criteria important to Paige.

One hour of mutual conversation and she was convinced deep down: it could really work with these three.

But now they're exchanging nervous glances. Not a good sign. Paige has that sudden feeling: Me against them. Or them against me.

Ellen is the first to speak up.

"Is this an advertising campaign?"

Of course it is Ellen who asks. She's the PR manager at a respected college. Single mom with two sons. Early forties, as they all are. Paige doesn't want any big age differences. Moreover, Ellen's Afro-Canadian. That's crucial for Paige: to have various ethnicities in the group. Looks good in the photos. Her company considers itself to be open and inclusive.

"The trip's a sponsored adventure, which is normal these days," she replies. "Can you get used to the idea? It opens up many more possibilities for us."

She doesn't want to come out with it right away, that this is a must for her.

"I don't know if I want to see my face in ads." Ellen's tone is more hesitant than dismissive.

"I'm sorry for not having told you right away," Paige apologizes. "Customers on most organized trekking tours consent to having their picture put up on the tour organizer's website and on social media. I wrongly assumed that's common knowledge."

"But we're organizing the trek ourselves," Carla interjects. "At least, that's how I understand it."

"Yes, that's basically the case. I'm just offering my company as a sponsor." She groans to herself: Is that so hard to understand?

"What do *you* think about this?" Carla turns to Sandy. Carla's the motherly one; Paige already figured that out during the phone calls before the meeting. She's a receptionist at a large veterinary clinic. With her empathetic manner, she weaseled it out of Paige that she was unhappy about being excluded from the Papua New Guinea expedition. Paige told her that Howard was still going. She made a note to herself afterward to be more guarded in the future.

As guarded as Sandy, who doesn't reveal much of herself. So little, in fact, that Paige harbored some doubts about whether it was a good idea to invite her on the tour. But Sandy seemed to have read up on the Ilungilak area more than the others did. She was extremely knowledgeable about climatic and geological conditions there, and about animals and plants. About herself though, she didn't say much, except that she runs a gas station in Elora. Paige had to look on the internet to see where Elora was. Not far from Toronto.

A gas station. She had to process this information. Maybe that wasn't so good for her company's image. But Sandy explained: "We sell your hats."

"In the gas station?"

"In the souvenir shop. A lot of tourists shop at our place."

Sandy looks like a mountain climber should. She's tanned and dressed in sportswear.

"I think your offer to sponsor the trip is awesome, Paige," she responds to Carla's question. "I'm wearing your hats anyway. I think we'll all take pictures of one another; it's a group trek after all. I expect photos to be posted on social media in any case, or are they banned on the trek? Am I looking at it the wrong way?"

"No, no," Carla assures her. "I'd like to send pictures to my friends. This isn't a secret military operation."

Paige blinks. Military? Is that an allusion to her decisive leadership style? She's certainly able to work in a team. For that's what they're going to be, a team. She'll make a note of it as a *pain point* in marketing speak.

"We must agree to a couple of things and establish some rules we can all accept," Ellen suggests. "For one, we must communicate if something's bothering us."

Paige wants to comment, but Carla beats her to it.

"Who's providing the tents? And who's taking care of the provisions? Any allergies? We must get enough calories."

Carla's excited and jumps from one thing to another.

But Paige has a checklist she wants to go through.

"I'll discuss that with all of you. Today I want to deal with some basics first."

"Do we have to sign a contract with your company?" Ellen asks.

"Contract?" Sandy looks at her, confused. "Paige, can you tell us what's in it first?"

"Yes, I can. It's a standard contract, nothing out of the ordinary."

"Have you got a copy with you?"

Paige really didn't want to get to this so quickly, but since she's been asked, she takes a file folder out of her briefcase. Fortunately, she's brought several copies of the contract.

Ellen starts reading.

"You don't mean that your company won't be liable for anything," she remarks.

Paige nods.

"Yes, I said it's a standard contract."

"Liable for what?" Sandy asks.

"In case something unforeseen happens—an accident, for instance."

"Or a grizzly attack." Carla makes a face. "There are polar bears up there too."

"They're nearer the coast," Paige says reassuringly, "so we don't have to worry about them."

"But *we* don't want to be liable," Carla says, rapping her index finger on the contract. "That should be in here. For example, if one of us goes bonkers and wants to go back."

Sandy stares at her.

"Why would one of us go bonkers?"

"That's really wild country up there, lonely and unpredictable."

Paige doesn't like the turn the conversation's taking.

"We're trekking on a route that others have walked before us. The risks are obvious. But we want to have an adventure, don't we? That's the point of the whole thing."

Ellen looks up from the paper.

"Of course we do. I get it that your company wants to protect itself against future claims. We just don't want to be sued either. Very simple. This is a standard contract, we can roll with it. We cross off what doesn't apply to us and add other things that do. For example: None of us will go bonkers. None of us will deliberately endanger the others. Everyone is responsible for themselves, not for the whole group."

She looks around at everybody. None of the women disagrees.

Paige would do the same if she were in Ellen's shoes. But she's not in her shoes. She's amazed at how readily Carla and Sandy submit to Ellen's proposal.

Minutes are passing. Even if she had time to look for new group members at this point, the discussion would surely be the same.

So she nods.

"That would be great if we're all agreed."

An inner voice immediately speaks up: I hope I'm not making the biggest mistake of my life.

21

Detective Sergeant Calista Gates
St. Anthony, Newfoundland
Tuesday, February 13

It's seven in the morning, and everyone's already at the station. I've told them we'll meet in the conference room.

Dustin's not enthusiastic when I assign them all to go door-to-door in Goose Cove. I can tell by looking at him. He's already questioned many people and probably sees it as criticism.

I feel obliged to explain my decision.

"People often hide things or need an extra push to tell something. Maybe they don't think it's important at first and so won't come to us."

I myself don't really have to do what I'm asking them to do. I'm the boss and can organize things as I see fit. But after Fred clued me in that Dustin's become rather prickly ever since his wife started training to be a dog handler, I've been more responsive to his needs. He's on my team and has good rapport with the locals, and I'm still a stranger to them.

He nevertheless has a gripe: "I'd have preferred to keep working on the red snowmobile the wildlife officer saw."

"She believes she saw something red, she thought it might have been blood," I correct him. "We're not sure what color the snowmobile was. If we find witnesses, we might learn more."

I leave it at that and organize them in pairs to go from house to house: "Heidy, you come with me; Dustin, you go with Fred. We'll take the homes below the main street; you take the ones above."

"And Woolly?" Heidy asks.

"He stays here with Rex."

They both looked chagrined: Heidy because she can't take Woolly, and Dustin because he isn't going with his wife. As if they don't spend enough time together as a married couple.

I'm in the car with Heidy shortly afterward, the men are following us. The road to Goose Cove is in excellent condition. What luck that it hasn't snowed for three days despite the forecast. Nothing's as unpredictable here as the weather.

I've got questions for Heidy.

"What do you know about Morris Tye?"

"You mean other than he fools around with other women and beats his wife?"

Wow! She isn't in a particularly good mood.

I keep my cool.

"Apart from that, hasn't he got a clean record?"

"Morris Tye wants to bring more mining to Labrador. But it's not so easy. The Nunatsiavut government won't be bypassed so quickly anymore. They want to have a say. And they want a big piece of the pie."

"Isn't it all above board?"

Heidy looks at me with raised eyebrows.

"When a politician campaigns for a mining company, he hopes to cash in on it."

"It benefits his voters—jobs are good for everybody." I play the ingénue to get Heidy going.

And it works.

"Sarge, do you still believe in Santa Claus?" she asks.

"Not every politician holds his hand out. If they're sincere, they get no thanks for it."

Heidy hits the brakes because a snowmobile's crossing the road. That must be exactly what happened to the wildlife officer.

Which leads to my next question: "How long does it take to go from St. Anthony to Goose Cove by snowmobile?"

"Half an hour, maybe even less. Ask Dustin; he's done it."

Heidy's the more athletic of the two. Quite muscular. She skis cross-country. Woolly's been going with her these days. Dustin's lost weight since I've known him. He has an electric bicycle, but he can't patrol on it in winter.

As I gaze over the snow-covered landscape, I have a sudden desire to go for a snowmobile ride. The winter's still holding; it's cold, but the wind has died down. Who'd have thought I'd enjoy blasting over the tundra? I don't like noise otherwise. It's all so white and peaceful. The snow looks almost fluffy; the bushes are wrapped in cotton. You can get to places by snowmobile that you can't in summer when the bogs aren't frozen: quiet bays, faraway hills, frozen lakes. You've just got to watch out for the creeks. In Labrador I fell through a snow bridge last winter and landed in ice-cold water. Several people here have lost their lives that way.

The distance between our cars shrinks. We arrive at Goose Cove harbor. My eyes turn to the spot where Nielle Helfrey was found.

Then I register some movement near the far end of the driveway. A snowblower is shooting white plumes in the air. I see the person behind it.

I shout: "Stop! I want to talk to that guy."

Heidy parks at the harbor while Fred and Dustin drive on. We tramp along in snowmobile tracks and footprints on the way to the house. The red blood spots have disappeared; somebody's covered them up with snow.

Not until we're very close does the man shut off the snowblower.

I introduce myself and Heidy and discover he's the son-in-law of the elderly gentleman Nielle cared for.

"We haven't told him anything," the son-in-law says. "It would upset him. Not good for his weak heart." He scratches his head through his wool cap. White ice particles dangle from his moustache. "Will she recover?"

"It looks like she's over the hump. She's still being treated in St. John's."

I just heard this morning that Nielle has regained consciousness and is communicating with the hospital staff. It's too bad the police can't question her. We're in contact with the RCMP there in case the situation changes.

The man spits on the snow.

"Who's the idiot behind it?"

I come back with a question: "What do you think Nielle was doing in Goose Cove on Sunday? Your father-in-law wasn't even in his own home; he was at your place."

"We've no idea. We told Nielle he would be with us."

"When was the last time you spoke to her?"

"My wife takes care of that. Probably when she told her he's going to be staying with us until I finish the driveway."

"How did you pick up your father-in-law?"

He looks at me in surprise.

"With the Ski-Doo, of course. My wife went."

"We didn't see any Ski-Doo tracks going to the house."

"We come up from the back." He points to the rear of the house. "It's easier."

I hadn't thought of that. You're out of sight behind the house.

"That's definitely the way she came," he adds.

"Who? Your wife?" Heidy asks.

"No, Nielle. I see her on her Ski-Doo now and then."

Heidy and I look at each other. Nielle didn't come by car

and didn't walk to the house. She came on a Ski-Doo. But how come she was lying some fifty meters from the house? And where's her snowmobile?

"What does Nielle's snowmobile look like?"

"Black. And silver."

"And her ski jacket?" Maybe she wore a different one than when she was attacked.

He frowns, thinks.

"Greenish. Green patterned." He rubs his gloved hands together.

I'm cold as well. Heidy acts as if the cold doesn't bother her.

"What am I going to tell the old man? He never stops asking for her. Nielle, Nielle, Nielle. The whole day." The man laughs, flashing his false teeth. "He's got a crush on her."

"Is she well-liked?"

"Oh, sure. She's good to the old guy." The man's expression is suddenly one of concentration, as if something had just crossed his mind. "Maybe she dropped by his cabin to see if everything was okay. He still has a log cabin, though he's never there. He doesn't want to give it to us because we already have one. He doesn't even let our kids in it. But he lets Nielle use it sometimes because she doesn't break anything." He grins and shakes his head. He obviously thinks his father-in-law is kooky.

"Where's his cabin?" I ask.

He explains the location to us.

I can't follow him, but Heidy nods.

"I think I know where it is. We need a snowmobile."

"And Woolly," I say, finishing her sentence.

22

Vyann Kippen, Caregiver for Seniors
St. Anthony, Newfoundland
Tuesday, February 13

Vyann turns off West Street onto East Street and onto Cabot Street right after. It's something new for her to visit Trina at her home. Previously, when Trina was still renting a small apartment, she never had Vyann over. They always met at Tim Hortons or Subway. About four times. Otherwise, it was always by phone. But Trina and her husband bought a house on Cabot Street last fall.

Trina's been a caregiver longer than Vyann. When her work at the fish plant no longer suited her, she looked for another job. Vyann has never regarded Trina as competition; there are enough seniors needing help in the area to go around. Trina's also always ready to fill in for her. But Vyann usually coordinated that with Nielle. Unlike Nielle, Vyann isn't from Newfoundland and Labrador but from the province of New Brunswick. She didn't want to go back there after her breakup with Noshi. She stayed because of Marcus. Her son means the world to her. Noshi and Kellyann don't have children—to Vyann's great satisfaction.

As far as she can tell, Trina has more luck with her husband. She got to know him in Alberta, where she grew up. He worked there in the tar sands. Trina didn't tell Vyann that, but Nielle did; she gets along well with Trina. Everyone likes Nielle. Including Morris Tye, unfortunately. She wishes Nielle would never have gotten involved with that sleazy politician. Vyann learned about it a few months ago. It was Noshi, of all people, who clued her in, but he didn't reveal his source.

Vyann parks in the driveway. Not a bad house. Trina's husband must make good money. He's half Inuk and originally from Labrador. Many people in and around St. Anthony have Inuit blood. Nobody used to mention it, but ever since the government started giving Inuit financial support, more and more people are discovering their Inuit roots.

Vyann goes to the front door, which has decorative frosted glass. Looks pretty; would look good in her front door, too. She won't be meeting Trina's husband, who's working in Labrador now. She learned that from some acquaintances. They all wanted to hear from her what happened to Nielle and who might have done it. Right now she's mainly worried about who's going to take over Nielle's clients until she's on her feet again.

That's what she must discuss with Trina. She knocks on the door because she doesn't want to simply walk into the house and shout hello, as is the local custom. Better to be cautious, considering it's her first visit. She doesn't know how Trina would react.

"Come in," she hears her call before coming into the hall. She's wearing leggings that look like leather and a turquoise tunic that doesn't even reach her knees. Trina's fashion-conscious.

Vyann takes off her boots and her outdoor clothing.

"You've come just at the right time," Trina says. "I've got to leave in half an hour."

They sit at the table in the modern kitchen. Ikea, Vyann guesses. Ikea kitchens are a status symbol in St. Anthony.

"Have you heard anything about Nielle?" Trina inquires.

"I've tried to reach her mother. But all I get is voicemail."

"Did the police tell you anything when they were at your place?"

"No, but I didn't ask. I was totally out of it because of Simmi . . ." She doesn't have to go on. She told Trina about it briefly on the phone.

"That's absolutely creepy," Trina says. "The business with Nielle and then your cockatoo."

"Are you afraid something could happen to you too?"

Trina fiddles with the cell phone in front of her.

"I've heard rumors that the new policewoman . . . that she was the target. Evidently a police badge was found in the snow near Nielle. Like the one Calista Gates has. Sergeant's insignia."

"Really?" Vyann mulls that over. How's that possible? Gossip spreads a lot of nonsense. "But what's that got to do with my Simmi?"

"That, I don't know. She found Simmi, didn't she?"

Vyann doesn't get it. A dead cockatoo surely can't scare a Mountie. "Who's saying that? That it was meant for Calista Gates?"

"Tornado's been saying it."

"You can't take *him* seriously. He rails against the new chief because she doesn't let him get away with everything."

Tornado's a troublemaker, Trina ought to know that. A poacher, drug dealer, vandal. Certain people in St. Anthony have protected him for far too long, as has his father. Calista Gates put a stop to his shenanigans. When she was in Vancouver for a few weeks, he probably thought he had free rein again. Then Constable van Heisen came back, and that was that. Now the police chief is back too, and Tornado's kicking up a fuss like a little boy who's had his toys taken away.

"Okay, so who do you take and who do I take?" Trina picks up her cell phone with the appointments app.

"I'm not going to the Robertsons'; their boys bullied Marcus." Vyann never forgives a person who does anything to her son. Even if there's a grandmother who needs care and nobody else in the family steps in to help her.

After ten minutes, they've cleared it all up. Vyann's workload has almost doubled, but that means more money, and she needs it, mostly for Marcus.

Trina's back onto Nielle's attack. She seems greatly concerned.

"Did the police say that you must look out for yourself?"

That's probably the reason she wanted to see me in person, Vyann thinks, to see how I react.

Trina has never let on that she knows about Nielle's relationship with Morris Tye, and Vyann has never mentioned it. And she won't do it now either. Let Trina get it from somebody else. Trina's very discreet; she never gossips and only talks about her clients whenever Vyann takes over for her. She says very little about herself, which may well be the reason they're not real friends.

"The police said they were trying to clear up the matter and asked me if I could help them with that." Vyann sighs. "And yet they should be helping us and not the other way around."

"They always say that. There's something I've noticed: Nielle was left lying where she could be found easily. I find that odd."

Vyann can't figure out where Trina's going with this. Doesn't she have an appointment soon?

"Why? That's a good thing. That way she could be taken to the hospital quickly."

"That's exactly what I mean. Somebody didn't want her to die."

"Of course not. For heaven's sake!" Vyann shivers suddenly despite the warm temperature.

Trina notices.

"Aren't you concerned for your safety?"

"Don't drive yourself crazy, Trina. There are characters who simply talk nonsense. Like Tornado."

"But he's got nothing against Nielle. At most, he hates Calista Gates."

"Maybe Nielle has enemies we know nothing about." Vyann regrets her words as soon as she says them, but it's too late.

"She would certainly have told you about it."

This time Vyann presses her lips together and says nothing.

Trina flips her cell phone back and forth from one hand to the other.

"Is it a warning?" she asks.

They look at each other, taken aback, and Vyann reads something in Trina's eyes she does not wish to see.

23

Detective Sergeant Calista Gates
St. Anthony, Newfoundland
Tuesday, February 13

Fred goes ahead on his snowmobile; Dustin and Heidy are following me. Woolly runs beside the two of them. Fred and Dustin broke off their door-to-door inquiry to come with us. It wasn't necessary, but I can't very well deny them this; they mustn't feel excluded. Besides, eight eyes see more than four. Dustin had scanned part of the snowmobile trail nearby on Sunday but found nothing suspicious. Maybe he overlooked something.

My eyes are watering. My visor's open so it doesn't fog up. My sunglasses are also fogged up. I really ought to spring for the seven-hundred-dollar helmet with built-in heating.

The snowmobile trail is obviously used by the locals: the snow in the middle is pushed down and the runner tracks are deep. We follow the route at a leisurely pace so Woolly can detect a scent. I'm doubtful the dog can help us because he's just begun his training, but you never know. It makes Heidy happy. It's very important to me that my team stays motivated.

My Ski-Doo steers well, not too easily and not too hard. Sometimes I hear the sound of my runners through the motor noise. We travel uphill and down and around some curves; it could almost be a family outing. The sun's peeking out but doesn't reduce the cold. When Heidy tried to put Woolly's protective booties on, the dog kicked up a fuss; too bad we didn't have time to coax him.

We stop at a fork; Heidy thinks she knows where the cabin is. From here we can't survey the area well enough, so we go a little farther up to a hilltop.

Once there, we see small, wooded spots with gnarled trees, but no building. I'm not surprised. Cabins are often built among fir trees in a hollow to protect them from the harsh winds. So, it's back to the fork.

Woolly runs ahead as if he knows where we're going. Heidy tries to call him back, but her helmet's in the way. She pushes up her visor and blows her whistle. Woolly stops, looks back, and then keeps running. I hope we don't lose him—that's the last thing we need.

We catch up with him at the fork, and right away he follows snowmobile tracks winding through the bush. We force our snowmobiles down the narrow route through some scrub firs. Then we hear Woolly barking. I follow Fred around a curve and see the cabin twenty meters ahead. The front is covered with an ugly, water-repellent black tarpaper. Footprints in the snow all around. Is somebody in the cabin?

We remove our helmets and put on wool hats. Fred approaches the cabin. He knocks on the door, but nothing is stirring. He tries the door, but it won't open.

Heidy's already at a spot in the snow that Woolly's pointing to.

"Sarge!" she shouts.

She gives the dog a reward, pulls him off, and points to the ground.

"We should dig here. It looks like somebody has piled some snow here."

Meanwhile, Fred has been able to get the rough-hewn door open.

"Nobody here," he shouts a little later.

"Is there anything we can dig with?"

We hear him rummaging around in the cabin until he appears with a shovel. He gets to work at once. Dustin stands beside him, as if frozen stiff. It's not long before red-colored snow is visible.

Heidy's face lights up.

"Woolly was right."

Fred sets the shovel aside.

"Was Nielle attacked here?"

"We have to consider it." I look around. "Suppose she came from St. Anthony by snowmobile and took off her helmet, just like us. At that moment, another snowmobile came up to her. Or several; we must examine the tracks carefully. But let's assume a single perp until we know more. He hit her. Maybe she didn't even recognize him if he still had his helmet on."

"Or she *did* recognize him and didn't expect any dirty tricks. Or maybe she came here with somebody else."

Heidy's fascinated by the blood. The red color is perfectly preserved in the cold snow.

"And then?" Dustin seems to have found his voice.

I look at Fred.

Two deep lines in his forehead indicate he's thinking about it.

"Then the attacker loaded Nielle on his snowmobile and took her to the site in Goose Cove."

Dustin is skeptical.

"In that case we'd have found more traces of blood in the snow on the way there."

"He probably tied her hood up tight. We found blood on it, along with some hairs stuck together."

"And nobody saw them?" Heidy shakes her head.

"How many people did we meet on the way here?" Fred shoots back.

"Not a single soul."

"Because people cross the road beforehand and drive on the other side," Dustin says. He'd evidently done that when he was out searching on Sunday.

"Then somebody disposed of her helmet and maybe a scarf."

I'm thinking out loud. So much effort just to send a warning? If indeed it *was* a warning.

Fred picks up the shovel.

"Best thing to do is not to mess up even more tracks with our boots."

"What's that over there?"

I see a sort of wooden shed through the stunted firs.

"I think it's an outhouse." Heidy pets a fidgety Woolly, who'd probably like to sniff around the whole area.

"Let's have a look." I carefully step beside the footprints leading from the cabin and tramp through untouched snow.

Heidy's right. On the side away from us there's a door held shut by a wooden bolt. It's frozen, so it takes a great effort for me to push it up. The door immediately springs open and something heavy falls out. I throw myself sideways and tumble into the snow. Pain shoots through me. Then a cold dread.

A human figure is lying before me.

A scream dies in my throat.

Fred's on his way to me.

I struggle to stand up. My foot hurts. Oh, not again! I try to ignore it. Stare at the man in the snow. Frozen like a block of ice.

I recognize him.

Trent Stolke.

His face is snow-white; his eyes are closed. He looks more amicable in death than I've ever seen him. He was always angry and rebellious in life. He was furious with me in particular.

"It's Tornado," Fred says.
Many know him by that nickname.
Something catches my eye.
"What's that?"
"He's wearing a police jacket," Fred says, baffled.

24

Tiffany Staid, Musher
Ilungilak, Labrador
Tuesday, February 13

Tiffany is totally exhausted. Pretor's been howling for almost the entire flight, and Rasputin's been tugging constantly on his leash. She can't wait for the earsplitting din of the motor to stop.

She'd hoped to catch a glimpse of Crater Lake from the air, but billows of mist temporarily blocked the view.

Only when the pilot gyrates one more time does she get a quick peek at the lake's almost perfect circle, completely covered in ice. The area around the crater is flat, which is why the higher rim of the crater juts up and appears somewhat darker. Tiffany wonders how long it would take to climb up to the rim. An hour? Longer? The horizon vanishes in a white veil. Sled-dog country.

The Cessna begins its approach. Patches of fog lie near the ground. Wasn't the visibility supposed to be good today? So said the weather report. How does the pilot know where the narrow, snow-covered landing strip is? She's flown with Vernon before; she trusts he knows what he's doing. She's only a bit nervous because it's such an important occasion. Pull yourself together, Tiff, the dogs need to sense that you're calm.

She can only see Gerald Hynes from behind. What might be going through his head? Maybe in his mind's eye he sees the finished lodge he'll build. Noshi's pretending that he and Kellyann think it's good to have tourist accommodations right beside Crater Lake. What's so good about it if tourists spend the night *there* instead of at Remote Point Lodge? Oh, sure, it will make the area more popular. Anglers will probably keep flying in to Remote Point Lodge because fishing's prohibited in Crater Lake. Yes, there are fish in it—Arctic char—she heard that from Noshi. But even Inuit don't fish for them. The trout belong to the Lake Spirit living in the crater. Inuit fish in Cloud Lake, not far from Crater Lake. Probably sport fishing will be permitted there, too, in the future. It would be in direct competition with Noshi's lodge.

The potential repercussions are confusing to Tiffany. She holds on tight to her seat. The Cessna's ready to touch down. She doesn't look at the dogs, or they might sense the nervous state she's in. At that second the runners hit the hard snow. The whole plane clatters and shudders. The dogs pant and bark. The Cessna comes to a screeching stop. At last. She's managed the flight. Just not all the other stuff.

She looks out the window and sees two dark figures on the edge of the temporary tarmac. They must be the helpers from Alliarkuk. She can use some assistance with the dogs. The pilot shouts to Gerald Hynes and asks if he can help unload.

She goes from dog to dog to see if everything's okay. She gives them all sorts of praise. The dogs are excited. They don't know what awaits them. Neither does she, but she must be the strong commander.

She exits the plane. It's much colder up here than in Tulliq, but the dogs can take it.

A man approaches.

"You've got the team?" he asks.

"Yes, eight dogs."

She doesn't have to ask him for help.

Inuit always help one another in these situations. It's in their blood.

Half an hour later, they have the team ready to go.

Gerald Hynes puts the sled together. He figured out how it works in no time.

Pretor's in his element. The rest of the dogs howl impatiently and strain at their leashes, held back by the two helpers. The dogs love something new, as long as it's not a Cessna. Several bite their leashes in their excitement. By contrast, Pretor watches what Tiffany's doing very closely.

Hynes sits down on the sled in front of the baggage and pulls the protective cover over him. She waits for the helpers' snowmobiles to start moving. Then she gives a signal, and they're off.

The dogs run like well-oiled wheels. Tiffany's tension wanes. The terrain is almost level. When the fog gets thicker, she starts worrying. At times she can barely make out the snowmobiles ahead. But the dogs have caught on that they're to follow the men. Tiffany hardly needs to change direction at all. It's pretty much straight ahead. Because the brakes don't grip very well on the smooth surface of the snow, she must count on Pretor following her commands immediately.

Hynes does not get a good shaking up thanks to the level terrain. She can't estimate the distance they've come, but the snowmobiles suddenly slow down. Three cabins appear out of the fog. They must be the hunting cabins.

She gives the signal to stop. Pretor obeys like clockwork. She has such a good lead dog.

Hynes gets off the sled. His eyebrows are already white below the line of his hood.

"Everything all right?" she asks him.

He nods.

"I love riding on a dogsled."

She gives each dog a treat. The men carry the boxes into one of the cabins. The structures look robust. Smoke rises from the chimney pipes. Nice—it will be warm inside.

But Gerald Hynes has other plans.

"I'd like to go to Crater Lake before the fog gets worse and before the crowd gets here. Can we go right now?"

She agrees. The dogs are full of energy; they want to run, run, run. And she'll be able to scout out the terrain before the VIPs arrive.

"I'll ask one of our guides if he'll come along," she says.

"No need. I've got a GPS."

She's packed one too, and a lot of batteries so the device will work for several days in the cold. But she'd like to ask the men from Alliarkuk as a courtesy. She and Hynes are guests on their territory.

"I'll do it," Gerald declares.

She sees a third man coming out of the middle cabin, and Hynes goes over to talk to him. The man raises a hand; they speak in English.

"All good," says Hynes as he comes back to Tiffany. "We're there in ten minutes." He points to the east. "It's straight ahead in this direction."

That conforms with her observations.

Even so, it takes longer than Hynes assumed because the ground becomes rockier when they're closer to the crater. The meteorite's impact scattered rock fragments all over. There's a painting depicting the scene in the Tulliq museum. Tiffany found the work impressive.

They stop at a high inukshuk that looks like a stone pyramid. A prominent path marker with a post projecting from the rock pile. The crater's rim is dimly visible.

Hynes wants to look around at the base of the crater.

"I must take in this place alone, by myself," he explains. "Come back in an hour, please."

He has Inuit blood, she thinks, he feels the mystical nature of the place.

She decides to go see Cloud Lake, which is on the way to the crater. They had ridden past it. She's got to pick up people from some cabins there tomorrow.

She arrives at the lake relatively quickly and finds two cabins on the right bank. All of a sudden a snowmobile looms up out of nowhere. The driver signals her to stop. The dogs do it against their will.

The driver raises his visor.

Not an Inuk, a white man. A *Qallunaat*.

"Who are you? What are you doing here?" he asks.

She introduces herself and tells him what she's doing there.

"And who are *you*?" she retorts.

"I'm responsible for security. Go back to the cabins near the airstrip, please."

"Gerald Hynes is at Crater Lake. I have to pick him up."

"We'll take care of it."

"But he's expecting me. I promised I'd be there in an hour."

"You must respect our orders. We're from the RCMP."

Police. The tourism officials had drilled it into her to always obey security people. They protect important persons.

She has a disquieting feeling as she takes the team back to the men from Alliarkuk and tells them about the encounter.

While the youngest of the men helps her take care of the dogs, she hears the other two in conversation in the cabin.

One of them comes out holding a satellite phone.

A creepy premonition steals over Tiffany.

25

Fred van Heisen, RCMP Constable
St. Anthony, Newfoundland
Tuesday, February 13

Fred helps Calista to her feet.

She grimaces.

"It's my foot, dammit," she mumbles. "Every time it's my foot." But she doesn't let it slow her down because she's just as stupefied as he is by what's there before them.

Trent Stolke is not only frozen.

He's in a dark blue RCMP jacket.

"What the hell's going on?" She stares at the dead man.

Fred would like to know too. First, there was the sergeant's insignia where Nielle was discovered. And now a corpse in a police jacket. A sergeant's jacket.

Heidy and Dustin join them after tying Woolly to a tree. The dog disapproves and barks his annoyance.

"Careful! Crime scene!" Calista warns.

"Understood, sarge." Heidy looks electrified.

Dustin is white as a sheet. Utterly aghast.

Fred can't recall whether Dustin has ever been the first

person to come across a dead body since he's been in St. Anthony. Dustin, he thinks, hasn't seen a single victim in the past year before the body landed at forensics.

"Good God! It's Tornado!" Heidy shouts on seeing the corpse, though it's already clear to everyone. "What's *he* doing here?"

Trent Stolke has always caused them aggravation. They caught him hunting caribou illegally last December. He hasn't appeared in court yet. And here he is, making trouble again.

"I can see a bullet hole in the jacket," Calista declares.

Fred looks more closely. Sure enough, there's a suspicious hole in the chest.

"Why's he wearing a police jacket?" Heidy asks.

Nobody answers. The situation's surreal.

"We're officially beginning the investigation." Calista sounds very formal. She's recovered from her initial shock and leaves no room for chatter.

Her modus operandi is nothing new to Fred. With rubber-gloved fingers, she opens the jacket and carefully removes the undershirt to expose the wound. Woolly continues to bark, but Heidy doesn't stop him. She's fascinated by what's before her.

Calista gives orders: "Fred and I will secure the crime scene until forensics gets here. Constables, you call an ambulance and Dr. Amaruntgamen." She's talking to Heidy and Dustin. "Wait by the road and bring the doctor here. Not a word to anyone, is that clear? I'll decide how and when we go public."

The police uniform, Fred thinks. This fact mustn't get out before they're ready.

"And Woolly?" Heidy inquires.

"Take the dog back to St. Anthony. He's done great work. We need the usual: tape, protective clothing, you know."

"Understood, sarge."

Dustin hasn't uttered a peep since the body was discovered.

"Then go back to going door to door in Goose Cove," Calista continues. "We need eyewitnesses."

"Got it, sarge." Heidy knows when to follow orders, even if she doesn't like them. She calls the hospital.

We're lucky to have reception here, Fred realizes. He hears Calista negotiating with Corner Brook on her smartphone. The colleagues there had helped them out on their last big case. They and their forensics team came to St. Anthony because a prominent archeologist had disappeared without a trace and a murder victim had been discovered. But he takes from what Calista's saying that this time it's more difficult.

She ends the call and slips her smartphone back in her inside pocket.

He also keeps his phone close to his body. Batteries die quickly in this cold.

"They're totally stretched. Nobody's available. You'd think a serial killer was on the loose in Corner Brook. They aren't about to send a helicopter to transport the body either. And the medical examiner is sick. Maybe we'll get a forensics guy tomorrow. For now, we've got to do it ourselves."

Fred's secretly delighted. There are advantages to being an investigator in an area five hours away from the next city. If the Corner Brook forensics team can't be mobilized rapidly, then Calista is their replacement. The crime scene can't wait; the first run-through must take place at once. Calista can do it; she brings extensive Vancouver experience with her. And the Corner Brook colleagues very well know it.

The Wilsons move out. The racket from their snowmobiles goes away, the barking has stopped. Silence settles over the trees.

Fred's more than ready. The crime scene belongs to them, and he's Calista's assistant. What more could he ask for?

She glances skyward.

"We have to hurry before it starts to snow."

Trent Stolke's death is regrettable, of course, but right now Fred's thinking about investigative work.

As does Calista, who's looking intently all around her. Registering details like a computer.

Then she brandishes her smartphone again.

"Pictures of the body first, the cabin afterward. Can you handle the footprints and snowmobile tracks?"

Fred takes out his phone. They set to work. The snow crackles under their feet with every step. Calista's limping. It doesn't escape him that she doesn't mention the police jacket again, although she leans over the body and scrutinizes everything.

"Here's a second bullet wound," she shouts, waving him over. "I can't be a hundred percent certain but is this . . . have a look."

He examines the spot. He can't see any abrasion around the edge of the wound where the bullet entered.

"There's no abrasion ring," he concludes.

"Exactly."

They stare at each other.

If a living person is shot, the entrance wound shows bruising because of the blood flow. That's not the case when a dead person is shot.

He draws the most obvious conclusion: "The victim was shot when he was already dead."

She nods, then pulls herself up and speaks into her smartphone's microphone in a clear voice: "The wound is shaped like a half-moon; therefore, the shot came from above at a steep angle. The shooter stood to the right of the body, as the widening of the wound shows."

Fred listens spellbound.

Good God. Shooting a dead man. The case is getting more and more bizarre.

He can tell by her expression that she's also mystified.

After a few seconds, she says: "It looks to me like the victim didn't die here. Or wasn't shot here. We'll search for shells anyway."

The case could get challenging—she doesn't have to tell him. It's always a disadvantage when the victim has been moved from the actual scene of the crime. But perhaps they'll discover dirt or vegetation or other clues on the body that don't originate from the present site.

Calista studies the victim from above.

"Confound it! When the body's frozen, you can't ascertain the time of death."

It's clear to him as well.

"Trent Stolke doesn't seem to be missed," he points out.

She nods.

"At least we haven't heard about it. Maybe he's only been dead for a short time. One night's enough to freeze a body."

She continues to photograph and then turns to him.

"Fred, what strikes you about the posture of the corpse?"

He doesn't need to think for long.

"If the victim had been shoved into the outhouse immediately after death, when the body wasn't stiff yet, it would have been frozen while sitting, not standing. But there's a high probability that's not the case. The victim was possibly frozen during rigor mortis."

He reasons further: "Rigor mortis ends between twenty-four and forty-eight hours after death. So was Stolke brought here when his body was still stiff?"

Calista picks up on his thought.

"Why was the victim brought here? And why was he stashed away in the privy?"

He finds it odd too.

"Did the killer assume that nobody uses this outhouse?" He can't believe it.

That hardly seems plausible to her as well.

"The perpetrator couldn't rule out that somebody might come to the cabin and make himself at home," she says.

"Did he know that Nielle comes by now and then? Was he watching her?"

Calista purses her lips and muses.

"Or did Nielle know about the victim's death? Did *she* see something? Was she attacked for it? Or was she party to it?"

"Whoever hit her certainly intended to have her found soon enough."

He loves brainstorming with Calista like this. Playing out various scenarios. It doesn't matter if something sounds crazy; they simply go on to the next possibility.

She arches her eyebrows until they disappear under the brim of her hat.

"Off the top of my head, I can't imagine Nielle knowing something about the body in the outhouse. I think it's a very low probability."

"Even so, she was at the cabin, maybe often. And she didn't use the toilet?"

Calista's face indicates skepticism.

"Many people hate these outdoor toilets. All Nielle had to do was to check and see that the house was in order. Or whether it had been vandalized. She probably never stayed long. But that's something we have to find out."

"Maybe the attacker hoped Nielle would find the body and didn't figure that she'd never go to the outhouse." He thinks a step further ahead. "How do you bring a dead body here without attracting attention? Under a tarp on a sled?"

He'd like to discuss the victim's police jacket with her. The shots penetrated the material. But since she doesn't bring it up herself, he holds off.

Why is she ignoring the jacket?

She limps toward the cabin. The door is still half open.

She suddenly stops moving.

"Take a look at this, Fred."

She points to a tramped-down spot in the snow. "Don't you see it?"

A dark object contrasting with the white surface, about the size of a grape.

He pulls an evidence bag out of his pocket.

She photographs the spot, then he picks up the object with his gloves on.

It's unmistakably a bronze button from a formal blue RCMP dress uniform.

He clearly sees the royal crest on it. A similar blue dress uniform is also hanging in his closet; the last time he wore it was to the RCMP charity ball in Happy Valley-Goose Bay.

"What stands out for you, Fred?" she asks.

"A needle in a haystack, and we found it."

She keeps looking at him. Finally, the penny drops.

"The button was deliberately put in trampled snow near the door, and not in the soft snow, so that we'd find it."

"I think so too. And another thing: This button didn't come from the victim's jacket. It still has all its buttons."

26

Tiffany Staid, Musher
Ilungilak Crater
Tuesday, February 13

The men from Alliarkuk won't tell her what's up. She hears their lively conversation, but she's too far away to understand words. They're speaking Inuttut, as the Labrador Inuit do; unfortunately, she's not fluent. Who were they calling on the satellite phone?

The dogs sense the commotion; they don't miss a trick. She's got to calm them down. Luckily the sled's snow anchor's holding. She ties one more long wire rope to the cabin that is allotted to her; one of the cabin's supports is ideal. Then she unties the dogs from the team one after the other and distributes them along the rope so they don't fight. The dogs could have made it through another sled run, but the men let her know that she was to stay at the cabin for the time being.

Gerald Hynes still isn't back. Is he staying with the policeman in one of the cabins at Cloud Lake? She doesn't understand any of this. The cop who stopped her had a heavy snowmobile. How did they get those machines up here? Certainly not in the little Cessna. By helicopter?

The opening of the national park must cost a lot. Her dog team is to provide photo ops for the media; it's to showcase Inuit traditions. Makes sense to her. She's proud of it. Her dogs are photogenic. All you can see of them now are round balls in the snow. Their furry tails are lying on their muzzles to protect their noses. Good: the dogs are behaving normally. And the fog has largely dissipated.

Standing around has chilled her. She'd like to warm up by the cabin stove. A door opens, and two men emerge. She sees Pretor open his eyes in the hope that he can go out running again. He always wants to know what's going on.

The men come over to talk to her: "We're going to Crater Lake. Tell us again what went on up there."

Something doesn't add up. Maybe it's all a misunderstanding. The police have acted without informing the Inuit. Same old story.

She relates once again exactly what she told the two men half an hour ago.

"Did I do something wrong?" she asks nervously.

"No, we're just going to check."

"Should I go with you?" She speaks softly so the dogs won't hear. They've got a sixth sense for things like that.

The men shake their head. One even cracks a joke: "We don't have to save Gerald Hynes; we have to save the Mounties."

She knows the drill. Her people often laugh to help themselves deal with serious situations.

"Go inside and wait until we're back," the man says, whose name she doesn't even know.

"Anuaktak needs company," the other man adds.

She waits until the two have left and checks on her dogs. Since they're keeping quiet, she goes inside and sinks into a wave of warmth.

The young man who helped her with the team earlier is at

the table. He's holding a knife and is busy cutting pieces of half-frozen, raw blubber. Tiffany's mouth's watering. She loves *muktuk*.

"Do the dogs need water?" he asks in English.

She's got to laugh to herself. A genuine Inuk's first concern is the dogs. They must be attended to before the owner can take a seat.

"Yes, later, with some dry food. They've had some snow."

"Come, eat and drink with me. It's been a long day," Anuaktak says. He has a likable face.

She takes off her boots and outdoor clothes.

While she's eating muktuk and biscuits, Anuaktak sounds her out. He wants to know everything about her and the dogs.

She'd rather find out what's up with the police and Gerald Hynes. Anuaktak doesn't say a word about them.

She can see how spacious the cabin is by the light of the propane lamp. The generators aren't making any noise yet. Clothes and tools hang on the walls over the bunks. There's a strong smell of hides and fur and tea. And burning wood.

"I've made a fire in your cabin," Anuaktak says. "You've got to add wood during the night."

"How many people will be here overnight?"

"Not many. The politicians will be at the opening ceremony tomorrow and fly back right afterward."

"And the cops?"

"They were already here today, checking everything out."

She puts down her cup of hot tea.

"They've got snowmobiles. How did *they* get up here?"

"No idea. Maybe a government helicopter put them down somewhere."

"You'd have heard the noise, right?"

"Not if it landed at Camp Pinnacle."

She knows about Camp Pinnacle. An Ottawa government facility. A military base. To defend the Arctic.

"Isn't that too far from here?"

"They've got Ski-Doos. It's really good training for them."

Yes, no reason to worry.

Or is there? Why did the cop feel he had to be on the lookout for people around Crater Lake? She chews her muktuk.

Anuaktak watches her eat and grins.

"We're serving the Qallunaat muktuk. And fish eyes."

She's pleased that Anuaktak uses the word *Qallunaat* for white people. And that he cracks jokes. It helps to find yourself in the same boat. He makes her smile. Fish eyes are a delicacy, but not for white people.

"When are the Qallunaat coming tomorrow, exactly?" she asks.

He shrugs.

"Dunno. If they're coming at all."

"What do you mean?"

"Dad says he can already hear a storm quite far away. He can sense things like that."

His father must be one of the men who've gone to Crater Lake. When will they ever be back?

"The weather forecast's good," she says. She knows that's not a persuasive argument. Arctic weather can change without warning.

Anuaktak gets up.

"And the fog wasn't predicted either."

She feels uneasy.

"I've only three days' of dog food."

The pilot wouldn't allow any more than that. He had enough freight on the plane as it was.

"Don't worry. If the Qallunaat don't come, we've lots of fish for us and the dogs."

He laughs again. His teeth are much nicer than Bud Abel's.

His expression suddenly changes.

Snowmobiles. She hears them too.

And she hears a dog barking. Sure to be Rasputin. He just

will not stop. She has to pay attention tomorrow that he doesn't bark when the politicians are making their speeches.

She'll have to stand beside him and stare at him angrily.

If the Qallunaat even get here tomorrow.

Boots tramping in the snow. The door's opened with a bang. They're back.

The men take off their boots and hang their jackets on nails.

Once a cup of tea is in front of them on the table, one of them says in Inuttut: "No cops at Crater Lake. No Gerald Hynes."

She freezes. Do the men think she made it all up?

He goes on: "Many snowmobile tracks at the crater, and warm stoves in the cabins. But no people."

"What direction were the tracks going?" Anuaktak asks.

"Southwest."

"To Camp Pinnacle?"

"That would be a long haul."

Anuaktak looks at the man who must be his father.

"Are you going to call the people in Happy Valley-Goose Bay?"

His dad nods.

"I don't like any of this."

27

Fred van Heisen, RCMP Constable
St. Anthony, Newfoundland
Tuesday, February 13

The body's gone, and the ambulance and Dr. Amaruntgamen along with it. It went amazingly swiftly and without a hitch.

It looks to Fred as if Calista expects the best in people and finds it. They're alone again. Dustin brought the white protective coveralls and a Bluestar Forensic kit before leaving. Calista prefers it to luminol because it doesn't have to be completely dark for it to pick up traces of blood. When the crime-scene forensic expert arrives—and they really hope he'll be here tomorrow—then he can easily use the Bluestar again without the luminescence decreasing. Any traces of blood will still glow.

But they discovered no blood during the first visual inspection. Not in the cabin and not in the outhouse.

Dustin was plainly unhappy that Calista was sending him and Heidy back to Goose Cove to search for potential witnesses.

Fred understands; he'd rather be on the spot too, where he can gain more useful experience for his new job in Saskatoon.

A pair of squawking Canada jays are hopping from branch

to branch up in the trees. Calista looks at them and is probably thinking what he is: if only those birds could tell them what they've seen. But the way it looks, she'll have to read it from the tracks in the snow.

There are tracks from many snowmobiles, along with drag marks where somebody must have pulled Stolke to the outhouse. Calista has already concluded from the footprints she's seen that only one person was able to manage that. A man, in all probability, given the large size of the boot prints. They found small, broken twigs in the privy and a roll of toilet paper. Nothing very exciting.

Fred's disappointed. There's little hope that the twigs will reveal anything about where the victim was shot. Or where he died.

Calista seems more optimistic.

"We're lucky that there's been virtually no snow for the few past days," she says, pulling her hood over her hat. It's grown colder since they arrived at the cabin. The fading daylight penetrates the firs more sparsely. Luck, Fred thinks, is exactly what investigators often need. It levels the playing field, because perpetrators are often lucky as well.

The footprints in the snow are frozen in the cold. They go inside the cabin again for another look around. Sometimes you unexpectedly catch something you missed. It's a typical cabin in the woods. A camp table with a beat-up Formica top that has seen better days. Three old chairs. Cups on nails in the wall. A tin teapot on a simple woodstove. A pile of chopped wood beside it, much too near the oven door to Fred's liking. An old nautical map on the wall opposite, covered with hand-drawn routes and arrows. A rough-hewn plank floor, swept clean; an old, frayed broom leaning against the doorframe.

A question's floating around in his head: "Assuming the killer intentionally planted the button, then why in the snow and not in the cabin?"

Calista wiggles her fingers in her latex gloves like claws,

clenching and stretching them. He feels the cold too but doesn't stick his hands in his pockets so as not to contaminate his gloves.

"I'm guessing the perpetrator wasn't in here at all." She scans the room some more. "I think he was deliberate, someone who only left evidence where he wanted to."

"We've got footprints."

"Yes, he might have worn boots that he otherwise never wears and disposed of them immediately."

"What does that tell us about the perpetrator?" She usually puts that question to him, but now he turns the tables.

"He's a sly one," she answers. "Not necessarily a complicated personality. He acts with purpose, with intent. I can't tell for now if he's following a rigorous plan. Not until I know the cause of death."

"And the police insignia?"

"Could that be a red herring? I mean, it's such a broad hint. Like, 'Look here, look here.' So obvious."

That's not the answer he was hoping for. Maybe she's being a little vague because she doesn't want to come out with all her ideas at once.

He tries another angle. "How are Trent Stolke and Nielle Helfrey connected?"

"I don't see a real connection." He tries to reply, but she cuts him off: "Let's assume that Stolke was shot after he died. Nielle, on the other hand, was beaten but not killed. She was deliberately placed where she could easily be found and helped. Those are two completely different starting points, to my mind two completely different motives behind each act. They don't have to be connected."

Fred's not convinced but says nothing because he can't think of anything persuasive to back it up.

She furrows her brow, like someone deeply worried. Then she looks at him squarely.

"Fred, brace yourself. This is going to push us to the limit."

He doesn't dare ask what she means exactly: To the limits of their capabilities? Or of their collaboration?

28

Detective Sergeant Calista Gates
St. Anthony, Newfoundland
Tuesday, February 13

I might have guessed. Somebody didn't keep his trap shut. The dead man's name is now public knowledge, and I've had calls from the media about Trent Stolke. I'd storm around the conference room to let off steam if I could. But I'm not about to lose my cool at the station.

Fred keeps on working, undaunted. He's printed out the photos of the tracks at the crime scene and is polishing up the press release—a job I handed to him. We installed battery-powered surveillance cameras and motion sensors around the cabin, and Rex keeps an eye on the situation using his laptop while working at the reception desk. So far, he's only picked up a fox and a female moose.

I don't suspect Dr. Amaruntgamen or the ambulance crew of leaking the Trent Stolke case. The doctor enjoys my complete trust; as my physician, she monitors the long-term consequences of the serious brain damage I suffered two and a half years ago. She sends a report to Vancouver from time to time, one of the conditions of my continuing to work for the RCMP during my recovery. I find their terms humiliating, but the doctor has made it as easy for me as possible.

"I'll see that nobody here but me has access to your medical file," she promised me.

I give her great credit for that. There are certainly some people who are keen to get their hands on more information about my brain.

I stop puzzling over where the leak is. Pure waste of time. St. Anthony is a town with barely two thousand inhabitants. The local population has a fundamental need to know everything that's going on in their community. This urge is often stronger than any privacy regulation. It was naïve of me to assume I could keep the affair under lock and key. Now it's a question of damage control.

We have the death certificate from Dr. Amaruntgamen. The victim's body will be kept in cold storage in the hospital until she can deliver it to Corner Brook for forensic examination.

Nothing turned up in the victim's pockets, no cell phone or credit card or anything people normally have on them. Nonetheless, Fred and I don't think a normal, everyday robbery is behind this suspicious death. We believe somebody's tried to eliminate evidence. I'm waiting impatiently for Stolke's bank and phone records. We obtained a warrant for them amazingly fast. It's all online now; we don't have to rouse the judge from her sleep by phone anymore. I love this improvement. We also want to inspect Stolke's home and car.

My ankle still hurts. I prop it up to take the stress off. It's not the first time I've twisted my ankle. It's obviously a weak point of mine.

Rex opens the door. He brings us a plate of his phenomenal sandwiches and sets it on the table. This time it's boiled snow crabs with strips of bacon, marinated tomatoes, and an addictive dressing—Rex gives his recipe to nobody. Woolly's been sleeping in the corner but gets up in a split second, hoping for a treat.

We're waiting for Heidy and Dustin, who have apparently found an eyewitness in Goose Cove.

Rex leaves and comes right back.

I'm bug-eyed as I see what he presents to me.

"Crutches? Rex, you're not serious."

"I can't watch you limping around like that, sarge. These will help you until your foot's better."

"Where did you dig them up so fast?"

"Lenny needed them once. They've been in the garage ever since."

Lenny's his life partner. He's the reason Rex moved from Halifax to St. Anthony. Lucky for me. He's an experienced dispatcher. And a good cook, just like Lenny. They're not married yet, unlike my brother Nikos in Vancouver, who's already adopted two children with his husband Maxwell.

"Woolly! Sit!" Fred shouts, because the dog has his muzzle on the table, threatening the sandwiches.

Woolly goes and lies down. He obeys amazingly well.

I can't protest about the crutches any longer because a call's coming in and Rex discreetly leaves the room.

The caller is one of the two RCMP officers stationed in Roddickton. It was his job to break the news of Stolke's death to his parents in Englee.

I put it on speakerphone so Fred can hear.

"His mother cried and said she was always afraid something would happen to him because he was so reckless," our colleague reports.

"And his father?"

"He was furious. The exact opposite of the mother." He hesitates before continuing: "He made *you*, sergeant, responsible for Trent's death."

"Why's that?"

"He said that you persecuted Trent, although he hadn't done anything."

Trent had already claimed that himself. His hatred was directed solely at me, rather than at any of my team.

"I had the feeling Mr. Stolke was drunk. He's well-known for his drinking."

So, Trent grew up with an alcoholic father. And maybe with an overprotective mother who spoiled him trying to compensate. That would explain a great deal.

"When did the parents last have contact with Trent?"

"A week ago," he says. "He called because he needed the trailer."

"What sort of trailer?"

"A boat trailer."

I write it down at once.

"A boat? That's odd."

The ocean's still totally frozen over. The ice in northern Newfoundland doesn't break up until April or May. Why would Trent be moving a boat? I ask my colleague.

"His father says he doesn't know either. I don't believe him. He simply doesn't want to tell us anything."

"Did Trent ever tell his parents or his friends that he had enemies? Or that he got mixed up with something illegal?"

"I asked that. His father said his only enemy was you." He sounds resigned.

I'd like to cheer him up.

"A cop's got to live with the fact he's become a bogeyman. It happens a lot."

Except in this case I'm the sole target. I seem to be an ideal object of hate for many people. Not only for men like Trent Stolke but for some RCMP men in Vancouver too.

"Sarge, about that uniform jacket, is it true?"

Good god, he knows about that too. The news has made it to Roddickton.

I play the ignoramus.

"What do you mean?"

"The father says Trent was found in an RCMP jacket."

I feel Fred's eyes on me.

"Did you ask him where his son got the jacket?"

"No, I thought he was making it up."

"I couldn't tell you that in advance, constable, because I first wanted to discuss it with HQ in St. John's to see how we should handle it."

That's a lame excuse. I don't want him to think I keep important things from him. I do intend to contact St. John's, though. Ever since that serial killer in Nova Scotia ran amok wearing an RCMP uniform and killed twenty innocents, the idea of people owning a police uniform has been a hot topic.

"Sure thing, sarge. Watch out, this will get around here fast."

"Where did his father get it from?"

"He wouldn't tell me, no matter what."

Of course. But we'll find out at some point. People like to talk—and say a lot.

"I can well imagine. Good work, constable. Thanks so much. Stay with it. Keep your ears open, and call again when you've got something."

The constable clears his throat.

"Sarge, whatever happens, we have your back."

I try not to sound emotional and reply rather dryly: "Thank you. We'll catch whoever did this."

Our conversation is over.

Before I can speak with Fred about it, I hear voices in the hallway, and the Wilsons burst in.

"Sarge!" Heidy shouts. "Guess what we found."

29

Tiffany Staid, Musher
Ilungilak Crater, Labrador
Tuesday, February 13

Anuaktak's father comes in. He's just spoken to Happy Valley-Goose Bay on the satellite phone.

"Nobody's flying tomorrow," he announces. "Too risky. The wind's not at storm level yet, but it's too dangerous. It's snowing and visibility's poor. They're afraid of the storm."

Tiffany's alarmed. Did she understand his Inuttut correctly?

"They're not flying at all tomorrow?"

Anuaktak's father shrugs.

"They're scaredy-cats."

"So when will the event with the politicians take place?" Anuaktak asks.

"Nobody knows. They're waiting for good weather."

"They cannot possibly know what it'll be like tomorrow," Anuaktak says.

Tiffany was about to say the same thing.

"Anything to do with bureaucracy is complicated," his father states.

It's just four o'clock but already dark outside the little windows.

The men are getting ready for a stormy night in the cabin. They've brought all the necessities: provisions and gas cans and extra firewood.

"You're sleeping in here," Anuaktak's dad says.

That's fine by her; she wouldn't feel safe in the other cabin by herself.

The dogs will spend the night outside in the storm. Straw's been put down for them, and their weight has pressed it into the ground. It's not for the first time, and she knows the dogs will survive. Still, she's concerned because the weather's changed so abruptly. Nobody saw it coming. What more can she expect to happen?

Gerald Hynes is not back.

Apart from her and the men from Alliarkuk, that seems to trouble nobody. Anuaktak's dad is upset. The people in Happy Valley-Goose Bay fobbed him off: "If he's with the security guys, nothing's going to happen to him." The men from Alliarkuk think that any responsible person must at least talk to the police before saying something like that.

Tiffany tries to keep her anxiety under control. She's an Inuk, after all. She ought to follow the example of the men in the cabin who've resigned themselves to an unavoidable situation and will make the best of it.

Anuaktak's father tosses a deck of cards on the table.

"I hope you're playing, because my pal here loves to cheat, so we have to teach him a lesson," he jokes.

The three men laugh.

Tiffany finds it infectious. It's how my people survive, she thinks to herself. They laugh off trouble and threats. The "pal" is Anuaktak's uncle, as she's found out in the meantime.

"We'll keep an eye on him," she says. "What's the game?"

"Hundred and twenties. But not for money, because my son always wins."

Laughter fills the cabin again.

The uncle's the dealer.

The wind howls louder outside.

All of a sudden they hear something. Snowmobiles.

They stop the game, get up, and go look out the window. Not much to see. Rasputin barks. Tiffany's stomach tightens. Stupid dog—he'll wake up the rest of the team.

Is Gerald Hynes back at last?

The tramp of boots in firm snow. Loud knocking. Two figures enter, quickly closing the door behind them.

They take their helmets off and introduce themselves.

Tiffany forgets their names immediately. All she hears are the words *constable* and *RCMP*.

Cops.

"We almost couldn't find you," one of them says. "We lost our way in the storm. Have you got room for us for tonight?"

Tiffany's heart beats faster. She can't tell if he's the cop who ordered her to go back without Hynes. His voice sounds similar, but the man had been wearing a jacket with a hood and had snow goggles.

"You can sleep in the cabin next door," Anuaktak's father says. "There's a stove in there too. You'll have to put on more firewood to stay warm." He doesn't bat an eyelash at their surprise arrival.

Tiffany wouldn't have expected anything different. Hospitality's in her people's blood.

"How did you find us, anyway?" Anuaktak asks.

"We followed the dog and sled tracks. But then it got dark. We turned on our headlamps and kept going slowly ahead."

"Have some tea with us." Anuaktak's father takes the cards off the table.

The cops don't need a second invitation.

Anuaktak and Tiffany look at each other as the visitors sit down with them.

Go ahead and ask, she prompts him wordlessly.

He gets her meaning.

"Have you seen Gerald Hynes?"

"Who?" one of the cops says.

"Gerald Hynes, the contractor from Port Brendan. He was at Crater Lake."

"No, we didn't see anybody. Where is he?"

"We don't know. Tiffany here took him to Crater Lake on her dogsled. Hynes hiked around a bit and wanted to be alone, so Tiffany went off to Cloud Lake. She crossed paths with a policeman there who sent her back to us. What did he say to you, Tiffany?"

All eyes turn to her.

"He said I had to go back to this cabin. He would bring Hynes here on his snowmobile."

"That wasn't a policeman," the other cop says. "We'd like to know *who* he was. What was he wearing?" He looks at her closely. His gaze promises no good.

"Dark clothes, like you. He said he was RCMP."

"Anybody can say that. Did he have on a jacket like ours?" He turns his back to her. *POLICE* is written on it in white letters.

She only saw the man from the front.

"Did you see this?" The second cop points to the letters.

"No," she admits. "He was on the snowmobile, and . . ."

"That was no RCMP officer," the first cop butts in. "Are you sure you saw someone?"

That takes her breath away. They had pounded it into her beforehand to follow any orders from security people and with no backtalk. And now this.

"Yes, I met a person. He sent me back here. Or I wouldn't have come back without Gerald Hynes."

"Whoever sent her back was posing as a policeman," Anuaktak confirms. "Or she would of course have brought Hynes with her. That's why she's here in the first place."

Tiffany's relieved that Anuaktak has come to her defense.

The other men don't reveal their thoughts. They let him do the talking.

"I don't know what went on there, and you don't know either," the first cop says. "It's impossible to look for this guy Hynes now."

The second cop seems to have an idea.

"Does anybody in Happy Valley-Goose Bay know about this?"

"My father and my uncle went looking for Hynes on snowmobiles. My father phoned somebody from the Nunatsiavut government."

"Who?"

Anuaktak's dad says nothing. He doesn't trust the cops, Tiffany thinks.

"The people who hired us," Anuaktak says. He doesn't trust them either. He names no names. Tiffany realizes that she has allies in these men.

The Mounties stand up as if on a given signal.

"We're very grateful we can stay in the cabin," one of them says. "Is there enough wood?"

"Yes, in a box on the wall. You can eat with us later. Say, in an hour." Anuaktak's father has found his voice again.

The cops thank him and leave the cabin.

Rasputin doesn't bark this time. Good; the dogs are asleep.

Tiffany is nevertheless in low spirits, still sitting at the table.

Anuaktak squeezes her shoulder.

"Don't be intimidated," he advises.

His father says something she's heard him say before.

"I don't like all this."

It's almost black out.

Where is Gerald Hynes?

30

Fred van Heisen, RCMP Constable
St. Anthony, Newfoundland
Tuesday, February 13

Heidy Wilson doesn't deliver her news immediately because Woolly overwhelms her with vigorous tail wagging. She can't help petting him. Dustin looks at the two in silence, and Fred observes all three of them.

"Shall we take a seat?" Calista asks at last.

Dustin grabs one of the sandwiches and eats while his wife looks around triumphantly.

"We have an eyewitness who saw somebody on a Ski-Doo drop something right where we found Nielle Helfrey."

We didn't find Nielle, Fred thinks, it was young snowmobilers, but he doesn't want to rain on Heidy's parade.

"We were at the Nobles', and old Mr. Noble said he saw it."

"How far away was he? Where's the Nobles' place located?" Calista asks. She constantly reminds her team how cautiously to treat eyewitness reports. They're not always reliable.

"Diagonally across from the harbor. So, relatively close.

Certainly not as far away as the houses on the other side of the bay."

"Why didn't Mr. Noble tell anyone about this until now?"

"He did! He says he told his daughter. And he told Trina Modeste, who comes to see him regularly."

"And they told us nothing?" Fred's irritated.

Heidy's not annoyed, apparently.

"Fred, you know what many folks here are like. They don't want to get sucked into anything."

"What did Mr. Noble say, precisely?" Calista asks again.

"A snowmobile comes over the hill, stops on the right spot, and something large falls onto the snow and stays there."

"He thought it was a moose calf," Dustin adds, putting the witness's testimony in an unfavorable light.

"That's what he thought *at first*," his wife hastens to correct him. "But when the snowmobile had left, he realized it was a person. From the way it was lying."

Calista's taking notes and looks up.

"Did he recognize the snowmobile?"

"No."

"Was it partly red?"

"He didn't exclude it out of hand. It was different from the ones he knows."

"Was he able to describe the driver?"

"Not really," Dustin answers.

Heidy gives him a hard look.

"Oh, he was: light-colored jacket, probably dark pants, very agile. So not an old person. Everything happened very fast."

Fred reminds Heidy of a question Calista taught her team, and he asks it now: "What was Mr. Noble's very first thought when he saw the scene?"

"I asked him that; I didn't forget to." Heidy almost sounds insulted, as if Fred were underestimating her. "He thought: Why's the guy going back over the rise where he came from and not toward the village?"

Calista lays her ballpoint down on the pad and rolls it back and forth.

"Thank you, Heidy, that confirms our suspicions. He immediately took the same route back."

But does it help us? Fred thinks.

"Why didn't Trina Modeste tell us what Mr. Noble saw?" he asks out loud.

"She was at Mrs. Eddison's yesterday. When was she at Mr. Noble's?" Calista looks at Heidy.

"At noon today. And I found out something else." Heidy's eyes sparkle. "Trent Stolke got his girlfriend pregnant. She just turned seventeen."

Calista looks surprised.

"What's her name?"

"Betty Burn, from Main Brook. I promised not to name my source, but it can be easily verified."

"Do we have a motive here?" Dustin asks.

"This case isn't so simple," Calista says.

Fred sees what she's about to do. Best not to reveal that he already knows.

Calista shows the Wilsons the photographs of the victim that Fred printed out.

"Do you see this bullet wound? What do you notice?"

Heidy and Dustin stare at the enlargement, frowning.

Heidy will find it first, Fred thinks.

And so it is.

"No bruises bordering the entry wound."

"And what's our conclusion?"

"The victim was shot when he was already dead." Heidy again.

Dustin shakes his head.

"But that's crazy. Then what did Tornado die from? There's no reason to shoot him when he's already dead."

Calista's voice stays calm.

"Forensics will have to determine the cause of death. We've got to find out the rest ourselves."

"And what's with the RCMP jacket? Do we know anything more? Why was he wearing it?"

Calista shrugs, which means she doesn't have the answer. Or it means she has a potential answer but doesn't want to reveal it.

Fred feels the need to join the discussion.

"Maybe Trent Stolke got inspired by the mass murderer in Nova Scotia who was in police uniform when he ran amok."

Dustin doesn't swallow that theory.

"So that he can trick his victims? But Trent's the victim here and not the killer."

Fred thinks of the press release he's drafted. The RCMP jacket isn't mentioned. Neither are the sergeant's insignia or the uniform button. But news of Stolke's jacket is already making the rounds among the locals. How is Calista going to explain it to the public?

Heidy pipes up again.

"Did Trent stage the whole thing? To thumb his nose at the RCMP?"

"Are you out of your mind? Why would he stage his own death? He wasn't at all suicidal."

They all stare at Dustin in astonishment. He's never snapped at his wife like that.

When he sees the team's reaction, he apologizes.

"I'm not in good shape. Must be a virus or something."

Heidy looks embarrassed but quickly recovers.

"Dustin's right: the pregnancy might be a motive for getting back at Trent. We should take a closer look at Betty Burn's family."

Calista agrees.

"Somehow, we've got to find out if he really fathered that unborn child. The main things we need are a forensic investigation and an autopsy report."

Fred can empathize with her impatience. He feels the same way.

"If Corner Brook doesn't get a move on, can we ask the Labrador team as an alternative?"

She nods.

"That would be an option in a pinch, but there would be some obstacles. It's not as if they're champing at the bit in Happy Valley-Goose Bay."

He can see why. Their medical examiner has enough on her plate what with drug overdoses and suicide victims.

Calista continues: "Our colleagues in Labrador could question Morris Tye in Happy Valley-Goose Bay. He's not flying to Crater Lake tomorrow. Nobody's flying. The event has been postponed for a day because a storm's come up."

Fred looks at her, amazed.

"They're supposed to question him about Nielle Helfrey?"

Her answer baffles him even more.

"They're to ask him why he recently bought a snowmobile with red stripes in St. Anthony."

Silence pervades the room for several seconds.

Then a confusion of shouts.

"Sarge, is that true?"

"How'd you find out?"

"Red stripes? Really?"

Calista reaches for a sandwich. Before she takes a bite, she tells all: "Very simple. I phoned the Ski-Doo store in St. Anthony and asked if Morris Tye had ever bought a snowmobile there. I can imagine he would give something like that to his mistress if he was head over heels in love with her. He'd pretend it was for himself, naturally, and not mention her." She nibbles her sandwich.

"But . . . aren't we assuming that the *perpetrator* has a red-striped snowmobile?" Heidy looks bewildered.

She's not familiar with Calista's convoluted way of thinking the way he is.

Calista nods.

"That was one option. It always pays to take other options into account."

Fred's just as perplexed as the Wilsons, but for a different reason. Why didn't Calista tell him about this? Why did she wait until Heidy and Dustin were back? He's annoyed.

Dustin wraps himself in atypical silence, but Heidy ploughs ahead: "So then the wildlife officer saw *Nielle* on the red-striped snowmobile and not her attacker?"

"It seems that way."

Calista notices that her revelation doesn't make everybody happy.

"It was pure speculation on my part. And lo! Bull's-eye." She takes a bite and eats as the rest of them watch. "Aren't you all hungry?" she asks. "Sometimes you just have to give it a shot. Now we're looking for that red-striped Ski-Doo. It's probably somewhere around the cabin where the perpetrator stashed it."

31

Paige Warner, Entrepreneur
Toronto, Ontario
Eight Years Earlier

Howard almost got wise to her. He found the four backpacks in the garage when he was storing some equipment for his New Guinea expedition. She'd ordered various backpacks to test the models and select the best one for the Ilungilak tour. A good backpack is almost as vital as a pair of comfortable hiking boots.

When Howard came into the kitchen with one of the backpacks—she was warming up a frozen dinner—she was lucky an excuse popped into her head immediately: "I might want to add backpacks to my inventory and need to check out the competition."

He grumbled an answer: "Why didn't you have them sent to your office? There's too much junk stored in the garage as it is."

They own a double garage with plenty of room. It's *her* house; Howard moved in with her four years ago when their relationship firmed up. He was pleased with the location in a green part of the city, quiet but not far from the city center.

He's a cleanliness freak. She wonders how he'll put up with the slimy, hot, and moist jungle of Papua New Guinea.

He found the two tents shortly afterward. Durable but surprisingly light.

"You're going to sell tents, too?" he asked with fake nonchalance covering his distrust.

"Probably not. Backpacks are more in line with our merchandise."

"I like this style. Can I try it out? Maybe it's better than mine."

"Sure," she replied. Then she had an idea: "Let's test it out tonight." She sent him an unambiguous look that he interpreted correctly.

It solved the problem of putting up the tent somewhere as a trial without him realizing why. They spent the night in the yard; it was a romantic one, and Howard kept the tent for himself: he was convinced. He'd always been quick to accept a gift. She ordered a new tent and had it delivered to the office. Howard didn't ask any more bothersome questions.

Paige settles in on the patio with some work papers on the garden table. Howard's out training and getting in shape for the expedition.

Her cell phone suddenly plays Mozart. It's not Howard but Ellen.

"Where did you get this number?" Paige asks, surprised. Only a few people know her personal cell phone number. She certainly didn't give it to the three women.

"From you, of course," Ellen explains.

Is that right? Paige searches her memory. Did she accidentally give Ellen the wrong number? How else could she have gotten it? It's secret. *Shoot!*

"Oh, this is the wrong number. Can you use the other number from now on, the one I gave you all?"

"Sure, no problem. But we have another issue."

Paige pricks up her ears. She doesn't expect everything to go smoothly; problems are there to be solved. She has considerable trouble-shooting abilities, or she'd never have gotten as far as she has.

"I happened to run into Sandy at the gas station where she's the manager. We shot the breeze for a while. And it came out that she's told several people about our trip."

What a bummer! "Told whom?"

"Family and friends."

Sandy, of all people, who talks so little about herself. That totally violates their agreement.

"I'll call her right away and talk to her. Thanks for the tip."

When Paige calls her, Sandy's nonplussed.

"Paige, you said no details. I didn't mention the place or who's going. I have to inform my boss that I'm taking a trip and for how long. And I've got to tell my family *something*. If I didn't say a peep, then they'll be all the more eager to know. You'd do the same thing in my shoes. Right?"

She's right, of course. Sandy certainly feels criticized, but Paige manages to placate her. What's important is that the public mustn't know anything, particularly Howard. She can't let Sandy know that she herself must clue some people in. The company lawyer, for instance. And the insurance company.

But this has left her with a bad taste in her mouth. Why is Ellen squealing on Sandy? Does she not like her? Ellen says she happened to run into her at the gas station. Paige doesn't find that kind of coincidence credible. Did Ellen want to suss Sandy out? She suddenly realizes how little information she has about these three women, despite her research. Paige hopes they'll all get along together although she doesn't know that for certain.

But so it goes in the business world. You must take risks to get results. It's only a trekking tour, after all, she tells herself. They'll have a satellite phone and emergency transmitters. And contact with a bush plane that can pick them up in the event of an emergency.

32

Detective Sergeant Calista Gates
St. Anthony, Newfoundland
Tuesday, February 13

Things are moving along. We tracked down Nielle's snowmobile before nightfall. It was indeed a good way off and hidden behind the cabin in some bushes.

I'm happy that we're getting a crime scene forensic expert from Corner Brook, thanks to the assistance of Inspector Terence Lametti; I'd worked with him very closely a few months ago. If the weather plays along, he'll be here in the morning. St. Anthony will continue to head the investigation, and the files will remain in my hands. My team and I could have finished documenting most of the tracks at the scene, but because a provincial member of parliament is involved, I want to have an outside expert backing me up who's well-versed in fingerprint analysis.

So far, so good.

Fred's still concerned about my health.

"You've done all you can for the moment," he argues. "We'll hold down the fort, and you go think about recent developments in total peace and quiet inside your own four walls."

But I intend to spend part of the night on a cot in my office, just in case. We have search warrants for Stolke's apartment, pickup, and computer. There's so much work to do.

I'm unable to turn off my thoughts. What happened to Nielle? I think somebody attacked her at the cabin, then took her to Goose Cove on her own Ski-Doo and left her in the snow, unconscious. But why? It sounds so crazy.

Fred insists I should go home and rest in a proper bed. He knows my brain needs a lot of sleep to recuperate. A consequence of my injury. Since the attack on me, I've had enormously productive spurts of work—until my brain slams on the brakes and demands rest. It's a real handicap in situations like this. I hide it as best I can. I should actually be happy, because most people with brain damage suffer from chronic insomnia and not from fatigue.

For all my protesting, Fred still drives me home. He tells the Wilsons: "Sarge has been sentenced to assess the crime scene photos." He knows me so well. He knows my best ideas come when I can think things over in peace and calm. It wasn't like that before I was attacked in Vancouver. I used to need people and noise around me. That's how I grew up with six brothers and sisters and lots of visitors in our home. My parents were very welcoming; it's their Greek heritage. Our house was "Little Greece" in the middle of Burnaby. They're taking it easy now; age brings many changes.

"Gates, has it hurt you professionally so far?" my doctor in Vancouver asked when I reported on my long periods of sleep. She always calls me by my family name.

Truth is, no, not really. Thanks to Fred. He keeps a watchful eye on me.

There's another reason to give into him today: my RCMP informant in Vancouver tried to reach me. I don't want to talk to her in my office. Our calls are confidential.

With Fred's help and in the light of the motion sensor, I hobble to the door of my house on crutches. Then he leaves for the station. Nobody's in the house to say hello. If I weren't away so often, I'd get a pet. Not a cockatoo, to be sure, like Vyann Kippen. I can't lock a bird up in a cage.

I make hot chocolate, pick up the files, and flop down on the sofa. The pounding in my foot settles down. Going through the photos of the cabin, I stop and study Trent's frozen face. I would never have wished anything bad on him. He wasn't even thirty. His parents have lost their son. What a tragedy for the family. And for the young, pregnant girlfriend. Trent was much less of a problem for me alive than dead. He turned people against me, of course. Troublemakers and cop-haters are everywhere. As a member of the RCMP, I've learned you've got to live with it. Those characters remind us not to abuse our power. That's how I see it.

It is a fact, though, that Trent said things about me that he really couldn't have known. For instance, he said on Facebook that I once tampered with the evidence at a crime scene in Vancouver. That's exactly what the defense lawyer for some criminal accused me of back when he was questioning me on the witness stand. The lawyer was clever, but of course he was lying. How did Trent dream up such a thing? A man from a small Newfoundland fishing village, Englee, who'd never been to Vancouver. That really made me wonder.

Now Trent's gone, and somebody shot him in the chest twice after he died.

I feel my ankle. Slightly swollen, but nothing to worry about. I go to the kitchen, get a bite to eat, and call my informant. It's four in the afternoon in Vancouver, half past eight in St. Anthony.

"Just a second," she says. She has to find a secure place where no one is listening.

"How are you?"

Normally she doesn't waste time with niceties; her question means something else.

"We've got a suspicious death," I say, "really remarkable. Bullet wounds postmortem."

"What's so remarkable?"

"The victim's a civilian but was wearing an RCMP jacket." I can tell her because Trent's father knows already. It's not a secret anymore.

A pause at the other end.

"Wow. That is . . . very remarkable. Be on your guard."

"Why? Are there problems?"

"I've heard that our enemies have set a spy on you."

"A spy?"

"Somebody's watching you."

"Here? In St. Anthony? Why?"

"You're the face of the enemy, a bogeyman." She almost says my name but catches herself in time. We're excessively cautious.

I know that "enemy" refers to people inside the RCMP. They see me as a traitor because three RCMP officers are under investigation, courtesy of my doggedness.

A spy. It's practically laughable.

"I can't hide in St. Anthony anyway. Everybody here sees everything. Who could it be?"

"I'd take it seriously. Maybe somebody's trying to pin something on you. A fabricated screwup, for example."

"Are they stirring up people against me?"

"And how! Don't trust anybody."

"There are good people, too. We shouldn't forget that. People who are on our side." *Our side.* My informant, who used to work for me, is among them, but also people who don't want corrupt officials dragging the RCMP's reputation through the mud. We want to win the power struggle that's smoldering between the two sides. We must win if we don't want to be sidelined.

"Don't trust anybody," she repeats. "Gotta go. See you."

Her last words sound frantic. Someone must have been approaching.

I feel like having a chat with Gerald. Too bad that's not possible today; he's somewhere near Crater Lake. Probably in one of the hunting cabins he mentioned last weekend. He might well stay there until the storm's over; it came up quite unexpectedly. He won't be taking any unnecessary risks, since he almost died on the Labrador pack ice a few weeks ago.

I go back to the sofa and study the crime scene photographs of the snowmobile tracks and footprints. Out of the corner of my eye, I see some movement at the large panoramic window. It's snowing in soft, puffy flakes. Great that we've already got the photos in the bag. The profiles of the snowmobile runners are all alike; it's hard to make out any differences. Still, I think I've found something after half an hour of looking.

At the cabin there were tracks from four snowmobiles that did not belong to our team: first, Nielle's and one belonging to the perpetrator. And then two more. I'm eager to see if the crime-scene forensics people come to the same conclusion. Drag tracks lead from one of the snowmobiles to the outhouse. That agrees with the footprints. To judge by the tracks, Nielle and two men were at the cabin. Or women with big feet. There don't seem to be any footprints from the fourth person. Strange.

It will take a lot of footwork to turn up the other snowmobiles. I'll leave that to Dustin Wilson. Hopefully that will cheer him up a bit; he seemed very depressed today. I need Heidy for the police jacket. She's to find out where it came from. Too bad we haven't come up with the object Nielle was beaten with. It could give us so much more information.

Maybe the solution to the puzzle isn't to be found in St. Anthony but in Labrador, where Nielle's from. I've texted Inspector Peter Allen in Happy Valley-Goose Bay because I couldn't get him on the phone. I'd like him to question Morris Tye about the red-striped snowmobile he bought for Nielle.

It's after nine, but I try to get Allen by phone one more time. Just the answering machine again.

I lie back on the sofa. The warmth in the house makes me drowsy.

I hear twittering, as if off in the distance.

My cell phone. I give a start. Where am I? I blink hard, trying to see properly.

Five forty-four. It's morning!

I recognize the number on the display.

David Pelletier. He was on my team in St. Anthony until six months ago. Now he's posted to Happy Valley-Goose Bay; Peter Allen's his boss.

"Sarge, did you hear about Gerald Hynes? He was on his way to Crater Lake, and now nobody can find him."

33

Tiffany Staid, Musher
Ilungilak Crater, Labrador
Wednesday, February 14

The storm is raging. It's rattling the cabin like a wild animal shaking its cage.

Tiffany rubs her eyes. She's hardly slept a wink. The howling outside and her worry over the dogs have kept her awake for a long time. And thinking about Gerald Hynes.

Anuaktak's father kept the fire going all night. He didn't get much rest either. The others are still not stirring in their bunks. She sloughs off her sleeping bag and goes into the cabin annex where the composting toilet is. It's ice-cold, but at least she has her privacy.

Her mind quickly reverts to the cops and yesterday evening. How dare they accuse her of lying! As if she'd made up encountering the third cop. They're rotten! The one thing that keeps her steady is the certainty that the men from Alliarkuk believe her and not the two cops. Maybe neither of them is the one who sent her back here. But why hasn't Hynes reported in? He must surely know what his absence means for her. Aside from the fact the storm outside is life-threatening.

She hears noises from the common space. Reluctantly, she leaves the john.

Anuaktak picks up a pot off the stove plate.

"Tea?"

"I must feed the dogs." The dogs always come first.

"I'll help you," Anuaktak says. "But you've got to get some tea in you before going out."

The hot drink does her good. She has a chocolate bar to top it off.

Not a murmur from the cops. You couldn't hear much in all the howling anyway.

Now the two other men start to move. They stretch, yawn.

A little while later, they're all around the table.

"We're going to look for him again," Anuaktak's father says. "You're coming with us."

Tiffany looks at him in amazement. When was this decided? Or was it always the plan?

"We'll go before the cops wake up," he continues. "Or they might keep us back."

"But the storm," she objects.

"We've got to go now. It will only get worse this afternoon. We'll be back by then."

"With the dogs?"

"Yes, they'll find the way there. You stop at the place where you left Hynes off."

They respect me as a musher, Tiffany thinks. I'm one of theirs.

She throws on her outdoor gear and takes some snacks for the dogs. Just a small bite; they don't run well on a full stomach.

Encouraged, she follows Anuaktak out of the cabin. The storm feels less severe than it sounds inside. Visibility's not so bad, maybe twenty meters. The dogs get up at once, shaking off the snow as though it were nothing. She greets each one separately, which motivates them all. Then she throws them freeze-dried meat cubes. Rasputin can't resist barking louder than the rest, the rascal.

Anuaktak helps her get the team ready. The dogs are euphoric. They want nothing more than to run. Just one big snow anchor holds them back. It's a bedlam of barking and panting. She sees the door of the other cabin open and quickly close. The cops are awake.

They've no time to lose. Anuaktak's father and his uncle are already on their snowmobiles. They provide some security. They have their rifles, as she does hers.

"Can you take me on your sled?" Anuaktak shouts. He needs to yell over the storm.

"Sure," she shouts back. The trip shouldn't be all that bumpy. "Here, take my gun and keep it warm." She passes it on.

He sits down on the sled, pulls the cover up, and ties it down. Tiffany gives the signal to start.

"Let's go, doggies!"

The team flies off like an arrow.

They're running into a white wall, but she can nevertheless occasionally spot runner tracks from the day before.

It's basically straight ahead. Pretor's capable of holding a dead straight line for a long stretch. Not many dogs can do that, Irvin told her. He'd buy Pretor from her anytime and race him, but she'd never let her lead dog go.

She must meet the storm head on. She leans forward to reduce wind resistance and make it easier on the dogs. Not a comfortable position, but it's not too far to Crater Lake.

She uses the metal claw brake to throttle down their speed; the team's simply flying along the straightaway. She mustn't leave the snowmobiles too far behind.

Pretor catches on and cuts the speed.

Good dog.

Anuaktak clings tight to the sled; it's a wild ride.

Suddenly a silhouette looms up to the east. A rise of land jutting up out of the white plain. Crater Lake.

Tiffany can hardly believe it. They've arrived so soon. She brings her team and the sled to a halt. The men slow down and finally stop.

This is the spot. Here's where Gerald Hynes began his march at the foot of the crater. She has a clear view of the pillar protruding from the inukshuk.

The fierce wind hasn't let up and tears at her clothes and the dogs' coats; they lie down and roll up into furry balls. Visibility is still limited but hasn't become any worse.

Her companions get their vehicles moving again. Tiffany watches them travel in circles and ellipses until the lead one stops. The other snowmobile comes up to it.

"What do they see?" Anuaktak yells. The dogs lift their heads in unison.

"Dunno," she shouts back. She'd like to know, too.

The men pick something up, examine it, lay it back on the ground. Then they go back to crisscrossing the landscape.

It seems like an eternity until they return. Anuaktak's dad points in the direction of Cloud Lake. She understands. He wants to go to the two hunting cabins on the shore.

The team picks up the pace again. Luckily, the dogs didn't create chaos by entangling the lines. She could give each of them a hug of gratitude.

They reach the cabins where Anuaktak helps her set the snow anchor, and together they tie the wire rope to a cabin support.

The men take off their helmets and pull their hoods on. Then they go into an unlocked cabin. Tiffany follows Anuaktak. The room isn't as large as the one they'd slept in, but cozy enough. Not freezing. Cups, sugar, and a can of condensed milk on a table. Anuaktak's father investigates the stove. There were a lot of glowing embers in it.

Somebody must have spent the night here, Tiffany thinks.

And it wasn't one of the cops who stopped off at their place. Was it Gerald Hynes?

"What did you find back there?" Anuaktak asks.

"A camera bag," his father says.

"Was there a camera in it?"

"Probably. The bag's heavy."

Tiffany can't hold back any longer.

"Hynes was carrying a bag over his shoulder."

Anuaktak's father nods.

"We'll report it to the cops. But we don't want to be carrying it if we meet anyone."

Tiffany understands his caution.

They leave the first cabin and go to the other one.

When Anuaktak's uncle tries to open the door, it doesn't give. He tries again, shakes it—no luck. The men go to a snowed-up window and manage to look in.

At that moment they hear motors.

They turn around.

It's cops on their snowmobiles.

They stop and take off their helmets.

"What are you doing here?" one of them asks gruffly.

Anuaktak's father stays calm.

"Why is this door locked?" he asks.

"We've got some equipment and things in there."

"We never lock cabins up here. They must be left open so people can rescue themselves in an emergency."

The cop approaches the cabin as if he owned it.

At that very second a shot rings out.

And another.

34

Detective Sergeant Calista Gates
St. Anthony, Newfoundland
Wednesday, February 14

I get up so quickly from the sofa that a sharp pain in my ankle immediately makes me fall back.

"What do you mean they can't find him?" My thoughts connect in a slow crawl because of my drowsy state.

"He was at Crater Lake with a dog team, apparently," Pelletier explains. "He wanted to be let off there and picked up later. But they haven't been able to find him. He's not there anymore."

I try to organize the information I'm being fed.

"With a dog team? Why was he going by dogsled?"

"I think they wanted it there for the media because it looks good in the photographs. The dogs belong to a young Inuk from Tulliq."

I connect some dots. David probably heard it from his girlfriend, another Inuk from Labrador. "Didn't the musher find Gerald later?"

"She wasn't the only one. There are three Mounties from Labrador looking for him, too."

"The RCMP is already there and searching? I heard that nobody can fly in because of the storm." My throat tightens. Gerald's missing in a storm!

"They've been there since yesterday morning to keep an eye on everything."

"You've got three men at Crater Lake? Won't the VIPs have their own security with them?"

"Oh sure, but they're coming later on the environment minister's plane."

"A minister from Ottawa?" Wow. This *is* a big deal.

"Yes. They're waiting for better weather."

"Gerald told me he would spend the night in a hunting cabin. Did they search all the cabins in the area?"

"I assume so. They'll know what they're doing."

I can only hope. It's probably all a big misunderstanding. Gerald doesn't simply go and get himself lost. He wanted to explore the site by himself to get a better idea of it for his construction project.

"Sarge, are you leaving St. Anthony?"

"No, why do you ask?"

"I've heard rumors that Austin Sullivan is applying for your job."

Sullivan? What's he got to do with anything?

"It really is just a stupid rumor," I say, baffled.

"I thought you would at least have heard about it."

It dawns on me once more how much I really miss having David Pelletier on my team ever since he took a posting in Happy Valley-Goose Bay because of his girlfriend. He's so young and talented. The opposite of Austin Sullivan, who was no shining light on my team in Port Brendan. Sullivan couldn't stand me.

David, on the other hand, was always loyal to me. Maybe I can pry a little more out of him.

"I've tried several times to reach Inspector Allen and can't get an answer."

"Doesn't surprise me," David says. "He's got his hands full because three of his men are at Crater Lake. Is it about the dead man in the police jacket?"

So, they already know about it in Happy Valley-Goose Bay.

"I wish I could give you a satisfactory answer," I reply evasively, hoping not to disappoint him.

Peter Allen's silence is irritating. You respond to a call from another station, even if you're under great stress. Maybe he's guessed what I want from him. He's heard about the attack on Nielle Helfrey and might be leery of getting involved. But *David* wants to help me. Can I ask him if his boss is taking Morris Tye into account here? No, I must find that out by myself.

"Thanks a lot, constable, keep me updated," I say, adding: "As far as it's possible." He will certainly understand what I mean by "as far as." In the past he's found explosive, hard-to-come-by things on the internet for me that helped solve some cases.

"*Avec plaisir*," he responds in the language of his Quebec hometown.

I stay on the sofa after the call, overwhelmed. There's still that throbbing pain in my ankle. Maybe I really should go to the hospital, but I don't have time. And there's that pain inside me too. How serious is Gerald's situation? Hard to say. He's been missing for one night. Maybe it will all be cleared up today. The area around the crater is huge. Hunting cabins are scattered far apart. The RCMP men probably don't know the place very well. Gerald was with a musher. She certainly won't be alone; other Inuit will be on the scene. It's their territory.

The thought calms me a bit.

Do Gerald's parents know they're searching for him? I can see them before me, so fragile and lost. I mustn't panic. That would help no one, certainly not Gerald. Besides, I've got two important cases to solve.

Smartphone in hand, I concentrate hard. Then it occurs to me how I can lure Inspector Allen to the phone.

I enter a text message: *We have a death with some suspicious circumstances. I want to interrogate Morris Tye. Can you help?*

If he's trying to keep Tye out of it, he'll want to know why I'm interested in the politician.

I hobble on my crutches to the kitchen and make some coffee. Decaf coffee—my stomach is in enough of a knot already. It just can't be that the contractor for the planned lodge, of all people, can't be found. All interested parties must be worried about his whereabouts. Including the Canadian environment minister.

Inspector Allen calls within five minutes.

"Sergeant Gates, what can I do for you?"

Well, now, we're off to a good start.

"Inspector, we've got a serious attack on a woman in Goose Cove, and word is that she's Morris Tye's lover. She's presently in the hospital in St. John's and not available for questioning. She works as a caregiver for the elderly, and one of her clients asked her to check on his cabin in the woods periodically. We found a dead body at his cabin."

"Do you suspect Morris Tye?"

His question's enlightening. He's not concerned about Nielle Helfrey.

"I'm hoping to get some useful information out of him."

"Because of rumors about a putative lover?"

I hear a giant question mark in his words.

"Inspector, if I didn't have some good reasons to question Mr. Tye, I wouldn't trouble you with it, believe me."

"Can you tell me those good reasons?"

I mention the red-striped snowmobile Tye bought in St. Anthony and that it's in Nielle's possession.

Inspector Allen doesn't conceal his skepticism.

"Maybe Mr. Tye sold her the snowmobile. What would he be doing with a snowmobile in St. Anthony?"

"That's exactly what I'd like to ask him."

Why is he coming to Tye's defense? It's clear to me that he'll only confront Tye as a last resort. Who wants to alienate an influential politician? But Peter Allen should be aware, meanwhile, that I'm not wasting my time on trivialities. He knows me from my time in Port Brendan when I was stationed in Labrador.

Nonetheless, he tries to shake me off.

"Right now, we're pretty well understaffed. I've got three men up at Crater Lake. They're looking for Gerald Hynes."

"Why? Has something happened?" I act as if David Pelletier had never called.

"Hynes has either cut and run or is doing something on his own initiative."

Allen's answer puzzles me. The inspector has apparently formed his own opinion regarding Gerald.

I must refrain with all my might from asking anything more. Allen's answer reveals that he's not going to come forward with anything useful about Gerald. I suspect he mentioned Gerald mainly to distract me from Morris Tye.

A text message comes in on my phone. Later.

I gather up my strength and continue, leaving Gerald out of it.

"It's better if Mr. Tye explains himself to the police before the case attracts more attention."

I can't say it any more pointedly without being impolite.

And he gets it. It won't look good for the Labrador RCMP if it turns out afterward that they were sitting on their hands.

"I'll question him and let you know."

"It's convenient that he's in Happy Valley-Goose Bay today," I remark.

He also understands this broad hint.

"You'll be hearing from me."

The connection's killed right then.

I go to my messages at once.

The last one's from Fred: *Nielle's mother is here in St. Anthony and wants to talk to us. I'll pick you up.*

35

Tiffany Staid, Musher
Not Far from Crater Lake, Labrador
Wednesday, February 14

The dogs are barking like mad.

The men stand there as if frozen.

Tiffany freezes too.

They all are listening.

No more shots.

Tiffany gets herself under control.

"No barking, doggies!" she shouts. "No barking!"

Reluctantly, the dogs quiet down. They see Anuaktak pick up the rifle on the sled. It's a reflexive reaction.

The cops turn their snowmobiles around.

"Stay right here!" one of them shouts.

Then they roar off in the direction of the shots. Into the white nothingness.

The three men from Alliarkuk stare at one another. The wind brings tears to their eyes and hers. She puts on her protective glasses.

"I don't like it," Anuaktak says, just like his dad did yesterday.

"We should take a look at the other cabin again," the uncle says to Anuaktak's father.

They peek through the glass. Shake their heads. Rattle the door again.

"Should we break in?" Anuaktak shouts, raising the rifle.

"Not with that!" Tiffany steps toward him. Her valuable gun.

The dogs strain at their leashes. The snow anchor and wire hold.

"We don't have much time," Anuaktak warns. "What do we do?"

An answer's unnecessary because they hear the noise of motors coming nearer.

Suddenly they can see the snowmobiles.

Two. Three. Then it's five.

One of them's towing a sled.

"No barking, dogs! No barking, Pretor!" Tiffany's voice is sharp.

The vehicles stop, one after the other.

Tiffany counts three cops.

She recognizes the two figures on the other machines after they take off their helmets. They're Inuit from Tulliq. One of them has a green ski jacket on.

The cops direct the two men into the cabin, then the others, so that nine people in total push into the small room.

Tiffany can see the men's faces now that they're bareheaded. She stands by the window to keep an eye on the dogs.

"I stopped these two," the third cop says. He's blond. "Take a look at what they had on them."

The camera bag.

She and Anuaktak exchange glances.

"They claim they found it at the foot of the crater." The blond cop sounds as if he doesn't believe them.

Tiffany stares at the camera bag. She doesn't risk looking at the men from Alliarkuk, revealing her thoughts.

Anuaktak's father doesn't make a move. What's going through his head?

"Where are you from?" the blond cop asks the new arrivals.

"Tulliq."

"Impossible. That would have taken you much more time."

"We've been here for two days."

"Where are you from?"

"I told you. From Tulliq."

Tiffany suddenly realizes who they are. They're often seen with Bud Abel. People who associate with the Fish. Not the sort she wants to have anything to do with.

"That's far away," the blond cop says.

"Yes, everything's far away here."

"Why are you hanging around Crater Lake?"

"What does that mean? It's our land."

"This bag does not belong to you."

"We know that. Do you know whose it is?"

"It belongs to Gerald Hynes," Tiffany bursts out.

"Where is this guy Hynes?" the man from Tulliq asks.

"We don't know," the cop answers. "Have you seen anything?"

"No. Not easy in this storm."

"We'll take your names for now," the cop announces. His colleagues silently give their permission.

The men from Tulliq resist.

"Why? We've done nothing."

"Just in case we need some information. Gerald Hynes has been missing since yesterday."

The men from Tulliq look at each other.

"Then you'd better find him quick," one of them says.

Tiffany glances out the window. She can still see the dogs. They're even lying down to rest. Nevertheless, she's antsy.

Anuaktak interrupts.

"Who fired the shots?"

The blond cop doesn't reply as he writes down the names the two men give him.

Tiffany knows these aren't their right names.

"So, who?"

Anuaktak doesn't give up so easily.

"Who fired the shots?" he repeats.

"I fired some signal shots," the blond cop replies.

"Signal shots—what are they?" Tiffany asks, offering Anuaktak some support.

"So we can hear where he is because we lost sight of him," one of the other cops explains. "People, you all go to your cabin now, and we'll come with you. Constable Sullivan, you keep watch here."

The man in the green ski jacket shakes his head.

"We're not going. This is our land. We can go where we want."

"Can we have your names too, constables?" the other man from Tulliq asks.

The tension in the room is mounting. Anuaktak's father makes his move and speaks to his son in Inuttut.

Tiffany understands most of it. He tells his son about the inauguration of the national park and the security measures for the prominent politicians and that it's better to give in because the police are under pressure and irritable. They argue back and forth until his father ends it with the words: "Nobody wants to attract the RCMP's attention at a moment like this."

That's a warning that even the man in the green jacket who gave the cop a fake name can't ignore.

Tiffany doesn't want to have anything to do with the Mounties either.

But now Gerald Hynes has disappeared, and she's the last person to have seen him.

Or perhaps not.

The police find it strange for the two men from Tulliq to show up here.

She does too.

36

Detective Sergeant Calista Gates
St. Anthony, Newfoundland
Wednesday, February 14

Nielle's mother has cried a lot in the last few days. I can tell just by looking. Though she's plump, her face is sort of pressed flat. That's just the way my mom looked when she saw me in the hospital after I was attacked two and a half years ago. The anxiety and pain of a mother who almost lost her child. I have three sisters; Nielle's an only daughter.

Mrs. Helfrey's sitting across from me in my office so that we can talk undisturbed. I'm lucky she's here. Her flight from Blanc Sablon to St. John's was interrupted in St. Anthony because of fog. She'll have to wait until this afternoon to fly out.

"Has your daughter ever felt threatened by someone or something?" I ask gently. I'm conducting this conversation by myself so that Mrs. Helfrey won't feel overwhelmed.

Her eyes fill with tears. Right now, I'd like to hug and console her, but my ankle prevents me from moving around spontaneously.

Nielle's mother lowers her eyes and studies her fingers. She seems to struggle with herself about whether she should mention her daughter's relationship with Morris Tye.

I help her out.

"You told someone in Port Brendan that Nielle has been having an affair with Mr. Tye," I say.

"It's probably no longer a secret," she admits, distressed.

"Not if a violent attack is the issue." I wait for her to offer more.

"His wife . . . she must have known something. She . . . she phoned Nielle and told her to keep her hands off her husband."

That matches up with Vyann Kippen's statement that Nielle felt threatened by the wife and her family. We'll have to poke around in this hornet's nest.

"So, Mrs. Tye knows about the relationship?"

"I told Nielle that you can't keep something like that quiet for long. Though they didn't meet up that often. He's in St. John's most of the time or in Happy Valley-Goose Bay."

"Where did they meet up?"

"In St. Anthony. And sometimes in St. John's. I wouldn't allow her to meet him in Port Brendan. Everybody would have known about it right away." Her voice is getting firmer.

"Mrs. Helfrey, why did you tell anyone in Port Brendan about it?"

Now she's struggling hard. She doesn't look at me when she replies: "We were always hoping that Nielle and Gerald . . ." She breaks off.

That's the way it is in sparsely populated areas. At some point the threads always cross. Gerald and Nielle, Gerald and me. Mrs. Helfrey can't have the slightest notion that, since this morning, I've been getting a pain in my heart at the mention of Gerald's name.

"I know that they used to be an item." I help her relax. "I also know that Nielle called Gerald recently because she wanted to talk to me. Perhaps you know what about?"

"A client of hers told her something. She didn't say what it was."

"A male client?"

"She doesn't say a word to me about her clients. She mustn't. But . . . she wanted your advice."

"Why from me, of all people?" I'm a stranger from Vancouver. I don't say it out loud, but it's hanging in the air.

Mrs. Helfrey wipes her hand over her mouth as if asking herself for permission to speak.

"After all those . . . cases. You solved them all. She rather trusted you."

I'm speechless for a moment. I've always worried that people here regarded me as an intruder. As someone who digs up old crimes and shoves them under their noses: Just look at how bad people are in your area! Now I'm hearing from a frightened mother that people value my work. That I'm trusted.

"Do you have any idea what she wanted to tell me? Or who the client was?" I ask a second time.

She shakes her head.

Yet another lead for us to follow up.

Tears in her eyes again.

"How's Nielle doing?"

I'm astonished she's asking *me*, though she probably heard nothing from the doctors while she was on the plane. But we're on top of it, because we asked the RCMP in St. John's to question the patient as soon as her condition permitted.

"The worst is over," I reply. "Everything's going to be all right."

The first sentence is correct, the second is born of empathy. I assume Nielle won't suffer permanent harm because the doctors are so optimistic. But we'll just have to wait and see, as it was in my case, only my head injuries were much worse.

Now Mrs. Helfrey's crying. I get up, limp over to her, put my arm around her shoulder. When she's calmed down somewhat, I have Rex bring in coffee and muffins. His muffins are terrific comfort food.

Thirty minutes later, everybody's assembled in the conference room. Nielle's mother is off to the airport. She told us Trina Modeste is driving her. If there'd been more time, I would have had some questions for Trina. Her connection to Nielle seems closer than she led us to believe.

"We must find out who this client is," I say, "and what was so explosive about what he told Nielle."

"Can't we talk to Nielle yet?" Dustin asks. "We'd save a lot of time."

"No, our colleagues aren't allowed to see her." Fred had dealt with this while I was questioning Nielle's mother. But it can't be long now.

I must admit to myself that Dustin was right. The prospect of dredging up all of Nielle's clients and bugging them with questions was not exactly enticing. Mainly because we don't know if one of those dear old clients consciously revealed something or was simply chattering on and inadvertently dropped some dynamite. It's the notorious search for the needle in the haystack.

"Is the forensics man coming today?" Heidy wants to know. "And when's Stolke's body going to the medical examiner?"

It's shortly after ten, and I haven't heard a word from Corner Brook yet.

"I appreciate your impatience. I'll ramp up the pressure. Until we learn more, we must go with what we already know. Fred and I will work on looking for clues at the crime scene. You two keep questioning Nielle's clients. It's always possible that something illuminating will come of it."

"We do have the judge's search warrant for the Stolke case. Why don't we work on that?" Dustin asks.

"We'll do it today. We'll begin with his car and his home."

Dustin would rather do that than quiz local people. But I'm doing the search for clues myself with Fred's help.

Dustin asks in a huff: "Do we also have to worry about Gerald Hynes?"

My jaw drops. I haven't heard that sarcastic tone of voice from Dustin before.

I give him a hard look.

"Where did you get that from?"

"A reporter phoned here this morning. He wanted to speak to you, sarge."

"Why didn't you tell me right away?"

"You said you were exclusively in charge of the media. I put it on our intranet."

Rats! I haven't had time to check our station's internal network. The press release hasn't come out yet either.

"Thank you, Dustin. I'll take care of it. When you go to Goose Cove, please see if anything's changed at the crime scene. Have the cameras caught anything at the cabin?"

"No. I've already looked into it." Fred hands the Wilsons a sheet of paper. "Here's the list of Nielle's clients and their addresses."

I look at him gratefully. Fred's in top form.

On the other hand, I'm worried about Dustin. He's probably ripe for a new posting. The Wilsons have been in St. Anthony longer than the normal four years. But I can't do without Heidy for the time being, since Fred's leaving.

He'll leave a huge hole behind.

37

Paige Warner, Entrepreneur
Remote Point Lodge, Labrador
August, Eight Years Ago

If Howard could see her now, his eyes would pop out of his head.

Remote Point Lodge lies at her back, a lake at her feet. The other women are getting settled in the little chalets. She rushed out into nature immediately to be alone with her thoughts for a few minutes.

Stands of fir line the lake that's steaming in the cool afternoon air. Veils of white rise from the water's surface. The far shore slopes upward to a bluff; behind it the treeless tundra begins.

Paige opens up to the landscape. She's here! A feeling of satisfaction fills her. Now she just has to break the news to the others that they will be leaving without a guide. She doesn't want a stranger to be part of it. She wants to share her triumph only with Carla, Ellen, and Sandy. Not *really* share—of that, she's fully aware. She will be the hero in the pictures and videos on Instagram, Facebook, TikTok, Pinterest, and her company's website.

She fans the mosquitoes away with her hands. She should have used a spray, but it reeks terribly and dinner's very soon. That's why the generator is booming and boisterous fishermen are having a beer by the lakeshore; luckily she'll soon be leaving the hubbub of civilization behind.

Suddenly Ellen's beside her. She's wearing a hat with the company logo. Paige notes it with pleasure.

"Vyann told me we probably can't leave tomorrow because it's going to be too foggy."

Paige's good mood goes down the drain at once. Why was Ellen informed and not her? Didn't she make it clear to Vyann that everything must go through her?

"We'll see about it tomorrow; the weather report's still favorable."

She tosses it off in a relaxed and friendly manner. The lodge owners still think that a guide's going to lead their group. She'll clear that up after dinner. For once *she*'s the paying customer and therefore the queen. A welcome role reversal.

"We must take the locals' advice," Ellen counters. "They know the area best."

Carla and Sandy arrive just as Paige is about to answer. Both smell of bug repellant. Good she has a room to herself, Paige thinks. On the trek, however, she'll be sharing a tent with Sandy. It's better because of the wild animals. Sandy knows her way around guns. That was a criterion for selection. And Sandy doesn't snore. At least, she says she doesn't.

"Can you swim in this lake?" Carla calls. "I'd love a cool swim."

"You're not serious?" Ellen shakes as if a cold shudder runs through her.

Sandy and Carla laugh. It was a joke, of course, but Ellen takes everything at face value.

Paige exploits the situation for her announcement.

"I think it's better if we go without a guide so that we're free. Other tourists have hiked the route by themselves and had no problems whatsoever."

"Super!" Sandy says enthusiastically right off the bat. "We don't need a babysitter."

Paige knew Sandy would agree. She's a genuine outdoorswoman. Sandy had even confided to her after the first group meeting that she thought a guide was superfluous. It played right into Paige's hands.

Carla, by contrast, looks concerned.

"Completely unaccompanied? Isn't that dangerous?"

"No, don't worry." Sandy gives Carla a friendly pat on the back. "We're just going along the ridge parallel to the river. That way you can't get lost."

Ellen hasn't said anything yet. Paige has been most worried about her reaction. Ellen's clever. She waits for all the other opinions so she knows where they stand before she gives her own.

Paige would do the same if she were her.

Ellen's words are surprise, nonetheless.

"Is it the money, Paige? Do you want to save on a guide?"

"No, that really isn't it." Paige tries not to seem prickly. "I saw the guide just now. She's very young, early twenties. She simply doesn't fit into our plans."

"But she does into mine," Ellen contradicts her. "She's an Inuk. She can tell us a lot about the history of the region. And she needs the money. It's her job."

What does she know about this woman anyway? Paige doesn't like the turn the conversation's taking.

"I'll certainly give her a tip; that's not the point."

Sandy comes to her rescue and says: "I think it's really great if we're independent. Otherwise, we'll be trailing after somebody the whole time, and we're old enough to do it ourselves. It's advertised as a self-guided tour as well." She looks at Carla.

"You did just say today that it was nice to feel really free for once."

Carla nods.

"Yes, I meant free from obligations."

"See? And nobody's going to tell you what to do and when."

Sandy can be very persuasive, Paige notes.

She looks at them all, one after the other.

"Are we agreed?"

"I'm outvoted anyway," Ellen replies.

That's relevant. They had agreed to discuss conflicting opinions and then vote on them.

"Are you totally against this?" Carla asks.

"No, it's okay." Ellen waves it off. "I can have a chat with Tiffany tomorrow about the area while we're waiting for better weather."

Ouch. Was that a well-aimed swipe at her? Paige wonders. Tiffany. Ellen already knows the woman's name.

Paige has the sudden thought that she might not have made the right choice with Ellen. Although her attractive, dark-skinned face will look good in the group photos. Paige wishes Ellen would laugh more and not be so critical.

"We won't be flying tomorrow?" Sandy asks.

"We'll decide in the morning." Paige resumes her leadership position.

But Ellen doesn't throw in the towel.

"Vyann thinks it could be bad weather tomorrow because thick fog's expected."

"Good, then I can get caught up on my sleep." Carla grins. "Because all the excitement has kept me awake."

Paige eyes her. How's Carla going to react to nights in the wild when only a thin tent wall lies between her and possible dangers?

She hopes none of the women will panic when they go off the safe trail and trek to the crater. To the forbidden lake.

She won't tell them until the third day. It will be too late for protests by then.

A shout comes from the lodge: "Soup's on!"

There's a damper on Paige's appetite now. She must face Vyann. She'd rather speak to her more laid-back husband, Noshi, but he's tied up with the fishermen. Vyann wears the pants at the lodge.

She's one tough nut.

38

Fred van Heisen, RCMP Constable
St. Anthony, Newfoundland
Wednesday, February 14

It's eleven o'clock, and a second search warrant has arrived. It concerns Trent Stolke's medical history. Heidy Wilson discovered he'd been treated in St. Anthony. Fred had already found out the hospital person he must talk to. And he'd accomplished something else: the press release had finally been sent. Some rudimentary information plus the usual concluding sentence: we can't say anything more because of ongoing investigations. Let's hope that will keep the reporters in check for a while. He *is* uneasy, though. The police jacket Stolke was wearing will be of burning interest to the media.

Calista is on the phone to Corner Brook again. He's looking at her notes about the pictures of the crime-scene tracks at the cabin. Nielle's Ski-Doo was there, and it was also in Goose Cove: the tracks matched the runner tracks he had photographed in the spot where Nielle was found. Calista believes the perpetrator brought his victim there on Nielle's Ski-

Doo. He must have parked his own machine near the cabin and not picked it up until later. Clever. That's why the eyewitnesses in Goose Cove and the wildlife officer saw Nielle's red-striped Ski-Doo and not the perpetrator's. That points to an attack that was planned. The perpetrator knew where he would find Nielle at a certain time. Or he arranged to meet her. In the latter case that would mean that Nielle and her attacker probably knew each other. It's time to take a closer look at the people Nielle associates with.

Calista finishes her call with relief on her face.

"Two forensics people will be here at one thirty on Friday, if all goes well. Not just one, Fred, two!"

He sticks his right thumb in the air.

She lifts her foot and gets up carefully.

"We're going to look at Stolke's place."

"Calista, I'm taking you to the hospital. You must have your ankle looked at before we do anything else."

She waves him off.

"It can wait; the swelling hasn't gotten any worse."

"Dr. Amaruntgamen wants to see you. She wants to talk to you about something."

That does the trick.

"Oh, good. Maybe she can shed some light on the cause of death."

Calista seems tense. The business with Gerald Hynes must be upsetting for her.

Fred doesn't bring that up right now and helps her to the patrol car.

There's still fog hanging over St. Anthony's streets; the headlights create a nebulous gloom. The snow from the previous night has been mostly cleared away; the white piles bordering the street have grown. Will Nielle's mother be able to fly to St. John's despite the bad visibility? The wait must be a crushing blow for her.

In the hospital they're taken directly to an examination room. Dr. Amaruntgamen has Calista's ankle X-rayed before joining them.

Calista thanks her for the swift treatment; it's a big favor the doctor's doing her.

"The ankle's slightly sprained," the doctor informs her after showing the X-rays. "Nothing serious, but you must go easy on it and not force it so it can heal quickly. It's good you're using crutches. I'll prescribe something to make the swelling go down completely."

Fred has the feeling that Calista's not at all interested in her ankle but rather in Trent Stolke's death certificate and the cause of death.

She asks about it right away: "Dr. Amaruntgamen, what struck you about the body?"

The doctor turns her chair away from her computer and closes the door.

"I manipulated the corpse as little as possible; that's forensics' job. Have you got a search warrant?"

"Yes, here it is."

Fred hands it to her, and she studies the document carefully. She doesn't want to take any risk of illegally violating confidentiality. Then she puts the paper down on her desk.

"Trent Stolke was treated for heart disease. I sent him to a cardiologist, who prescribed medications. I saw the results of hard drug consumption on his body. I warned him that drugs like ecstasy could lead to cardiac arrest."

"Do you think that's what happened in this case?"

"That's certainly something the medical examiner will look at."

"We're waiting for a decision from Corner Brook before we can send the body there. And the bullet wounds?"

Vertical lines appear in Dr. Amaruntgamen's forehead.

"I don't believe I'm telling you anything new if I conclude these wounds occurred postmortem."

"Is there anything else you can tell us?"

"I tried to help Mr. Stolke. I found a withdrawal program with methadone for him, but he refused." She sighs softly. "It's too easy to get your hands on drugs, as you probably know too."

"Doctor, we're doing our best to stop the illegal dealing. Did Mr. Stolke's parents know about the risk their son could face by taking drugs?"

"I don't know for a fact, but it's possible. That heart condition is genetically determined, so the father must be at the same risk."

The father's an alcoholic, Fred recalls. What a vicious circle addiction is.

Dr. Amaruntgamen stands up.

"Please go easy on that ankle, Sergeant Gates. If you've any questions, do call me. I'll send you the death certificate by email right away."

Calista expresses her thanks.

"Forensics will get in touch with you directly about the medical records," she says. "I'm leaving that to Corner Brook."

On the drive back to the station, she discusses the fresh information with him.

"Let's assume Stolke went into cardiac arrest after taking ecstasy. Who would shoot him after he died?"

"Might it be because he was wearing a police jacket, and somebody hated the RCMP?"

She claps her hands softly.

"Why was he wearing that damn jacket?"

"To aggravate people? Maybe he antagonized somebody with it so much that this somebody had to send him a big message."

"Sounds rather bizarre if you ask me."

"Maybe somebody was playing the avenging angel because Stolke was making life difficult for you."

She looked at him in horror.

"Do you really think it's something like that, Fred?"

No, not really. He quickly switches to his next hypothesis.

"Maybe Trent didn't pay some of his drug debts, and it's revenge or anger because the dealer can't get his money anymore when Trent's dead."

"Did Trent have any cash on him, any credit cards? Did somebody try to get his money in another way?"

"We haven't got his bank records yet. Or his phone records."

Fred knows those things never move quickly. He's frustrated nevertheless. During his last trip to Saskatchewan, he'd had to explain to his friends that in real life it takes much longer than in the police procedurals on TV.

There's one more question he must clear up with Calista while they're alone in the car. Nothing should come between them when they're in the middle of an important investigation.

"Calista, what did Dustin mean about Gerald Hynes? What's up?"

She seems more than willing to talk about it.

"He's at Ilungilak Crater Lake and they can't find him."

"Who's *they*?"

"RCMP from Labrador are up there because the minister for the environment is coming from Ottawa to announce a new national park. Gerald's invited. He's supposed to build a tourist lodge right on Crater Lake."

"How long has he been missing?"

"Since yesterday. He went by dogsled to the lake. The musher let him off there because he wanted to look around by himself. She was to pick him up later. But he wasn't there. They can't find him."

Fred has the impression that Calista is trying her hardest to keep it together. He knows her well enough to realize she certainly won't want anybody to think this incident is jeopardizing her work in St. Anthony.

"Who'd you get that from?"

"David Pelletier."

From his predecessor. Fred replaced David, the young computer geek, in St. Anthony.

She's still in contact with David and gets information from him, Fred thinks. He must make a mental note of that.

39

Noshi Mercer, Owner of Remote Point Lodge
Labrador
Wednesday, February 14

Noshi's anxious about Kellyann. The weather's so rotten. He can barely make out the lake from the lodge. It's all blurry, white, and gray. The tips of the firs rock back and forth in the wind. Not a day you'd choose to go outside. But Kellyann insisted on being taken from Tulliq by dogsled to the lodge.

"If Irvin thinks it possible, then I'll trust him," she told Noshi on the satellite phone.

She actually preferred to go by bush plane, but Vernon's not going up because of poor visibility, and Kellyann's too impatient to wait for better weather. She was at the hospital for some tests because she suffers from recurrent joint pain. The Labrador climate is probably not ideal for her, though there's nowhere else she'd rather live. She wants to be with him in the lodge together. She makes no secret about it, even to the guests.

His heart's one hundred percent in the lodge, but doctor's visits cost a bundle. First, there's the bush plane to Tulliq; second, the flight to Happy Valley-Goose Bay. They're expensive. You usually have to pony up for several nights in a hotel. Kellyann's been gone for five days. He can't wait to see her again.

He keeps looking out the big window of the lounge, the room where guests meet and mingle in summer. The focal point is the huge woodburning stove. The tourists love the cozy log cabin atmosphere. He and Kellyann spend many days here by themselves in wintertime, except when a party of snowmobilers comes by. He treasures his time with her because in summer they're totally tied up with the guests, and there's hardly time for each other.

He goes to prepare a meal in the kitchen. Kellyann and Irvin will be hungry by the time they get here. He's already thawed some leftover meat for Irvin's sled dogs. He freezes the bits after every fall hunt, and for Tiff's dogs as well.

He keeps the rest of the meat well hidden; he doesn't want to get caught with it. It's caused him enough problems; somebody must have blabbed. Even though he'd taken great care, some people found out, and it got to Morris Tye. It certainly wasn't Tiff who betrayed him. Tiff's an ally. She's at Crater Lake now, in this nasty weather.

He hears something. They're here!

He opens the door, shouts words of welcome, and closes it at once. The cold and wind are overpowering. Kellyann was right: Irvin knows what he's doing. You can rely on him and his dogs.

When they're finally sitting around the table and eating, Noshi can still feel relief in his heart.

"It was a wild ride," Irvin acknowledges with his mouth full. "It bounced you around hard, eh, Kellyann? You've probably got bruises everywhere."

She laughs and looks at Noshi. She looks so pretty with her

blond braids and thin, colorful cap. She wears it because she thinks it gives her a bold air.

"Noshi, you can find that out later."

He feels hot.

"Black or blue, I take them all," he jokes.

Kellyann has no fear of outdoor adventures. She's strong and athletic. The right woman for a lodge. So was Vyann, but they grew apart. The incident of the missing women drove a wedge between them. That's what he's persuaded himself so he wouldn't feel so guilty.

"I almost feel bad for sending Tiff up here," Kellyann says.

Irvin puts down his fork.

"*You* sent her?"

"I told the tourist people of the Nunatsiavut government to take Tiff because you didn't want to do it."

Noshi's well aware that Irvin wants nothing to do with politicians or bureaucracy. His passion is dogsled racing, and that's it. Noshi just now notices that Irvin's beard is totally shaved off. Practical in winter when everything freezes. He looks ten years younger, but he's still got his bushy eyebrows. He should trim them back, too.

"I hope she's got enough food for the dogs," Irvin says. "Vernon didn't go up yesterday afternoon."

Noshi grins. The dogs. That's Irvin's world.

"You know Tiff. She leaves nothing to chance."

Irvin chews his moose meat.

"Wouldn't surprise me if the politicians forget about flying to Crater Lake and do their thing in Happy Valley-Goose Bay instead. They're searching for the contractor; two Inuit have vanished into thin air as well."

"How so?"

"I heard in Tulliq that two of us were up there and some Mounties wanted to detain them, allegedly for security reasons. Imagine that. They flew the coop."

Kellyann frowns as she always does when something has her complete attention.

"Gerald Hynes from Port Brendan has disappeared at Crater Lake. He's supposed to build the lodge this summer."

Noshi acts baffled, because he doesn't want to let slip that whatever involves that new lodge is of huge interest to him.

"He's disappeared? At Crater Lake?"

Kellyann plays along and nods.

"Yes, there's a search on for him. People in Happy Valley-Goose Bay are talking about it."

Noshi gets on his hobbyhorse.

"The cops are freaking out because they've got to protect the VIPs out in the boonies. They don't have a clue what it's like up there." He has no qualms badmouthing the police; Irvin doesn't like them either.

Indeed, his friend doesn't let this opportunity go by: "The two men from Tulliq, they simply made their getaway. So would I. The laws up there are different. That rubs the cops the wrong way, of course. I think they're particularly on edge. They found a dead man in St. Anthony."

"A dead man?" Kellyann almost knocks the wine bottle over.

"Yes, in Goose Cove near St. Anthony. And you know what?" Irvin raps his knife on the table. "They say he was wearing a police jacket, though he's no Mountie."

"A dead man?" Kellyann stares at Irvin. Noshi looks at Kellyann.

"Yes, his name's Trent Stolke, from Englee. The RCMP lady from Vancouver has got her claws in the case. She was Stolke's archenemy. He was always slandering her. And now somebody's knocked him off."

"Who'd you get this from?" Kellyann asks. Her voice is scratchy.

"You can find it all on Facebook," Irvin says.

"Do you know anybody in St. Anthony?" Kellyann hangs on his words.

"I don't, but the Fish does."

Now it's Noshi who stares at Irvin.

"You're buddies with the Fish?"

"Sure, I don't want anything to happen to my dogs. The Fish will see to that if I'm good to him."

Good to him. Does Irvin slip the Fish money? The thought's nothing new to Noshi. He's paid people to keep quiet too.

Irvin's got something more to report.

"Shortly before that, a woman was discovered who was badly beaten up. Also in Goose Cove."

"A woman?" Kellyann asks.

"And now comes the kicker. The word is, she's Morris Tye's lover."

40

The Spy
St. Anthony, Newfoundland
Thursday, February 14

A most satisfying sight. Calista Gates is limping out of the hospital on crutches with Fred van Heisen beside her.

He records the scene on his cell phone. Not even rolling down his car window.

What a huge building the hospital is, a clay-colored monument in a remote town. Trent Stolke's frozen body's lying in the basement. The forensics team from Corner Brook will find out the truth when the thawed-out body's lying before them.

Will this thing finally destroy Calista Gates? Signs of her slow collapse are already visible.

In his police files it says she sometimes has problems with her right leg, ever since the attack on her in Vancouver. Episodic acute pain. Whenever she's under heavy stress, her leg drags slightly behind.

So those incidents are doing their job. She's bending over from the weight on her shoulders. Vancouver finagled it well. You can't miss it. And he's documented it on his phone.

At some point she won't be able to do it anymore.

She's got two tough cases to crack. One is Trent Stolke. The RCMP jacket. The bullet holes will give her plenty to do. The victim shot after his death. A mysterious death.

The other is Nielle Helfrey, a genuine stroke of luck. If Calista digs deeper into it, she'll have a snarky politician around her neck. Morris Tye will pull every string he can. He's got a lot to lose. With all his connections, he'll be a powerful opponent.

And of course there's the fretting over Gerald Hynes. It must be torture for her. Painful and potent.

He starts the car and has some coffee from his cup. He'll find Gates and van Heisen again. The world of St. Anthony is small. It makes monitoring them so easy.

He takes the cloth from the seat beside him and wipes the fogged-up windshield clean. What crappy weather. Lucky the visibility was better than in the morning so he could get those pictures.

Other than that, it's all running smoothly. Calista Gates has been crippled since her shortish visit to Vancouver. At least, that's his impression. Three RCMP officers have been charged because of her. Nobody's safe, not even colleagues. If she'd stayed in Labrador longer, she might have had him arrested, too. Maybe she'd have discovered his shady sideline. That he sometimes takes in a little cash. Now he can play a part in putting her out of commission.

Gates's family is involved in the Vancouver case. It could come to a trial. That means several weeks of intense media interest. There'll be a lot of talk about the Gates clan. What a strain on her nerves. Maybe it will break up the family.

Couldn't wish for anything more. The psychological profile in her dossier says Calista's large family is the foundation of her mental health. That's vital information. You know where you can start drilling. Where you can cut down the pillars.

Best of all: Fred van Heisen will soon be gone. He might have been dangerous.

As menacing as a wild bull moose. Van Heisen would never let Calista fall; he's been with her through thick and thin.

He scrolls through his cell phone. Let's take a little look on social media. Once you could count on Trent Stolke railing against Gates. Now he's hors de combat. But Stolke can be replaced. There are always people who have a bone to pick with the RCMP. Particularly with Calista Gates.

Here! He didn't have to look for long. A woman says on Facebook:

St. Anthony is no longer a safe place since the new police chief's been here. Not even our kids are safe anymore. Kids were not being murdered before she was here. Now women are being attacked. I don't dare go out of the house.

The following comments are music to his ears:

These days, we've got the reputation as an unsafe place. Never used to be like this. Not until the new lady worked here.

She wants to make a big splash in the media. That will scare off the tourists even more. There are already fewer bookings for accommodations than last year.

Why didn't she stay in Vancouver? The Wilsons and the Mounties in Roddickton can do it all without her.

It's all part of a Deep State plan. Make work for the police!

A man comments:

Who needs cops anyway? They should be abolished. Freedom for Canadians!!!! Vote the government out! Do it!

Nobody's on Calista Gates's side, he notes with schadenfreude. Probably the woman who made the Facebook post deleted any positive comments. Or Gates's supporters don't dare speak up. Group pressure's a scary thing. But a good scary thing.

He sends off the video from the hospital and screenshots of the Facebook comments. Proof that he's doing his job. That they're getting somewhere.

His pulse quickens when he thinks of the missing Gerald Hynes. That will finish Calista off.

If it breaks the right way, she'll never get over it.

He could jump for joy in expectation. But he doesn't want to draw attention to himself. He's the last person they'd suspect.

And it better stay that way. Noshi stops eating. He asks the obvious question: "Is she still alive?"

41

Mick Hudson, Reporter for the *Labrador Tribune*
Happy Valley-Goose Bay, Labrador
Thursday, February 15

Shit. He saw it coming.

The environment minister is going to speak at a media event. Not at Crater Lake but in the Hotel North ballroom in Happy Valley-Goose Bay. She's pressed for time. The weather upset her plans. Full appointment calendar blah blah. Can't wait blah blah blah.

He shoves a slice of bacon into his mouth. Breakfast at Pep's Diner usually means a good start to the day. Not this morning. The frustration could drive him up the wall.

How can he get to Morris Tye now without him clamming up? It would have been a cinch on the plane, away from the TV cameras. It's that much harder at an official press conference—he can't out Tye in public. If he did, he could kiss his job in Happy Valley-Goose Bay good-bye.

He pokes around in the fried egg on his plate. Nobody's about to tell him what's going on at Crater Lake. Why can't they find Gerald Hynes? The RCMP has several men on site.

And a couple of experienced Inuit who know the region like the back of their hand.

Suddenly he has an idea. He gobbles up the rest of the hash browns, washes them down with coffee, and throws his ski jacket on. Then he drives to the military airport.

Even in the car he can feel the unimpeded wind. It must really be something else up there at Crater Lake. The whole area is cast in a murky light. He can hardly see what's coming at him down the road. Halfway there, he turns around. It's totally stupid to go to the airport. There won't be any planes or helicopters going up in these conditions to search for Hynes.

The weather is more powerful than anything else. Much stronger than his wanting a scoop. So, he goes to the office.

Where his boss takes him aside.

"What's new?" he asks.

"We should call Search and Rescue and find out when they're going to go look for Gerald Hynes."

"Why? Is he officially missing?"

"I'll drop in on the police. Better than a phone call. I don't want them to brush me off." He's getting ready to go when his uncle, who's also his boss, says: "I'm sending you to St. Anthony."

Mick freezes on the spot.

"But there's the press conference today with—"

"*I'm* going to that. St. Anthony is more important."

Mick looks at his uncle in amazement. Since when is St. Anthony more important than Labrador?

"There are rumors we can't ignore. Nielle Helfrey and Trent Stolke. Maybe it's got something to do with Calista Gates." His uncle half sits down on his desk, one leg on the floor, the other flapping in the air.

"What kind of rumors?" Mick asks.

"Trent Stolke was wearing a police jacket."

"We already know that."

“Apparently a sergeant’s insignia was found near Nielle in the snow.”

“What’s that supposed to mean? Calista Gates attacked Nielle?” Mick doesn’t even try to hide his mocking tone.

“Really odd about the insignia, don’t you think?”

Mick shakes his head, incredulous.

He’s angry that his uncle wants to keep him out of Happy Valley-Goose Bay. But what can he do? He’s twenty-two and only been with the *Labrador Tribune* for a few months. His uncle got him the job. The newspaper mainly exists because a diehard Labradorian who got rich in mining bankrolls it. Unfortunately, that also muzzles any criticism of mining companies in the paper.

“Who made up that horseshit?” he asks. “Gates was in Port Brendan on Sunday as far as I know.”

“Where Nielle’s mother lives.” His uncle folds his arms across his chest. He fails to mention what many found out in the meantime: Nielle Helfrey is Morris Tye’s lover.

“So what? Where’s the connection?” Mick doesn’t know where his uncle’s going with this.

“Calista Gates was in Vancouver. She’s barely back in Newfoundland when Nielle is beaten up. And Trent Stolke is found dead shortly afterward. It could be a coincidence or not. We’ve got to go down that track.”

“You don’t mean . . . ?”

“I don’t mean anything. But people talk.” His uncle gesticulates. “Just take a peek at the social media. They’re all saying that murders arrived in St. Anthony along with the new chief of police. That’s surely no coincidence.”

“Mindless gossip. It’s probably some bots.”

“Doesn’t matter if it’s robots or who the hell knows—we’ve got to check it out.”

Mick finally gets what his boss is driving at. Morris Tye’s a friend of the *Labrador Tribune’s* owner. If Tye is involved in a big story that will make waves outside the province, then the

Tribune cannot look the other way, and Tye would be fair game. But if that can be averted, then his uncle is the one to stop it. Calista Gates is a welcome diversion to take the spotlight off Tye.

Mick gazes out the window. Is the fog better now, or is it just his imagination? Is his luck so bad that flights are no longer delayed, and so he must fly to St. Anthony?

"Stolke has apparently been carrying out a private war against Gates," he says. "The rumors are coming from that quarter for sure."

"That's exactly what I mean. And now this guy Stolke is dead. I've heard he's got two bullets in him," his uncle says.

Dammit! Mick's fed his boss exactly the wrong words and made it easier for him to spout off this nonsense.

It used to be that the *Cape Lone Courier* in St. Anthony would have taken up this story. But the paper folded after a media conglomerate in Nova Scotia took it over.

"What about that amateur freelance reporter who writes for the *Tribune*?" he asks with hope. "Can't she do it?"

"She's on holiday in Mexico," his uncle says.

Mick makes one last stab at it.

"And what about Morris Tye?"

"You can ask Calista Gates if she's going to put him through the wringer."

Mick gives up all hope. Unlikely that the police chief will tell him anything. Yesterday's statement to the media said they had nothing more to comment on because of ongoing investigations. He'd have gladly flown to St. Anthony in any other situation, but now he can't shake the feeling that somebody's trying to keep him away from Morris Tye.

His boss slides off his desk and says: "You can sleep in the old *Courier* office, and the company car's still there."

Those schemers have cooked this up very cleverly, Mick thinks to himself. His uncle doesn't want to lose his job, and so he beats up on Calista Gates. But they've counted their chickens too soon. It's going to backfire—he'll do everything to see that's what happens.

"By the way," his uncle remarks, "Calista Gates is involved with Gerald Hynes. And he's disappeared off the face of the earth. Another of those strange coincidences. Did Hynes know too much? Maybe those wicked tongues were right after all."

42

Fred van Heisen, RCMP Constable
St. Anthony, Newfoundland
Thursday, February 15

All of a sudden, a massive snowplow is coming straight at their car near the airport. Fred can barely veer out of the way. He sees that Calista's been thrown against the side door.

"Jesus! Where did that come from!" Fred's able to keep the SUV under control—no mean feat on the icy, sloping road.

"You all right, Calista?" he inquires anxiously.

She looks worried, but this was the case even before the snowplow. It must be her concern for Gerald Hynes.

"Yes, nothing broken. You handled the car so well, Fred. Hats off."

He's in shock from the near collision. A few years ago, a driver was killed in a similar situation.

Maybe we should concentrate on the road and not discuss our cases, he thinks to himself. But if they don't talk, then his thoughts will drift to Gerald Hynes, as hers are sure to do as well.

They're on their way to Trent's parents' home in Englee.

They want to find out who Trent's friends were, what he did in the days before he died, who he got the police jacket from, who sold him ecstasy. He probably kept his drug habit from his parents. They still hope to get some useful information from them before the forensics folks arrive tomorrow. The two colleagues in Roddickton are helping with the investigation, but Calista wanted to talk with Trent's parents in person.

Trent's computer and cell phone are nowhere to be found. Fred's still waiting for the phone company records. The only thing that was discovered in Trent's old pickup parked in front of his apartment in St. Anthony was a hunting rifle under the back seat. Nevertheless, they took the pickup with them, along with his snowmobile. The Corner Brook team will deal with them.

Fred turns down a lonely road by the airport that takes an hour and a half to deliver them to Englee. Small white flakes whirl in front of the windshield. Hopefully the wind won't get worse. Since Calista's not saying anything, his thoughts snap back to Gerald. He saw on the internet that they'll send a plane to search for him as soon as the weather improves. Gerald's been missing for two nights now in that ice-cold wasteland up there. Whatever happened? Calista must know more. If she would only clue him in.

There's an incoming call on her phone.

She puts it on speakerphone so he can hear.

St. John's RCMP.

"We've been able to speak briefly with Nielle Helfrey," their colleague reports. "She says she has no recollection of the attack. She went to the cabin to see if everything was okay. The last thing she remembers is a snowmobile motor. After that, she blacked out."

Fred's listening intently.

Calista exchanges glances with him before asking, "Constable, did you have the impression she was telling the truth?"

"Hard to determine because the patient's still pretty groggy.

But the doctor's talking about transferring her to the St. Anthony hospital in two days. Then you can talk to her."

"Did you ask if she had any enemies?"

"Yes, but she said no. Sergeant . . ."

"Yes?"

"She did babble some incoherent stuff about a dead cockatoo. I asked her what she meant, but she said she had probably been dreaming."

Calista gives a start.

"One of the caregivers for seniors in St. Anthony kept a pet cockatoo. We found it dead at her front door when we came to her house. Its wings were cut off. Did Ms. Helfrey mention that?"

"No, just that the cockatoo was dead. It was really confusing."

Calista thanks him for his work and ends the call.

Fred feels her eyes on him when she asks: "Don't you think it's odd?"

"That Nielle remembers nothing?" he asks. "Or the cockatoo business?"

"That Nielle remembers nothing is possible, given her head injury. The technical term is *retrograde amnesia*. But still . . . her injury doesn't seem so serious that it would have blocked out everything right up to the attack."

"She was unconscious when we found her."

"If she can be moved to St. Anthony in two days," she points out, "the CT scan probably didn't turn up any severe brain damage."

"You think Morris Tye silenced Nielle?"

"We can't exclude it."

Fred reduces speed because the snow's getting heavier. This means the forensics will have to look for tracks *under* the snow. Good thing they've got the photos.

A thought comes to him out of the blue.

"Maybe Tye didn't have to tell her that in the first place. She keeps quiet out of preemptive obedience."

"It's possible. But whatever can she mean with the cockatoo?"

So strange. Who would have thought they would be wrestling with a dead pet bird? Police work's full of surprises.

"You mean the cockatoo you sent to the lab for an autopsy?" he remarks dryly.

"I know you think that's crazy, but I want to chase down every lead," she says. "So tell me: How could Nielle know about the dead cockatoo? That happened *after* the attack on her."

"Vyann Kippen probably phoned her and told her about it." A logical explanation, in his view.

Calista begs to differ.

"You think Vyann phoned her *before* the police spoke to Nielle?"

"Vyann and Nielle are friends."

"All the same . . ." Calista shakes her head. "I could ask Vyann if that's what happened." She looks at her phone. "We're in a dead zone. No reception."

When they arrive in Englee, he's relieved. They made it despite the snowfall. The Stolkes' house is white like every other one around it. White's the cheapest vinyl siding. Their colleagues in Roddickton had been monitoring the house so Fred and Calista could be sure they weren't making the trip there in vain and would actually find somebody home.

They park in the driveway. The path to the front door looks slippery. Not ideal for Calista and crutches.

He says on the spur of the moment: "I'll carry you."

His boots are equipped with fully spiked soles. Before she can protest, he picks her up vigorously.

She's got no choice but to put her arms around his neck. He walks toward the house, stepping firmly.

A woman's waiting in the open doorway. She looks careworn. Lines from lifelong worries.

Taken by surprise at the sight presented to her, she lets the visitors in without a word.

They find themselves directly in the living room, and Fred slips Calista into a chintz-covered armchair. The room smells of dog, but he can't see one.

"My husband's not in," Trent's mother says.

Calista introduces them, explaining her injured ankle. Mrs. Stolke acts dismissive. Desperation is written all over her face.

When Calista expresses her sympathy, Mrs. Stolke doesn't even look at her. Calista goes ahead: "I discovered your son's body. I'd like to find out why and how he died."

Mrs. Stolke reacts forcefully.

"Died? He was murdered!"

"That's just what we're investigating. Mrs. Stolke, did your son have heart trouble?"

Trent's mother sits down and bursts into tears.

Calista glances at Fred. He knows what she means. Tears are always good; the dam has broken. They wait.

Mrs. Stolke wipes her face with the sleeve of her light-blue sweatshirt.

"He always had a weak heart, from birth. But we kept an eye on it. For twenty-four years. For nothing, nothing at all."

"I can imagine how terrible this is for you, Mrs. Stolke. Please help us find out what happened to him."

"Do *you* have anything to do with his death?"

She stares Calista in the face, who after a little hesitation says calmly: "No, of course not. Whatever gives you that idea?"

"It's what people are saying on Facebook."

43

Detective Sergeant Calista Gates
Englee, Newfoundland
Thursday, February 15

For a second I'm tempted to check my phone to see what's being spread around about me on Facebook. But that would send the wrong signal. I don't want to create the impression for Mrs. Stolke that I take these things seriously.

So, I say, unfazed: "I want to get at the truth, and I'm turning to you."

She fights back.

"Why did you arrest my Trent? He did nothing. Absolutely nothing."

"Mrs. Stolke, he was driving way too fast when I stopped him. He couldn't even stand up straight. I had no choice. He could have caused a fatal accident and killed himself in it too."

She waves her hands around. "I know a lot of people who drive too fast. The police never stop *them.*"

I'm not interested in discussing other people. I want to know more about Trent before his father comes home.

"Mrs. Stolke, does Trent have a computer?"

Her eyes flit about the room. She must process a lot in a little time.

"A tablet. But not here."

"Does he still have a room in your house?"

"He sometimes sleeps upstairs."

"May we take a quick look around?"

"What are you looking for?" she asks warily.

"We just want to be sure that nobody's stolen his tablet."

I expect some resistance, but she stands up and we follow her out.

Fred helps me up the stairs.

Mrs. Stolke takes us to a bedroom. It's cleaned up, the bed's made. There are several posters that a young man would hang: snowmobiles, motorcycles, pickups. And Sidney Crosby, the famous hockey player from Nova Scotia.

I open the closet door. T-shirts, lumberjack shirts, a pair of jeans. No police uniform. Drawers filled with stuff. Not a single book except for *Man on the Ice*; I've seen it in some St. Anthony shops. I flip through it. Something's in the pages. A ticket to last year's RCMP Ball in Happy Valley-Goose Bay. Interesting.

I hold the book up.

"With your permission, we'll take this with us."

Ms. Stolke shrugs. Evidently a book is no loss to her.

I slowly scan the room.

"Where do you think Trent got the police jacket?" I ask.

"You'll certainly know better than me." She folds her arms.

"Was he fascinated by uniforms?"

"Uniforms? No, why would he want them?"

"Did he like to dress up?"

"No. Only once, as Santa Claus."

I saw that on Trent's Facebook page. A photo of him as Santa. Two years ago. He apparently didn't post a picture of himself dressed as a policeman. Not even to make fun of me.

"Who were his friends? Who did he hang around with?"

"He didn't have many pals anymore; they moved away. To Alberta or Ontario."

"Who did he see of those who stayed?"

"No idea; they're in St. Anthony."

We've identified two of his buddies in Facebook photos. They aren't from Englee. We'll deal with them next.

Mrs. Stolke's in tears again.

"He should have stayed here. St. Anthony is not for him. He could have been fishing for Corn. Then he'd still be alive."

"Corn?"

"Cornell Seary from Main Brook," Fred informs me.

I remember. Our colleagues in Roddickton told us about that fisherman. He said he'd noticed a change in Trent over the years. He didn't want to tell my colleagues directly it was from drugs, but he hinted at it. Trent lost interest in fishing, was unreliable, and then Seary had to look around for somebody else.

He didn't want to name any of Stolke's friends to the Roddickton RCMP but asked a rhetorical question: "Where did Trent get his money? After all, he hasn't got a job."

That's what we'd like to know too.

Some banging downstairs. The front door. Then a dog barks.

"He's back." Mrs. Stolke seems frightened.

"We won't provoke him," I whisper to her.

Paws scratching on the stairs. The dog appears in the room. A mongrel.

"We've got a cat too," Mrs. Stolke says. "She's hiding somewhere."

I take her remark as a sign that she's not so hostile toward us anymore. Her face seems to say: I can't hide like the cat when my husband comes home drunk.

I quickly press a card with my phone number into her hand.

She slips it away in the belly pocket of her sweatshirt.

"Anytime," I say, softly but emphatically. "We're here for you."

Her husband comes swaying up the stairs. He must have seen the police car. He bellows: "Get out of here! Out!"

I hesitate.

"Do you want . . . ?"

But Mrs. Stolke motions for us to leave.

"He'll lie down and go to sleep," she whispers.

We can't accomplish much if she doesn't want our help. Intoxication is not a crime in itself.

I think of Mrs. Stolke as I'm cooling my ankle with an ice pack late that evening. It's quiet in the house. Does she have any relatives to support her? Friends to help her? Daughters she can turn to?

I know by my own experience that you can't always confide in somebody even in the worst of situations. My fear for Gerald is driving me crazy. It digs its claws into my flesh like a crazed animal. But I can't burden my family with this. They've got enough to worry about because they may have to give testimony in the trial of the RCMP officials. My oldest sister is usually my wailing wall. But she's involved in the case. Daphne has three kids and a part-time job in a fabric shop. My younger sister, Aretha, writes romance novels. I don't think she can give me any advice. And the youngest, Maria, lives in Costa Rica.

My brother Nikos is under permanent stress with his auto repair shop. And he's got two little kids. Frank lives in the States, and Elias, the inventor, stays in his own isolated world. Who can I turn to? David Pelletier keeps me au courant. I can't expect anything more from my young colleague.

My body temperature's rising. A sign of panic. My throat's tight; I'm not getting enough air. I ought to eat something, but my stomach rebels. Gerald, please get in touch. I've called his phone any number of times in the last several hours out of pure desperation, although it doesn't do any good. I'm calling him now—no luck.

In my distress I consider reading the Facebook rumors about me, to distract me from Gerald. But Fred's ordered that it's strictly forbidden.

Fred. He never talks to me about Lucinda. Why should I talk to him about Gerald?

I hear a twittering. My phone's ringing.

"Are you home? I'm in the neighborhood." It's Heidy Wilson.

"Yes, ring the doorbell, and I'll let you in."

When I hear a car, I get my crutches and hobble to the door.

"Nice and warm in here," Heidy says, following me into the kitchen.

"Would you like some tea? Coffee?" Heidy seems like an angel of light to my eyes.

How many times has she been in my house? Not very often.

"I wanted to see how you were doing," she explains.

I give her a grateful look.

"Because of Gerald Hynes," she says more precisely.

I didn't see that coming from Heidy. She's not the sentimental type. I must be careful not to let my eyes mist up. Not to burst into tears.

"What have you heard?" I ask, quickly going to the kettle.

"That he disappeared near Crater Lake, and they're searching for him. You must be beside yourself with worry, sarge."

"I just don't see how it's possible. What's happened. He would never take any risks up there. He's level-headed no matter what he does. What else did you hear?"

"Not much."

"The worst of it is there's nothing I can do. I can't help him." My voice cracks.

Heidy nods.

"No, you really can't. You must leave it to our guys in Happy Valley-Goose Bay."

She's right. Crater Lake isn't my territory. I haven't heard from Inspector Allen since our last call. Not a word.

"It's so hard not to keep thinking about it," Heidy says. "When Adam went to university in St. John's, I was so apprehensive. I thought, Maybe he'll hook up with the wrong friends or start doing drugs. Or have an accident on his motorcycle. It's so dangerous."

Adam's her twenty-one-year-old son. The Wilsons' only child. Trent Stolke's death must remind them of Adam. Of the dangers young people face.

She sighs.

"But life goes on. It changes. Sometimes in a direction you don't expect. Relationships aren't for all eternity." She takes my hand and gives it a little squeeze.

I'm floored. This isn't the Heidy I know. Is she talking about herself?

She sees my inquisitive expression and quickly strokes her short, bleached hair.

"It hasn't been very long, and Gerald has it in him to protect himself," she continues. "People know where they need to search. It's good that colors stand out so clearly against the white ground."

I don't know what to say. She doesn't seem to expect a response.

"A coffee would be nice," she says. "Let's talk about Nielle Helfrey."

44

Paige Warner, Entrepreneur
In the Crater Lake Area, Labrador
Eight Years Earlier

"Time for a break!" Paige shouts. They've been hiking eastward for three hours, high above the canyon.

Sandy set a fast pace, but Paige pointed out that they weren't in a competition. They'd like enough time to take in all aspects of nature. And time to take videos and photos, of course.

Sandy's the strongest of them physically. She carries one of the tents and the rifle and a good share of the provisions. Paige has food on her back as well, and Carla carries the cooking utensils. The second tent's hanging from Ellen's backpack.

"Good idea!" shouts Carla, who complained she was hungry an hour earlier.

They drop their backpacks. At first they're speechless because the view is breathtaking. They can see beyond the canyon into the tundra. The brownish green is sprinkled with tiny white dots of snow. Blue-green patches light up among them, little lake after little lake, when hit by the sun's rays.

Paige takes care that the women keep their distance from the canyon's rim. The walls drop off vertically down to the river; the huge rock crevasses will form a magnificent background for her videos. She thinks the cliffs look dangerous, a fantasy landscape. She's nearly dizzy from looking into the depths of the canyon. This would blow Howard's mind.

The sun bathes everything in a golden light. A soft wind's blowing, keeping almost all the mosquitoes away. Vyann, the lodge owner, was right, even if Paige didn't admit it publicly: today was a good one for beginning an adventure. Yesterday's weather was miserable and would have dampened the group's spirits.

Paige wasn't in a good mood because Vyann criticized her for not taking a guide. But that couldn't stop them; Paige had the last word.

Even the bush plane pilot who dropped them off up here had been grumpy. Do those lodge guys have any idea how to treat their paying guests? She could teach them how to handle customers so that they get raves on the internet afterward.

She hopes the pilot has deposited the container with the extra food at the place they'd agreed upon. But she relaxes at once. Of course he did. He doesn't want to ruin the lodge's reputation. It's a one-time opportunity, Paige reasons: her photos and videos will be fantastic advertising for the place. That should more than compensate for her refusal to take a guide. Paige suspects that Ellen slipped the Inuit guide some money, feeling guilty because the young woman had lost the assignment.

Ellen is being Ellen in this regard. But Paige can live with it so long as she doesn't interfere with her decisions. So far, so good.

Paige reapplies her sunscreen. Ellen probably has less need of it, what with her dark skin. It really would have been good to also have a woman with Asian facial features in the group, but there was too little time for that. So, she's just happy that Ellen's along.

"We made it!" Ellen shouts with gusto.

"Not quite," Sandy corrects her, grinning. "This is just the beginning."

"Yes, a successful start, and from now on it's only going to get better."

Sandy's grin evaporates. She nibbles thoughtfully on a slice of carrot.

"Hey! Something's moving down there."

"Where?" Carla shouts.

Ellen points to a spot on the wide canyon floor. Now the others see it.

Sandy takes out her binoculars and looks down. "Muskox." And adds immediately: "The Inuit call them 'animals with a coat like a beard.'"

Carla unpacks her camera.

Paige notes in amazement that she has the most expensive camera of them all, with a powerful zoom lens.

But that doesn't help her.

"Too far away, unfortunately," she says, disappointed.

"You don't want to get too close to them," Sandy warns.

Now's my chance, Paige thinks.

"We'll soon be climbing down into the canyon," she announces.

"What? Aren't we staying on the ridge all the way?" Ellen looks askance at her. "So we don't get lost."

"That's one option. But we can also hike in the canyon itself. It runs in the same direction as the ridge. The view's not as good from down there. But we'll see animals to make up for it."

"I don't know if that's advisable." Ellen looks at Carla, who's indecisive and still holding her camera.

Sandy backs Paige up again.

"If we want to see wild animals, we should go down there. The animals are at the river."

Ellen crosses her arms.

"Wild animals can be dangerous. We're pretty safe up here."

"We do have this here." Sandy holds up the hunting rifle.

"And we also have bear bangers." Paige is fully in boss mode. "There has never been an incident involving wild animals and tourists here."

Carla tips the scales.

"If I'm lugging this thing around, then I want to shoot pictures."

Perfect, Paige thinks. Ellen's outvoted. Couldn't have worked out any better.

She saw a good place earlier where they can climb down.

She shoulders her backpack.

"Let's get going."

By three in the afternoon, even Ellen's happy. The descent went off amazingly well, even if they all seemed a little nervous. The footing wasn't always stable, but nobody slipped. Once they were down, they all hugged one another with joy and relief. Overcoming obstacles is the glue that binds groups together, Paige muses.

It's distinctly warmer in the canyon than on the ridge. The roaring river is like a live creature, a friend in the calm and barrenness of the tundra. They discover delicate little flowers in beguiling colors among the boulders and hassocks.

"Sandy, tell us something about the vegetation," Paige calls. She'd assigned some homework to each woman, who could then feel she was an expert in her subject. That's good for group dynamics.

She didn't have to ask Sandy twice: her knowledge bubbled over like a waterfall. The women eagerly photographed wildflowers, Carla getting down on her stomach to catch the best angles. They didn't get any pictures of muskox because the animals had left by the time the women got down there, but they did spot caribou and snow grouse.

And now they see something else. Yellow blotches on the riverbank.

Rubber dinghies.

Carla can't believe it.

"How'd those get here?"

"They're definitely from the lodge," Sandy explains. "For the adventure tourists."

"The pilot dropped them," Paige adds.

Vyann had told her about them and said they mustn't touch the boats. Which planted a fantastic idea in Paige's head.

She looked at everyone.

"I've arranged a surprise for you all. We're having a little river cruise."

She'd seen on her map that rock bluffs farther down made another climb up to the ridge impossible for a long distance. Sandy noticed it too and drew her attention to it. Sandy's a good map reader.

Carla and Ellen look at the river with worried expressions. It doesn't flow gently along but hops choppily over the uneven riverbed, foaming white in some places.

Ellen shakes her head. "I don't want my things to get wet."

Paige suppresses a sigh. "We've got a watertight cover for our backpacks, and your shoes are also waterproof."

Sandy comes to the rescue once again. "Do you think the lodge owners would do something like this with seniors if it were dangerous?"

"With seniors?" Carla's amazed. "They take seniors down the river?"

"Sure do," Sandy replies.

Paige realizes with surprise she isn't the only one who can be free and easy with the truth. She asks herself for the first time whether Sandy suspects that Paige intends to go to the crater. And how long Sandy might have seen through her.

She trots out her best argument in a relaxed tone of voice: "This way you don't have to go all those kilometers on foot and lug your heavy backpacks. These rubber dinghies are virtually untippable."

"And it'll be great fun for us." Sandy puts her arm around Ellen's shoulders. "Come on, it'll be the adventure of a lifetime."

Ellen grimaces. "If it doesn't kill me."

45

Vyann Kippen, Caregiver for Seniors
Goose Cove, Newfoundland
Friday, February 16

"Where's Nielle?" Mr. Grant asks for the fourth time.

It's slowly getting on her nerves. Why are they all asking about Nielle? She has no answer. She tried to find out some news, naturally, but got no reply to her text messages. She feels cut off from Nielle. Hopefully it's not a bad sign.

"In the hospital in St. John's," she repeats.

"Why doesn't she come anymore?"

Gosh! These questions are really getting to her.

"She'll come when she's healthy." She wipes up the crumbs around his plate and takes the rag to the sink.

"When is she going to come here again?"

"I don't know exactly," Vyann replies, shoving Mr. Grant's dirty clothes into the washing machine.

He doesn't always get to the bathroom in time. Nielle should have made him wear diapers, but she avoids it for as long as she can. Nielle finds diapers humiliating, she confessed to Vyann.

Isn't it humiliating for her to see soiled underwear like this? Vyann thinks more practically. If something must be done, then it must be done. Mr. Grant shouldn't eat so much cabbage and beans. Just tell that to a Newfie. She likes cabbage and beans herself.

Vyann goes through the rooms hunting for more dirty underwear.

Mr. Grant asks again: "When's Nielle coming back?"

"When. She. Is. Healthy."

"What's wrong with her, anyway?"

Mr. Grant's daughter asked Vyann not to say anything about the attack because it would get the old man too upset. His heart might not be able to take it.

"No idea."

"But you're her friend."

He knows that? Did Nielle tell him? You've got to chat about *something* with the elderly. Mr. Grant is cared for by Trina when Nielle can't do it. But now everything's topsy-turvy.

She cannot hold back her curiosity.

"Did Nielle tell you that?"

"Yes. Nielle tells me a lot. I'd find out nothing otherwise."

Mr. Grant's one of the few who don't own a computer and aren't on Facebook. That makes him lonely. Too bad, really; he'd feel a lot more connected if he were online.

"So, what else did she tell you?"

"That she's got a new Ski-Doo. I saw it out the window."

Vyann throws a dirty terrycloth towel into the nearly full washing machine and turns it on. She must talk louder to drown out the machine.

"Where did she get it? At the Ski-Doo store or at Arctic Cat?"

"She didn't say."

Nielle never told her either how she got the new Ski-Doo. Vyann would like a new one too. The one in the garage is her son's. When he's away, she sometime takes the machine through the woods.

"I told her to pay attention." Mr. Grant is genuinely concerned for Nielle.

Vyann joins him at the table. He still hasn't finished his soup, but she wants to keep talking.

"Why should she pay attention?"

"Somebody was following her."

Vyann's heart skips a beat.

"Who?"

"Somebody on a snowmobile. I saw it more than once."

The old man's not as scatterbrained as she thought.

"Do you know who it was?"

"I told my son." Mr. Grant leans forward like a conspirator. He's obviously enjoying the moment before he bursts out with "Tornado."

Three seconds go by until it clicks. Trent Stolke. Trent, who's dead. Found frozen stiff near Mr. Elliott's cabin.

A wave of relief washes over her. There's a suspect! Trent's the suspect. He must be the suspect. But who bumped him off? Trent was stalking Nielle! One more thing Nielle kept from her. She was truly leading a double life. And she calls herself a friend!

Mr. Grant looks at her expectantly.

He probably banked on a different reaction. She points to his soup.

"Wouldn't you like to finish it?" Then she has an idea. "Did your son tell that to the police? About Trent Stolke and Nielle?"

"Yes."

"Were the police here?"

Mr. Grant doesn't reply. Looks out the window.

She follows his gaze. A police car.

"They're here," Mr. Grant says, all excitedly.

Let's hope this doesn't hurt his heart.

She sees two people get out. One is Calista Gates—again. The other one's named Heidy.

There's a knock at the door. Police are the only people to knock at the door before entering. That's not the custom around here.

"Come in!" Mr. Grant shouts.

Vyann was so wrong about this man. The elderly need exciting entertainment to perk up. She can't tell him she's less than enthusiastic about this visit.

Nevertheless, she gives the women a friendly welcome as they take off their jackets and boots. They obviously intend to stay for some time.

"Hello, Mrs. Kippen. Can we have a word?"

Vyann stares at Calista Gates.

"With me?"

The police chief nods.

"Can we go to another room? Constable Wilson will see to Mr. Grant."

Vyann has no choice but to follow her to Mr. Grant's bedroom. Fortunately, she'd put new sheets on the bed that morning and aired out the room.

Calista Gates closes the door.

"Did Tornado attack Nielle?" Vyann asks instantly.

"What makes you think that?" The Mountie looks at her searchingly.

"Mr. Grant saw him following Nielle a number of times on his snowmobile. He told his son about it, and he reported it to the police."

"When was that?"

Calista Gates seemed to be in the dark. Did Mr. Grant make something up again in order to appear important?

"I don't know. Mr. Grant's son can tell you," Vyann says.

The police chief thinks for a few seconds before sitting down on the side of the bed.

"We've got good news for you, Mrs. Kippen. Nielle Helfrey can speak again and is recovering better than expected."

What does she mean by that? Calista does not look well. That strikes Vyann right away. Gerald Hynes is missing at Crater Lake in Labrador. Nielle once told her that Hynes and the police chief are an item. Nielle herself went out with Gerald many years ago, but he supposedly had no time for her. How ironic! As if Morris Tye would have *more* time. Nielle is apparently impressed by his public status.

The police chief goes on: "Many patients need time to regain their speech completely. But Ms. Helfrey can already speak normally. That's a good sign."

Vyann has to sit down too. Not on the bed. Not beside the policewoman. She sits on the rocking chair near the little window.

Calista Gates looks at her with her big, dark eyes.

"Maybe you already know this. Have you spoken to Ms. Helfrey?"

"No, I . . . I couldn't get her. I also tried Nielle's mother, but . . ."

"Ms. Helfrey knew about your dead cockatoo. Can you explain how that's possible?"

Simmi, her poor Simmi. Her hands grow moist.

"She talked about Simmi?"

"Yes. We're wondering how Nielle knew your cockatoo was dead."

"No idea. Probably somebody told her."

"But Ms. Helfrey had only spoken with her mother before then."

Vyann shakes her head. Where's the policewoman going with this? she asks herself again.

"I haven't talked to Nielle since she's been in the hospital."

"When did your cockatoo die?"

"I don't know. I only know how long he's been missing."

The Mountie keeps her eyes steadily on Vyann. She doesn't miss a thing.

"We know the cockatoo's wings were cut off *after he died*. Was that you, Mrs. Kippen?"

Vyann begins to quiver inside.

46

Bud Abel, Part-time Cook
Tulliq, Labrador
Friday, February 16

It's easy to see: the Fish is on edge. Bud just phoned him. Something's happened he hadn't counted on.

Bud would like to stay out of his way because the Fish can take his moods out on the person who happens to be standing next to him. But he's got news from his friends in Alliarkuk: something's been going on that should be of interest to the Fish. That will boost his stock with him.

Bud threads his snowmobile around the houses in Tulliq. Smoke's billowing from the chimneys into the icy air. The wind's slackened a little, and the snow has stopped. He sees a gang of teenagers heading toward the community center. They're showing the film *Atanarjuat: The Fast Runner*; it's screened once a year. He feels a stitch in his side. A longing. Schooldays were the best, but he'd never tell anybody that. He liked the teachers even though he rebelled against them now and then. He felt he was in good hands. When he lost the solid structure of his youth, he lost himself along with it.

At the harbor he takes the curve and drives to the other end of the town, where there are fewer and fewer buildings. He slows down.

Bud doesn't see any familiar vehicles in front of the trailer. The Fish is by himself. Strange. Where are all the others?

He parks and opens the trailer door when he hears the Fish talking. Maybe he ought to wait.

But the Fish gets up and gestures for him to come in.

"Are they out of their mind?" he roars into his cell phone. "They're fucking crazy!"

Bud hears a voice shouting at the other end.

"You guys better get yourselves out of that shit before you drown in it! Got it?" The Fish flings the phone down on the table.

A bad moment to be here, Bud thinks.

The Fish scowls at him.

"What do you want from me, Pint-size?"

The nickname reminds Bud how thin and unimpressive he is. But he does know something: knowledge is power.

"I heard two cops sheltered with the guys from Alliarkuk because they didn't trust a third cop as far as they could throw him."

"What's this crap coming out of your mouth?" The Fish's eyes are glinting.

Shit, now he's made him madder. Just because he can't properly describe what his friends told him.

So, he begins a second time.

"Three guys from Alliarkuk are up at Crater Lake because they're . . . because the park . . ."

"I know that," the Fish interrupts.

Not a good sign, Bud thinks.

"They slept in the cabins near the airstrip. The cops were at the cabins on Cloud Lake earlier, nearer the crater. The three cops were supposed to stay there, but two of them went to the

Alliarkuk guys because they . . . because the third cop gave them the creeps."

Now he's grabbed the Fish's attention; Bud can see it.

"How so, gave them the creeps?"

"The guy was firing his pistol."

"He was shooting at people?"

"He wanted to scare people. Did you know that two guys from Tulliq were up there on snowmobiles?"

"Why do you even ask? There are always people up there, not only from Tulliq. Not only from Alliarkuk."

"The third cop fired over their heads. The other two cops heard it and drove off right away. The third cop claims the Tulliq guys had Gerald Hynes's camera bag on them."

The Fish's face twitches.

Bud's not sure if the Fish knows that part of the story or not. But maybe the rest of it.

"The two other cops went off with the Tulliq guys."

"How do you know they wanted to get away from the third cop?"

"That's what the Alliarkuk guy said. On the satellite phone. The two cops had already spent the first night in the cabin near the airstrip."

"Sure, they wanted to keep an eye on the guys from Alliarkuk. That's why they stayed there."

That's something Bud hadn't thought of.

He doesn't know if he should go on, but the Fish pushes him to.

"The two guys from Tulliq"—he avoids saying *your friends* from Tulliq—"went missing on the way back because of poor visibility." Bud did *not* say they pulled a cut and run.

"And how did the cops take it?"

"They told the guys from Alliarkuk that the ceremony for the national park was being moved to Happy Valley-Goose Bay because the environment minister couldn't wait for better weather. And that they would keep searching for Gerald Hynes."

"And did they say anything about the Tulliq guys? Are they looking for them?'

"Not a peep. Not a peep. And the guys from Alliarkuk didn't ask."

The Fish clenches both fists.

"The cops haven't got a thing on them."

And the camera bag? Bud wants to ask but bites his tongue. If it turns out that the Fish's Tulliq guys have something to do with Gerald Hynes's disappearance, then everything must be kept quiet.

"Go to the airport," the Fish orders. "Vernon flew to Crater Lake today to pick up Tiff Staid and some boxes. He'll be back at some point. See if you can find out some more."

Nothing could be more to Bud's liking.

He scrambles outside and starts up the snowmobile.

It's not long before he's waiting impatiently at the airport in the shed beside the runway. The warmth inside makes him more fidgety.

Vernon's Cessna lands two hours later.

Bud feels his heart spinning. It takes forever for the propeller to stop.

Vernon climbs out.

Then Bud hears barking. The dogs! Tiff appears at the door.

He hurries over to her, sees her face. And is shocked.

"What the hell did they do to you?" he shouts before he can stop himself.

She doesn't object.

"A nightmare," she says.

47

Fred van Heisen, RCMP Constable
St. Anthony, Newfoundland
Friday, February 16

Fred's petting Woolly, who licks his hand eagerly. Dustin Wilson, who's just come in, ignores the dog. No greeting, not a pat, nothing. It seems he leaves Woolly completely to his wife.

How can Dustin be such a curmudgeon just because Heidy has found a new passion? After all, a search dog is useful. Besides, their only child is in St. John's, so she needs a little more life in the house.

Since he came back from Vancouver, Fred's noticed that the two of them are not so keen on going out on patrol together. Heidy's with Calista in Goose Cove today; Dustin's asking residents in St. Anthony about Trent Stolke.

Fred adopts a friendly tone.

"Well, find anything interesting?"

"Not much," Dustin answers, making himself a coffee.

Maybe Dustin's sore because he, Fred, is working in the office while he has to knock on doors. Dustin used to jump at the chance; he doesn't like sitting behind a desk. So why's he back so soon?

Fred's staying at the station because the forensics people could arrive at any minute. He's spent the time making phone inquiries in Labrador. Calista knows nothing about it, doesn't need to for the time being. She's got enough on her plate. Besides, she can't encroach on Inspector Allen's territory. If she gets mixed up in the search for Hynes, the inspector might take it as a criticism and get all huffy. Peter Allen wants to keep a firm hand on the reins in this search because of the politics involved. The contractor for the planned lodge disappears into thin air the day before Canada's environment minister is to announce a new national park. Allen certainly won't want to drag Morris Tye into it unless external circumstances compel him to.

But Fred has had good connections in Labrador ever since he was stationed in Port Brendan. You get to know a lot of folks in four years, even though he's not the most genial person. He's got nothing to lose; he's out of here come May. He doesn't have to show deference to anybody, the way Calista must; he can make inquiries behind Inspector Allen's back. There are always people who love to gossip. That's how he learned that Austin Sullivan's running around up at Crater Lake.

Sullivan's a son of a bitch. When Calista came to Port Brendan, he always made fun of her. He thought she was a spoiled city slicker who didn't have a clue about pack ice, snowstorms, and snowmobiles. Well, she showed she certainly was *not* spoiled and put on a great performance, solving three murders in record time. That got her promoted to St. Anthony's chief of police. Sullivan thought it was unfair. What a nasty piece of work he is.

Fred shakes off those thoughts and turns his attention to Dustin.

"Did you have a look at the photos of the snowmobile tracks?"

Dustin knows all about snowmobiles. Fred hopes he'll warm up if he treats Dustin as an expert.

Dustin sips his coffee before answering: "Yeah, I did. Nothing struck me that we didn't already know. Somebody drove from the cabin to Goose Cove, dropped Nielle there, and went back."

Fred's disappointed. Why didn't Dustin take into account the two snowmobiles at the cabin that did not belong to the police? He must surely know about them. Drag marks and boot prints lead from them to the outhouse. He's about to face Dustin with this when he hears some noise in the hallway.

Heidy's the first through the door and immediately hugs her dog. Calista has a word with Rex at the reception desk, then enters with a plate of cinnamon buns.

Fred and the Wilsons dive into them.

"Did Mr. Grant's son tell any of us that Tornado used to stalk Nielle on his Ski-Doo?" Calista asks.

"Me," Dustin replies.

"Why didn't we know about it?"

"The old guy makes up things like that all the time. Even his son told me he didn't know if it was right."

"Every detail's important in investigations. We—"

Dustin interrupts her. "Trent doesn't make sense as the perpetrator. He's got an alibi for the time of the crime. He was chopping wood for the old folks' home. You should know that, sarge. It's part of his punishment for his last crime: fifty hours of community service."

Fred's amazed at Dustin's tone.

And further amazed at how she gives it all short shrift.

"Are there any witnesses?"

"Yes, several. I've got their names."

"You ought to communicate these things to us, constable."

"I intended to put them on the intranet; didn't get around to it yet." Dustin takes a big bite out of the cinnamon bun as though nothing happened.

Calista changes the subject. She'd forgotten at times to post things to the intranet too.

"We got a surprise from Vyann Kippen," she announces. "Her cockatoo was dead by the time the business with Nielle occurred. She told Nielle about it."

Fred stops eating.

"She lied?"

"Yes. She staged it herself and put on an act for us."

"And the wings?"

"She did it herself."

"She cut them off herself?" Dustin suddenly perks up. Maybe it's the bun. Sugary icing sticks to his lips. "Where'd she get that idea from?"

"She said it's a ritual of some sort. So that the bird stays with her and doesn't fly away."

"Is she out of her mind?"

Dustin's words could have come out of Fred's mouth if he weren't so dumbfounded. He asks instead: "Do you believe her, sarge?" He doesn't call her by her given name when other people are present.

"I don't know yet. It sounds a bit crazy. She's got no plausible explanation for why she put the bird in a box at her front door. She misled us. We must scrutinize her closely. Check her alibi, quiz the neighbors. And we'll pick up Trina Modeste again too."

The scent of cinnamon hangs in the room. Fred notices Calista's the only one not eating. She looks pale. Not a good sign.

He visualizes Vyann before him, dissolving in tears when she saw the dead cockatoo.

"Why didn't she tell us about this ritual?"

"Because she was scared we'd think she was batty." Calista makes a face that speaks volumes.

"She is." Dustin speaks with his mouth full.

Calista taps her fingers on the table.

"First of all, Vyann can't explain why the cockatoo was the

first thing Nielle mentioned when she was being questioned. Why does a dead bird matter so much to her?"

"She can't think straight yet because of her head injury and talks nonsense," Dustin explains. "Maybe that's the reason."

"This is not the proper time for jokes," Heidy corrects him.

"That's the way it is. People with head injuries often talk nonsense."

Dead silence.

Fred stares at Dustin. Does he realize he's just made a faux pas?

Heidy pulls herself together fast: "Apparently, people who don't have head injuries do that too, as you've just proved."

Calista intervenes and puts her foot down: "I'd like everyone to behave like professionals so our investigation can move ahead." She looks at Dustin. "Have you found out anything about the unidentified tracks at the cabin? Can we match them to specific snowmobiles?"

Dustin says no. "It's impossible. Hundreds of snowmobiles leave tracks like those."

Fred looks at Calista. They've already determined together that for one of the snowmobiles, the tracks in the snow are sixty centimeters wide. Not many snowmobiles in St. Anthony are that wide. With most of them, it's forty or fifty centimeters. Furthermore, some skis have double runners, and you don't see those around St. Anthony very often. Calista raises her eyebrows and says nothing. She probably doesn't want to straighten Dustin out when his wife's present. So, she too has spotted how delicate the situation is between the Wilsons.

"What's this here?"

Dustin holds up a book Calista put on the table, an attempt to distract her from his disappointing report. He reads out loud: "*Man on the Ice.*"

"Oh, yeah, my bedtime reading," Calista replies.

"It's in an evidence bag."

"So it won't get wet."

Fred's taken aback. Why doesn't she tell Dustin what's really going on? They took the book from Trent Stolke's parents' house. Between its pages they found a year-old ticket for the Royal Canadian Legion in Happy Valley-Goose Bay; it was probably just a bookmark. *Friends of the Force Charity Ball*, it says. The annual RCMP ball. How did Trent get his hands on a ticket like this? And why is Calista keeping her discovery from the Wilsons? She throws him a look that says: I'll explain afterward.

Fred can see only one reason why: she wants to do some research in Labrador but on the down-low. Just like him.

Rex sticks his head in the door.

"The forensics team isn't coming until tomorrow evening. The flight's been canceled."

48

Paige Warner, Entrepreneur
In the Crater Lake Area, Labrador
Eight Years Earlier

The journey goes amazingly well for the first few kilometers. The river looks wilder than it is. The four dinghies glide almost leisurely over the foaming water. Paige stops her boat on the shore once and lets the rest of them paddle on while she records them on her cell phone. She has extra batteries and chargers. There's no reception around here, but she's got the smartphone for pictures and videos.

The women are nearly euphoric. They'll have such terrific pictures to show back home! The impressive canyon cliffs tower high over them on both sides of the river. The sky above is visible in shimmering blue strips. They feel as if they're on a fantastic film set. Carla's fear that her gear could get wet has dissipated. Sandy's always way out in front, and even Ellen's stopped griping.

The mood changes when the flat riverbank disappears and the steep rock wall on both sides seem never-ending. Paige shouts to the women it's only for a short stretch, then they'll come to flat land again where they can pitch their tents. She's glad they're finally passing through the tunnel-like cliffs, which are an important landmark on the route to Crater Lake. But she won't tell the group.

The river narrows and the waves churn. Carla cries out at times when her boat hits an unexpected bump. Sandy turns around every time and shouts soothing words to her. That really should be my role, Paige thinks, but she's too busy keeping her boat in balance. Does the lodge really take their guests down this river?

After a while they all realize that nobody's tipped over. Carla stops panicking. She even takes pictures of the cliffs.

Paige sees that Ellen's bringing up the rear.

"Everything okay?" she calls.

"I've got to go," Ellen answers.

That's really not possible. The narrow tunnel's taking longer than Paige expected. She feels a little uneasy now. The dinghy's abrupt movements are hard on her back.

She hears a roar from Sandy. She doesn't understand why at first. Then Sandy raises an arm as a victory sign. Paige gets it: they've reached the end of the narrow canyon. A first victory.

That evening Sandy prepares the food on the camping stove. She collects the ready-to-eat meals and ingredients from all the backpacks, which takes quite a bit of time. The result is a delicious dinner, and they're all very hungry.

Good food can save many a situation, Paige has read. She didn't skimp on top-quality, freeze-dried meals.

As they sit around the fire in front of their tents having tea —they were able to find some wood in the area—Ellen says: "I saw someone up on the cliffs when we were down below. A man."

All eyes pivot to Ellen.

"How could you see him from the boat?" Sandy responds. "Impossible. Your eyes were deceiving you."

A man? That's the last thing they needed: for somebody to see them in the boats. In the stolen boats. The lodge owners would soon find out they weren't staying on the route above the canyon that they'd agreed upon.

"I suggest we head north," Paige says as nonchalantly as she can. "Then we'll come to Crater Lake. That would be a big win for all of us."

"What?" Carla almost drops her aluminum cup. "Why Crater Lake all of a sudden?"

"It's a sacred Inuit site. The lake was created more than a million years ago when a meteorite hit. It's not far from here."

"How far?"

"About a long day's march."

"Are you sure?"

No, she's not sure, maybe it's two or three days, but there's no sense saying as much. The route is manageable.

"That would be fantastic," Sandy enthuses. "I'm sure very few white people have ever been there."

Ellen doesn't let that pass without comment: "White people? What's with us Black people?"

"I didn't mean it like that. Don't get in a huff."

Ellen, who's sitting next to Paige, turns to her.

"Do you even know the way there?"

Paige sighs inwardly. Ellen's interfering again.

"It's quite easy by compass. And we have GPS on our cell phones. I have long-life batteries."

Sandy nods in agreement.

"I do too." She looks at Carla. "We can take terrific pictures."

It's a familiar constellation. Three against Ellen.

Paige has an important ally: money. If one of the women should want to peel off, she'll buy her acquiescence. Very discreetly, without anybody noticing. She's brought enough cash to buy off any number of people. She's not letting herself be held back by other people's misgivings so close to her goal. In her backpack, she's got a thick stack of bills. She's stowed the rest in a bag that's waiting for her at the lodge.

The four of them stare into the fire for several seconds.

Ellen knows she's outgunned.

"We'll always keep the group together," she warns. "Sandy, you've got the rifle. Keep that man on the cliffs in mind."

Nobody giggles or makes a snide remark.

Paige puts on some dry branches. Flames flare up.

Why must Ellen always make the others feel afraid?

The man's probably a tourist like them. Someone who's sticking to the route on top of the cliffs.

The next morning they set out in the first light of day. Paige is impatient: Carla and Ellen take way too long to pack up their tent.

They climb from the bank up a slope and must fight their way through a stretch thick with firs and bushes. Staying together is more easily said than done. Carla has the most trouble keeping up with the others. Even Paige's backpack keeps getting caught on sharp little branches. The ground is unpredictable and sometimes gives way unexpectedly. They're victimized by mosquitoes in the scrub. There's no wind to cool them. Sweat soaks their clothes, but rain would be worse.

Paige is irritated. At some point they *must* come to the barren tundra. But they're still slogging up the overgrown slope.

Sandy stops before they reach the top, waiting for the rest of the group to catch up.

"I'll go and see what's ahead," she suggests. "You can wait for me here."

Ellen protests at once: "No, no way, we're going together. You've got the gun. What if a grizzly shows up?"

"Here's the gun, quick, take it," Sandy offers.

Ellen refuses, and Sandy makes no move to hand the weapon over.

"It's not far, and anyway, you've got the bear bangers and pepper spray. We haven't seen a single bear."

"I hope I won't go home without any pictures of them." Carla wipes the sweat from her forehead, and the mosquito spray with it.

Who would have thought it could be so warm in the subarctic?

Sandy looks at them all. "Do you guys really want to scramble up here, and then, if it turns out to be the wrong way, go back down and up again?"

Nobody feels like doing that, not even Paige.

Sandy starts out, carrying her heavy backpack. Does she want to show them how athletic she is?

They wait. Time passes slowly. The mosquitoes show no mercy, yet nobody tries to put their bug netting on in the scrub, or they won't be able to see anything.

Paige finally loses patience.

"I'm going to see what's keeping Sandy."

"No, we're staying in a group."

This time Ellen won't be talked out of it.

Now they all speak at once.

"She has the rifle. Why doesn't she fire a shot to let us know she's okay?"

"Does she have any ammunition in her backpack, or who does?"

"She's got the satellite phone," Paige says. Maybe she shouldn't have mentioned it because Ellen immediately looks through her backpack.

"I can't find my emergency transmitter."

They all root around in their backpacks. The transmitters are gone!

"She took them when she got our food out last night." Carla

looks around almost in triumph: she's proud of her powers of detection.

Paige, in contrast, is alarmed. It can't be true.

"We have to go look for her," she decides. "We have no choice."

They put on their backpacks and fight their way up, one unsteady step after the other. It's a laborious climb. They force their way through bushes with whiplike twigs; thorny branches lash their faces. They protect their eyes with their bare hands. One of them occasionally stumbles into a hidden dip in the ground or over a root.

"Ow!" Ellen cries as she slips and falls to her knees.

Pray that nobody breaks a bone, Paige thinks.

They finally get the bush behind them and can see the rocky hilltop. They ascend the remaining hundred meters and drop their heavy burdens on the ground. They look around. No trace of Sandy.

"Where the hell is she?" Carla swears, her face shining with sweat.

They shout Sandy's name. Over and over. Louder and louder.

Look hard all around.

Suddenly Ellen says: "Do you know that Sandy Miller isn't her real name?"

49

Detective Sergeant Calista Gates
St. Anthony, Newfoundland
Friday, February 16

Vyann Kippen isn't home, something I'd expected because her workload's been increased. She has several of Nielle's clients to take care of.

That suits me fine: we can question the neighbors without any bother or upset. I let Heidy handle it; she explains to people that the police want to protect caregivers from any further attacks after the one on Nielle. The first two neighbors are mainly interested in Trent Stolke's death. We don't get much out of them.

Fred and Dustin are investigating the Stolke case; they want to track down his buddies. Heidy and I concentrate on Vyann. We're lucky at the third neighbor's: we meet an elderly woman with mobility problems who is pleased at the unexpected visit and talks a blue streak. She drops a bit of important information amid her flood of words: she saw Vyann get out of a car with an unfamiliar woman on the day Nielle was attacked.

"Did you recognize the woman?" Heidy asks.

"No. They went into Vyann's house. I only saw them for a little while. I don't think it was anyone from here."

"Why do you think that?"

"I would have recognized her. Vyann sometimes has people staying at her house who come from far away and need to go to the hospital. They sleep at her place."

"Do you mean relatives?"

"Yes, relatives, or people she knows."

"Did you see them again that day?"

"I heard a Ski-Doo and went to the window. But I didn't see anything. I'm not so quick on my poor legs. I saw Vyann get into her car afterward. By herself."

"What time was that?"

"It was shortly before nine in the morning. Because my daughter always calls me at nine o'clock. Every day."

Heidy exchanges quick looks with me. That correlates with our information. Vyann was at a client's from nine to twelve, then drove to another client in St. Carol's, and stayed there until shortly after three. She seemed to have a solid alibi.

"And the other woman? Did you see her again?"

"No, but I heard a Ski-Doo. I don't know who was driving. When I went and looked, the Ski-Doo wasn't in front of Vyann's house. Her garage door was open. She has a big garage. She can't use it most of the time because her son stores so much junk in there. She's already complained about it."

"Is her son here?"

"No, he works in Alberta. He only comes now and then."

"Do you sometimes see him on his Ski-Doo?"

"Yes, he has a big machine. He earns a lot of money in Alberta and can afford it. He'll probably take over the lodge from his father someday. You know it, the Remote Point Lodge in Labrador."

"What does his Ski-Doo look like?"

"Blue. Or blue-black."

"A Ski-Doo? Not a Polaris or Arctic Cat?"

She hesitates. "I know he bought it at the Ski-Doo shop in St. Anthony. He told my nephew about it. He paid a pile of dough for it."

Heidy glances at me once again. This lady's a piñata of information.

We thank her and decline a cup of tea because we have to move on. As we leave the overheated house, the cold washes over us like a shock.

I type a text message to Fred when we're in the car. I want him to inquire in the Ski-Doo store if Vyann's son's snowmobile has a double runner on the skis.

"Maybe Trina Modeste was at Vyann's place," Heidy speculates. "If she was wrapped from head to toe in winter clothing, the neighbor maybe couldn't recognize her."

"Where's Trina now?"

Heidy looks in her notes.

"In Goose Cove, at a Mr. Field's."

"Super. You're really up-to-date. Let's go there."

We've just gotten to West Street when there's a call on my cell phone. I recognize the number, David Pelletier.

My heart's in my throat.

I don't want to speak to him when Heidy's around; I must protect him as a source.

"One minute, please," I tell him. And then to Heidy: "Can you get us a coffee? I could use one."

"Yes, I can tell by looking at you," she says and stops at the Rebel Coffeehouse. She gathers at once that it might have to do with Gerald. "Decaf for you?"

I nod, and she disappears into the brightly painted little coffeeshop.

"Heidy Wilson was in the car, with me," I explain to David. "She's gone for coffee."

"I'll be brief, sarge. A reliable source tells me Gerald's camera bag was found at the crater. No pictures on the memory card. Seems he hadn't begun to shoot any."

Finally. Some sign of Gerald! My heart beats wildly. But what did the find mean? My joy fizzles out instantly.

"Are there any footprints? He left on foot."

"Evidently not. The wind keeps smoothing the ground over up there. I also can imagine that any footprints were destroyed by snowmobiles."

"The search parties didn't find anything?" I know I sound rather desperate.

"Some Alliarkuk people were the first to search for him. No luck."

"What did Austin Sullivan find out? He was in the vicinity when Gerald was last seen. Fred told me."

"Are you by yourself, or is Heidy back?"

"No, shoot."

"You do know Sullivan from Port Brendan days. A perfect bastard, if you ask me. He would not be unhappy if Gerald Hynes never turned up."

"What are you saying, David? You're not serious!"

"Sullivan wants your job, sarge. He's already applied for it. It's an open secret around here. And he wants to take his pal Delgado to St. Anthony with him."

"But that's got nothing to do with Gerald."

"Sullivan didn't like you in Port Brendan. That's another open secret. There are people who want to do you harm."

"Hurt me by not rescuing Gerald?"

"I could imagine."

"You mean they'd kill him?"

"No, they probably wouldn't go that far. But maybe they wouldn't have their heart in the search."

I'm stunned.

"When you say it's an open secret, does that mean Inspector Allen knows?" I ask.

David doesn't hesitate.

"I can imagine that's the case."

"Is Sullivan still up at Crater Lake?"

"No, he's been taken off the case."

Before I can ask him why, David says: "Something else, quick, about Morris Tye. He used his influence to send wildlife officers up to Remote Point Lodge last January. We got a report in our office that the owner, Noshi Mercer, is illegally selling caribou meat on the quiet. But the wildlife officers didn't find any at the lodge. I've heard Morris Tye's brother-in-law wanted to buy the lodge, but Noshi refused to sell."

"You think . . ."

"Gotta go." And he's gone.

I sit there, overwhelmed. Letting my thoughts wander. I can't come to a clear conclusion. I don't want to be helpless; I want to fight for Gerald. I want him back! It takes effort not to slam my fists on the car's dashboard. I hammer on the seat cover instead until my arms grow weak.

I must call Gerald's parents. I think about it with a heavy heart. There's nothing I can do to comfort or console them. My distress over Gerald weighs on me so much that I'm afraid it will only make it harder on them.

50

Tiffany Staid, Musher
Tulliq, Labrador
Friday, February 16

Tiffany examines Pretor's paw. At least it's healed. One problem less. She nestles her head against the dog's coat and rubs his body. Pretor pushes back, thankful for the attention. She could stay like this forever, her face in the dog's fur, the happily trembling animal in her arms. She feels the warmth under the shield of thick hair, the warmth that allows the dog to survive and that she herself needs to survive at this moment.

She's back. She made it. She escaped.

The police didn't arrest her. But she doesn't know what's down the road.

Bud's still there in front of the pen. He helped her with the dogs but doesn't make a move to leave. What's he want from her? Is he going to pump her for information? Did the Fish send him? What were his guys doing at Crater Lake?

"The Fish wants to talk to you," Bud says as she proceeds to close the pen door. The dogs are so tired that they're already lying down, exhausted from the excitement, not from running.

Here it comes. Just what she was afraid of.

She wants nothing to do with the Fish. She'd been able to keep out of his way until now.

Bud seems to read her mind.

"Don't be afraid, the cops can't lay a finger on you; we'll all stick together."

"I've done nothing wrong," she says, "I can't be accused of anything." Maybe the Fish's guys did something, and they want to buy her silence.

"It's not about Tuesday or Wednesday."

She looks at him.

"So, what *is* it about?" But she's already guessed.

"The missing women."

"What's the Fish got to do with it?"

Wrong question. She ought to have asked: What have I got to do with it?

She'd been waiting for this. Someday she'd pay the price. The price for her help. The price for her dogs.

She's got no choice. She must find out what the Fish knows.

"I'll take you there." Bud gets on his Arctic Cat.

Resigned, she sits down behind him.

They drive to the village, past the church, the community center, the arena, the houses on stilts with smoke coming out of their chimneys into the cold air. It's the same as always: snowmobiles in front of the doorsteps, gray satellite dishes on the houses, oil tanks beside them. She sees it all through different eyes today. This village is her home. She must come to terms with the people here whether she wants to or not. She cannot brush off the Fish.

His trailer home is at the edge of town, around a bend. It's only visible from the ocean side; you can see what's going on only from there. From boats. Or from the pack ice, like now.

Bud stops the snowmobile.

"Go on in; he's inside."

"You're not coming with me?"

"I'll wait here. I'll take you back afterward."

"It's too cold to wait." She speaks not out of empathy. She wants to be sure he's not leaving her alone with the Fish.

"It won't take long."

How does he know? But she has no time to think about it.

She opens the door and finds the Fish at a table rolling a cigarette.

"There you are," he welcomes her. "Make yourself at home."

His friendly greeting takes her by surprise. A dog is asleep under the table. The Fish looks different; he's clean-shaven, hair cut short. The last time she saw him, from a distance, his hair was shoulder length. He looked ferocious back then.

She's on her guard. He puts a cup in front of her, a teabag in it, then some hot water. She's to feel like a guest. It's weird.

She doesn't touch the tea, though she's longing for a hot drink.

"Why aren't you having any?" the Fish asks. "Have the cops scared the hell out of you?"

"I've done nothing wrong." She'll repeat these words until she drops.

"We've got your back."

Who's *we*?

"Nothing's going to happen to you," he reiterates.

"Why should anything happen to me?"

"The cops need a scapegoat because one of them made a mistake. The blond cop. Sullivan."

What's the Fish mean by that?

"He sent you back to the cabin near the airstrip."

She screws up her courage and asks: "How do you know that?"

"I've got eyes everywhere."

It must have been the men from Alliarkuk. They know about it. And the cops themselves. But the Fish didn't get it from them. She nevertheless can't imagine that those guys from Alliarkuk told the Fish. Why would they?

"That blond cop stinks. He wants to cook my guys' goose because *he* made a mistake. He says they stole Gerald Hynes's camera bag, that they got rid of him. Now we're going to cook *his* goose." He looks at her. A somber look. "You can help. You help us, we help you."

"I've done nothing wrong."

"We know. Neither have my people. The cops still say my guys have something to do with Hynes's disappearance."

What's the Fish want from her anyway?

"We know it's not true. You say the blond cop stopped you at Cloud Lake?"

"Yes."

"The cops are saying that's not correct. But we've got witnesses. My people saw him there. With you."

That can't be. She didn't see anybody around.

"He stopped them too," she says evasively.

"I mean before. They saw him before. At Cloud Lake. With you."

"How's that possible? We'd have heard their motors." She fingers the string holding the teabag in her cup.

He regards her with an inscrutable gaze through slightly reddened eyes.

Finally, the penny drops.

And he realizes she gets it.

"They saw you with him. And he threatened you with his pistol. He sent you back to the landing strip that way. Just the way he did to my people. Because he did something illegal." He stresses the words like a judge. "We're gonna turn this joker in."

If she agrees, she'll have to lie. She'll make herself an enemy of the cops.

The Fish leans back. Looks at her like she's his quarry.

"We'll help you too. That's our pact." He takes his time before firing. Then he shoots: "Nobody needs to know you followed the missing women back then."

That hits like a blow to the head.

Somebody had seen her!

Sweat's forming on her forehead, but she doesn't want to take off her coat, or the Fish might notice.

"It's of no interest to us what you were doing there," he continues. "And it's of no interest to us either why you didn't tell the cops."

Why you didn't tell the cops.

Suddenly she flashes back to Remote Point Lodge. Back then, eight years ago.

She's cleaning the common room when one of the women takes her aside.

"I'm sorry they dumped you. It's the others who were against taking you along as a guide. I'm Sandy."

Tiffany doesn't know what to think or do.

"You deserve some compensation. Come, I've got something to show you."

Sandy goes ahead, and Tiff follows her to one of the chalets.

They go in, and Sandy opens a drawer in a dresser and shows her a red bag. She undoes the zipper and takes out a thick stack of bills.

"When we've gone, you can help yourself. Nobody will notice."

Tiff shakes her head.

"Not interested."

"Don't worry. The woman has no idea how much money she's got. She's swimming in it."

Tiffany wants to get out of there as quickly as possible. Not be seen with this Sandy.

She'll secretly follow the group because Vyann and Noshi want her to. They don't trust the women at all. They're planning something that isn't kosher.

And tail them she did. She left a day earlier and followed the opposite riverbank, where the vegetation was thicker and the terrain more difficult. She saw them stealing the rubber dinghies. She hadn't seen that coming. On the river, the women could move faster than she could. She lost sight of them. By the time she discovered the remains of their campsite, it was too late. She didn't find the women anywhere.

She reported to Noshi and Vyann by satellite phone and hiked back to a small lake. Vernon picked her up in his Cessna. They agreed later not to tell anyone about it.

"Or else the cops will think you have something to do with the women's disappearance."

Nevertheless, somebody had seen her and kept his mouth shut until today.

It can only mean one thing: that particular somebody won't want to tell the cops what he was doing there himself.

She'd seen the money in the red bag again, in an airtight container where the women stored things they didn't want on their trek. She took none of it before the cops showed up at the lodge. But when she was cleaning the women's chalets afterward, she discovered more bills behind a moose head on the wall she was dusting—and she took them. Nobody knows about it. She bought her dogs with the money two years later.

She must take the deal with the Fish. No two ways about it, because it's evidently not a secret she followed the four women back then.

"Tiff, are we agreed?"

She nods.

51

Detective Sergeant Calista Gates
St. Anthony, Newfoundland
Friday, February 16

What did David Pelletier just say? Austin Sullivan hates me. He wants to be the police chief in St. Anthony. He made no effort to search for Gerald.

My head's spinning. I shut my eyes.

Concentrate, Calista. Concentrate.

I must go to Labrador. I must go to Crater Lake.

Inspector Allen can go hang himself. Come what may.

I can't stand it. I must find Gerald.

The driver's door opens. Heidy hands me my coffee and gets behind the wheel. She puts her cup in the cupholder between the seats, and I do likewise. The coffees are still too hot.

"Any news about Crater Lake?" she asks.

I struggle to get the words out; my tongue sticks to the roof of my mouth.

"It's almost more than I can stand, to be here and unable to do a thing."

"You couldn't do anything up there either, sarge. They've got a plane and a search party with snowmobiles. They're making a huge effort. Hopefully they'll be using tracking hounds as well."

She says tracking hounds. Not cadaver-sniffing dogs. Every ounce of hope counts.

I can hardly breathe; my throat muscles are so tight.

Heidy puts her hand on the gearshift.

"He wouldn't want you to put your life in danger on his account, would he?"

Truth is, I don't know. I don't know what Gerald would advise me to do. We haven't spent all that much time together. We've lived in different worlds. I didn't even know Nielle Helfrey was his girlfriend in her younger days. Nevertheless, the bond between us is strong.

Some people are coming out of the Rebel Coffeehouse. Two women with two little children in brightly colored ski jackets and matching hats with white pompoms. We hear their chatter. My body's taking deep breaths without my help. I've got a responsibility for the local people as their police chief. I must be their protector. They're entitled to it. It's my duty. Above all, I mustn't let Nielle down. She suffered the same ordeal as I did. Only her attacker didn't hit her as hard as mine did. Or as many times.

A dam inside me breaks. I let my tears flow freely. No sense holding them back. When was the last time I cried? I cannot remember. Heidy's sitting calmly beside me and doesn't prod me to do anything. After a few minutes, I take a tissue out of the glove compartment and wipe away my tears.

Heidy hands me the coffee cup without a word, and I take a drink. The coffee feels like an icebreaker, the warmth does me good.

I can't afford a crisis. That would be a win for the RCMP hyenas who want to push me out.

"We've got to carry on. So, off to Goose Cove," I say.

Heidy turns the key and asks: "Have you checked on Trina Modeste again? It's so peculiar."

I share her opinion. When Heidy did her research, she didn't find much about Trina, and that bit of information didn't go back very far. Heidy asked me to try because she wasn't sure she'd thought of everything. Unfortunately, I didn't get any further.

"Best to take the Ski-Doos, don't you think?" she suggests.

She loves riding the snowmobile. We can move around on them better than in the SUV or the pickup. And there's no snow coming today.

"Okay."

"What's Dustin doing, actually?" Heidy asks shortly before we reach the station.

I'm astonished by her question. She usually always knows what her husband's doing.

"He and Fred are supposed to track down Trent Stolke's buddies and question them."

"I see." Then nothing more.

I feel more composed as we drive along the snowmobile path to Goose Cove. Steering the machine takes my full attention. The white landscape is soothing. I do hope we don't meet a polar bear, because we can't see what's around the next curve. Heidy seems not to give it a thought as she roars along the trail without braking. She's a more experienced driver than I am.

We go past the turnoff to where we found Trent Stolke's body. I'd like to take another look around there before the forensics people come, but I'll have to worry about that later. We want to catch Trina before she leaves.

Mr. Field, her client, lives near the white church, the largest building in Goose Cove. There's a wooden wheelchair ramp up to his front door; the snow almost comes up to it. No vehicle in front of the house. Trina must have walked up from the main road.

When she opens the door, she gives no indication that our coming is a surprise. She certainly heard our snowmobiles. Or she'd long expected we'd want to talk to her a second time.

Heidy and I do what worked well previously. She takes care of the old gentleman in the kitchen, and I go with Trina to another room.

This time it's a storeroom with a washing machine and dryer.

I first ask Trina about Vyann, wanting to know who her friends and acquaintances are.

Trina leans on the washing machine.

"I've told you, I'm not close to Vyann and Nielle."

And yet you're close enough to drive Nielle's mother to the airport, I'm thinking.

I notice how put-together Trina is: strikingly good haircut with highlights, careful makeup, separately applied eyelashes, perfect eyebrows. I think that's evidence she respects her clients; it matters to the old folks what she looks like.

"Somebody saw Vyann on Sunday morning with a woman who probably isn't from here. Do you have any idea who that might have been?"

"No." Trina doesn't say one word more than she needs to. That doesn't necessarily mean she's lying. Suspects often deliver long, convoluted explanations to mask the truth.

"Did she tell you she was expecting a visitor?"

"No." Trina stands before me with arms crossed as if she'd like to get out the door as fast as possible.

"Do you like your job?" A surprise question to test her reaction.

"What's that supposed to mean? Of course I like it, or I wouldn't be doing it."

She doesn't have a Newfoundland accent. Somebody told Heidy that Trina met her husband in Alberta.

"How long have you been living here, Mrs. Modeste?"

"I don't know exactly. I'd have to think about it."

I don't let her off the hook, although Heidy has already found out this information.

"Could you do that, please?"

"Six years, I think."

"Where did you live before that?"

Now Trina's getting a little nervous; her fingers dig into her arms.

"Why are you asking these questions? Do you think I'd . . . Nielle . . ." She eyes me suspiciously.

"I'm only trying to get to know Nielle's circle. You can help me with that."

"I'm not in her circle," Trina repeats.

An interesting statement. To what circle *does* Trina belong, in that case?

She won't tell me here, in this storage room, I'm sure of that. I can't keep her any longer; she has a client to attend to.

Heidy looks relieved when I liberate her from the kitchen.

Mr. Field, on the other hand, seems disappointed as we leave the house.

We get on our snowmobiles and set out. At the harbor I wave for Heidy to stop.

"We've got to think more about Trina's background," I tell her. "She's hiding something. Second, find out if Vyann drove anybody to the hospital last weekend. And whether she picked anybody up from the airport. It won't be easy, but we ought to give it a try, anyway."

Heidy's right there.

"I'm on it."

I've got something else to do in the meantime.

"I'd like to look at the cabin by myself before the forensics team gets here. And after that, Dustin's to come with me to look at the tracks at the crime scene again."

I can't see Heidy's eyes anymore because she's closed her

helmet visor. But I don't fail to notice that she doesn't ask me why I want Dustin for this. I don't tell her that I also want to speak with the eyewitness who told Heidy he saw the driver on the snowmobile after that individual left something heavy behind in the snow. Or else Heidy might think I don't trust her interrogation.

52

Mick Hudson, Reporter for the *Labrador Tribune*
St. Anthony, Newfoundland
Friday, February 16

Everything's frustrating him right now. The St. Anthony RCMP is giving him nothing. That was to be expected, but he's frustrated anyway. His boss wants to keep him off Morris Tye. There's nothing worse for a reporter than a superior blocking him from a hot story.

All he can do is watch where the police are traveling. Chief Calista Gates and a female constable, Heidy Wilson, called on Vyann Kippen's neighbors. He observed them from a proper distance. Then they went by snowmobile in the direction of Goose Cove. Probably to the cabin where Trent Stolke was found.

Mick didn't follow them; he doesn't have a snowmobile. Besides, he'd been watching something else that he also found interesting. Dustin Wilson—he's known him since the RCMP ball in Happy Valley-Goose Bay—had driven to the harbor on his Ski-Doo and parked near the fish factory, where he got into a parked car with the motor running.

Mick parked the company car higher up and waited. Ten minutes later Wilson climbed out of the car and left on his Ski-Doo.

Mick didn't see the driver of the car because the guy didn't come his way but took the other exit from the harbor. Mick moved too late and lost sight of him. He didn't get the license plate either. He could have whacked himself on the head for it.

Now he has taken up a position in the parking lot at the Viking Mall from which he could see the Ski-Doo store. It's in a huge black building that looks rather new and modern.

Fred van Heisen has gone into the store. He knows Fred, who was with the RCMP in Port Brendan before Calista Gates hauled him off to St. Anthony. The constable will certainly want to find out who was on that snowmobile at the cabin and brought Trent Stolke there and who brought Nielle Helfrey to Goose Cove.

Mick imagines it's a tough case to investigate unless the snowmobile tracks are somehow different. He'd love to eavesdrop on the conversation in the shop, but van Heisen would certainly not let him listen in.

Suddenly there's some movement at the store entrance. Fred hurries out. He runs over to a run-down pickup directly in Mick's field of view. The constable talks to the driver, and they exchange a few words. The man gets out, goes around the truck, and climbs into the passenger seat. Fred gets in on the driver's side.

The motor kicks in noisily, smoke comes out of the exhaust, but the pickup stays put. Aha, they don't want to be overheard. This time he notes the license plate. The pickup driver looks rather down-at-the-heels.

Mick's on pins and needles. What are they talking about? First Dustin Wilson and now Fred in vehicles that aren't theirs. Is that poor soul a police informant?

They both get out of the truck a few minutes later. They go to the police car, get in, and head toward the main road.

Mick doesn't tail them. He's got something else in mind. If Calista Gates is hot on Vyann Kippen's trail, then he should pursue that. The police chief has a great lead, for sure. What's more, Vyann's a link to Labrador, because she worked at Remote Point Lodge, and that might be interesting.

When he arrives at her house, there's a car in front. It appears she's home. Full of hope, he rings the bell.

A woman soon comes to the door. It must be Vyann.

"Mick Hudson from the *Labrador Tribune*," he introduces himself. "May I have a brief word with you?"

Her eyes narrow. "What about?"

"About Morris Tye."

"I've got nothing to say."

She tries to shut the door.

He's got to talk fast. "Kellyann bragged that somebody had tipped her off that wildlife officers were coming to the lodge. She named a name."

That does the trick. Vyann hesitates. She doesn't want the neighbors to hear their conversation. "Come in."

They stand in the hallway where jackets and scarves are hanging, boots on the floor in an orderly row.

She looks at him. "What's the *Labrador Tribune* doing here in St. Anthony?"

Her curiosity is encouraging.

"I've been sent here because certain things are going on." Then he zooms in. "How did Morris Tye know Noshi was selling caribou meat illegally?"

Bull's-eye.

Her mouth twitches, but she recovers fast.

"That's wrong. The wildlife officers didn't find anything."

She doesn't answer my question, he thinks. He plows ahead: "One of Noshi's customers must have squealed. Maybe somebody got drunk."

"I've just told you: it's all a pack of lies. Noshi would never do a thing like that. Certain people want to put him in a bad light."

"My source is reliable."

"Then you would have gone to the police long ago."

"Did Nielle Helfrey tip Morris Tye off?"

Vyann frowns. "What's Nielle got to do with it?"

The question gives him hope. She wants to know more; she could have cut off the conversation here.

"Nielle is having an affair with Morris Tye. It's all over town. You've surely heard. You and she are often together." He's not completely sure about that, but he assumes so.

"What do you want from me?"

"Did Morris Tye sic the wildlife officers on Noshi so he'd have to sell the lodge? That's what Kellyann claimed."

"Then you'd have to ask Kellyann, not me. I've nothing more to do with the lodge."

"She's been badmouthing Morris Tye."

"She's not the only one. Kellyann doesn't mince words. She calls it the way she sees it. If she's accusing somebody, she'll certainly have her reasons."

Strange. Vyann's defending the woman who stole her husband.

"I tried to talk to Kellyann, but Noshi told me she's in Happy Valley-Goose Bay."

Vyann shakes her head.

"He would never have told you any such thing. That's nobody's business."

Mick makes a tactical withdrawal. "You're right. I'm wrong. I got the thing about Happy Valley-Goose Bay from another source."

"What kind of a source might that be?" Her voice is sharper.

"I never reveal my sources. I'm discreet."

That finally makes her angry. "Then be so discreet as to get out of my house."

He has no choice but to say good-bye.

Back in the car, he makes notes on their conversation. Why does Vyann defend her rival and the man who left her? She ought to hate them both. Remote Point Lodge was her life, her pride and joy. So his uncle told him.

There's only one logical conclusion: she's not defending Noshi or Kellyann; she's defending the lodge. She shares a son with Noshi. He'll take over the lodge one day. She's doing it for him.

Mick feels a sudden surge of optimism. Good thing he came to St. Anthony. He must be wherever Calista Gates is because that's where the music's playing. He can already hear a drum beat.

He has a hazy inkling a fabulous story awaits him.

53

Fred van Heisen, RCMP Constable
St. Anthony, Newfoundland
Friday, February 16, an Hour Earlier

The young woman behind the counter lets Fred know that the owner of the Ski-Doo store isn't there. But she's sharp enough to fetch a veteran employee. It takes a while for the man to appear. He probably has a lot of repair work in the winter, especially when the owner's away.

"Can we talk somewhere in private?" Fred asks. It's always better not to have an eavesdropper around.

The man takes him to an office at the back of the store.

Fred shows him the photographs of the snowmobile tracks. "Does anything strike you?" he asks.

The employee picks up his glasses and studies the photos.

"Something that distinguishes the tracks from one another?" Fred adds. He's getting impatient because the forensics people haven't come yet. He wants to get ahead of them. He wants results. He used to be more deliberate; now he's more like Calista.

"There are several machines," the man answers cautiously.

"What differentiates them? Can you somehow identify them?"

"This one's a wider model." The man points out a track. Then he holds one of the photos up to his eyes. "This one here. A double runner." He taps a finger on it. "Here the carbide's broken off. The driver probably hit a stone."

Fred holds his breath. He suspected something like that. But he plays the clueless guy. That's how you get more information out of people.

"Carbide? I don't really know my way around it."

The repairman looks at Fred as if he were from another planet.

"I've got to know precisely," Fred goes on, "for the report on my investigation."

The man clears his throat. He's probably never had to explain it to anyone before. This is a part of the world where three-year-olds drive all over the place on mini-snowmobiles.

"Runners . . ." He corrects himself, "Write *wear bars* in your report. These bars let the underside of the ski make contact with the ground. They're important for steering. You can't steer without these bars. Nowadays almost all runners are coated with carbide. I can show you . . ." He turns toward the office door.

Fred waves him away.

"No, no need to. I know what you mean."

"Okay." The man picks up from where he left off. "The runners protect the snowmobile's skis; the skis are made of plastic, so they wear down fast. They do that particularly quickly on ice."

He glances up to see if Fred's able to follow.

"Logical," Fred says.

"The runners are made of carbide, not like the skis. But here"—he holds the picture under Fred's nose—"you can see right here that the runner's broken off."

Fred sees the irregularity in the ski tracks.

He rejoices. Exactly as he'd thought, and Calista had noticed it too. Now it's confirmed.

"The track's deeper, right?" Fred says. "It's not only a *worn-down* runner but a *broken-off* runner."

The repairman nods, delighted that the policeman got it. Fred feels like an idiot. But what wouldn't you do to get at the information you want?

"Yes, the track's deeper than with a worn-down runner."

That's what Fred wanted to hear.

"Have you come across a vehicle like this recently?" he asks. "A wider model with a broken runner?"

The man ponders.

"There aren't many wide machines around here. But we're selling more than we used to—they're the next big thing. Really in demand. Your colleague has one. Have a look at it."

"You mean Constable Wilson?"

"Yes."

At first Fred's disappointed. Then he takes a closer look at the photos. Strange. Dustin never took his snowmobile all that close to the cabin. He and Heidy stopped at the edge of the clearing. But the deeper tracks lead directly to the cabin. Good God. He must seriously check it out. But not here.

"Nobody else comes to mind?" He wants to make sure.

"I'll think about it," the man says. He escorts Fred to the door and asks: "Any news about Trent Stolke? How he wound up in the outhouse?"

"We're considering all the possibilities. Do you know anything we'd be interested to know?" Calista would do just what he's doing. Taking advantage of every situation to ask questions.

"See that guy over there? He's one of Stolke's pals."

Fred watches a man crossing the parking lot. He looks thin, despite his winter clothing. And wobbly, as if he could trip over his own boots any minute.

"Thanks," Fred says and rushes outside.

A few long strides and he catches up to the man, nearly slipping on an icy spot in his haste.

"Constable Fred van Heisen. I'd like to have a brief word with you."

The man's face is hollowed out, although he probably can't be more than forty. Many years on drugs, Fred thinks.

"What? What do you want? I've done nothing."

"Come, we'll sit and talk in your pickup."

The man's about to get in on the driver's side, but Fred stops him.

"The other side."

He waits until the man's inside and then gets into the driver's seat.

"Can you show me your driver's license, insurance and the car registration?"

"Up there."

The man points to the sun visor and fumbles for his license.

Fred takes the documents from behind the visor. Made out to Reginald Goode.

"Your insurance has expired," Fred declares. A nice coincidence.

"That's why I'm in St. Anthony, man . . . inspector," Reginald Goode protests.

"Constable. Best we talk at the police station."

"Why? I've got to get to the insurance office. You can drive me there if you think that's better."

"I'll drive you, but first I'm taking you to the station. Come on."

The man keeps protesting in the police car and as they're going through the station door.

Fred lets him rant.

"Is Dustin in?" he asks Rex at the reception.

"No, they're all out."

Fred would prefer to have somebody there at the interrogation but has to do without. God only knows where Dustin's gadding about. He sends him a text message, but there's no reply. If even the man who works in the Ski-Doo store knows Reginald Goode and Trent Stolke are pals, why hasn't Dustin mentioned his name? Dustin's been working here for four years. He can't have missed that.

He takes Goode to Calista's office. It's tight and uncomfortable but serves the purpose. In the warm room, he can smell the man's perspiration. Sweat, unwashed clothes, cigarettes. And mainly fear.

Fred enters Goode's name in the computer.

Just what he thought. Drug offenses. And not only that: the man's on parole. Fantastic.

Fred puts his phone on Record.

"Can I smoke?" Goode asks.

"Afterward. Sit here, in this chair." He looks him straight in the eye. "If we search your vehicle, will we find something?"

"No, of course not. Why am I here, anyway?"

"I'm sure we'll find something. Better you help us."

"What do you want from me?" Goode's voice is cracked, like the skin on his face.

"When did you last see Trent Stolke?"

Goode slides back in his chair.

"Is this about Trent? Is that why you brought me here?"

"I'm asking the questions, Mr. Goode. When did you see Trent for the last time?"

"Reggie to you, inspector. Haven't seen him for a long time."

Fred realizes at once that he's lying.

"We know that's not true. When, Reggie?"

"If you know, then why are you asking me?"

Offense is the best defense, but he's making a mistake. Fred decides to put the screws on.

"You really don't want to get involved in a murder investigation, Reggie."

"Murder? No way that's murder."

"What makes you so confident about that?"

Reggie thinks about it. Fred doesn't leave him any room to maneuver.

"If I arrest you now, then you'll spend the best years of your life behind bars, Reggie."

"You can't arrest me, inspector. I haven't done anything."

"So, prove it."

Reginald Goode's hands shake.

"Is it because of the shit Trent said about Calista on Facebook?"

Calista. So that's what Trent and Reggie and all of them called her. It makes Fred furious.

"Detective Sergeant Calista Gates to you, Reggie."

"I said to Trent: stop it, you'll only make problems for yourself. But he just laughed. I didn't understand . . ."

"What didn't you understand?"

Goode's eyes dart around wildly. Then he says: "You'll get something from me when we make a deal, inspector."

54

Paige Warner, Entrepreneur
In the Ilungilak Area, Labrador
Eight Years Earlier

“Her name isn’t Sandy?” Carla looks at Ellen in amazement. “How do you know?”

“Because I ran into her at the gas station, and somebody called her Ina. I thought the person had it wrong, but Sandy didn’t say anything.”

Paige feels she must say something because they’re both staring at her, puzzled.

“Maybe her middle name’s Ina; happens all the time.”

She’d hurriedly researched the women’s backgrounds. Looked at Sandy’s and the others’ credit scores: her credit history was spotless. Maybe she should have dug deeper or stopped in at the gas station as Ellen did. But Ellen never told her about the other name.

Paige didn’t want to get lawyers or colleagues involved. She was afraid Howard might discover her plans. Sandy is the most congenial of all of them to her; she has backed Paige’s decisions one hundred percent.

But now she's got a problem: Sandy's gone missing. That could jeopardize the whole project. She really ought to alert Search and Rescue or—even worse—the police.

But then comes a saving insight: nothing's happened to Sandy. She planned to defect right from the start. She purposely took the emergency transmitters and the satellite phone so the rest of them couldn't reach anybody. That can only mean one thing.

"Sandy wants to beat us to Crater Lake. She wants to achieve something on her own," she announces.

Ellen takes off her sunglasses.

"What's that supposed to mean, achieve something on her own?"

"She wants to be on social media as the first white woman to reach Crater Lake. She's always posted similar adventures on Instagram. That's why she interested me. Because she had so much trekking experience."

Paige sees the pictures in her mind's eye. Sandy on mountain peaks. At Mount Everest base camp. On Kilimanjaro. Crossing an Alaskan glacier. Her smile of triumph. And she looked good in a hat. She was always photographed wearing a hat and sunglasses. That's how she could picture Sandy so well as an advertisement for her products.

"You think she took the transmitters and phone on purpose? So that we'd have to turn back?" Paige can tell from Carla's expression that the terrible realization is slowly filtering through.

Ellen's jaw is working. She's struggling to hold it together and asks: "Doesn't that break the contract?"

Paige hadn't even considered that possibility. The contract's the least of her worries. She doesn't want to put her expedition at risk. She doesn't want Howard to say: *See, you can't even hold your team together. Not taking you to Papua New Guinea with us was the right thing to do.*

"She can talk her way out of it; she can claim she got lost and happened to land at Crater Lake," Paige says. Or worse: She could say Paige Warner organized the whole project terribly.

"What do we do now?" Carla's face is shining with sweat. It can't only be the physical strain that's making her perspire.

"We won't simply let her get away with it, right? We're so close to our destination." Paige activates her inner motivational speaker.

Ellen doesn't argue. That's progress.

"How long from here to Crater Lake?" she asks.

"If we step on it, we could be there before nightfall."

But Carla seems undecided.

"Suppose something happens to us and we can't get help? Sandy has the gun too."

Before Paige can answer, Ellen gets there first: "We still have the bear bangers and the signal pistol. Sandy didn't find them in my backpack."

Is she deluding herself, or is there something like triumph resonating in Ellen's voice? Can it be that Sandy's betrayal triggered something in Ellen? Paige isn't sure, but Ellen's answer persuades Carla.

"There aren't bears this far inland, they're on the coast," Paige adds.

"Too bad, I'd have loved to get some shots of them."

Paige and Ellen look at each other.

All at once they're in agreement.

"Let's get going. We'll catch up to Sandy." She picks up her backpack.

55

Fred van Heisen, RCMP Constable
St. Anthony, Newfoundland
Friday, February 16

Fred grants Reginald Goode a smoke and pushes a paper cup toward him. Calista won't be happy that her office stinks of smoke, but she'll understand. Reginald's ready to sing, and Fred's eager to hear what's coming.

"Trent was nuts. A crazy guy." Reggie sucks on his cigarette.

Fred opens the window a crack. Weak sunbeams filter through the glass pane into the room.

"He thought he was tougher than all of us. No way."

Fred says nothing. He resists the temptation to speak, waiting for Reggie to go on.

"I warned him, but he didn't listen."

He'll lay it all on Trent, Fred thinks. After all, he's dead.

Then Reggie said: "They paid him."

"Who did?"

"Dunno. He never told me."

Reggie's hands are shaking again. Some ash tumbles from his cigarette.

"They pushed him. So he'd slander the new lady."

"They gave him money to do it?"

"So he said. They wanted something more." Reggie looks directly at Fred. "If I tell you, will you let me go?"

"Depends on what I get from you. If it's helpful, I'll take you to the insurance office, and we forget the whole thing."

Fred wonders what Calista would say to that but he can't let the opportunity slip away. Investigators frequently cut deals with petty criminals.

"They wanted to plant something on Calista. A little ecstasy. So she could be caught with it. I think in her car. Not exactly sure."

Fred tries to evaluate this assertion. A character like Reggie lies all the way through his wretched existence. Matter of survival.

Reggie's face twists into a crooked grin.

"What bullshit! They're idiots. Trent doesn't let go of anything he gets. He keeps it for himself." He looks at Fred as if he expects him to find it laughable, too.

Fred does him a favor and grins back. Good thing nobody's watching.

"How do you know it was ecstasy?" he asks.

"Ecstasy or whatever shit made him croak." Reggie puts out his cigarette and quickly lights up a new one. "Trent had a weak heart. Like me. Half of Roddickton has heart disease, if you ask me. Englee too. And St. Anthony. People are dying like flies. Don't you know that, inspector?"

"Were you there when Trent died?"

Reggie coughs. "No."

He's lying, Fred is sure about that. Reggie's scared; he can tell by looking at him. Now's the moment when Calista would change tack in her interrogation.

"Why was Trent wearing a police jacket?"

Reggie's relieved Fred is asking something different and answers at once: "He got it from somebody."

"Who?"

"Dunno. So Calista would get mad when she saw Trent in it."

"She could arrest a person for it. It's illegal to impersonate a police officer."

That's half right. You can dress up as a policeman, for example, for Halloween or a costume party, as long as you couldn't be confused with a genuine policeman. Fred finds that much too lax, and it makes him angry.

Reggie isn't grinning anymore.

"Calista can't lock Tornado up now—he's dead as a doornail."

Trent's demise probably hits Reginald Goode harder that he lets on.

Fred exploits it. "If ecstasy killed him, then why the bullet holes in his chest?"

Reggie's face twitches. His lips open and close. "You're letting me go, right, inspector, sir?"

"It's still 'constable.' So far, so good, Reggie. But I need more."

"What do you think it was, inspector, sir?"

"I have my ideas, but I want to hear it from you."

"Does the word start with *w*?"

Fred nods. That's not on the recording: *w* as in warning.

"Then we're thinking the same thing, inspector, sir."

Reggie's so afraid that he doesn't want to talk about it. Who's scaring him so much?

"Where's Trent's laptop, Reggie? His cell phone? His wallet?"

Reggie reacts at once.

"I didn't take nothing, inspector! You can't pin it on me."

Fred believes him. Somebody scrubbed the place clean. Somebody who knows what he's doing. Who knows how to get rid of evidence.

During their investigation on the case before the last one,

Calista coached him: "Don't just look at what we find; look for what's missing as well. That's just as important."

Reggie's squirming in his chair.

"Can I go now, inspector? They'll for sure know I'm in here. They always knew where Calista was too."

"Who's 'they,' Reggie? Who are these people?"

"No idea. That's just it. I don't know."

The best always comes at the end. *They always knew where Calista was too.* A sinister suspicion dawns on Fred.

He ends the interrogation and drops Reggie off at the auto insurance office, fully aware that Reggie probably doesn't have the cash to renew his policy. He could have grilled him some more, but there was a more pressing matter. He can deal with Reggie later.

He phones Calista from the car. An automated message comes back: *The person at this number is temporarily unavailable.* All his alarm bells go off at once.

He tries Dustin's cell phone. The call goes through, but only to voicemail.

Heidy's next. It rings and rings. It takes forever for her to answer.

"Where's the sarge?" he almost bellows.

"At the cabin. She's meeting Dustin to review the snowmobile tracks again."

What? Why does Calista need to look at the tracks again? That's odd.

"Where are you, Heidy?"

"Going to the hospital. I've got to find something out."

Should he take Heidy with him? No, the risk is too great.

"Did the sarge send you to the hospital?"

"Yes. What's up?" She suspects something, naturally.

"I interrogated one of Trent's pals. I went to the Ski-Doo store too. Gotta go."

He doesn't hear anything more from Heidy and races toward Goose Cove.

The road feels safe. The sun's warmer now. It takes him eight minutes to get to where the paramedics and Dr. Amaruntgamen tramped through the snow up to the cabin. Further along he sees an SUV by the side of the road. The discovery sends terror through his whole body. He hopes it's not too late. He parks his car and frantically follows in the paramedics' partly snow-covered footsteps to the cabin. Now he hears a snowmobile. Is it Calista? Or Dustin?

He's almost behind the cabin when the motor stops. He can see through the trees that somebody's getting off the snowmobile. He recognizes Calista when she takes off her helmet.

At that moment he's aware of some movement among the firs. A man. He has something in his hand. A pistol. It's aimed at Calista, who has her back to him.

Fred does two things simultaneously. He takes his pistol out of his holster and yells: "Gun down! Hands up! Police!"

The man turns around and aims his weapon at him.

Fred throws himself on the ground, as a shot whizzes through the air over him, then another.

In a flash he aims and pulls the trigger.

The man staggers and sinks into the snow.

Brandishing his weapon, Fred gets up and goes toward him.

Out of the corner of his eye, he sees that Calista has drawn her pistol. She keeps it aimed at the man in the snow.

Then he sees Dustin appear from behind the cabin.

"Dustin, hands behind your head!"

Dustin looks at him, openmouthed.

"Fred, I . . ."

"Behind your head!" Fred's ready for anything.

And Dustin realizes it. He obeys.

Fred removes Dustin's pistol from its holster. "Don't you move an inch!"

He looks over at Calista, who's standing over the wounded man in the snow, making sure the guy doesn't get to his handgun.

"Fred, I'll call an ambulance. Give me your phone. Mine's quit, for some reason."

He comes over to her, his gun still trained on Dustin.

When he sees the man in the snow, he freezes. "What the hell?"

Calista shakes her head. "Unbelievable, isn't it?"

56

Detective Sergeant Calista Gates
Goose Cove, Newfoundland
Friday, February 16

Frank Delgado.

I'm stupefied.

It's Frank's blood that's soaking into the snow.

It's Frank who's moaning and groaning at our feet. The bullet hit him in the leg. Fred's a really good shot.

But I know for a fact that he'll be blamed for using his pistol and not his taser. As if that would have been an option at that distance and with trees everywhere.

I still can't get my head around it. Frank tried to kill Fred or me.

A colleague. Not a helpful one. He made my job at the Port Brendan station as miserable as he could. He and Austin Sullivan, an evil-minded twosome. I remember their malicious comments all too well. Always ready to make me look ridiculous. They were forever waiting for me to make one wrong move.

They couldn't get over the fact that I'm more experienced.

That I have more of a profile. That I came to Port Brendan, Labrador, from a metropolis, Vancouver, British Columbia. And that I was later promoted to chief of police in St. Anthony. A posting that Sullivan apparently has his eye on.

Frank Delgado.

Why is he here and not in Labrador, for heaven's sake?

Why does he want to knock one of us off?

While waiting for the ambulance, Fred stops Frank's leg from bleeding. He gets the first-aid kit from my Ski-Doo and skillfully applies a compression bandage.

I can't help Fred because I have my boss in St. John's on the phone and I'm keeping Dustin Wilson in check.

An RCMP officer shot by another RCMP officer—that's something the boss should know about immediately. There'll be a special commission, that's obvious. Most of all it will be a huge media circus. I feel like throwing up when I think of the consequences.

I don't take my eyes off Dustin. He looks white as a sheet. Even whiter than the last time, when we found Trent Stolke.

He's in deep shit, and he knows it.

The voice at the other end snaps me out of my thoughts: "We're sending two men to St. Anthony right away. Leave Frank Delgado to us. Don't move him. Wait for the ambulance."

I was afraid I wouldn't be allowed to grill Delgado. But they didn't say anything about Dustin because they don't know how he's wrapped up in the whole business. Basically, I don't know either, but I'm determined to find out.

"I assume the Corner Brook forensics men aren't on site yet?" my superior in St. John's asks.

"They're coming tomorrow," I say, "if all goes according to plan. They should have been here today but put it off to tomorrow."

"Good. Don't touch anything at the crime scene. Hands off. Understood?"

"Understood." And how. The boss is in panic mode. There

can be no screwups. Or, more accurately: there can be no more screwups than there have been already. Good grief! As if the RCMP needed yet another scandal.

Frank Delgado. Who'd have thought it?

"You'll do nothing for now, Sergeant Gates." The voice on the phone repeats.

But surely they don't want to take away my other investigations?

Investigations that have become hellishly complicated. Or maybe they've become quite simple. I don't know yet.

"I've got two other cases here to worry about."

Silence.

Not good.

"I need to see them through," I emphasize. "We really don't want any more victims. We shouldn't be kept from doing our duty because of violence and intimidation attempts. It's important for my team."

I've got to keep breathing down their necks. My boss knows I can make big trouble for them if I want. They also know I have two eyewitnesses.

It works.

"We'll send our men as fast as possible. It's important for you to cooperate with them."

"Sir, that goes without saying."

"I'll call again."

His final words.

I photograph the scene with Delgado from every angle, just in case. We've got to watch our backs.

I keep Fred's phone because he hasn't got a free hand.

Now we hear the ambulance siren. Not that there's heavy traffic on the Goose Cove road or people speeding. The siren's a warning to reckless snowmobilers who sometimes cross from the side of the road.

I breathe a sigh of relief. The sooner Delgado gets medical

attention, the better. We're so lucky to have a hospital in St. Anthony.

"You can put your hands down," Fred tells Dustin.

The two paramedics are shocked when they arrive at the crime scene. I can understand it. Do they believe what's on social media? That the increasing violence in and around St. Anthony is *my* fault? That I'm a controversial figure with many enemies?

Doesn't matter. They act professionally and lay Delgado on the sled. They're off in no time, and we hear the siren howl briefly.

Now it's quiet. Fred and I look at each other.

"Thank you." I can't get anything more out than that. It seems like a bad dream. Did it really happen?

Dustin Wilson is still standing on the same spot, as if consigned to the corner as punishment.

"This is not what I wanted," he stammers. Desperation's in his eyes.

"We have to talk." I point to the cabin. "In there."

I don't want to wait until we're at the station, despite the cold. I'm afraid Dustin's about to collapse. Besides, I don't want Heidy in the way. Maybe he won't utter a word; he'd be so ashamed if she were standing right there.

It's not as cold in the cabin. We won't contaminate much here; we were already inside before we found Trent Stolke.

I indicate to Dustin he's to sit in one of the old chairs; Fred stays standing, as always. It hurts to see how distraught Fred looks. He must be fully aware that this day will thoroughly reshape his life for a long time.

I take Fred's phone out of my pocket and press the Record button. I name the place, date, time, people present. Dustin doesn't object.

"We're putting this on record for our files," I explain. "Why did you bring Constable Frank Delgado to Mr. Elliott's cabin?"

"I didn't know Delgado was here. I didn't know until I saw him."

Dustin speaks like a broken man. Resigned to having it all come out. Knows he's a goner.

"Did you meet him before?"

"Yes, several times in the last few days."

"When was the first time?"

"Quite a while back. At the RCMP ball in Happy Valley-Goose Bay two years ago. Then again in December. Delgado and Sullivan had a talk with me."

"Constable Austin Sullivan?"

"Yes. They picked up on my frustration. They wormed it all out of me. That I want to get out of St. Anthony, but I can't get out because Fred's leaving, and you haven't got a replacement for him."

"What's the hurry, constable? You seemed quite happy here even last fall."

A long pause. He takes off his gloves and rubs his fingers over his face; it's still ghostly pale where there was always a rosy glow. He can't get a sound out.

"Is it because of Heidy?" I ask.

57

Vyann Kippen, Caregiver for Seniors
St. Anthony, Newfoundland
Friday, February 16

Vyann puts her feet up on the coffee table and leans back on the sofa.

The stressful day is over at last. Time for Netflix. Or Disney, Prime, HBO, or whatever they're called. She's subscribed to lots of streaming services.

An entertaining film relaxes her best. She's just finished an addictive series and is looking for something new. She more or less has a drama in mind, one with suspicious deaths or missing persons.

Not that she really needs a series for drama. She's got plenty of it going on in her own life. She could write a book about it.

What stage of the plot is she at right now? *The noose is tightening?* Maybe that's what Calista Gates wants her to believe. Her neighbor told her the police chief had just been to her house and quizzed her. And that she'd gone to other neighbors as well.

"What did you tell her?" Vyann asked.

"That my legs aren't what they used to be. I found her hard to understand; she talks like people who come from away."

The old woman always used to rush to the window whenever she heard something outside. But her hearing's bad now, as it is with nearly all seniors, and she can only get around slowly. Vyann dreads growing old.

Now she's found something relaxing: an opulent costume drama, a sweet little flight from the everyday. She snuggles down into the sofa cushions. That reporter from the *Labrador Tribune* annoys her more than Calista Gates. He thought if he mentioned Kellyann, he could lure her into a trap. He probably speculated she'd badmouth her. She'd get carried away and make indiscreet remarks she'd regret later.

What a jerk. She didn't believe a word he said. Kellyann would never brag that somebody had tipped Noshi off that wildlife officials were coming to inspect the lodge. She'd never do that. Whatever else Kellyann is, she can keep her trap shut. She can keep secrets to herself. She's calculating but not stupid. She'd never risk everything she's managed to get: her life with Noshi and her role at the lodge.

Pompous music fills the living room. The British queen and her entourage enter the on-screen ballroom. A flowing, glittering dress; jewels sparkling in her crown. The monarch is wise to every court intrigue, pulls all the strings, punishes traitors.

Just as in real life, actually, Vyann thinks.

58

Detective Sergeant Calista Gates
Goose Cove, Newfoundland
Friday, February 16, Late Afternoon

Dustin Wilson cringes when I mention Heidy.

"Did she tell you anything?" he asks.

"No. Just wondering."

He stares at the wooden floor as if it could help him out. He stares for a long time.

He finally comes out with it.

"Heidy has been flirting with another man. At dog training. I saw the texts they were sending. I want to leave St. Anthony, with her, so she can get away from this guy."

Fred and I exchange glances. His face is in semidarkness. Daylight's getting weaker, and we haven't lit any lamps in the cabin. I avoid doing anything to stop the flow of Dustin's confession.

Heidy. Another man. Really? I try to think back to my talks with her. Were there some hints I didn't catch because I was preoccupied with Gerald and me?

Maybe Dustin's just anxious because Heidy's taking a leap now, because she's learning new things, developing her own interests.

Dustin continues with his revelations. I hope he wants to share it all.

"Sullivan told me he was getting your job in St. Anthony. Then he'd let me leave, he promised. He said you had your eye on a Vancouver posting, but you couldn't make up your mind just yet. The process can be sped up, he said. If she ran into problems, and if things got uncomfortable for her in St. Anthony, he added, then she'd be out of here faster."

It's not only my decision, and Dustin should know that. It's headquarters' call. But I don't want to interrupt him.

"Sullivan claims you had a lot of enemies at HQ. You were completely isolated there, had no support. So, the folks in St. Anthony must be mobilized against you, he said. And if you didn't have the confidence of the population anymore, you were toast." He puts his gloves back on; he needs the warmth. He keeps his eyes lowered. "I was very receptive toward his ideas."

"Are you behind the smear campaign on Facebook?" Fred asks.

Dustin shakes his head.

"No, it wasn't me. But I put the sergeant's insignia in the snow beside Nielle. And the jacket button next to the cabin."

I'm perplexed.

"Why did you do that? What did you hope to gain?"

He lifts his gloved hands in a gesture of helplessness.

"I was furious. I felt I was in a prison. I wanted out. I . . . I blamed you, sarge, for Heidy's radical change. But I also saw that Sullivan and Delgado were going too far. They worked on Trent Stolke. I didn't agree to that. Trent's bananas. I told them so."

"What happened to Trent?" Fred asks.

"I don't know. I have nothing to do with Trent. When we

found him here in the outhouse, I was just as surprised as you. But there's something I *can* figure out. Delgado wanted me to come here and look for any security cameras around the cabin or on the trees. That was before we installed our cameras here. I had to tell Delgado where you were all the time, sarge. That's how he knew you and I would be here today. And he knew on the day we found Trent that the four of us would be going to the cabin."

Insane, I think, completely insane. All this was going on and I didn't have a clue.

"So it was Delgado who brought Trent's body here?"

Dustin answers without hesitation.

"Yes, I'm dead sure. It was definitely a warning to me because he and Sullivan had noticed that I was finding the whole thing scary and wanted out. They were afraid I'd squeal. I think that's why Delgado put two bullets into Trent when he was dead. To intimidate me."

"But he took a huge risk when he came here and stuffed the body in the outhouse. Did you ask him why he did it?"

"No, I never let on that I suspected him. I was too afraid of him. But he made a remark today I'll never forget. He said, 'A body in the outhouse—Calista Gates will never get that image off her back. A picture's worth more than a thousand words. Whenever her name comes up, people will associate it with the corpse in the outhouse.' That's what he said. And it's right on. Social media is full of it, and the papers, too. TV. If Trent had been found dead in his apartment, with no bullet wounds, nobody would say a word about it."

It's grotesque but not illogical.

"Do you think Delgado wanted to kill me?" I ask.

Dustin shrugs in resignation.

"Maybe he's nuts. He's on drugs. Maybe he's turned paranoid and thought you and Fred wanted to kill *him*."

Sounds absurd. But in my job, everything's possible. I'll have to bring this up with the special investigators who will be here soon. I make a quick mental note: Delgado—blood test for drugs.

Maybe the man also panicked because he was afraid we were on his trail.

"I'm such a dumbass, sarge. I'm so sorry. Delgado should have shot *me* instead."

Dustin covers his face with his hands; his body's shaking.

The sight does not leave me cold. How could it? But one thing I do know: I've got to make a quick decision before the investigators arrive from St. John's.

I stop the recording and put the phone in my pocket. I say as soberly as I can: "Constable, Fred and I must have a discussion. We're stepping outside for a minute to talk. Give us your cell phone; we don't want you calling anybody. Sit here at the window so we can see you from outside."

He does it all meekly. He knows I'm his sole chance of survival.

The sun's about to go down. The cold air feels like a freezer as we go outside. We don't have much time. If Heidy or the hospital tried to call me, they wouldn't have gotten through. Nobody's tried to reach Fred on his phone, but that could change at any moment.

I pull out the headlamp from under the Ski-Doo seat and put it on. The light makes the snow sparkle and lends the firs a Christmasy air. It's surreal.

"I've got something important to tell you," Fred says for starters.

What he tells me almost bowls me over. He questioned a man named Reginald Goode at the station, Trent's pal. Goode revealed that people unknown tried to get Trent to plant drugs in my car. Trent was given ecstasy for that purpose but took it himself. Which led to his heart failure.

"He must have gotten it from Delgado," Fred concludes.

I had the same thought.

"This Reginald Goode is our most important witness. Where's he now?"

"I had to let him go because I was afraid something was happening to you. I just sensed that you were in danger."

For a moment the wall I've built up around me threatens to collapse.

"Oh, Fred. What would I do without you?"

It's all so overpowering. So much goes unsaid between us.

Fred doesn't follow up but wants to move on.

"I believe Reggie was mighty scared because Delgado's one of us. That's why he didn't mention him by name."

"Delgado's not one of us anymore. I'll see to that. What do we do with Dustin?" I look over at the cabin window and can see his silhouette. "He's our eyewitness to what Delgado did, firing those shots."

I let my words echo through the quiet woods.

Fred immediately gets what I'm driving at; I can tell by his silence.

An eyewitness on whom so much depends.

I elaborate on my reasoning.

"Do we really want to turn Dustin in? What crime has he committed anyway? He slandered me, but Sullivan and Delgado certainly goaded him into it. He didn't tell us that Delgado could have been connected to Trent's death and to the bullet wounds. And he didn't tell us that Delgado persuaded Trent to mobilize people against me."

"Dustin planted fake clues at two crime scenes," Fred adds. "The insignia and the button."

That's serious. But he confessed it voluntarily when he didn't have to. He came clean right away.

Fred and I are marching on the spot in our boots in the cold, avoiding the ski tracks. The beam of light from my headlamp jiggles back and forth.

The matter is terribly complicated, and yet I've got to find us a viable path forward. That path might be a hidden trail through the bushes.

"Fred, I'm convinced Sullivan and Delgado weren't acting on their own. All that talk about my having enemies at headquarters. Yes, there really are. Those two wouldn't have gotten involved in something as crazy as this if they didn't have influential people backing them."

"So that makes Dustin merely a sacrificial lamb who was sucked in at a moment of weakness?"

"I don't know if *sacrificial lamb* is the right term. But I do not want to see little fish caught while the big ones get off scot-free, as so often happens."

I can't look at Fred without blinding him with my lamp. But I can see that he's looking at me.

"We need Dustin," he says, "and he needs us."

I hoped he would say that. Fred agrees with me. I can really count on him. Now I see the path: we've got Dustin over a barrel with that recording. But we won't turn it over to the special investigators. Dustin's eyewitness testimony will get Fred off the hook and pin the shooting on Delgado. It's more important to me that Fred comes out of an external investigation unscathed than that Dustin gets punished.

"That's exactly how I see it," I say. "I'm afraid Dustin might do something to himself in the state he's in. I think he sincerely repents everything. I've gotten to know him pretty well since I've been here."

"Calista, would you have considered it possible for Dustin to do what he did?"

"No, but what are any of us capable of doing in extreme situations? I often ask myself that question." Maybe I'd have killed Delgado if he threatened Fred with a gun. You never know.

There's a ringing in my jacket pocket. Fred's phone. I hand it to him. The phone with the recording of Dustin's confession.

"Are we agreed?" I ask.

His instant reply: "Yes, we are."

He takes the call and turns to me after a few words.

"It's Heidy. What do we tell her?"

"That nothing's happened to Dustin. We're bringing him back in our car."

59

Detective Sergeant Calista Gates
St. Anthony, Newfoundland
Saturday, February 17

Mick Hudson, the reporter for the *Labrador Tribune*, is waiting in ambush for me on the way from the parking lot to the hospital entrance. He's written a long article beginning with the sentence *High waves are hitting St. Anthony on the northern tip of Newfoundland, although the ocean is still frozen everywhere.*

The reporter reveals that Constable Delgado officially reported in sick at his post in Labrador last week. He is said to have caught COVID-19, but this appears to have been a pretext, Hudson writes.

He found out among other things that an internal RCMP investigation of Delgado is underway because he's alleged to have misappropriated drugs from a raid. Hudson emphasizes that now, counting Delgado, a second RCMP officer from the south of Labrador is entangled in shady incidents: *Previously, Constable Austin S. was recalled from the Ilungilak Crater when locals accused him of threatening them with his service revolver.* I found a detail in the report interesting: Sullivan is supposed to have volunteered for the assignment in the Ilungilak area.

The reporter must also have confronted Morris Tye at the event for the environment minister in Happy Valley-Goose Bay. But Tye claimed to have no opinion on the purported abuses, which doesn't surprise me.

Naturally, Hudson called me as well, and I assured him that the St. Anthony RCMP are carrying on with the investigations in the Nielle Helfrey and Trent Stolke cases.

I hobble past him at the hospital entrance. He takes a video; it's probably required for reporters today. I can't get mad at him. I could never have imagined what happened yesterday. Others surely feel the same way. The locals, who only listen to rumors because we're not permitted to say anything, conjure up all sorts of scenarios, of course. A woman in the Viking Mall says in his article that she didn't take her kids shopping because she feared for their safety. He quotes her as saying: *Will there be gunfire at our mall sometime soon?*

I'll look awful in the *Tribune* video, harried and tired-eyed, but that's the least of my worries. Fred looks like a ghost. The external investigation will put the worst demands on his patience and nerves.

"Fred, I'm with you no matter what happens," I said to him in the car.

He only nodded gloomily.

I phoned the two RCMP colleagues from Roddickton yesterday for help in guarding the crime scene all night. I don't want to take any chances that somebody messes with evidence or destroys it before the forensics team gets there today.

Dustin and Heidy surely had a sleepless night too.

I have no idea what went on behind closed doors, but Heidy whispered to me in passing: "Dustin's going to support Fred."

I report to the hospital reception and am taken to Nielle's ward. It's on the same floor as Frank Delgado's. Warsame, who occasionally works as a security guard at the hospital, helps us keep a sharp eye on him. The rooms here are chronically crowded, but I pleaded for Nielle to be kept in isolation because she's a crime victim. Only her mother is with her when I open the door. I suppose I have her to thank that Nielle's ready to talk. Mrs. Helfrey's expression is tired and strained like mine, but she smiles and stands up as I come in. I'm relieved. Most people accept me despite the smear campaign on social media. Mrs. Helfrey even leaves me alone with her daughter. If that isn't a vote of confidence!

"I'll get you a coffee, sergeant," she offers. "I need one too."

I thank her and go over to the bed. The door closes softly. Nielle's head is bandaged up in two places. She's lightly made up to preserve some dignity. I know from personal experience how important it is, despite an injury, to remain the person you were before the attack.

"How are you?" I ask, drawing up a chair to her bedside.

"Very well, given the circumstances. What's up with Gerry?"

Of course she wants to know. She's Gerald's former girlfriend. An unusual situation, but everything's been unusual these last few days.

"They're still searching for him."

"He can't simply disappear," she says in a surprisingly firm voice. "Gerry's tough; he's a survivor."

She means it as consolation, which I think is nice. But speaking of Gerald brings me almost to the breaking point.

I change the subject.

"Ms. Helfrey, you shouldn't worry about him. You must recuperate. Are you able to answer some questions? Why did you talk about Mrs. Kippen's cockatoo to my colleagues in St. John's?"

The question seems to surprise her. Did she expect me to ask her about Morris Tye? It can't have escaped her or her mother that there's gossip about the affair with him. But I don't want her to clam up and not tell me more.

"I don't know why the bird was the first thing to cross my mind." Her manicured hands knead the bedcovers.

Somebody painted her fingernails, or she did it herself. Does she think her lover's going to visit her? He won't. Morris Tye wouldn't dare show his face in St. Anthony. It's only a matter of time until more reporters arrive, and Tye will certainly want to duck their questions.

"I gave Simmi a bit of noodle salad," Nielle suddenly says. "Simmi loves noodles. Cockatoos love pasta. Hard to believe, eh? Somebody put a cold plate with ham and salads in my car. People do that sometimes because I don't always have time to cook."

I believe her. We often have food like that at the station. Women in St. Anthony and elsewhere make cold plates for sale and donate the money to charity.

"I took the plate with me and fed Simmi when I went to Vyann's. Simmi loves me. I took the rest to work. Vyann called me right away and told me that Simmi wasn't well and that I shouldn't touch anything on the plate. Simmi died that evening."

"When was that?"

Nielle thinks for a moment.

"Two days before . . . the incident."

She still has no recollection of how the attack took place. Her hands shake as she goes on: "I . . . maybe it was something in the food that wasn't good for Simmi. You have to watch out with animals. Onions aren't good for dogs, for instance. And avocados are dangerous for cockatoos. I think avocadoes were mixed in with the noodles."

I've known since this morning the cockatoo did not die that way. The lab sent me a report much faster than expected. Somebody in the lab must be a bird lover. Simmi died from Pacheco's disease, caused by a herpes virus. The cockatoo caught the virus long before eating the noodles, which were completely harmless.

My phone pings: an incoming text.

I read it quickly. It's from Rex. *The men from forensics are at the St. Anthony airport. Heidy is picking them up.*

At last. The two experts from Corner Brook are what I absolutely need. We're still waiting for the special investigator from St. John's. That gives us a breather.

I continue questioning Nielle: "Did you tell Vyann that you were going to see if everything was okay at Mr. Elliott's cabin?"

"Possibly."

"Did you say when you were going?"

"Probably. I often drop in on the way to Goose Cove."

"Why were you going to Goose Cove?"

"I wanted to look at a quilt at Petrina Holt's place."

"Who's that?"

"Someone I know."

"Did Ms. Holt know you were coming? And when?"

"Yes."

Petrina Holt. This woman has never come forward. One of those people who want nothing to do with the police no matter what. That doesn't indicate guilt but rather fear of authorities.

"Do you know whether Vyann had any visitors that day?"

"No. I can't recall that she mentioned anything."

Strange. Vyann doesn't tell her best friend something like that when she otherwise tells her everything?

"Can you remember going to the cabin?"

"Yes, and that I got there and took off my helmet. That's the last thing I remember."

"Why did you want to talk to me when I was on my Vancouver leave?"

"Because of Tornado. He's been following me and hitting on me."

"Trent Stolke?"

"Yes. I don't know why he's been going after me of all people. He chatted me and Vyann up once in the RagnaRöck, and we exchanged a few words."

"How did he follow you?"

"On his snowmobile and in his pickup. Again and again. I wanted to ask you what I could do about it."

Why did she want to talk to *me*? Why not Heidy, for instance? She must have heard that I pulled Trent over for speeding once and took him to the station. She apparently trusts me to take her seriously because of it.

Nielle's mother comes in with a tray holding three cups of Tim Hortons coffee and a box of doughnuts. She hands me a cup.

I conclude the questioning because I've got to meet the forensics guys.

But first I want to relieve the patient from some psychological stress.

"The cockatoo was not poisoned; we had it tested in the lab. It wasn't your noodle salad, it was a virus. Vyann was wrong, and you're not to blame for anything."

Did Vyann really believe it? Or did she just make the poisoning up? The way she made up other things about the cockatoo? To make her friend anxious and horrified?

"Have you found out who did that to my daughter?" Mrs. Helfrey asks, still with the tray of coffee and doughnuts in her hands.

I expected Nielle to ask that question, but she didn't. Weird.

I stand up and say good-bye with these words: "I can't tell you anything definite yet, but I'm confident we're quite close."

60

Fred van Heisen, RCMP Constable
St. Anthony, Newfoundland
Saturday, February 17

Fred roars across the frozen bay on his snowmobile like a maniac. He can hardly see the houses on the distant shore. He's accelerating faster than he ever has.

The office felt suffocating. He had to do something, get outside for some air to keep from going crazy. Calista's on her way to the crime scene with the forensics people. Fred recalls that the last time those same colleagues helped out in St. Anthony they investigated the crime scene with great care, concentrating fully. That's important for him because they'll secure evidence of the two shots that Frank Delgado fired, luckily before the special investigators from St. John's arrive. Two extra pairs of eyes are worth their weight in gold.

The forensics team thought the material that Calista showed them was good: photos, videos, and notes that the St. Anthony team had put together. Presumably nothing has changed at the crime site in the meantime. The two RCMP colleagues from Roddickton spent the previous night guarding the crime scene.

The ice surface is bumpy; Fred is thoroughly shaken up. He didn't even inform Rex when he stormed out of the station. He was loaded for bear. What else is coming down the pike? He still hasn't been suspended for shooting at Delgado, which surprises even him. But that could change at any minute. He doesn't even want to imagine what that could mean for him.

He must phone Lucinda before the rumors get to her. He makes a sharp turn and speeds toward shore. Before reaching it, he stops, removes his helmet, pulls off his gloves, and takes his smartphone out of his breast pocket.

Lucinda's voice sounds like a signal from a completely alien world. She's far away, in Saskatoon, her hometown, where he's to start a new posting in a few months.

"Fred! Alison is here, and we were just talking about you. Is that not telepathy?"

Bad. She's not alone. But he can't let that change anything. He must speak to her. Now.

"Can you go to another room, sweetheart? I have to talk to you about a private matter."

"Oh . . . of course. Let me . . ."

He hears her explaining to Alison. Seconds go by until she's back on the phone.

"What's the matter, darling?" She doesn't sound as cheerful; his urgent tone must have brought her down to earth.

He outlines what has happened. He leaves out the details but doesn't sugarcoat it.

"What's this all mean?" she asks, bewildered. "Will they put you in jail?"

"Probably not, it was self-defense." He listens to his own words and doesn't find them persuasive. Can he tell her the unvarnished truth?

"It was a murder attempt in my opinion," he continues. "But the special investigators must confirm it first. If I know the RCMP bureaucracy, it can take weeks or months for the results to come out. Until then I'm still under suspicion."

He hears nothing for several seconds. She must be processing what she's just heard.

"What about your job here?" she asks at last. "You *are* coming back to Saskatoon, aren't you? You really don't *have* to stay in Newfoundland."

Her voice trembles, sounding almost scared.

"I can't say yet. Don't you worry. I have to wait until the investigators arrive. Then I'll know more. Can you please keep all this stuff to yourself?"

Her answer comes instantly: "It's not good for you to be on Calista's team. She has enemies in the RCMP. Maybe they can make you a scapegoat. Because you help her."

Her reply astounds him. He'd always assumed she didn't know anything specific about the hostility toward Calista. Or that she'd heard something but wasn't interested. Was he ever wrong.

He must admit to himself that Lucinda's right. As a rule, the RCMP protects its members as well as it can. But Calista has enemies within its own ranks who must know he's loyal to her. They might want to make a public example of him, to show that they will act firmly against their own people in similar cases without making flimsy allowances.

Lucinda interrupts his silence: "You don't have to protect Calista, darling, you must protect *yourself*. Your career. And me. Our future."

His head hurts in the cold; he has almost no feeling in his hands now.

"I'll call you tonight. Then we can talk about it calmly. And please don't tell anybody anything."

Before he has finished the last sentence, he knows his request is futile. Lucinda will call her parents immediately. He can't even hold it against her; she's all alone in Saskatoon, and he's in St. Anthony. Thousands of kilometers away.

"I want you to come here," she says by way of good-bye.

"Talk to you tonight," he answers.

Back in the warm office, he has time to make a coffee. He's all by himself. Heidy and Dustin are taking Woolly for a walk. Together. The couple and the dog are for now no longer part of the Nielle Helfrey or the Trent Stolke investigations. Calista's orders—internally, not officially. From the outside, however, the team is a bulwark of defense; they're sticking close together.

Now he hears Calista's voice in the hallway.

What's he going to do when one day soon he doesn't hear that voice at work? He can't envision it.

She comes in, closes the door, tosses her cap on the table, and takes off her jacket. The cold air has reddened her cheeks. She looks feverish.

He doesn't know how she can withstand it: the strain of Delgado's attack on them, Dustin's betrayal, the pace of the investigations, the external inquiry. And Gerald Hynes's disappearance. It must drain her completely. How long can she take it? Her voice sounded calm but fragile when she conferred with forensics. It might also be lack of sleep. It's as if she were pushing with all her might against a landslide that's threatening to sweep her away.

Fred suspects the landslide could bury him as well. He'd like to hold her hand tight so they won't be torn apart.

She starts talking while making a coffee: "We can't afford to exclude Heidy and Dustin from the investigations any longer. It doesn't look good if they're sidetracked for too long. We'd be sending the wrong signal."

He doesn't argue. Dustin may be desperate, but he didn't go along with planting the drugs in Calista's car, Fred's convinced of that. Delgado would ultimately have pushed Dustin too far, even if he couldn't see any other way out. Dropping the police insignia at the crime scene was his limit. Delgado got scared when he was afraid Dustin would rat him out. But this case should be solvable with Reginald Goode as a witness. He's not an ideal one, for sure, but credible enough to nail Delgado. Thank heavens for Reggie.

Fred gives Calista something different to consider: "Frank Delgado will accuse Dustin. Then Dustin's officially under suspicion. And our investigations are seen as compromised."

She takes her coffee to the table.

"In a perfect world I'd agree with you. But we're fighting for our survival, Fred. I'm not going to let corrupt people destroy my work. At some point, enough's enough."

She sits down and looks at him. Fire's smoldering in her eyes.

"These guys want to dismantle the rules. We can give them a taste of their own poison."

He looks out the window because he can't take that gaze anymore.

"Delgado's fighting for his survival, I mean, inside the RCMP," he counters.

"Let him. We'll simply say Dustin was working under cover. That he pretended to go along, and that's how he met Delgado."

She picks up her cup, her hands aren't even shaking.

She has made up her mind, Fred thinks. She's fighting with any weapon she can lay her hands on. She's not squeamish about the means.

He understands her perfectly, but should he go along with her?

"You'd swear that under oath?"

She takes a sip and replies: "It won't come to a trial, Fred. I firmly believe that. The bosses will know how to stymie it. They don't want to have a scandal hashed out in public. The incident will be portrayed as an accident or misunderstanding. Delgado had no business being at the cabin. He'll be forced to leave the RCMP, and for that he won't go to prison for his drug offenses. They'll persuade us to consent to it. This affair will have no implications for you, Fred, and that's why we can agree."

"It's not like you to compromise like that, Calista."

She makes a dismissive gesture.

"I've got other battles to fight. I can't have wars on all fronts. And I particularly don't want them to pin anything on you. I also don't want those gangsters to bring me to my knees."

"Shouldn't we be fighting for the truth?"

She looks at him thoughtfully.

"What is the truth? The truth is, corrupt forces in our ranks are trying to destroy good cops. They've declared war on us, and in war the rules are different. We must defend ourselves with all our might."

He makes no reply.

One thought is constantly whirling around in his head, a question he has no answer for as yet: Should he let himself be drawn into the maelstrom with her?

61

Ava Zittner, Criminology Student
Toronto, Ontario
Several Days Earlier

It's peaceful in the Istanbul Café. Ava chose the place on Eglinton Avenue because she knows Martha better now, in particular her passion for Turkish coffee and revani cake. It's not loud in the café, which makes it a good place for a rendezvous; luckily, the cozy corner table in the window nook was unoccupied. She munches on a vegan breakfast cookie, the flavors of cinnamon and nutmeg tingling on her tongue.

She's made a special trip from Windsor to Toronto for the meeting. She's elated because she was able to convince Martha Calambaro, the well-known journalist, to reexamine the case of Joe Salomon, the sex offender who was shot and killed.

She's about to pick up her chai latte when she sees Martha coming toward her.

The journalist offers no excuse for being late but greets her with the words "Now let's see what we have."

As a matter of fact, it was Ava who gathered all the information, but Martha can weave a more gripping story out of it. And

Martha knows what she can legally publish without risking a libel charge. Besides, she has assured Ava that both their names will be on the byline.

"I've more statements from people who knew Fiona Gelp," Ava says, waiting for Martha to place her order with the waitress. "They all say the same: Fiona's ex-partner was controlling and a bully. Fiona ended the relationship with Colin Hatterbush twice, but she went back to him again."

"Was he physically violent?"

"Looks like it. Friends noticed bruises and scratches and spoke to her about it, but she always maintained she'd bumped into something or that a cat scratched her. But she didn't have a cat."

"Did she ever report Hatterbush to the police?"

"No. That's why domestic violence didn't come up during the trial."

"We did consider the possibility it was Fiona who shot Colin and Joe Salomon was not the killer. A lot points in that direction. The surveillance camera, for example: it wasn't working during the crucial moments but did record everything before and after. And the revolver was lying at Salomon's right hand, but he was left-handed. Moreover they also never found out who owned the stolen gun. The neighbors heard two shots, but they were spaced quite far apart. And Fiona didn't wait that long to shoot Salomon after she found him with Colin's body." Martha gives Ava a meaningful look. "I've got another theory."

The waitress brings the coffee and cake.

Martha drinks her Turkish coffee down in one gulp but holds off on the cake, which pleases Ava. She can't wait for what Martha wants to tell her.

"Probably friends and acquaintances weren't the only ones who realized that Fiona was in an abusive relationship. Her family must also have been aware of it. Particularly because Fiona twice tried to leave Hatterbush."

Ava can't hold back her excitement.

"You think there was a third person present in the house! That crossed my mind too."

"Who were you thinking of?"

"Her sister. Ann Price. She was very close to Fiona. And her fingerprints were everywhere. She visited Fiona occasionally when Hatterbush wasn't home."

Martha nods.

"Ava, you're very much on the ball! If we assume that a third person was involved, very different scenarios are possible. Have you thought about that?"

"For example, the scenario that it was all planned and Salomon was lured into a trap."

"Exactly!" Martha's eyes sparkle. "Then a lot adds up that logic can't account for."

She devotes herself to the cake and lets Ava continue.

"Fiona met Joe Salomon in the bar. She flirted with him and fed him enough information about her house to entice him to break in. She could see him on her computer monitor while the surveillance camera was filming. Somebody turned off the camera after Salomon was inside. He got into the bedroom where he thought Fiona was sleeping. Hatterbush was already dead at this point. Somebody had shot him. It is possible because the neighbors heard a shot during the night before Salomon got into the house. The surveillance camera footage confirms it. The neighbors heard another single shot about two hours later. Somebody shot Salomon and put a stolen pistol in his right hand. During the trial Fiona's lawyer cast doubt on the testimony of the two elderly neighbors because they hadn't called the police."

Martha nods. "Yes, they supposedly thought it was firecrackers. I suspect they didn't want to have anything to do with it. The trial was a farce, as I see it. So many inconsistencies. The question is: How could the sisters know when Salomon would break into the house? Their plan would work only if they knew that."

Ava has asked herself the same question. "I can't say yet. But witnesses at the trial mentioned that on the same day a suspicious man on a bicycle kept going up and down the street nearby." She watches Martha taking notes. "Did Fiona in fact know Joe from somewhere before she happened to meet him in the bar? I haven't found that out."

"But I have," Martha says, shoveling another piece of cake into her mouth.

"Fiona's sister, Ann Price, went to the same elementary school as Joe."

"Wow. Wow. Wow." Ava's eyes and mouth open wide. "I didn't find her name in the school records."

"Because Ann Price was registered under her mother's name and not her father's."

"Brilliant!"

"Now it's your turn, Ava. You said you have some sensational news for me."

She did indeed. She didn't tell her over the phone so the rendezvous with Martha would be well worth it for her. "I found Fiona's grandma. She has a different family name from Fiona's."

Martha's reaction doesn't disappoint. "What? That's fantastic! How? Where?"

Ava could say it was thanks to her criminological streak, but it was a lucky break. "A fellow student told me purely by chance. Her grandma lives next to Fiona's grandma. Fiona sometimes paid her a visit. That was long before the trial."

"And? Did you go see her?"

"Yes. I pretended to be an old friend of Fiona's. Grandma was very nice. Not wary, but rather sad that she hadn't seen Fiona for years. Just Ann Price comes to visit now and then. Fiona wrote her on her eightieth birthday."

Martha's staring at her. Waiting for the big reveal.

And it comes.

"She showed me the birthday card and the envelope, but not

what was written on the card. Nevertheless I could read the postmark on the envelope. It was mailed in St. Anthony."

"Where's that?"

"In the province of Newfoundland and Labrador."

"Labrador!" Martha exclaims, as if she'd been given a magic word. "Ann Price twice went on holiday with her boyfriend to a fishing lodge in Labrador. I found out thanks to a photo of them on the internet." And she's got more for Ava. "It's the same lodge where four women started out on a trekking tour back then and disappeared, never to be seen again."

"When was that?"

"Eight years ago."

Ava bumps her knee against the table in her excitement, nearly knocking over her cup. "Do you know what, Martha? The women disappeared eight years ago, you said. Grandma's eightieth birthday was one year afterward. Isn't that a huge clue or what?"

Martha exhales from between pursed lips so fast that she whistles. "It's so hot that we need to dive into it some more."

62

Detective Sergeant Calista Gates
St. Anthony, Newfoundland
Saturday, February 17

Fred's driving and saying nothing. He keeps a close eye on the road to the St. Anthony airport for icy patches.

I'd prefer for him to talk, but maybe it's all been said. When I broke it to him two hours ago that I'm going to Labrador, he didn't seem surprised. He's probably been wondering for days how long I could stand not being up there myself. Nevertheless, his silence troubles me. Maybe he feels I'm deserting him in a situation that could turn out badly for him.

But he simply asks: "And the colleagues from Corner Brook?"

An idle question. He knows forensic experts can work alone; they don't need an investigator supervising them.

"You're my deputy, Fred, that's good enough."

"And if the St. John's people come for the external inquiry?"

The special investigators. They must be giving Fred nightmares.

I'm afraid of them too, but I mustn't show it.

"I'll be back in St. Anthony by then. They won't be here that quickly. You know from experience how bureaucracy is exceedingly slow." They told us the special investigators would be sent as soon as possible, but I'm sure it will take three days or more.

Before we left, Fred also wanted to know if I'd arranged my trip with inspector Peter Allen in Happy Valley-Goose Bay. Labrador is Allen's domain.

"I informed him that I had to find out a few things in connection with the Nielle Helfrey case. He couldn't refuse me that."

Fred just nodded.

Peter Allen has his hands full with Frank Delgado and Austin Sullivan. I also told him it has nothing to do with Morris Tye. I had to make that concession so that Allen would let me onto his turf. I know the limits of my competence.

Fred looked at me skeptically after I finished explaining all this to him. He's convinced I want to go to Crater Lake. He always sees himself as my protector, like during our stay in British Columbia. Or like at the cabin in Goose Cove.

I do want to back him up during the external inquiry, but now I'm leaving him by himself in St. Anthony. I've no choice. The only place I'll find answers to my questions is Labrador. And Gerald's there. Somewhere. It's almost suffocating to think about it. I can justify it to my bosses if I really must.

I break the silence because there's something else I have to tell Fred: "I've left some business for you on the intranet. I haven't gotten to it yet, and maybe it's a non-issue. You must talk to Mick Hudson, the reporter for the *Labrador Tribune*. It seems he's been contacted by a journalist from Toronto. She's supposed to have some information on a woman who might be in St. Anthony and who was involved in a killing in the town of Amherstburg, Ontario, some ten years ago or so. I've a vague recollection of the case. The woman was acquitted. A criminology student at the University of Windsor is supposed to have found an important lead pointing to St. Anthony." I give Fred a sidelong look since he didn't show any reaction while I was talking.

He's looking straight ahead at the road. Sometimes he's so inscrutable.

I don't let him stop me.

"The journalist from Toronto isn't ruling out the possibility that the woman might have something to do with the disappearance of the four tourists eight years ago," I continue. "The Happy Valley-Goose Bay RCMP evidently wouldn't tell her anything, which doesn't surprise me because of the Delgado and Sullivan business. That's why she turned to Mick Hudson. And Hudson talked to me about it because there's supposed to be a connection to St. Anthony. Maybe you can follow this up? I gave you Hudson's cell number."

"Permit me a question, Calista: Since when do we pursue dubious leads from the press?"

I hadn't expected such a brusque response. We're all near the breaking point.

I can see that Fred might not feel like talking to Mick Hudson. Especially in his situation.

Still, we must follow up.

"Just find out who the Toronto woman is and talk to her. Can't hurt."

"Why are we bothering with women who've been missing in Labrador for eight years? Haven't we got enough on our plate?"

"If there is in fact a lead to St. Anthony, we should follow it up. The families of the four women need an answer. It must be terrible not to know what happened. For now, we just make a phone call. Then we'll see."

Fred doesn't reply. I shut up. I don't feel well, and it's not the drive. It's the thought of Gerald. My stomach nerves are vibrating. In the past few days, I've called anyone in Labrador that I know had some connection to him. I was frantic with hope they could give me any clue as to what might have happened to him. I'm tortured by nightmares. When I finally sink into a restless sleep, I wake up terrified and bathed in sweat, my heart hammering.

Fred's going as fast as the precarious road conditions allow. I absolutely must catch that plane to Happy Valley-Goose Bay and then the one to Tulliq. The odds are good. The predicted snow hasn't started yet. I thank the universe for that. Because under these conditions, the forensics team will be able to see clear evidence from where the shots were fired. They are reliable and conscientious colleagues.

And that's what Fred is for me too. As we turn off the highway onto the road to the little airport, I'd like to say something to him. Something he can hold on to. That will give him courage. But I can't pull it off: my thoughts about Gerald completely possess me. If I can only see him again soon, touch him, hear his voice, and laugh with him. I long for nothing more than that. The painful uncertainty is eating me up. I keep back my tears with great effort. The corners of my mouth twitch. I bite my lips until it hurts.

Fred parks and looks at me.

"Be careful," he says. "I don't want to lose you."

"Fred."

I reach out my hand for his and squeeze it. Then I quickly get out of the car.

I've got twenty minutes in Happy Valley-Goose Bay before my flight to Tulliq. Everything goes as planned. I stuff my backpack under the seat. The Twin Otter takes off with a dozen passengers, most of them Inuit. It's two o'clock; it will still be light when I arrive in Tulliq.

David Pelletier gave me the names of two people to contact who could help me. A man called Iqaluk, also known as the Fish. A somewhat inscrutable person, but one who knows an awful lot about what goes on in the area. And the pilot Vernon Lindental who's been flying passengers and freight all over in his Cessna for years. I'd like to talk to Tiffany Staid, who took Gerald to Crater Lake with her dog team. Whether she wants to talk to me is another matter. I can imagine that my colleagues in Happy Valley-Goose Bay gave her a proper scare. Did Austin Sullivan intimidate her with his service revolver?

I'm still waiting for Heidy's list of women who were outpatients in St. Anthony on the ninth or tenth of February. It would be easier to get the list directly from the hospital, but a search warrant would be out of the question. Our suspicion's too vague and patient privacy too important. Vyann Kippen told Heidy that her neighbor had made a mistake and she, Vyann, did *not* have a houseguest, saying the neighbor was senile and got things mixed up at times. We don't believe her.

Heidy's now on another tack. She's drumming up patients who were in the waiting room at the time. I'm confident she will turn up something with her method. I've sentenced Dustin to giving our helpful Roddickton colleagues a meal to thank them for their nighttime guard duty.

I sink into a light sleep, with the Twin Otter's engines as my lullaby.

The little plane lands on the lonely Tulliq runway on time after an hour and twenty minutes. A layer of snow covers the gravel, and the landing is tolerable. I can make out a mountain on the left. David said as long as you can see the peak, you can fly. I was really lucky; sometimes there are no flights into Tulliq for days on end. I feel the cold as I disembark but almost no wind. Unbelievable. I accept my good luck with thanks. A blue pickup is waiting for me on the edge of the tarmac. Another tip from David. There are ordinary people in Tulliq who provide taxi service to visitors for a fee. It's cheaper than a car rental.

The driver's a woman whose age is difficult to estimate. I explain that I want to go to the hotel briefly—the only one in town—but then I must keep going.

"Do you know where Iqaluk lives?" I ask.

She looks at me in astonishment.

"You really want to go there?"

"Yes, I must talk to him."

As a local she'll certainly be familiar with Iqaluk's reputation, but she observes my request. After I've deposited my bag at the hotel, we go down a bumpy street to the edge of the village.

A poorly lit mobile home comes into view.

The driver stops.

"He's here, I can see his snowmobile. Shall I wait until you're finished?"

"It might take half an hour."

She thinks for a moment.

"I'll come back in half an hour."

"Good," I say. "Honk when you get here."

She leaves the headlights pointing to the trailer so I can more or less see my way.

I place a foot on the icy metal step before the door. I've left my crutches at home. The medication has reduced the swelling around my ankle considerably.

Before I can knock, the door opens and swings toward me.

I stumble backward and barely manage to catch myself. Pain shoots through my half-healed ankle.

A voice pierces the cold air.

"What's a cop doing at my place?"

63

Detective Sergeant Calista Gates
Tulliq, Labrador
Saturday, February 17

I can barely make out the outline of a man's face in the semidarkness. Is he alone? I don't hear any voices, only music.

"I'm looking for Gerald Hynes and need your help," I say.

These situations are unpredictable. I've always told my team to show up in pairs, and I'd thought about doing that. But two policemen might put Iqaluk on the defensive. Here am I, alone, in civilian dress and without a police car; everything is supposed to hint that I represent no threat to him. I don't want to provoke him.

He recognized me at once. Who tipped him off? David Pelletier? Can't imagine. Then it occurs to me that my face is everywhere in the media, and not just this past week. Yes, the Fish lives in a remote village—only accessible by air in wintertime—but he doesn't live in isolation.

The Fish retreats inside his shelter; the door stays open. I take it as an invitation. Once again, I put my healthy foot on the metal step, bring up the other one, go up hand over hand, and dive into the warmth. It smells sweetish. Marijuana. Quick as a flash I survey the room, noting the table with things piled up on it, the small cookstove, the battered kitchen cabinets, the passageway leading to the darkened back section. Then my eyes pick up the brawny man of average height watching me, hands on hips. Nothing that would instantly trigger alarm.

Iqaluk sits down on an upholstered bench; I sit on the other side of the table so I can see the doorway and the dark passageway. And now I notice the dog dozing under the table. It didn't even get up on its feet to sniff me. Maybe it's an old dog slumbering its way toward its final days. It would say something about the Fish that he doesn't simply shoot it because the dog's now useless.

"Tea? Coffee?" he asks.

An Inuit's hospitality is stronger than any mistrust.

I turn it down.

"I'd sleep badly with caffeine," I explain. A little acknowledgment that although I'm a police officer, I'm just a human being.

Of course, he puts a cup down before me anyway.

I would like to get right down to business, naturally, but I must rein in my impatience; anything else would be considered rude.

Iqaluk seems relaxed, his movements are loose; maybe he enjoys having a cop needing his help.

He reaches out his hand; there's something in it wrapped in tissue paper.

"You might like this."

He pushes the thing across the table.

I unwrap it. A carved figurine, merely as tall as my hand. A drum dancer. He's holding his drum up high.

I turn the figure around on the tabletop.

"It's very beautiful. Who carved it?"

He names a name I don't know.

"Made out of caribou antler."

I know it's not a gift to me. Carvings like this one command a high price. Iqaluk makes some money by supplying them to art dealers. So the taxi driver told me.

But I'm not his usual customer, I'm certain of that. He's testing me to see if I'm a "flexible" cop. If I'm prepared to meet him halfway. Not a bribe, but a transaction in a gray area.

"How much?" I ask.

"Three hundred."

A fair price. The drum dancer would cost twice that in a Vancouver shop.

"Okay, I'll take it," I say.

The bargaining has begun.

He accepts my bills, pleased.

"The cops in St. Anthony are bumping one another off."

Of course he's heard about it.

"There are rotten apples everywhere," I say cautiously. "What happened at Crater Lake?"

"A cop threatened two men from here with a gun."

"Who was the cop?" I feign ignorance.

"Austin Sullivan. We'll bring an action for coercion."

"Why did he threaten them?"

"Maybe he was trying to hide something."

"Well, what?"

"You tell me."

"Something to do with Gerald Hynes?"

"Are you two an item?"

"It's probably been going around. Do you know what's happened to him?"

"No."

"What have you heard? The two men up there, what did they see?"

"They found a camera bag. The cops took it."

Strange. Why would Gerald leave his camera bag behind? After all, he wanted to take in some impressions of the area and get them on film.

I'd love to have questioned those men from Tulliq. But now that they're going after Austin Sullivan for coercion, their lips are sealed.

"Did the men see Gerald's footprints?"

"They weren't looking for them."

What were those two from Tulliq doing up there? Why did they get in Sullivan's face?

I must feel my way forward gently. Very gently.

"Is the new national park a good idea?"

"That's Inuit territory."

"Yes, and it will stay Inuit territory," I say. "The park will be administered by Inuit. The Nunatsiavut government has the final say."

"The money's coming from Ottawa. Money always rules. Always."

"You don't think the Nunatsiavut government is doing the right thing?" I ask.

"We don't trust Morris Tye."

Morris Tye procured the building contract for Gerald. Did it make Gerald any enemies?

"Do you trust Gerald Hynes?"

The Fish suddenly looks at me hard.

"My guys have nothing to do with his disappearance. Absolutely nothing. You're barking up the wrong tree."

My guys. The Fish sent his allies to Crater Lake. They were probably supposed to torpedo the grand announcement of the national park and wreck Morris Tye's fancy show. But it all turned out otherwise.

The dog under the table stirs. A muzzle presses against my foot. I rub the coat on the bony skull.

"You're a good dog," I say, praising it. "You don't hurt anybody. You don't play with people's lives."

The dog presses its muzzle into my hand.

Iqaluk clears his throat.

"Crater Lake is not Disneyland. Not a playground for

tourists. The terrain is damn dangerous. My grandfather warned me about it. He warned everybody. He said the evil spirit of the lake blows through its open jaws above ground. If its breath hits your face, you'll be swallowed up." He looks at me penetratingly. "Your life ends in its guts."

In its guts.

What does that remind me of? I frantically search my memory.

Suddenly a cold shudder runs down my spine despite the warm air.

64

Fred van Heisen, RCMP Constable
St. Anthony, Newfoundland
Saturday, February 17

Rex comes into the conference room carrying a pizza.

Right then Fred realizes how ravenous he is.

"It's from Pizza Delight; I didn't have time to cook," Rex apologizes, laying his cards on the table. "Dustin's providing pizza and hot drinks for the forensic guys. Heidy's keeping an eye on Vyann Kippen."

Rex is one smart cookie. He guessed Fred wants to be kept up-to-date on the Wilsons' whereabouts.

It's a welcome break for Fred. He always loves a pizza, whether it comes from Rex's oven or Pizza Delight. But he's not enamored of the task Calista has sentenced him to carry out.

Every fiber in him resists contacting that Toronto journalist. Who can guarantee it's not a ploy to question him about what went on at the cabin? He feels Calista's leading him down the garden path; his mood is at rock bottom. For the first time ever, he can empathize with someone who commits a rash act or strikes a liberating blow against oppression. He called Lucinda again on the way back from the airport. She ignored the events that were depressing him and chattered on freely. Lucinda's a past master at repression. She tried to show him how much she was looking forward to his move to Saskatoon, to a cozy life together. House, family, children, stability. Lucinda is sweet. Everybody loves her; she has no enemies. He feels the undertow emanating from all of that. Isn't it the ideal combination: adrenaline rush at work, relaxation at home? If it weren't for the pitch-black shadows that have beset him . . .

The picture of a domestic idyll puts him off. Lucinda will always know only half of him. The dark side of his everyday life will be hidden from her. His own, personal dark side too. There will be an invisible barrier between them. There is already.

Calista, on the other hand, understands him instinctively. She's like a mirror. But she also poses a danger.

He'd rather put it out of his mind.

He pushes a slice of pizza into his mouth and rereads Calista's notes on the intranet. A piece of evidence is supposed to lead to St. Anthony, a postmark. Mick Hudson's cell number's in there.

That's all? He's disappointed. Nothing that Calista hadn't already told him in the car.

Why is she following up a farfetched lead like this? He's more than skeptical, though he must admit that Calista's good nose has seldom deserted her.

He makes a coffee and dives deep into various online reports. She won't be able to scold him for ignoring orders.

The Amherstburg case, then, was twelve years ago. He tries to go back in his mind to that time when he wasn't in the RCMP yet but a government official in the finance ministry in the province of Saskatchewan. And what a totally frustrated civil servant he was.

This case is completely new to him. He can't help but find the information he dugs out extremely fascinating.

A previously convicted sex offender, Joe Salomon, broke

into the home of a woman living in Amherstburg one night, Fiona Gelp. She was separated from her former partner Colin Hatterbush, who was able to insinuate himself back into Fiona's life. It was assumed that Salomon knew nothing about this and intended to rape Fiona. Salomon found Hatterbush asleep in Fiona's bed instead. Fiona was in another room because, as she claimed, she didn't want to disturb Hatterbush in his sleep. She heard a shot, grabbed a pistol that was registered to Hatterbush, and went into the bedroom to check on him. There she found Salomon. She shot him in self-defense. The trial was scheduled relatively quickly and went to a jury. Salomon's revolver had been stolen. He also had a knife on him. His family accused Gelp of murdering him and Hatterbush. The prosecuting attorney felt the same way; however, his murder theory proved unpersuasive. Fiona Gelp was acquitted on all charges.

She disappeared from the scene after that. Fred reads in a media report that she's said to have fled abroad because Salomon's family threatened her.

Something's fishy. Not one of the women reported missing in Labrador is named Fiona Gelp.

He can't find any information about where she went.

But his curiosity is piqued enough for him to bring himself to call Mick Hudson.

"It's about that journalist in Toronto," he explains. Hudson mustn't get the idea he can pick Fred's brains in return.

"Finally," Hudson exclaims. "I was beginning to think St. Anthony was as uninterested in this as Happy Valley-Goose Bay is."

"I don't know yet if I ought to be interested. Maybe my colleagues in Labrador have good reason to hold back."

"Because then it might come out how they bungled the investigation eight years ago," Hudson retorts. "Four tourists don't just simply vanish."

Oh, yes, they do, they might easily disappear in the vastness of Labrador. Fred can well recall from the four years he was stationed in Port Brendan how rapidly it can happen. Hundreds of people disappear in the wild every year on the North American continent.

Mick Hudson has a quick tongue: “Your colleagues told Martha Calambaro it was pointless to call St. Anthony because the RCMP there isn’t allowed to speak to the press.”

Fred doesn’t dismiss the possibility that something like that happened.

But he doesn’t want to get himself into a tricky discussion.

“I’m pressed for time,” he responds. “Would you like to give me Martha Calambaro’s number?”

“I want something from you, too, constable. I want to be the first to get the story if something comes of this.”

“Won’t you get that from the journalist in Toronto?”

“No, she doesn’t want the story taken away from her.”

“I’ll have to leave that decision to Sergeant Gates, but I’ll put in a word for you.”

Hudson had barely given him the number when Fred signs off and phones Calambaro.

At first he only gets her mailbox. He leaves a message.

Not twenty seconds later, the journalist calls back.

“I think it’s great you called, Constable van Heisen,” she says breathlessly. “Where did you get my number?”

“From Mick Hudson.”

“How collegial of him! Do you have the files on the missing women?”

“No, they’re in the hands of RCMP Happy Valley-Goose Bay in Labrador. I’m stationed in St. Anthony in Newfoundland.”

“Are you familiar with the Fiona Gelp case?”

“With the basic outlines, yes.”

“Good. Then I can come right to the point, if I may. Fiona Gelp wrote her grandma a letter postmarked St. Anthony. I hadn’t known for a long time where Fiona was living. The letter’s an important clue. But I wanted to tell you mainly about this: Fiona has a sister called Ann Price, who's supposed to have gone fishing with her boyfriend several times at the Remote Point Lodge in Labrador. As you know, that's where four women disappeared on a long hike after spending a night or two at the lodge. Fiona probably turned up in St. Anthony a year after the women disappeared. And we have her sister staying at the lodge before it happened."

Fred listens up.

"What years was her sister at the lodge?"

"I couldn't find out. I phoned the lodge, but they said that information about their guests is confidential. For instance of prominent guests who have a right to their privacy."

He expected nothing different. The lodge's owners will certainly have had their fill of reporters.

"What was her sister's name again?"

"Ann Price. Price with a *c*."

"Fiona Gelp has a different name from her sister?"

"Yes. They have different fathers."

He looks at the words on his notepad. Ann Price. A run-of-the-mill name.

"Can you send me photographs of the sisters?"

"Sure. But they're several years old."

65

Detective Sergeant Calista Gates
Tulliq, Labrador
Saturday, February 17

I get into the taxi that came back.

The driver seems relieved that I'm still in one piece. She takes me to the village.

"Have you ever heard of an evil spirit in Crater Lake?" I ask.

"Yes. As a kid I heard it eats people who get too close to it. We have many stories like that. There's an evil spirit on the pack ice too, who lures kids out there and has them disappear in the cracks in the ice."

"Do they tell the stories to make people more cautious? Or to scare them away?"

"Maybe to scare them off. Crater Lake is a sacred place for us. It must be treated with respect."

Will tourists do that? I don't ask the woman what she thinks of the planned national park and the lodge. My instincts tell me to steer clear of the subject; as a policewoman, I don't want to take sides.

I tip her generously when she drops me off at the hotel.

"I must be at the airport tomorrow by eight. Could you drive me at that time?"

"My husband can. I'm cleaning at the hotel in the morning."

"How many jobs do you have?"

"I also work at the culture center in summer and lead tours for the visitors. I like it. I meet many people and learn a lot."

"The tourists will certainly learn from you too. One day I'll visit the exhibit if I can find the time."

She looks at me sympathetically.

"I hope you find him."

It is immediately clear to me that she means Gerald. Word has gotten around everywhere. Her concern wraps around me like a warm blanket.

Not all people hate me. They don't hate all cops. Really don't.

"Have you heard anything that might be of help?" I ask.

"A couple of men from Alliarkuk were up there when it happened. They still are."

"At Crater Lake?"

'Yes, my husband's relatives, they've got hunting cabins there. They've got a satellite phone too. You can certainly stay with them in a cabin."

"Where are the cabins?"

"Not far from the landing strip where you'll arrive."

"Very good. I'm glad to have this information."

"Gerald's one of us. You must find out what's happened to him."

Overwhelmed with emotion, I thank her and go to find my room.

There I see that Fred has tried to call me repeatedly.

He'd left a short text message but nothing specific.

Why didn't I hear the phone ring? Isn't there reception everywhere here?

I call him immediately.

"Where are you?" he asks.

"In the hotel in Tulliq. Has something happened?"

"I talked to the journalist in Toronto." He summarizes their call.

It's puzzling. Fiona Gelp in St. Anthony. Her sister, Ann Price, in Remote Point Lodge. What's it all mean?

Before we can talk about it, he brings up more news.

Heidy gave him the long-awaited list of people who were in the St. Anthony hospital waiting room during the time in question. Fred reads me the names. He's meticulous, not wanting to leave anything out. I'm impressed at how many names Heidy was able to dig up with her labor-intensive search.

She flagged one name in particular, and Fred verbalizes what I'm thinking: "Calista, I think we've got a lead."

It is an understatement, but we don't want to get carried away by any premature enthusiasm. Disappointments during investigations are a given.

We need concrete proof is my immediate thought.

"Forensics must have found fingerprints. Are they finished?"

"Yes, they worked like fiends."

"Great!" Not everything's going wrong. Certain people are still reliable.

I sign off with the words "Tell Heidy how highly I think of her work. And of yours, which goes without saying, Fred."

I call Vernon Lindental immediately afterward to see when we're flying to Crater Lake tomorrow.

"The way it looks, we can't fly in the morning," he informs me. "Too much fog. Afternoon should be possible."

I think for a minute. I can't sit here in Tulliq and do nothing; worrying about Gerald would drive me up the wall. I already have my nighttime torture. I've got to keep busy.

"Can you land at Remote Point Lodge tomorrow afternoon on the way to Crater Lake and pick me up from there?" I ask.

"That costs extra. Why do you want to go to the lodge?" The pilot sounds suspicious.

Not good; I don't want my scheme to go up in smoke. I can only convince a man like Lindental with a plausible reason, or he'll really get suspicious.

"Gerald's parents told me he had something to discuss with Noshi Mercer. In connection with the construction project at Crater Lake. I'd like to talk to Mr. Mercer about it."

"How will you get to the lodge from here?" he asks.

"I'll figure it out. Maybe somebody will take me by snowmobile."

The pilot appears to accept my explanation. He knows Gerald; he's one of the last people to have seen him. That can't leave him cold.

And he's sure to phone Noshi Mercer about my intentions.

I say good-bye and call the number on the taxi driver's card. She's now my contact in Tulliq.

I tell her that my plane's not leaving until tomorrow afternoon, and I want to go to Remote Point Lodge.

"How can I get there? Could somebody take me by snowmobile?"

"It's a long way for a snowmobile. There's some difficult terrain. It's better by dog team, particularly in fog. You can ask Irvin. Irvin Clad. He's got a team."

She gives me his cell number.

"What about the fog?" I ask.

"The dogs always find their way. They know the route."

66

Tiffany Staid, Musher
Tulliq, Labrador
Sunday, February 18

She hitches up the dogs. Anaisha's in heat and will stay put. Otherwise, she'd drive the pack crazy. She doesn't understand why she can't go along, and her whining is heartrending.

The St. Anthony police chief is in Tulliq. The Fish ordered Tiffany to keep her mouth shut.

"She might try to get in touch with you," he warned.

Tiffany needs his protection, as the RCMP won't protect her. The Fish and his pals have a lawyer. They're preparing a lawsuit against the blond policeman. She knows his name: Austin Sullivan.

Ever since the cops learned about the threatening lawsuit, they've been more circumspect toward her. They are *so* deep in shit. Not only in Labrador. The Fish said a cop in St. Anthony shot at another cop, a guy who cooked up nasty schemes with Sullivan. Now the cops are eating one another up. They're too involved with themselves.

That's good for her.

Irvin inquired if she could take over a taxi job to Remote Point Lodge for him. Sure can. She's back in business despite the debacle at Crater Lake. They still haven't found Gerald Hynes. Did the blond cop whack him and do away with his body? But why? Gerald was so nice to her; he's one of them. Who'd want to do anything to hurt him?

She must see to the dogs. Irvin didn't tell her who the client was. She knows what that means: it's somebody who's picking up stuff from Noshi. Nobody must know. She can easily imagine what it is. Noshi's selling caribou meat. It's against the law, but you've got to survive somehow. Like her. The dogs help her get by. She'd never have had the money to buy them. The dead don't need money. It's been well invested.

A snowmobile approaches. Bud Abel for sure. She doesn't ignore him anymore because he keeps her up to speed. She needs to know what's happening.

The dogs bark frantically. They sense they'll be taking off in a minute. The snow anchor's holding them back, nothing more.

A person dismounts from the rear seat. Takes the helmet off.

Tiffany realizes at once who she is. The cop from St. Anthony.

She looks so foreign. Black hair like her but eyes as round as full moons. And those lashes. No makeup. A sad expression. Gerald Hynes's beloved.

She comes toward her, limping slightly.

Irvin. That rat. He fooled her. She's suddenly furious. He knew exactly who the client was. He didn't want to take the cop to the lodge himself. The dirty rascal.

What was she to do? Just take off with the team? Run away?

Too late. The policewoman pulls on a woolen cap and speaks to her: "Tiffany Staid? I'm Detective Sergeant Calista Gates. Can you take me to Remote Point Lodge?"

Tiffany is paralyzed. Is she supposed to warn Kellyann and Noshi about the cop?

No. Irvin has certainly done it already. He's not that dense.

Or someone else has told the lodge about Calista Gates.

Many people in Tulliq are undoubtedly watching her every step. The way Bud's watching her and Calista right now.

She gives in to the unavoidable situation.

"Do you have any baggage?"

"This backpack. How long will it take us?"

"About two hours. Maybe two and a half."

Can the cop take it? She looks petite even in her thick winter jacket.

"You were with Gerald Hynes at Crater Lake?" the policewoman asks out of the blue.

Now she's going to put the squeeze on, Tiffany thinks.

Watch out. I must watch out.

"I only dropped him off there; he wanted to be alone and sent me away for an hour." That's the statement she made to the other cops and since then repeats it constantly.

"Did he say what he was going to do?"

"I can't say anything about that. Lawyer's advice." Good that the Fish coached her to say this.

"You can help save a life." The policewoman looks at her with those big, dark eyes.

Tiff feels as if she's on camera. She tries not to let it show and says: "I don't know where he went. You have to ask the RCMP officers. They probably know more."

If the Fish could hear her now, would he approve? She doesn't want to be unfriendly or provoke the policewoman unnecessarily, or she might really take greater interest in her. That's the last thing she needs.

She secures the backpack to the sled with bungee cords.

It's hard to carry on a conversation over the dogs' yapping. Just as Tiffany wanted.

But the cop has one more question: "Did he mention the evil spirit in the Lake? That the spirit's breath is dangerous, say?"

Tiffany hesitates with an answer, lowers her eyes.

She hesitates too long.

The cop guesses that he did mention it. She holds her gaze on her for a long time.

Then she gives Bud a sign and climbs on the sled: "I'm ready."

Tiffany hands Calista Gates a helmet, spreads the caribou pelt over her, then the waterproof canvas cover and ties it all down tight.

From now on, *she* calls the shots. The cop is in her hands.

She trusts me, Tiffany thinks. In spite of the incident with Gerald Hynes.

She pulls out the snow anchor, and the dogs race ahead.

No time anymore for dark thoughts; she must concentrate on her job. The fog is still thick, but the dogs know the way and so does she. If there's one thing she's learned, it's that she must never relax, never take her eyes off the dogs. Only on the long plain before the rocky hills can she sometimes let go a little. But not in this fog. And not with a client on the sled.

It hadn't really snowed much for several days. The snow's had time to firm up. The wind today is unusually weak. That makes the trip easier for her and the dogs. Still, the weather can turn at any time.

She'd like to have asked the policewoman why she wanted to go to the lodge. Why didn't she fly directly to Crater Lake?

It can't have to do with Gerald Hynes.

Then what?

The sled rumbles over uneven ground. A constant up and down and back and forth. Enough to slow the ride down a bit.

Until they finally reach ice-covered Lake Poqii, where the dogs shoot off like a rocket.

This is usually exhilarating for her and her team.

But today she has the feeling she's racing toward her doom.

67

Detective Sergeant Calista Gates
Remote Point Lodge, Labrador
Sunday, February 18

I stagger toward the lodge entrance, my helmet still on my head. I can hardly believe we've arrived at last. Have I gone mad to get involved in something like this? Tiffany Staid could have dumped me on the foggy, ice-cold tundra. Nowhere to be found, like Gerald. The trip was supposed to take two and a half hours. It seemed unending to me. My body feels as if I've been tortured.

The dogs, on the other hand, are in high spirits. Tiffany had to curb their enthusiasm. She knows what she's doing.

I leave my backpack behind without a word; I just want to get to a warm place.

Nobody opens the door to welcome me, so I must let myself in. In the vestibule I take my helmet off and can see winter clothes hanging and shoes in a row. I take off my boots and jacket. Still, nobody has shown up. The lodge owners must surely have heard the dogs.

I open the next door and find a large living area.

Now a man finally appears from an adjoining room.

He peruses my ID as I say: "Hello, I'm Detective Sergeant Calista Gates from St. Anthony."

"Noshi Mercer. To what do we owe the honor?"

He doesn't sound aggressive so much as somewhat sarcastic. He knows I bring trouble. Where's Kellyann? Isn't she here?

I feel too miserable to wait for an invitation.

"Could I have a hot drink? I'm frozen to the bone."

"Sure. Best come to the kitchen where it's warmest."

His hospitality is greater than his displeasure. I probably look pathetic with my half-undone bun, runny eyes, and frozen face. I can only move with some effort.

He glances at my socks. I just now take a close look at the design on them: a shark's open jaws showing two rows of sharp teeth. Perhaps I ought to have chosen something more discreet for my visit, but the socks are thick and warm.

The kitchen doesn't look as industrial as normal restaurant kitchens do. No pans on metal hooks but a lot of glossy wood instead—all tidy and livable. I blow my drippy nose and quickly detect the smell of fresh bread. I hope he gives me a piece.

"Are you hungry?" he asks right on cue.

I nod. How dependent we are on others in this rough, inhospitable environment. I wish Gerald were with me. He can deal so well with the locals. I've often admired him for it. A lump forms deep down in my throat.

I choose a seat at a large table against the wall. Probably where the staff eat during the season.

Noshi Mercer sets a big plate of bread, butter, cheddar cheese, and cold cuts before me. Along with muffins and a bowl of stewed peaches.

As he pours my coffee, I hear voices. Doors open and close. Tiffany brings my backpack into the kitchen; an athletic-looking woman comes behind her. A thin cap covers her long, blond, loosely braided hair. An appealing face. Her eyebrows are too perfect to be natural.

"I'm Kellyann," she introduces herself. "We've been expecting you. What brings you here, Sergeant Gates?"

She sits down across from me. I can well imagine how good she is with the guests. Affable, robust, a doer. But so is Vyann. Why did Noshi swap wives? Did he want to make a new start after the uproar about the missing women? Just as my ex-husband in Vancouver wanted a new beginning after I was assaulted; he wanted a life that didn't remind him of my brain injury and slow recovery.

Tiffany fills a cup at the kitchen counter and picks up a muffin. She knows her way around the place.

I put down my coffee mug.

"Can you recall a guest by the name of Ann Price? She was apparently here several times with her boyfriend to go fishing."

Kellyann and Noshi exchange looks. It dawns on them that I'm not here about Gerald.

Noshi's expression is serious.

"We don't give out any information about guests, for privacy reasons."

"My question is part of an investigation. I can get a court order, and then you must allow me to see your guest list."

"Why are you investigating this woman?" Kellyann's smile has vanished.

"I'm not investigating her, but she can help me with my investigations in St. Anthony."

"What's being investigated, actually?" Noshi asks.

"I'm looking for the person who attacked Nielle Helfrey in Goose Cove."

"What's that guest got to do with it?"

"That's what I want to find out. Maybe you can help me with it."

"As I said, our rules don't allow us to do it."

I look at the two of them. We won't get anywhere this way.

Out of the corner of my eye, I see Tiffany sitting perfectly still in her chair.

I address my next question to Kellyann.

"Mrs. Mercer, what were you doing in St. Anthony on February the eleventh?"

"What's that? My wife wasn't in St. Anthony, she was at the hospital in Happy Valley-Goose Bay." Noshi's voice sounds irritated for the first time.

I ignore him and don't take my eyes off her.

"Mrs. Mercer?"

"Noshi's said it already: I was at the hospital."

"At which hospital?"

"In St. Anthony."

Noshi looks at his wife dumbstruck.

"But you were . . ."

She interrupts.

"I wanted to go to the ear doctor because of the noises in my ear, all that ringing and whistling. I didn't want to tell you, darling, because you think I'm just imagining it. They did tests on me in St. Anthony."

"Why go *there*?"

"Because they have a good ear specialist."

I take charge of the conversation again.

"Where did you stay in St. Anthony?"

"In the hospital."

"Where did you spend the night?"

She hesitates before answering.

"At a friend's."

"Which friend?"

"Begging your pardon, sergeant, why are you asking me these questions?"

"Because I'm investigating the Nielle Helfrey case."

"My wife has nothing to do with it." Noshi stands up abruptly.

I repeat the question: "At whose place did you spent the night?"

Kellyann gets up too. "I don't like these innuendos. I'm not saying anything more. I want a lawyer."

"That is your right, Mrs. Mercer. But it looks like you might have something to hide. Wouldn't you like to assist me with my investigation?"

I'm disappointed and encouraged simultaneously. Disappointed I didn't get more out of her. Encouraged because my suspicions are firming up. Kellyann wasn't in St. Anthony just to be treated by an ear specialist.

Noshi crosses his arms. I can see he's concerned.

"What are you accusing my wife of, sergeant?"

"Nothing. I've just got some questions for her. Why she kept her visit to St. Anthony secret, and . . ."

"But she just explained that."

"And why she went around on a snowmobile; she was seen."

I'm simply speculating. A bit of pressure can't hurt.

Kellyann reacts at once.

"I have nothing to do with Nielle Helfrey. Why would I have done anything to her?"

I let the question hang in the room. I watch Noshi's face, where something's going on. A hint of panic. He's putting two and two together.

Nielle knew about Noshi's illegal meat sales because Vyann was imprudent enough to tell her about them after Kellyann told her. Vyann still had no clue at the time that Nielle was having an affair with Morris Tye. Nielle, the betrayer. Was the assault on her an indirect warning to Morris Tye not to do anything more vis-à-vis Remote Point Lodge?

Noshi turns to Tiffany, who hasn't uttered a word so far.

Her face is frozen stiff. She surely hadn't expected a conversation anything like this when she left with me for the lodge.

"Tiff, take Sergeant Gates back. We've said all there is to say."

I cut myself a slice of cheese.

"Mr. Mercer, *you* don't determine how long I stay here. Vernon Lindental will come pick me up."

I open my backpack and feel around for my satellite phone.

68

Fred van Heisen, RCMP Constable
St. Anthony, Newfoundland
Sunday, February 18

Fred's at the window watching the snowmobiles tearing back and forth over the ice.

They're buzzing like aggressive wasps. Young people wanting to work off steam. The ice in the bay is still thick enough for those wild games.

He, by comparison, feels like a person walking on thin ice who might fall through at any moment. Calista called him from Remote Point Lodge on the satellite phone. They couldn't talk for long, and she hadn't received his text messages. Communication with her won't be easy in the coming hours and days. The lodge owners say their internet is down. Calista doesn't believe it, but what can she do? The Mercers now see her as the enemy, which couldn't be prevented.

Calista asked him to put Vyann Kippen under some pressure in the hope that she stops resisting and tells the truth about Kellyann, the cockatoo, and Nielle. He puts on his heavy jacket and leaves Heidy in charge; she makes the sacrifice and is writing up the outstanding reports on the investigations. A job he can't stand. As a government finance official back in the day, he would write reports constantly. Dustin's taking the forensics team to the airport. They did superb work that can only be helpful to him.

Fred wants to catch Vyann before she leaves Mr. Grant's home in Goose Cove for her next assignment at two o'clock. Her clients seem to be primarily single men. Women are more independent in old age; they can take care of themselves longer.

The trip to Goose Cove seems like the calm before the storm to Fred. He expects to be taken off the job as soon as the special investigators arrive. As a matter of fact, it's puzzling it hasn't been done already. Calista must have control over whatever's protecting him for now. What a screwup. But then he goes back to the reason he quit his job in the finance ministry in Saskatoon and joined the RCMP. He hates being bored. And it is never boring with Calista.

He parks in front of Mr. Grant's house.

When Vyann opens the door, her face registers immediate disapproval. But she lets him in.

On the other hand, Mr. Grant's delighted.

"I heard you were arrested after the shoot-up, constable," he exclaims.

Fred takes no offense. Elderly people may take more liberties and cross red lines. They don't have to be polite or considerate all the time because they don't have a career to lose.

"I have to bathe my client," Vyann interjects.

"It can wait," Mr. Grant argues. His watery eyes sparkle with pleasure.

"We have to take your hearing aids out before your bath," Vyann explains, "or they'll get wet."

The scene reminds Fred of Mrs. Eddison and Trina Modeste. The caregivers seem to fight a daily battle with hearing aids.

Mr. Grant's protest is futile. Fred watches as Vyann

patiently but firmly gets him to obey. She probably did that in the lodge too. She convinced the guests to move more cautiously through the wilderness. Not to get too close to the wildlife. Not to cross the river at the wrong spot. Not to leave litter behind outdoors. To drink water after physical exertion.

She was only unable to impose her will on the four missing women. Paige Warner, an entrepreneur who led the group, was used to having people obey *her.* That must bug Vyann to this day.

Fred puts his phone on Record and discloses it. She doesn't object, to Fred's astonishment, so he kicks off the questioning.

"Detective Sergeant Calista Gates is at Remote Point Lodge."

Vyann freezes. A good reaction, Fred thinks. He'd secretly hoped she didn't know that, though the odds were minimal because news travels so fast. Particularly between the lodge and Vyann. But for some reason she hadn't gotten the word.

A second push.

"She's questioning Kellyann Mercer."

Vyann stays on her feet but changes her body position, as if she wanted to hide her face from him.

"What does she want from Kellyann?"

"What do you think Sergeant Gates wants from her, Mrs. Kippen?"

"Why ask me?" Vyann's tone is more concerned than aggressive.

Fred likes that too.

"Why do you think I'm coming to you after Sergeant Gates talked with Kellyann?"

"You tell me, constable. I can't read your mind."

"I'll give you a hint, Mrs. Kippen. Our colleagues from Corner Brook found evidence and fingerprints at the cabin in the woods yesterday."

She says nothing.

He must keep pressing on until her resistance is broken.

"Why did you lie to us? Several times, Mrs. Kippen. You said you didn't have a visitor. But we know Mrs. Mercer was in St. Anthony when Nielle Helfrey was attacked. Mrs. Mercer admitted it to Sergeant Gates. Why are you lying to the police?"

Vyann Kippen sits down on a chair. Fred's rejoicing inside. The first step toward a confession. She won't hide behind a lawyer.

"Kellyann asked me to. She didn't want Noshi to find out and be worried."

Fred curses to himself. That's what Kellyann said to Calista. The women have colluded.

But he doesn't give up so quickly.

"You would have me believe that you'd obey the wishes of the woman who married your ex-husband?"

"Why not? We're not enemies."

An unexpected confession. That agrees with Calista's hypothesis: Vyann and Kellyann—incredible as it sounds—have joined forces to save the lodge.

"Did Kellyann take your son's snowmobile to the cabin?"

"No idea, constable."

"To wait for Nielle and take revenge on her?"

"But that's absurd, don't you think so?" Vyann has pulled herself together.

She's sly. She realized that even if they've found Kellyann's fingerprints at the cabin, they aren't evidence of guilt. *Crap.*

He hopes that Kellyann left traces on Nielle's Ski-Doo. The results are still forthcoming from forensics. But it's probable she wore gloves; it was winter, after all.

"Why should we believe your statements, Mrs. Kippen? You've lied to us again and again. About your cockatoo as well. We know your bird was already dead before the attack on Nielle occurred. We have a witness."

"Witness? You mean Nielle? She can't remember anything right, with her banged-up head. Who'd believe Nielle?"

Fred feels the questioning slipping away from him. Vyann

knows every trick in the book. She admitted being defeated eight years ago by Paige Warner, and that ended catastrophically. Vyann will do anything to avoid getting herself in a situation like that again.

He's thinking frantically. What cards has he got left to play?

"You can't protect Kellyann, Mrs. Kippen. But you can protect Noshi. And the lodge."

Vyann doesn't take the bait. He's underestimated her. Kellyann doled out the punishment to Nielle, and Vyann thought it was just. A traitor must be punished. And her lover Morris Tye needed a warning shot across his bow. Kellyann did it for Vyann. And Vyann wouldn't turn Kellyann in.

"Did you know an Ann Price who often vacationed at the lodge?" he asks instead.

For an instant Vyann's eyes twitch, but the moment quickly vanishes.

"I'm not allowed to give out any information about the guests. Privacy concerns." Her mouth narrows to a slit.

He realizes he mustn't appear helpless despite his defeat.

"This isn't our last conversation, Mrs. Kippen. We'll be asking you to come to the police station soon," he informs her.

"I understood something," Mr. Grant cackles. "Without my hearing aids. I hate those things. I've always said I don't need them." The old man looks around in triumph. He's the only one who's happy.

Fred leaves the house. He's achieved nothing. Absolutely nothing.

The worst is yet to come when Nielle's mother phones the station two hours later: "Nielle doesn't want her case investigated any longer. Perhaps she only fell off the snowmobile, she says. She just wants to be left in peace."

What nonsense. She didn't just fall off the snowmobile. Then how did the machine get back to the cabin?

"Sergeant Gates isn't here at the moment. Your daughter should speak to her. She . . ."

“I don’t understand it either, but Nielle won’t listen to me.” Mrs. Helfrey sounds just as beaten down as he feels.

Now it’s not just that Vyann has bested him. Morris Tye has certainly muzzled Nielle. How much did that cost the politician?

Fred sighs; it feels like one of the blackest days of his life.

69

Detective Sergeant Calista Gates
Ilungilak Crater, Labrador
Sunday, February 18

The aircraft takes off and gains altitude. I'm the only passenger and share the Cessna's cabin with a heap of boxes. My throat feels dry, my head seems to be roaring like the plane's engine. I've been waiting for this moment for five days. Since Gerald's been missing. It feels like an eternity. The worst thing is not being able to act. But what can I expect? Why have they still not found him? Is he stuck somewhere? Or has he completely lost his sense of direction for some reason? I'd like to walk around in the cargo area to keep my tension at bay. Instead, I'm tied to the seat and afraid I'm going to explode.

That scares me more than my bosses' potential punishment. I can already hear their voices: "Sergeant, you didn't coordinate this with colleagues in Happy Valley-Goose Bay. You abandoned your investigations. You evaded the external inquiry."

Whatever. I must risk it.

Fluffs of mist waft along outside the little window. However, visibility is better than yesterday. Vernon Lindental didn't leave me high and dry. I'm eternally grateful to him. If the RCMP won't pay for a flight that should have been officially approved, it will cost me a pretty penny. More expensive than the ride on Tiffany's dogsled. I'm also grateful to the musher for getting me to the lodge safely. Will Noshi and Kellyann take it out on her? Hopefully not. I think they've got enough problems to keep them busy. For example, that Kellyann deceived Noshi about going to St. Anthony instead of Happy Valley-Goose Bay. And that she didn't tell him what she did there, and why she needed a lawyer all of a sudden.

For the time being, I must leave it to Fred to see where we go from here. He's on his own, just as I am.

The fog's lifting more and more. I see canyons far below that rivers have carved out. Then white, unscarred plains. I feel uneasy. It's an inhospitable region where I've no business being. But I have lost something there: the man who made me believe in relationships again.

The Cessna suddenly veers and circles. Now I can see it plainly and distinctly: an almost perfect circle. Crater Lake. Its high rim juts out from the whiteness around it. The frozen surface is smooth and level, as if a machine had stamped it out.

The Ilungilak Crater.

Somewhere down below is where Gerald was last seen.

I realize the pilot isn't circling to show me the frozen white lake. He's scanning for anything suspicious.

I hold my breath. Now things get serious.

The Cessna begins its approach. The hunting cabins that the Tulliq taxi driver told me about come into view. I've got no snowmobile, no dogsled. I'm becoming very conscious of how unprepared I am.

The Cessna's skis bounce hard on the ground, then glide and bump along the runway that I couldn't make out in the flat landscape.

What do I do now?

One step after the other, Calista.

The pilot helps me clamber down. The cold hits me like a slap in the face, taking my breath away. I blink hard.

Vernon Lindental puts my backpack down on the snow and points behind me.

I turn and see two Indigenous people on snowmobiles towing sleds for transporting freight. The men from Alliarkuk. One gets off and lifts a box the pilot had unloaded onto his sled.

The other one waves me over. I pick up my backpack and go to him.

"Get on," he says, handing me a helmet.

That's a load off my mind. I won't simply be left to my own devices up here.

We ride to one of the cabins. The driver points to the door without a word and gets off.

I remove my helmet and follow him.

Inside, I meet two more men, one of them rather young. I feel the wave of warmth pouring from a woodstove.

When I give my name and rank, the men show no surprise. They've obviously been informed that Gerald and I are an item. I take off my outer shell.

The young man takes a step forward.

"I'm Anuaktak. That's my father and that's my uncle. Would you like some tea?"

His words are an invitation for me to sit down and tell the men why I'm here. I do it, though they seem to know already.

As they don't comment, I proceed straight to my concern: "May I ask you some questions? Where is Search and Rescue?"

"In the cabins on Cloud Lake."

"Where's Cloud Lake?"

"About four kilometers from the Ilungilak Crater."

"What are the search teams doing?"

"We've heard the helicopter sometimes. But not today."

"Do you see search parties on occasion?"

"We saw some yesterday. They were on snowmobiles. We've gone out looking for Gerald many times."

I ask the most urgent question on the tip of my tongue: "Did you see Gerald after he arrived?"

"Yes, he was at this cabin," Anuaktak says. "He wanted to go right away to Crater Lake."

"With Tiffany Staid's dog team?"

Anuaktak's father nods.

"Tiff's not to blame for anything," Anuaktak interjects.

"I've met Tiffany. She and her team took me from Tulliq to Remote Point Lodge." It's important to let the men know I'm not after Tiffany.

Anuaktak seems relieved.

"She took Gerald Hynes to the foot of Crater Lake; he wanted to be there by himself."

"For how long?"

"An hour," he says. "Tiffany went to Cloud Lake in the meantime. A cop there sent her to our cabin. He told her he would bring Gerald back on his snowmobile."

Anuaktak isn't reciting this course of events for the first time, I think. A smart young man. He probably suspects it's important to never deviate from the original version.

"Did he do it?" A dumb question, I know. But sometimes an investigator must play dumb to elicit information.

"No."

The men look at me to observe my reaction.

I shake my head. "As far as I know, that's being investigated by the RCMP Happy Valley-Goose Bay. His whole conduct is being examined. I've heard that some people from Tulliq are going to sue him. Were you there when he threatened those men with the weapon?"

Again, it's Anuaktak who answers; he's more outspoken than his father and his uncle.

"They found the camera bag, and the cop insinuated they had something to do with Gerald Hynes's disappearance."

That agrees with what the Fish told me.

They'd have done better to leave the camera bag lying there;

it would have helped the cops to determine which way Gerald had gone. But locals don't think that way.

"Do you know where the Tulliq men picked up the camera bag?"

Pause. Then Anuaktak's father shrugs.

I take that not as a no; they don't want to come right out and say it. That's encouraging.

"Tiffany surely told you when she came here what had gone on. What did you do then?"

I hope my questions don't sound like a police interrogation. I don't want to intimidate my hosts.

Anuaktak's uncle rouses himself.

"We went to look for Gerald. Twice. But we saw nothing."

"No footprints?"

"There was a storm."

My hands are very hot because they're clutching the tea mug.

"Can you show me the spot Tiffany showed you?"

"Sure."

I close my eyes to suppress tears of relief. When I open them again, the men have already stood up.

I take a few unimportant things out of my backpack that I want to take with me but leave the well-packed satellite phone in there.

70

Detective Sergeant Calista Gates
Ilungilak Crater, Labrador
Sunday, February 18

It's beginning to snow. I hope it won't turn into a storm. The airflow doesn't hit me full force, fortunately, because I'm sitting on a snowmobile behind Anuaktak's father's broad back.

So, this is the very route Gerald took with Tiffany's dog team. What was going on in his mind? I can't dwell on my thoughts; I must concentrate on not falling off. And this ride too—the second one today—seems long although it is much shorter.

Suddenly the two snowmobiles in front of us stop. Anuaktak's father follows suit.

How can they even know where they are in all this overwhelming whiteness?

I remove my visor. Now I can barely detect the outline of a post. A sign is attached.

I get off and walk over to it. *DANGER! AUTHORIZED ENTRANCE ONLY* is the warning on it. Visibility is still not too bad despite the swirling snowflakes. I look to the west, where I can make out the ascent to Crater Lake. This is where the meteorite fell more than one million years ago. The boulders scattered by the impact are hard to make out under the snow. The deep gaps between them are even harder to see. You'd be crazy to try to go up there on foot. Gerald isn't crazy.

The feeling of an invisible threat comes over me but I am fascinated at the same time. Was this fascination strong enough to make Gerald throw caution to the wind?

I turn to my companions.

"Do you think Gerald went up there?"

Anuaktak's father says no.

"Absolutely can't imagine it. It's an hour and a half to the rim of the crater. Much too dangerous. You can't even see where you're putting your foot down."

It would be hard to avoid disappearing into a crevasse. Gerald's not through with life. He's an experienced outdoorsman. He'd never have dared to do it. Not on foot.

It seems more probable he tried to record the terrain at the foot of the crater. Not for very long, because he'd left his camera bag elsewhere. He surely intended to turn around immediately.

I walk back to the snowmobile.

"Can we make one slow pass around the crater?"

I haven't the foggiest idea how far that would be, but the men are on board right away.

I get back on behind Anuaktak's father. The ride's jerkier, and I can't see much.

The snowmobile stops after a while.

"Do you want to keep going?"

I get off and let my eyes wander.

The climb looks steep from here. I can't see the rim of the crater anymore.

But I spot something conspicuous.

"What's that?" I point to a high, iced-up pillar. It stands in clear contrast to the terrain.

"Never seen it before," Anuaktak replies.

His uncle thinks otherwise.

"Maybe the remains of an inukshuk."

I get out my binoculars.

"It looks much too tall for an inukshuk."

"Every winter the ice accumulates, and it grows in height."

While he's speaking, an image comes to my inner eye. A similar ice tower, but much, much higher. A tiny man in front of it. Snow and ice all around. Where *was* that? My pulse quickens. If Gerald stood right here, he must have discovered the pillar we're looking at. Like me, he must have felt the urge to investigate it.

"I'd like to go over there," I declare.

This time the otherwise so helpful men hesitate. It's the uncle who comes out with the reason: "It's the spear of the evil spirit of Crater Lake."

I, on the other hand, think it's something very different. But I'd never have expected to find it here in the Canadian Arctic.

"I believe it might be a fumarole," I say.

"What's that?"

"A smoke hole found in volcanic regions. Gases stream up and out from them."

"This is not a volcanic area." Anuaktak's father sets me straight.

That's correct. That's why I'm so astounded. The Ilungilak Crater isn't a volcanic crater. It was created by a meteorite that fell to earth.

"There are fumaroles in northern British Columbia," I explain. "They're mostly in very remote locations; that's why almost nobody sees them."

My youngest brother gave me an article about fumaroles, which I read years ago. He teased me with it. He said: "I'll give you a murderer you've never, ever heard of." And then he showed me parts of the article he'd emphasized with a marker. I remember them well: *. . . a silent and invisible murderer . . . maybe Canada's most lethal geological phenomenon . . .*

It became a running gag for us. Whenever I was after an unidentified murderer, he'd joke: "Well, if that's not a fumarole, what is?"

"The First Nations in British Columbia call them 'the guts.'" I'd barely spoken the word when I remembered the Fish's words: *Your life ends in its guts.*

Now nothing can stop me. I barge ahead. Warning shouts behind me penetrate the cold air. But I can't do what the men want. I've got to get to the ice pillar. I must.

Despite my ankle injury, I gasp my way up the slope and then go across to the ice formation. I can hardly make progress, but every step brings me closer; that's all that counts. I hear crackling steps somewhere below, but I ignore them. I must get there.

A scuffling noise. Then a curse. Somebody must have fallen. I don't look back. Climb some more. My regular jogging pays off, but the ice-cold air hurts my lungs. Along with a pain in my ankle. I can't give it a moment's thought.

The ice pillar's coming closer.

I double my efforts. Once, I almost fall over and manage to catch myself at the last second. Suppose I get a foot caught in a rocky crevice? What then? I can't think about it.

Now I understand why Gerald left his camera bag behind. It would have slowed him down. And it also marked the spot where he'd have to go downhill.

The ice tower is so close. I suddenly slip and land on my rear end. I try to get up, but my smooth gloves can't grab on to anything, I take them off and claw my way with my bare hands firmly in the snow. Blood clings to my scratched hands but I want to go on.

A bit above me I suddenly see a figure. Anuaktak.

I scream: "Don't go on! Don't go on! It's too dangerous!"

As it is for me too. Nevertheless, I stumble ahead toward the ice pillar.

Then I smell something, despite my stuffed nose. Sulphur! I can't smell the other gases.

The silent murderer.

I stop and stand, breathing heavily.

With the little air I have left, I shout again: "Don't go any closer! There are deadly gases!"

Anuaktak replies: "You shouldn't be here either. We're going back."

The ice pillar is somewhat higher up from where we are. Looking at the front, nothing indicates an opening.

What's at the back side?

"I want to take a quick look at the other side, then I'll come back. You stay here."

I take a deep breath, press a glove against my mouth and nose, and go around the pillar.

Something dark in the snow.

I stumble backward in horror.

A backpack on the edge of a partly covered crevice in the rocks.

I recognize it. It's Gerald's.

Broken sunglasses.

A scream pierces the quiet ice.

It comes from me.

71

Detective Sergeant Calista Gates
Ilungilak Crater, Labrador
Sunday, February 18

I want to stay at the ice pillar, but I can't expose myself to the deadly gases. Anuaktak guides me back to the snowmobiles.

The looks of the men from Alliarkuk are worried. Though they're afraid of the evil spirit in the lake, they didn't hold Anuaktak back when he followed me. They can certainly tell by the way we look how serious the situation is.

I speak with difficulty, as if a solid mass were in my throat.

"Gerald's backpack is up there. He must have slipped into the crevice behind the pillar. We need people with gas masks to lift him out."

What I can't bring myself to say: we must recover his body.

I've lost Gerald forever.

The thought is unbearable.

Only one important mission keeps me standing upright: I must see to it that his parents can bury their son.

"Would you please take me to the Cloud Lake cabins?"

They nod.

As if in a trance, I climb up on the snowmobile behind Anuaktak's father.

I can't say how long it takes us to reach the cabins. I'm numb.

As we arrive, two men emerge from one of the huts.

"Are you with Search and Rescue?" I ask.

They confirm it but don't recognize me right off. I fill them in with a few words.

The men stare at me.

"Are you sure?" one of them gasps, as if I'd told him a ghost story.

"Yes, please hurry. We need gas masks."

They bring me and my companions into the cabin.

Inside, a man and a woman in police uniform are seated at a table.

"Sergeant Gates, what are *you* doing here?"

They're new colleagues from Happy Valley-Goose Bay. I don't recall their names. They look at me as if seeing a phantom. They obviously hadn't expected to find me here. How ironic. The men from Alliarkuk knew about me but not the police.

It takes great effort to take off my gloves; the blood on my hands sticks to the lining.

"I believe I've found Gerald Hynes."

"You *believe*? Where is he?"

I repeat what's happened.

"We'll go up there first and check it before we make a plan."

I warn them immediately: "It's deadly without gas masks, believe me. The gases can kill you in no time."

"What kind of gases?" the policewoman asks.

"Mainly carbon dioxide." I think about how much I should explain, my colleagues have to be persuaded that they must proceed with caution. "The gases come from deep in the Earth where there's volcanic activity. They melt the snow, making steam in the process that freezes and often forms a pillar of ice."

I'd never have dreamed my brother's newspaper article would one day be vital for survival.

"Up here? But that's an inukshuk covered in ice. We've seen it."

"No, believe me, it's not that. It's a fumarole."

The other RCMP colleague is skeptical as well. "Nobody's ever mentioned anything like that." He turns to the Alliarkuk people.

"I smelled sulphur," Anuaktak says.

"Sulphur, like from the devil?"

The policewoman would like to grin but doesn't quite dare to, seeing my serious expression.

"Sulphur that's often emitted from fumaroles."

I'd expected some resistance. Most people have never heard of fumaroles. I only know about them thanks to my brother, who used to tease me. Something else crosses my mind that I read in the article he showed me.

"Carbon dioxide is the deadliest gas fumaroles emit. About twenty years ago members of a ski patrol on Mammoth Mountain in California fell through the snow in a dip in the terrain near a fumarole. So much carbon dioxide had collected there that they all suffocated."

A man from Search and Rescue speaks up immediately. "Like that farmer in Ontario. My cousin's neighbor. He climbed into a manure pit because a valve or something got stuck. Then he lost consciousness because of the gases in there. His wife tried to help him, climbed into the pit, and fainted as well."

I feel my patience nearing its end. My ankle's throbbing, but it could be worse.

"It's already starting to get dark. We ought to hurry."

"We're on it," the policewoman decides. "Where do we get gas masks?"

No problem for the man from Search and Rescue.

"We've got full-face respirators. They'll last forty-five minutes."

Luckily, my RCMP colleagues haven't thought to inform inspector Peter Allen. Or they don't want to involve him yet in case this is all a farce; they don't want egg all over their face.

I'm happy because otherwise I might have been excluded from the recovery effort.

Nobody says we ought to wait until tomorrow. Search and Rescue are prepared to operate in the dark as well. We still have a little daylight, but not much.

The men from Alliarkuk are ready to show us the way to the ice pillar again. A column of snowmobiles starts out. I keep my feelings under wraps. As a cop I know it's bad enough to find a body. But it's even worse not to know what's happened to a missing person.

Daylight is already very low when we come to the foot of the crater again. Isolated snowflakes are still falling from the gray-white sky; it's a soft, white dance. The column follows the still-visible tracks of our first trip.

Anuaktak's father stops, and we all follow suit. The ice pillar is only visible in outline.

I see a Search and Rescue man bringing along a body bag. Most of them have crampons on their boots. I'm given a pair and a headlamp. The climb goes more slowly this time because these people are more cautious than I was earlier.

As we near the ice pillar, I can smell sulphur again. It's time to put on our masks. The policewoman films the ghostly scene. Two rescue men go around the pillar. I approach it in their wake. The backpack's still there, somewhat whiter than before. The men shine their flashlights into the partly snowed-in crevice and wipe away a layer of snow. Then they shine it in again.

I'm glued to their every movement.

Shapes become visible.

A ski jacket. Legs. A body's hanging halfway into the fissure.

"We've got him," somebody says.

A camera clicks repeatedly.

The men tie a rope around the body and pull it up. My

colleague continues to film the scene. She knows what's to be done.

Finally, the stiff body emerges. The frozen limbs are slightly twisted.

Even before they turn him over on his back, I know it's Gerald.

His face looks peaceful. The gases put him to sleep without him knowing. He died without fear, without pain.

To see him like this is overpowering but I don't want to collapse in front of my colleagues. I've had a feeling for days he's no longer alive. To see him here before me, dead, to know that he'll never come back, that I'll never again hear his voice, feel his touch—knowing this drives a knife into my heart.

I crouch down beside him. But I mustn't hold him. Or stroke his face. The body will be examined to determine the cause of death. I begin to shake.

Suddenly a shout of surprise from one of the rescuers.

"There are more bodies down there!"

72

Detective Sergeant Calista Gates
Ilungilak Crater, Labrador
Sunday, February 18

The flashlight beams latch onto a red windbreaker.

Red. Blue. Orange. Yellow. The jacket colors of the missing women.

Paige Warner, the entrepreneur, wore red.

Gerald's body must have melted the snow on her when he was still warm and covering her. Everything else is white from the flashlights above.

I'm forced to correct my assumption at once.

"Hynes must have wiped off the snow from the red jacket," a rescuer speculates, "before the gases knocked him out."

So Gerald had discovered something in the crevice that made him investigate it. Did he have any suspicion about what he could find?

"Look over there! A piece of yellow material!" the Happy Valley-Goose Bay colleague shouts. "Looks like a backpack cover."

She has a sharp eye. Now I see it. Yellow. This means another dead woman might be lying in the crevice.

"Forensics has to get here before we do anything," the RCMP man decides.

The correct decision in this situation. I'm feeling more confident about my new colleagues.

"And the body?" the man from Search and Rescue asks.

Please don't leave him here, I beg silently. Please don't leave Gerald alone in the cold and dark.

"We'll take him with us."

I could weep with gratitude, but my tears would freeze. I must make the tricky climb down to the snowmobile successfully.

There's hustle and bustle in the Cloud Lake cabin. Inspector Allen is informed immediately. Events are coming at him thick and fast. First the Delgado and Sullivan business. Then Gerald's body is found. And now probably two female corpses. I can imagine, despite my brain fog, that it's rather frantic in his office right now. Questions must be cleared up: how and when the bodies will be recovered. When Gerald's body will be transported to Happy Valley-Goose Bay. When the media will be informed. I understand that Peter Allen doesn't want to sit on that for too long in order to nip any rumors in the bud. He's announced that he'll be sending out a press release at two o'clock tomorrow, with a press conference to follow in a few days. Surely the inspector wants Gerald's parents to receive the terrible news beforehand. I'm not allowed to contact them until after the RCMP goes to their house in person. Gerald's brother at the least must be with them when they are told—I drummed that into my colleagues.

Everybody will know by tomorrow at two that I was the one

who led my colleagues from Happy Valley-Goose Bay to Gerald's icy grave.

"People will wonder how you knew where to find Mr. Hynes," the policewoman warns me. "They'll also wonder what your position is here."

I didn't *know* where Gerald was, of course, and my colleague wouldn't seriously suggest that. She's trying to prepare me for the rumors and speculation. A joint statement must be drawn up. It's ultimately a matter of protecting the RCMP.

I've got urgent questions too that are crying out for answers. Why didn't the police search the very spot where I found Gerald? Why didn't the ice pillar attract any attention when it's such a prominent feature in the landscape? It can easily be spotted from a helicopter. The search parties should definitely have looked there. I don't get it. The ice pillar doesn't exist in summer, only in winter, when the temperature falls below freezing. Now, in winter, it was evidently taken for an iced-over inukshuk. Nobody could know what a fumarole is because it hasn't been documented in this region. There are some in the Antarctic, but it's a geological phenomenon unknown in Labrador.

Until now.

The policewoman couldn't answer my questions. Instead, she grilled me about every detail regarding my activities since coming to Ilungilak. She'll interrogate the men from Alliarkuk as well. Those poor guys. They've walked into a whirlwind of events.

I repress my grief with all my strength. It's as if a voice is whispering to me: you can't give in to your emotions now, Calista, you've got to wind up pressing business beforehand.

Gerald's body is laid out in the third—unheated—cabin. My thoughts turn to his parents. Who will inform them? And when? It's important they hear it from the police and not the media. Gerald's brother will have to care for them from now on.

I'd like to be alone with Gerald, just for a few minutes. But police protocol doesn't permit it.

My colleagues empathize with me; at the same time, they're under pressure. They mustn't make any mistakes.

I must call Fred.

The colleagues confer. They want to ask Peter Allen first, inexperienced as they are. Good heavens, they can't supervise me all the time. I'm a witness, nothing more. In the end they agree.

I dress warmly and leave the cabin, satellite phone in hand. I expected pitch blackness, but now there are will o' the wisps all over the sky. Aurora borealis. Green and yellow shimmering northern lights, dancing, flashing. A light show against a black background.

I stay on the spot, entranced, observing the spectacle. The fog has lifted completely, and there's no more snowfall! How fast the weather can change at this latitude. Is it Gerald, giving me a sign? We once watched the northern lights together in Labrador. He'd seen them so often, but they were new to me. He was delighted by my amazement. He was often delighted by me, and I by him.

The cold yanks me back to reality. It's biting in my face but also drains the phone's battery faster.

Fred's on the line immediately. He's probably been waiting all evening for my call.

Hearing his voice brings tears to my eyes. They freeze to my eyelashes.

"What's up, sarge?"

He only calls me sarge when there are people around. He's not alone.

"I've got some sensitive information for you."

He understands and finds a suitable spot somewhere.

"Mick Hudson came to the station. I'll tell you later why."

I say: "We found Gerald. He's dead."

Silence. Then: "Calista, I . . . I don't know what to say."

Fred's not one to simply offer his sincere condolences. He really does not know what to say.

"Who found him? You, Calista?"

I haven't got much time. My hands are getting numb. I say in a few words what's happened.

"There are more bodies in the crevice. I believe they're the missing women."

"How many?"

"Probably two. Could be more."

"Calista, I think I've got some evidence that the fourth woman's still alive."

"What? How?"

"The Toronto journalist sent me pictures. One is of a certain Fiona Gelp, who was acquitted of killing in self-defense in Amherstburg. That was over ten years ago. The second photo is of her sister, Ann Price, who vacationed at Remote Point Lodge before the women disappeared eight years ago. She was there at least twice—Heidy dug that up by going through old pictures on social media."

"And?" I'm pushing him. I'm afraid my fingers will fall off and the battery will die.

"Ann Price, the sister, she looks a lot like Kellyann Mercer."

"Oh, my God!"

"Fiona Gelp doesn't remind me of anyone, unfortunately."

"And Heidy doesn't recognize her?"

"No. But a crazy idea came into my head."

"Yes?"

"Fiona Gelp could be the fourth missing woman."

"What gives you that idea?"

"If Kellyann Mercer is Ann Price, then she was familiar with Remote Point Lodge."

"Yes, but . . ."

"And her sister Fiona was apparently in St. Anthony a year later and sent her grandma a postcard from there."

I'm getting colder. I can't think straight. The shock over Gerald's death feels like a frozen face mask. But Fred's on the ball.

"When are you coming back, Calista?"

73

Detective Sergeant Calista Gates
Ilungilak Crater, Labrador
Monday, February 19

Inspector Allen watches me put some firewood into the stove.

We're in the smaller cabin where I spent the night but hardly slept a wink; the RCMP colleague and a woman from Search and Rescue slept in the other bunks in the room. They'd helped me out with toiletries, since I'd left most of my things in the cabin at the airstrip.

I'm amazed I can have even one clear thought because since I was assaulted my injured brain needs huge amounts of sleep. I want to get back to St. Anthony as soon as possible, but this morning, I was informed Peter Allen was flying up and wanted to talk to me. He already arrived at eleven by Cessna, but first went with the forensics team to the ice pillar.

I wasn't allowed to go with them—Allen's orders. He condemned me to twiddling my thumbs while terrible thoughts tortured me. My Happy Valley-Goose Bay colleagues kept a watchful eye on me the whole time, which didn't escape me.

Peter Allen should be happy that the weather didn't put a

crimp in his plans. Weather conditions aren't ideal—cloud cover has been building—but the wind is moderate and there's no snow. He hasn't told me anything about the investigation of the ice pillar so far. I sit down opposite him on one of the boxes that probably contain things intended for the politicians and their entourage.

He's sitting on a rough-hewn chair.

"Detective Sergeant, I'd like to express my deepest sympathy" are his opening words. "It must be a very painful loss for you."

He catches me off-guard. No one here has expressed sympathy so far. They were probably as floored by events as I was.

"Thank you, inspector," I reply because I don't know how else to respond. I'm determined to carefully conceal any sign of weakness that he might take advantage of. If he wanted to.

Allen changes the subject quickly. He asks to hear again exactly what happened yesterday.

I struggle with my concentration, but the events are so deeply burned into my memory that I can recall them one after the other. When I look at Allen's face more closely, I discern the same traces of exhaustion I know are in mine.

He conducts our conversation with no witnesses present. He doesn't record it either. The policewoman did that yesterday. The inspector has as much at stake in this as I do. He must have mixed feelings about me. The discovery of the corpses at the ice pillar will divert public attention from the corrupt scoundrels Delgado and Sullivan. The inspector surely can't object to that. But sooner or later somebody will ask if Sullivan had anything to do with Gerald's disappearance.

After twenty minutes, there is a pause in the conversation.

The wood crackles in the stove, and we hear snatches of voices as if from far away.

Now he's coming to a decision. Should he make me his

antagonist, or does he need me to be favorably disposed toward him?

He crosses his arms and leans back. For a police inspector, he has rather transparent body language.

"Sergeant Gates, we'll make every effort to get to the bottom of the shootings in St. Anthony."

I'm wary.

"We? I've been informed that the special investigators are dealing with it."

"What I mean to say is I will be cooperative. I will not protect any criminals, even if they are my subordinates."

That's a white flag of peace.

But not one that puts an end to all the problems. Maybe Peter Allen won't shove any obstacles in the investigators' way, but Sullivan and Delgado most definitely will.

The inspector clears his throat.

"I hope you understand that I nevertheless must clear up some things with you. I'll be brief."

I'm waiting.

"It was not part of our agreement for you to come here, sergeant."

I was ready for this rebuke.

"I told you it concerned the Nielle Helfrey case and that was why I had to come to Labrador. I was at the Remote Point Lodge because I suspect Kellyann Mercer was the one who attacked Ms. Helfrey."

Surprise is evident all over his face.

"Is that true?"

"She was in St. Anthony in the days around the assault and even kept that from her husband. She was in the hospital for the ear doctor and was seen in the waiting room. She was also seen talking to a seniors' caregiver, Vyann Kippen, who denied that fact. Kellyann would also seem to have a motive."

"Which is?"

I don't really have to tell him because he's not my boss, but I'm going to need his help later.

So I let him know: "Kellyann and Vyann believe that Nielle told her lover, Morris Tye, that Noshi Mercer was selling caribou meat illegally. Mr. Tye apparently sicced the wildlife officers on him. It was an act of revenge."

As I see it, both wanted revenge: Morris Tye, because the Mercers didn't want to sell the lodge to his brother-in-law, and Kellyann, because Tye got her husband into real trouble.

"Has Mrs. Mercer confessed?"

"No, she'll only talk to us through her lawyer, which is really peculiar."

"What evidence do you have that it was Mrs. Mercer?"

"I'm certain the forensics team from Corner Brook have confirmed it was her boot prints in the snow and that there were traces of her on Nielle's Ski-Doo because Kellyann took the victim to Goose Cove on it."

"Well, then, good luck, sergeant."

The way he reacts to my account indicates to me that he doesn't want any friction between us. I think he doesn't have anything against my being in Ilungilak; I could just as well be here as Gerald's partner, which is absolutely legitimate. The inspector however wants a plausible justification for the public.

"Something else," I say. "It might be that the missing women case is connected to my case in St. Anthony."

"The assault on Nielle Helfrey?"

"I think it could be connected to Kellyann Mercer. That's something I'd ask you to please treat as confidential. Can you tell me how many bodies were found in the crevice?"

He thought for a moment and then said: "Three, not counting Mr. Hynes."

"Three of the missing women?"

"It seems so for now." He hesitates again before confiding to me: "Unfortunately, we didn't recover any of the women's backpacks."

"The backpacks weren't there? Where are they?"

"That's what I'd like to know too. What do you think happened there, sergeant?"

I don't need to think for long.

"Probably one of the women fainted and fell into the fissure. The others tried to save her, and the gases overpowered and killed them one after the other. It can happen very fast."

"Do you think that's what happened to Mr. Hynes as well?"

"Yes."

"Did he know about the fumarole?"

"Difficult to say. I don't think anybody knew about it except the Inuit, but for them it was a mythological phenomenon and not a geological anomaly." I tell him about the evil spirit in Crater Lake that kills people and swallows them up.

Your life ends in its guts.

Peter Allen strokes his chin. "There were no witnesses or reports back then that the women were at Crater Lake. My predecessor was convinced that they did not hike to the crater."

I think that over.

"Maybe they *were* seen by somebody. The backpacks might have been stolen. Tents, cooking utensils, pocketknives, emergency transmitters and other equipment—that's all worth something. And the thief didn't want to blow his cover."

I still have Fred's words from yesterday ringing in my ears. *The fourth woman.*

Should I tell the inspector?

I decide to do it because now's not the time for playing games like hide-and-seek.

"We're investigating a possible scenario where the fourth woman is still alive. There might be evidence linking her to St. Anthony."

74

Paige Warner, Entrepreneur
In Ilungilak, Labrador
Eight Years Earlier

She plants her foot carefully, slips, and sinks at once into the boggy ground. This is not how she imagined the tundra would be: wet and unstable, full of sodden islands of grass that don't provide footing. The rocks beneath the surface knock her off balance. It's no different with Ellen and Carla. Paige can hear their cries of frustration. They're all splattered with mud and near tears. They're wearing waterproof boots, but the pools of water are deep and muddy. The splatter will probably look good in photos and videos, they'll look adventurous.

But right now, they would all have to force themselves to smile for the camera.

The mosquitoes are the worst. The women defend themselves with netting, but every time they try to drink or relieve themselves, the bloodsuckers make a dash for any exposed skin. If just a few of them are able to crawl under the net, all hell breaks loose.

At least it's no longer as hot as it was a few hours before.

Aren't they in the subarctic, goddammit? Paige reminds the others that rain and cold would be worse, but she's not so sure about that at times.

She can see the Ilungilak Crater through binoculars at last. But between them lies a seemingly endless plain. Theoretically, she thinks, they should have arrived at the foot of the crater ages ago.

"How much longer?" whines Ellen, who at every stop throws her backpack down on the ground like a sack of potatoes, a burden she'd probably like to be rid of forever.

"Two hours," Paige replies. She hasn't a clue how many hours it will actually take, but she knows it's better to say something false than nothing at all. People must be able to orient themselves with *something* in times of uncertainty.

Carla, who's not as agile as Ellen and Paige, and who is lugging a heavy camera, is holding up amazingly well. Paige believes Carla's mentally stronger than Ellen. Perhaps it comes from her working in a veterinary clinic.

The responsibility for this adventure does not rest on Carla's shoulders, to be sure. That's something for Paige to cope with.

She wonders why they haven't seen Sandy anywhere. Their gaze roams freely over the flat tundra. Paige has scanned the surrounding area with her binoculars time and again. She should have spotted that orange jacket long ago. Sandy can't have that much of a head start. Yes, she's the most athletic of them, but she can't make good time on the boggy tundra either. It's just as unlikely that she's gone off in a different direction.

Paige nevertheless uses Sandy as an excuse to push her little group onward. She shouts: "Our timing's good. Sandy will be amazed. We'll show her what we think of traitors."

Her words have a rapid effect. Two hours are long but doable. There's light at the end of the tunnel.

They're tired after a few kilometers, but Crater Lake has come much closer. That spurs the women on. Soon they'll have done it! Ellen falls once, but she's not hurt. That's Paige's nightmare: a sprained ankle or a broken arm. What would they do without a satellite phone or an emergency transmitter? Sandy's going to pay for this. Paige knows many ways to punish disloyal people. Not through public scandal. That would be bad for her company's image. No, unseen and anonymously, naturally.

On the other hand, she feels a growing admiration for Ellen and Carla. How swiftly an extreme experience like this one can bond people together!

The final kilometers push them to the limits of their strength. But when they finally reach the foot of the crater, they shout for joy and hug one another. A triumph that tastes delicious despite all their toil. They sit down on some boulders still warm from the sun. But the air has turned pleasantly cool and the circling mosquitoes are not as thick and aggressive anymore. They take off their nets and spray themselves. Too exhausted to take off their sweaty clothes, they keep warm with their windbreakers.

"I'm so proud of us," Ellen exclaims.

"And I'm even more so," Carla responds.

You wouldn't be here without me, Paige thinks. You would have given up long ago. But she would never say this out loud.

"You are the best," she praises them instead and looks around. She discovers a dry spot. "We can put the tents up here."

"The sunlight right now would be perfect for photos." Carla looks up at the crater's rim. "Who knows what the weather will be like tomorrow?"

"It's too far to the lake for today. And we'd have to come back down as well. We don't want to try to find our way in the dark." Paige can't wait to climb up to the lake. How rewarding that will be!

Where the hell is Sandy?

Ellen asks: "Do you two think Sandy's already up there?"

Paige shakes her head.

"We would have seen her for sure."

"Maybe she climbed up from the other side."

"Even then, we would have seen her from the plain."

"What's that up there?" Carla points to the east, where a little rise has caught her eye.

Paige picks up her binoculars.

"An inukshuk, but it's fallen apart."

"Does it show the way to the lake?"

"Probably." Paige wants to get going with the tents.

"We could at least climb to the inukshuk," Carla says.

"For heaven's sake, Carla, aren't you tired?" Ellen shakes her head.

"This is a once-in-a-lifetime experience. We've got to make the most of it."

Paige thinks. If Sandy came through here, maybe she followed this Inuit signpost. Maybe she left her backpack there, because she certainly wouldn't have climbed up the crater with the tent and her very heavy equipment.

"Okay, let's do it before dark," she says. "It's really not far. Ellen, will you watch our backpacks?"

Ellen shrugs. "We can just as well leave them here. Nobody's going to steal them. Besides, we can still keep an eye on them from up there."

Carla hesitates. "We shouldn't risk it. We don't know where Sandy's roaming around. She's already made off with the emergency transmitters and the satellite phone."

Paige doesn't want Carla to panic. It's not worth it. "We'll stick them behind the rocks where nobody can see them."

They shove the backpacks into the space between two huge boulders they can easily recognize when they come back. Problem solved.

What Paige didn't think possible just half an hour ago is now happening: they're climbing diagonally over boulders up the slope. Footing on the rocks is more secure than on the sodden subsoil of the tundra. They just have to pay attention when crossing crevices. Everything's easier without the burden of backpacks.

They still haven't gotten to the collapsed inukshuk after fifteen minutes when Ellen shouts: "It smells like sulphur here. Do you smell it too?"

Carla, who's juggling her camera, stops.

"Yes, like at the hot springs in Italy. Come on, let's go see if there's a sulphur spring."

"Girls, we're not in Italy. We're in the subarctic."

Paige sits down on a boulder. She doesn't want to show how exhausted she is. Tomorrow's climb will be a test of her character that already scares her.

"I'm going to take in the view. Sulphur baths make me feel sick." The last sentence is meant as a joke, but Carla and Ellen are serious.

Oh, what the hell. Let them go.

She drinks greedily from her water bottle. The voices of the others grow more distant. They're moving first in the direction of the inukshuk but later more to the east. Paige's thoughts revolve around Sandy. She picks up her binoculars again.

Suddenly she hears shouts.

"Carla! Carla!"

A scream of fright.

Then a terribly long, drawn-out "Paige!"

And then nothing.

Paige hurries uphill and climbs, breathing heavily, to the right, where she last saw Carla and Ellen.

What's happened? A wild animal?

Why doesn't she hear anything from them?

"Ellen?" she gasps. She hasn't the breath to shout.

The smell of sulphur is getting stronger. She takes a handkerchief out of her jacket pocket and presses it to her nose.

She stumbles forward as fast as she can.

Suddenly, a yawning crevice in the rock stands open before her. She can just barely catch herself.

Down in the fissure, she can see Ellen's blue windbreaker and the yellow of Carla's jacket.

"Ellen? Carla?"

The bodies aren't moving.

Paige feels dizzy. The smell of sulphur is overpowering. She instinctively moves back from the crevice. She can breathe again.

"Ellen! Answer me! Carla!" she screams as loud as she can. Again and again.

Not a sound from the crevice.

Her mind's racing.

And then she freezes.

She knows—deep down she knows—it's too late.

Everything's too late.

Ellen and Carla are unconscious.

And they'll be dead before help comes. They're probably dead already.

Falling into the crevice didn't kill them. It's not deep enough to do that.

It's the gas.

Paige knows that.

Two dozen pigs on her parents' farm died in their pen, poisoned by hydrogen sulfide from the cesspool.

Her parents were lucky. Their farmhand turned back in time when he smelled the gas. Or he might have been killed too.

She drops down onto a rock.

What is she to do?

Her dream's exploded. Her triumph has turned into a nightmare.

Two dead women. Another one disappeared. Everything is her responsibility. Her fault.

A catastrophe.

They're not supposed to be here at all. Not at Crater Lake.

Her reputation's ruined. It will be the end of the company.

It will be the end of successful entrepreneur Paige Warner.

The families will sue her.

An unbearable thought.

She sits on the rock, transfixed, Crater Lake at her back, the vastness of the tundra below.

The sun is setting. It will be dark soon.

She stands up.

There's only one road to take.

It's quick and easy.

She shoves her handkerchief into her jacket pocket.

Approaches the crevice. Stands at the edge.

She bends forward and inhales deeply.

75

Fred van Heisen, RCMP Constable
St. Anthony, Newfoundland
Tuesday, February 20

Passengers are streaming through the glass door into the small airport building. Fred's stretched to the breaking point. Calista will appear at any moment. But which Calista? In what state?

She found Gerald dead.

And he has only bad news for her. No consolation.

He didn't want to tell her over the phone; he prefers to be with her when she hears it.

There she is. She's wearing a colorful headband instead of a cap. A ponytail instead of the bun.

She spots him and raises a hand in greeting before she picks up her backpack. He walks over to help her carry it.

While he was waiting, he'd thought about what he'd say to her. The words for bridging the unspeakable.

But he can't get a single word out. Instead, she hugs him for several seconds.

They are his best seconds in a long time. He presses her to himself with both arms.

They separate quickly because people are stopping. Naturally. It's the St. Anthony airport.

"We'll talk in the car," Calista says. But she's silent for the first few minutes.

He waits. They spot a caribou herd from the highway.

Calista seems composed, although he caught sight of tears in her eyes when he took her backpack. Sadness can present as numbness; he knows that from experience. Or as a strange calm. Nothing can frighten a mourning person; they've already experienced the worst; all else is trivial.

She turns a pale face toward him.

"What have I missed?"

No sense trying to fool her. She wants to work because it helps her go on living. He'd feel exactly the same way.

"Nielle Helfrey doesn't want her case to be investigated any longer. Her mother called me with the news. Nielle says she might have had an accident on the Ski-Doo."

"Oh, really? And who's the person who took her to Goose Cove and dumped her in the snow when she was injured?"

"Nielle doesn't want to talk to us anymore."

"Well, that takes the cake! By the way, I've got a glass that Kellyann Mercer drank out of. All set for testing. And now this."

"That's not the whole story," he says. "The special investigators arrived at the Haven Inn today. We're meeting them right now at the station."

"Wow. They're going at top speed. Is Delgado still in the hospital?"

"Yes, though they normally always kick patients out unbelievably fast. I think the doctors don't want to run any risks because he's RCMP."

"Good. We're not responsible for Delgado now. What was the reaction to Inspector Allen's press release?"

"We're getting a lot of inquiries from reporters about the discovery at Crater Lake. They don't understand why you haven't made a statement since you were up there at the time. I keep referring them to the colleagues in Happy Valley-Goose Bay, of course."

"Is Mick Hudson still hanging around?"

"Yes, he wants info from us, especially now that the missing women are everywhere in the media. Martha Calambaro from Toronto is nearly ballistic because she's afraid of losing the scoop."

"Can I see the pictures she sent you?"

"In the glove compartment."

She retrieves the copies and says at once: "Kellyann is Ann Price, that's for sure. You can see it very well, though it's a rather old photo." She looks at the second picture. "And this is supposed to be Fiona Gelp?"

"Have you ever met her?"

Calista shakes her head thoughtfully.

"Maybe Fiona Gelp visited her sister and was staying for a little while in St. Anthony when she sent the birthday card to her grandma."

"Calista, don't you think Fiona might be one of the four missing women?"

She nods, to his surprise.

"It's not entirely farfetched. There were only three female bodies found. So, where's the fourth? Did she get lost? Break off from the group?"

"Did somebody kidnap her?" he adds.

"Or did she begin a new life somewhere and lead everybody to believe she died in the wilderness? Her sister, Ann Price, alias Kellyann Mercer, never filed a missing person's report."

"Nobody else seems to know where Fiona got to after Joe Salomon's death was tried," he says. "Martha Calambaro thinks she's living anonymously somewhere abroad."

"That's also possible."

Calista studies Fiona Gelp's photo with knitted eyebrows.

"We ought to interrogate Kellyann Mercer," he suggests.

"We? Inspector Allen would object to that. His nose was already out of joint because I showed up in Ilungilak."

"But you solved a high-profile case for him, and he waltzes off with all the credit. He can bask in it. Isn't he a happy camper?"

"He's got a lot of new, tricky issues to clear up. Delgado and Sullivan will make life difficult for him with all their scheming."

They're doing that to us too, Fred thinks. They and the special investigators.

76

Anuaktak's Uncle
Ilungilak Crater, Labrador
Tuesday, February 20

He knew it. When the policewoman ignored his warning and lurched her way up to the ice pillar, he was dead sure.

The spirit of Crater Lake has spoken. It has defended the lake against the intruders.

The policewoman and Anuaktak almost stumbled into the spirit's mouth. But she saw the danger in time and warned Anuaktak. The evil spirit showed forgiveness toward her. It's a whimsical spirit.

Now people are up there with gas masks, recovering the bodies. Better to leave the victims in the crevice, in the guts. They belong to the spirit of Crater Lake. Disaster won't be long in coming.

Maybe they'll finally listen to the people who've ranged over this land for thousands of years. They move from their summer pastures in the north to the forests in the south. People must not disturb animals, nature, rocks, water. Caribou herds need this unpopulated vastness. And the people of Alliarkuk, Tulliq, and Sivinganik need the caribou. Since time immemorial.

The women thought nobody saw them. They thought they could simply march in here without asking. They tried to deceive everybody: Noshi and Vyann, Vernon Lindental—but mainly the Indigenous guardians of Crater Lake.

What were we to do? the guardians asked. Chase them away? Strike fear into their hearts? Send them back?

The women didn't belong here. They were arrogant, presumptuous; they showed no respect for the people who have hunted and picked berries in this region for generations.

Leave it be, he'd said. The spirit of the lake will put it in order.

His sons and nephews protested. His daughters and nieces too. We can't wait that long, they said. By then the women will be at the sacred lake.

Patience, patience. The spirit of the lake will put it in order. He said it time and again.

And so it came about.

They watched the women climb up to the inukshuk. But before they reached their destination, they turned off in another direction. They never came back. The spirit swallowed up their backpacks also.

And everybody kept silent.

One woman went off from the party. She did not want to go to Crater Lake. She hiked to Okak Bay on the east coast. She had helpers. A stranger would never find the bay by herself. A boat took her to Tulliq and farther down the coast from there. She'd never have made it on her own.

Not a soul knows where she is now. Not even her helpers.

Nobody will ever say a word about what took place.

His people know how to protect themselves. Protect the lake, and the caribou.

Gerald Hynes bet on the wrong horse. He did not believe in the evil spirit and paid the price.

Will the lodge still be built? After all that's happened?
He doesn't know.
He leaves the answer to the spirit in the lake.

77

Detective Sergeant Calista Gates
St. Anthony, Newfoundland
Tuesday, February 20

The special investigators are well over fifty. Probably close to retirement. A woman and a man. The woman is a sergeant, the man a superintendent. The hierarchy is thereby established. A question arises in my mind: When will there be more women in the upper ranks of the RCMP, as Commissioner Jill Perrier promised in her inaugural speech?

The investigators have introduced themselves, and then the superintendent says in the conference room: "Sergeant Gates, I'd like to have a brief word with you alone, with your permission."

I'd like to reply: "Can't we do that here with these people present?" Particularly Heidy and Dustin shouldn't think I'll say things about them behind their back.

When the superintendent notices that I'm hesitant, he adds: "It's about some administrative issues."

I can't refuse, I must appear cooperative. So, I take him to my small office. I smell smoke at once. Somebody has authorized a cigarette in there. It was probably for that petty drug dealer, Reginald Goode, when Fred questioned him. Reggie, our key witness in the Stolke case and the entanglement with Frank Delgado.

We take a seat, me behind the desk, he in front of it. The order of seating is determined by the constriction of the room. His face is pleasant, almost fatherly, but I mustn't let it deceive me.

"Sergeant, if circumstances were different, I'd be congratulating you. Thanks to you, the families of the deceased in the Ilungilak Crater will no longer live in uncertainty. I'm aware of what a tragedy it is for you personally. I'd like not to make the situation even more difficult for you, nevertheless . . ."

I interrupt because I cannot speak about Gerald's death at this minute. It's too painful.

"Superintendent, have you spoken with Constable Delgado?"

"Yes, we saw him in the hospital. Sergeant Gates, during our inquiry, I will not be telling you anything concerning our conversations with him. You will surely understand. It's important for me to have everything proceed correctly so we can conclude this business quickly. That is also certainly in your interest as well, is it not?"

"Will the results of your inquiry be made public?"

"That's not for me to decide; my superiors will. But what I can tell you is: I will give it my best."

I can't defend myself against the inquiry; I can't obstruct it; I must comply. As I see it, Frank Delgado has a bad hand to play. But will the special investigators see it that way? It's absolutely futile for us to go up against them.

My fingers twitch, so I interlock them and say: "If there's anything we can do to make your work easier, please let me know."

He presses his lips together briefly before answering: "There *is* something that will make our task easier, Sergeant

Gates. We would like to reassign the Nielle Helfrey case elsewhere."

I was afraid of this but I try to stay calm.

"The case is effectively solved. A reassignment would endanger the success of the investigation. Surely nobody would want that."

"We wouldn't want that either, sergeant. We simply don't want anyone to say the investigation was manipulated."

Manipulated. As if I were the perpetrator. As if I had done something incorrectly.

My blood pressure's going up, and I ask: "What do you imagine will happen? Who would wrap up the case? You?"

"No, the RCMP in Happy Valley-Goose Bay."

I stare at him in disbelief. "You're not serious."

"Inspector Allen feels all the threads lead to Labrador. I think it's reasonable that the investigations are concentrated there."

"That means I'm being eliminated?" I'm no longer choosy with my words.

"No, you can take care of other cases, as always."

I'm steaming inside. So, Inspector Peter Allen is *not* biased, unlike me? Despite Delgado and Sullivan? This is getting better and better.

"Superintendent, let's be frank about this. To all outward appearances, the investigations are being taken away from me."

"We do not in any way wish to convey that impression. The investigations will simply be shifted geographically." His voice is emphatic, his eyes are just as penetrating. "Sergeant Gates, I have no choice if I want to conclude this inquiry seriously and without prejudice. As long as you're investigating the Nielle Helfrey and Trent Stolke cases, you are—purely optically—also tied to the events involving Frank Delgado. And optics is sometimes all that matters to the public. We want to keep you out of it, you understand?"

I know what he means. Nielle Helfrey was attacked at the

cabin. Frank Delgado showed up there with a firearm. Presumably Delgado hid Trent's body in the outhouse. I haven't received the forensics report yet—it will still take some time—but they probably secured a lot of good evidence in the woods that points to Delgado. In my opinion, the two cases have nothing to do with each other, but the media will see it differently.

The special investigator draws the proper conclusion. But I'm so furious inside, I could sweep everything off the desk, I could turn the piece upside down. Set everything ablaze.

I can't hide my fury. My facial expression gives me away.

The superintendent leans forward.

"You must trust me, sergeant. I know what I'm doing. I'm already retired. That's why they gave me this assignment. I don't serve any master, only my conscience."

I don't reply for fear of regretting what might come out of my mouth.

There's a loud beep.

The superintendent looks at his cell phone and stands up.

"I must go. We have a search warrant for Delgado's car and his cell phone and so on."

I nod. He's concentrating on Delgado. Not on Fred.

That's a good sign.

I think Delgado ditched Trent Stolke's cell and notebook but wasn't so cautious about his own devices.

I repress my anger with all my strength and stand up.

"I shall inform my team, superintendent."

78

Detective Sergeant Calista Gates
Dominican Republic
Three Weeks Later

I dive into the surf and glide down beneath it. With fierce strokes, I cut through the warm water, only coming up for air.

What a blessing.

The sun glistens so hard I need to squint.

I hear voices from the beach, happy children shouting. Still, I feel far away. I do the crawl out toward the distant horizon.

Aretha normally comes swimming with me for safety reasons, because you mustn't underestimate the ocean. But Ari's chatting with a young man at the beach bar right now, and I was getting hotter and hotter on the deck chair, even in the shade. I waited for her until I couldn't stand it.

Ari has the excuse that she's doing research for her erotic romance novels. She selected this beach resort—all-inclusive—because it was less expensive. I simply went along with her plans, too lethargic to give any input.

My parents and siblings hounded me because I sounded so beleaguered on the phone. They thought I needed to recuperate in the sun in some faraway place. We've been here for two weeks, and I must admit they were right. I've had the feeling for some time now that I can breathe comfortably.

I'm getting tired and swim back to where I left the beach slippers I bought from a vendor who had a portable shop around his waist. The sand's hot even right after breakfast, but the many palms offer shade. The heat. It seems so surreal. Wasn't I just in the icy cold of northern Labrador? Must have been somebody else. Not the Calista walking over to her deck chair dripping wet, drying herself with her terrycloth towel and looking around for her sister.

Ari's still perched at the bar with the same young man. I'd like a fruit drink too but would rather wait. I want to be alone with my thoughts and have no desire for a friendly but banal conversation. Especially no desire for questions. Where are you from? Where do you work? Where's Newfoundland and Labrador? Ah, I remember. The iceberg. The *Titanic*.

I once accidentally overheard Ari explaining to a man who wanted to talk to me that I was a policewoman and just needed to relax. The word *policewoman* had a chilling effect on the man, which suited me just fine.

I stretch and snuggle down on the deck chair and close my eyes. The air smells of sunscreen lotion, salt, and cinnamon. I have some success, for a few moments, in blotting out Crater Lake, Gerald, St. Anthony, and my team from my mind. And the special investigators too, who questioned me thoroughly before my trip and green-lighted my trip.

Fred drove me to the airport. Actually, he needed a break from work, but there's one already planned for May, shortly before he leaves for his new job. We've only got a little time left together. And now even less with my vacation.

I couldn't bring myself to go to Gerald's funeral in Port Brendan, although Heidy offered to go with me. So kind of Heidy. But I wouldn't have been able to deal with the inquisitive faces from the village. Gerald told me once he wished to be cremated and have his ashes scattered over the ocean or the ice. Unfortunately, he'd never made it official in writing, and so his parents had him buried in the cemetery. It's surely a consolation for them to be able to visit his grave.

I went to see them before my trip. Gerald's brother and his wife were there as well; it was heartrending for everybody. As a policewoman, I've experienced again and again how terrible it is for parents when their children die before they do. Meeting Gerald's mother and father churned me up inside. I wish I could have offered them better comfort.

"Lista, I've brought you something." Ari's voice.

I open my eyes.

She's standing before me, suntanned and beaming, with a glass in her hands; the straw's yellow and the drink is blue, with a red blossom floating in it.

"How sweet of you!" I'm delighted.

Aretha and I come from different planets: she creates dramatic stories about love, betrayal, sex, and seduction, and is successful with it. She even had in mind a novel about attractive police agents, about domination and submission, but I've made it crystal clear she should back away from it, as she had confided in me that she'd been inspired by Fred's looks and that she finds him very sexy.

Since Gerald died, these topics have been taboo for us. Aretha doesn't want me to be perpetually sad.

She flops down on the deck chair next to me.

"Good that you're not on the phone for once."

That's a gross exaggeration, but I don't hold the remark against her. I just can't get angry at my little sister. After all, she's brought me my favorite drink: papaya, coconut, and mango, with a spritz of white wine and blue vodka for the color.

It's true that I've had several phone conversations during our vacation because I want to keep up-to-date on what's happening in St. Anthony and Labrador. I'm in regular contact mainly with Fred. It's so good to hear his voice.

Heidy called twice. After I returned from Labrador, she insisted on spending the night in my guest room because she was so concerned about me. And because Warsame, my household help, has had to clear pushy media types off the property. Apart from that, it was important to Heidy to let me know that Dustin has really found his way back onto the right path.

I was most interested in the forensics report. They had sent it to our team by mistake, though the case files are now in Happy Valley-Goose Bay. The results were surprising and sobering at the same time. No unequivocal, useful evidence of Kellyann could be found on Nielle's snowmobile, though there were other footprints from a woman's boots found near the cabin, apart from Nielle's. But it's still an open question whether they're Kellyann's because we couldn't examine her boots. And the snow around the spot where Nielle was found was trampled down by so many different people. It would have been hard for me to build an airtight case out of all that. Hard, but not impossible. We'd have simply needed more time.

Frank Delgado's case, on the other hand, is richly documented. Boot tracks, fingerprints, even threads from his clothing on Trent's police jacket. What a gold mine. I wonder how the RCMP bosses will take it.

Aretha tears me away from my thoughts.

"What do you think of my new book?"

"I envy you," I reply.

"Why?" She props herself up on her elbows.

"You're writing something many female readers love; they read it with pleasure; it makes them happy, and so they can hardly wait for your next novel."

She pushes her sunglasses up to see if I'm serious.

I'm absolutely serious.

"Basically true." She sinks back in her beach chair, satisfied.

Do I make people happy in my profession? My drink cools me right down to my stomach.

I can see the Nielle Helfrey case more analytically from a

distance. If Kellyann is arrested—I'm not counting on it—Morris Tye might be able to force Noshi to give up the lodge so Tye's brother-in-law can buy it for a song. Noshi and Vyam had rotten luck when the four women foolishly changed their plans, deceived people, risked their lives—all as part of a marketing scheme for an outdoor clothing company. Noshi's life's work was almost destroyed because of it.

Somebody told me—it was David Pelletier, but nobody's to know—that a contract preserved in plastic tubing was recovered from the pocket of one of the dead women, a contract the group members signed with Paige Warner. The document survived the eight years unharmed. It covered exclusive rights for images on Instagram, TikTok videos, Facebook posts, stories on Paige's blog, and so on. Did the women know what they were signing? Too bad that no personal notes or diaries were found.

How far away all that seems right now. Lazing and pleasantly sleepy, I watch the bikinied beauties and Adonises in tiny speedos sashay past. Aretha's taking notes. Writing books takes work.

She'll certainly get a pile of ideas for her main characters. Describing faces isn't easy. I observe it time after time when eyewitnesses have problems remembering details like lips, chin, eye position, eyebrows, forehead.

The straw abruptly drops in my glass.

Details.

Eyebrows.

How could I miss it?

79

Mick Hudson, Reporter for the *Labrador Tribune*
Happy Valley-Goose Bay, Labrador
March 25

The conference hall in the Hotel North is filled to overflowing. Mick takes a little pride in the number of media people from all over Canada who have come to Happy Valley-Goose Bay. It's a home game for him.

Martha Calambaro is sitting beside him—that makes him even happier. He and she find it striking that the special investigators from St. John's and the Happy Valley-Goose Bay RCMP are holding a joint press conference. As if the Delgado case and the missing women had anything to do with each other.

"It's intentional, meant to divide attention between the two cases," Martha said. "*Divide et impera.*"

In response to his questioning look, she explained: "Divide and conquer. They want to confuse the media."

He must make a note of that.

Prior to the conference, a press release was sent around that summarized the special investigator's report in a few sentences.

Mick noted it down, paraphrasing: *Constable Frank Delgado*

had no business being at the crime scene at the cabin. He was not recognizable as a police officer because of his outdoor clothing.

One round was fired from his pistol accidentally. Constable Fred van Heisen is in no way at fault for anything. Calista Gates is a competent and proven police chief.

As Mick sees it, the press release raises more questions than it answers. He would have loved to have heard Martha's opinion, but she's not interested in Delgado, just in the four missing women, three of whom have been found. When he told her five weeks ago that the RCMP Happy Valley-Goose Bay was taking it over exclusively and Calista Gates was pulled off the case, she was pissed.

He gives Martha a sidelong look and can tell from her expression how annoyed she still is. He can empathize. The Nielle Helfrey case will soon be forgotten because nobody's interested in solving it: not Nielle herself, nor Morris Tye, nor the police, who have very different problems in the meantime.

RCMP officials are gathering around the microphones with Inspector Peter Allen in the lead, the special investigators next, a man who's introduced as a geologist, and the RCMP press secretary.

Calista Gates is nowhere to be seen. They will definitely praise her to the skies to divert attention from the rumor that she has been taken off the two cases.

The question period is now open. Mick puts his smartphone on Record and takes notes on the answers in shorthand.

Question: "Why did the search eight years ago never focus on the inukshuk, though it's visible from a good distance?"

Answer: *The inukshuk and the ice pillar are not at the same location. The inukshuk has collapsed and is not visible to the naked eye at a distance. The crevice in the rock that emitted gases is approximately one hundred meters away from the inukshuk in an easterly direction. It is well concealed, in summer too, but particularly in winter under snow cover behind the ice pillar. In addition, one must not forget that we are talking about a huge search area, and the search was intensive by air and on the ground. (Peter Allen)*

Mick adds: *If anybody had found the crevice, his corpse would be lying there.*

Question: "How come nobody knew about those lethal gases until now?"

Answer: *According to our previous knowledge, there was no evidence until now of fumaroles in the Canadian Arctic. These gas emission locations can apparently form constantly anywhere or dry up, a result of activity in the Earth's crust. On the basis of these tragic events, we will be carrying out an extensive geological investigation of the area. (geologist)*

Question: "Where's the fourth woman's body?"

Answer: *We don't know as yet. The most probable explanation is that Sandy Miller did not want to go to Crater Lake with the others because it seemed too dangerous to her, and instead she wanted to go back to the Remote Point Lodge by herself and died on the way when the weather suddenly turned bad. (Peter Allen)*

Question: "Is it possible the fourth woman is still alive?" (Martha's question)

Answer: *We have no credible evidence concerning that. (Peter Allen)*

Question: "Where have the women's backpacks gotten to?" (Martha's question)

Answer: *That investigation is ongoing. (Peter Allen)*

Question: "Why isn't Sergeant Gates here? She found the women, who'd been missing for years, and Gerald Hynes, who'd been missing for days. Why can't she provide any information?" (Martha's question)

Answer: *As you know, Detective Sergeant Calista Gates is stationed in Newfoundland, in St. Anthony. But these investigations are being carried out in Labrador, which is why the RCMP in Happy Valley-Goose Bay is responsible for them. We'd like to thank Sergeant Gates for her admirable dedication.*

Question: "Then why did Constable Delgado show up at a crime scene in St. Anthony when he's stationed in Labrador?" (my question)

Answer: *According to Constable Delgado's statements, he wanted to just say a brief hello to Sergeant Gates. They had worked on the same team earlier in Labrador. (special investigator)*

Question: "Am I correct in assuming that you do not find Constable Delgado's explanation credible?" (my question)

Answer: *We cannot go into that here because of ongoing investigations. (special investigator)*

Question: "Did Constable Delgado fire two shots at Trent Stolke? Why was Stolke wearing a police jacket?" (my question)

Answer: *That is still under investigation. But we can inform you that, according to the medical examiner's report, Trent Stolke died of heart failure.*

Mick scribbles: *Have they found out anything at all?????*

Question: "Where do things stand with Austin Sullivan? There are rumors that Sullivan and Delgado wanted to harm Sergeant Gates." (my question)

Answer: *This is the last answer for you, Mr. Hudson. Other reporters must also have an opportunity to speak. As you probably know, an action has been brought against Constable Sullivan. Therefore, we cannot say anything concerning this. Furthermore, we have no evidence Constable Sullivan's and Constable Delgado's actions were directed at Detective Sergeant Calista Gates. (Peter Allen)*

"And we're supposed to believe that?" Martha Calambaro says it loud enough for everyone in the room to hear.

Mick could have hugged Martha for her parting shot.

80

Detective Sergeant Calista Gates
St. Anthony, Newfoundland
March 25

For several seconds, nobody says anything; everybody just stares at the screen. The headline shines like a neon sign. We were about to rewatch parts of the press conference in Happy Valley-Goose Bay to discuss it. But suddenly that's of no interest anymore.

Labrador Tribune—BREAKING NEWS

RCMP CONSTABLE SUSPECTED IN ST. ANTHONY SHOOTING IS DEAD
Friends found Constable Frank Delgado dead in his home in Port Brendan. A hypodermic needle was found beside the body.
Overdose?
RCMP has not yet confirmed his death.
Full Report Follows

"What the hell!" Dustin shouts, the first one to get a hold of himself.

Fred and I look at each other, thunderstruck.

Heidy throws her pen onto the table with a bang.

"We monitored Delgado in the hospital continuously so he wouldn't do anything stupid—even though we're so short-staffed. Then Happy Valley-Goose Bay takes over, and he's dead!"

"His death isn't confirmed yet," I interject, an automatic response.

"The *Labrador Tribune* wouldn't print something like this if they didn't have reliable sources." Heidy's really outraged. "Why was Delgado at home at all and not in custody if they're investigating him for drug violations? Would somebody please explain *that*!"

That's what I'd like to know, too. Nobody asked the question at the press conference; the media were much more interested in the dead women at Crater Lake.

"Good that it didn't happen when he was here," Dustin says. He looks shaken. "That would have been a catastrophe."

"Now he can't talk," Fred states soberly, though it's a shocking realization.

Delgado can't create any more trouble for Dustin and Fred. But he also can't tell anyone what drove him to commit those crimes. Or who drove him to fire at Fred and aim his weapon at me.

"How did they manage to bring Delgado to the point where he'd com—?" Heidy doesn't finish her sentence. What it would imply is too monstrous.

Such a convenient suicide. If that's what it was.

"Maybe the special investigators discovered things we haven't got a clue about," Fred remarks. "On Delgado's smartphone, for instance. We should have examined it."

I look at him, speechless. Fred can only mean I should have disobeyed orders from St. John's.

In hindsight, he might be right, nevertheless. We're all furious at being sidelined. Rage binds us together.

We should also be relieved, but of course we can't show it openly.

I'd like to talk with Fred alone. He's been avoiding me since I came back from vacation, and he seems more uncommunicative than usual.

The countdown to his inevitable departure is ticking. I still haven't found a replacement for him, though David Pelletier has shown some interest in coming back to St. Anthony. He's not happy in Happy Valley-Goose Bay.

"I need to do a little shopping," I say.

We've got time for such banal things now; nothing's going on in St. Anthony.

Everyone accepts my explanation, but Fred's eyes are following me to the door.

Fred, talk to me, I'd like to say. *Get rid of what's eating you.*

At the same time, I'm afraid of what his answer might be.

Does he suspect I don't just want to shop but have something else in mind? I didn't let on in any way. He'd have to have X-ray vision to know what it was.

81

Fiona Gelp
Amherstburg, Ontario, Canada
Twelve Years Earlier

Fiona opens the porch door with trembling hands. Ann slips into the semidarkness of the kitchen.

"Shhh," she whispers when Fiona begins to sob. Her whole body is shaking.

"What am I to do? What am I to do?" she asks repeatedly.

Ann hugs her tight. "Is he in the bedroom?"

"Yes, in bed. Blood everywhere."

"Where's the gun?"

"Upstairs, in . . . in the bedroom." Fiona's speech is shaky.

Ann takes off her shoes and goes upstairs first.

Fiona sees she's wearing gloves. What's she going to do? She follows her reluctantly. She doesn't want to go to the bedroom again and look at what she's done.

Ann peers through the open bedroom door. She turns on a light. The floor lamp casts a feeble glow into the room. Ann walks over to the bed. Pulls back the covers.

Fiona can only see her sister's face from the side.

She seems to be studying the scene. The blood. The bullet hole in the back of the head. The whole blood-covered mess. She throws the covers back over the body.

"Where's the gun?"

Fiona points to the chair beside the door.

Ann's voice is determined. "We must get rid of your fingerprints."

"But the police . . ."

"Colin got this revolver illegally—he told you that, didn't he?"

"Yes, yes." Colin didn't want to have it traced back to him. Part of his diabolical scheme.

"Get me a rag," Ann says, picking up the revolver.

They go downstairs to the kitchen.

Fiona gets a rag from the cleaning closet.

She watches Ann slowly and carefully wipe the gun.

One hell has ended—the hell with Colin—but a new nightmare has begun.

"What's that?" Ann points to the laptop beside the toaster.

The screen has suddenly lit up.

"The surveillance cameras."

"Are they on?"

Fiona shakes her head. She turned the cameras off so they wouldn't record Ann.

Ann frowns.

"Turn them back on, or it will look suspicious."

The cameras were Colin's idea. The alarm system would have been enough for Fiona.

Currently the alarm is turned off—Colin's orders. Just as he'd ordered her to mention casually to Joe Salomon that she didn't have an alarm system. Colin wanted her to tell Joe in the bar that she needed a new alarm system but didn't have the money. And she was to lead Joe to believe that she'd been living by herself in the house since her divorce. Although Colin and she never married.

"Do you have any pets?" Joe asked immediately when they met.

"No pets," she acknowledged.

She flirted with Joe in the bar. Following Colin's instructions. Flirted energetically. With a convicted sex offender.

"He won't be able to resist you," Colin boasted. "He'll walk right into the trap."

She'd also walked right into a trap in the past. Into Colin Hatterbush's trap. She'd first met him at the yacht club. He was her sailing instructor. She wanted to learn to sail because her deceased parents loved to sail.

Colin was exactly her type: dark, curly hair, athletic, beautiful teeth. Women were all over him. Though she found him too loud at first, too domineering, too vulgar. Besides, she had a boyfriend. So she gave Colin the cold shoulder.

That must have spurred him on. He helped her learn to sail. He encouraged her. Praised her when she made progress. He also stopped drinking so much with the guys at the club bar.

He switched tactics; she realized that later. He showed her the most beautiful corners of the Muskoka Lakes region. She fell in love with him before she could put on the brakes. She'd just turned nineteen.

He wanted her to move in with him at once. Her girlfriends envied her. Even Ann was happy for her. But that changed when Fiona showed up at her place with bruises and makeup over a black eye.

She initially made excuses for her bruises. She once even said the cat was responsible, though she didn't own a cat.

Colin didn't let her have a pet. He also didn't allow her to see Ann.

"She can't stand me," he claimed. "She gets you worked up against me."

She met Ann secretly, fearful of his beatings. And even more so of his guns. He owned several. He taught her how to shoot at the beginning of their relationship. Later, he stopped. Maybe because she had such good aim.

Ann wrapped up the polished gun in the rag and laid it on the counter.

"Was he expecting Joe Salomon today?" she asked, with her eyes on the laptop.

Fiona nodded wordlessly.

"Why today in particular?"

"Because I . . . I had to meet Joe again yesterday. I saw him today riding his bicycle past the house several times."

Ann keeps staring at the screen and what the cameras are recording.

"Joe didn't find out that Colin was living with you?"

"He never said he had suspicions. Colin parks his car farther away and comes into the house through the backyard. We keep the curtains and shutters closed except on the yard side."

"Joe's been scouting out the house. Good." Ann says it as a matter of fact. That's Ann. Pragmatic, judicious, composed. She'd never have gotten mixed up with a guy like Colin. She'd never have shot him out of fear and desperation. Ann's boyfriend doesn't own a gun, just fishing rods.

"Why good?"

"Joe will probably try something today."

Fiona shudders. That's what Colin said too. He ordered her to watch the monitor until late into the night while he was sleeping.

It was clear to her what Colin intended. A man who owns so many guns wants to use them someday.

"Colin wanted to make it look like self-defense," she explained.

"Self-defense." Ann grabs her by the arm. "I don't believe it. Colin wanted you out of the way because you know too much about his true nature, and then he'd pin the murder on Joe. That's why he bought that revolver illegally."

Fiona stared at her sister. Was that possible? Her mind was

screaming for clarity, but her thoughts were racing off in all directions.

"Where can I find Colin's guns?" Ann asks.

"He's locked them up. Except . . ."

"Except what?"

"Except for this revolver. And a Colt he bought today."

"Legally?"

"Yes. At the gun store on Cruise Street."

"Where is it?"

"In the garage. He wanted to shine it up, but instead he watched sports and Westerns in the bedroom. I had to make him a Rusty Nail. I . . . I impulsively added a sleeping powder. I wanted to be free of him and the whole awful plan. When I went upstairs later, the TV was still on. It was so loud that the noise drowned out the shot."

They went through the laundry room and into the garage. They didn't have to look for long. The Colt was lying on a toolbox still wrapped in cloth.

Ann unfolds the cloth. "Where's the ammunition?"

Fiona shudders again. "Why? What are you going to do?"

"We lure Joe into the trap exactly as Colin planned." Ann's voice is icy.

It takes Fiona's breath away.

"How?"

"We frame him for Colin's death. Just let me do it. Joe's death will be purely in self-defense."

Fiona finds the package of ammunition.

Ann slips some cartridges into the Colt and looks at Fiona.

"It's your best chance."

82

Detective Sergeant Calista Gates
St. Anthony, Newfoundland
March 25, Afternoon

The Honda's in front of the house. I drive one street past it, park, and walk back on the icy path. Her car is unlocked. I open the door and sit in the driver's seat. I know her work schedule; it can't be long now.

Maybe she heard or saw me, but she can't very well leave her car to me. She'll get in because she knows what I have to say to her.

And that's how it goes.

She hesitates briefly when she sees me. Then she gets in on the passenger's side.

Her coat looks chic. It could be merino wool or some other expensive material. The wool has a pleasant smell.

She doesn't ask what I want from her. She's well practiced in wariness.

"Your sister did something bad in Goose Cove," I begin. "And that jeopardized your precarious situation as well. But you've probably told her that already."

She says nothing, clutches her leather bag on her lap.

I watch very carefully to see that she's not fiddling with her cell phone. I don't want to be on the record.

"I'm amazed your sister risked that attack on Nielle. She usually does everything to protect you. Maybe she felt too safe after so many years."

I put a hand on the steering wheel and take it off immediately. It's cold in the car. I intend to keep this short.

"I'm not taking any action. You don't have to be afraid of me."

That must stun her. She'll wonder why the police chief doesn't throw her to the wolves. But that must remain unspoken. I can't tell her I won't let any more of my cases get screwed up by outsiders. Or that there are powers within the RCMP that massively and systematically destroy my investigations, trying to drive me to the brink of despair. I can't show her I'm seething inside because dirty tricks were played on me and my team. Above all, I can't explain that I'm fighting against it all with my own means. Means in a gray area I've never employed before.

"I should like you to know what I've concluded," I continue. "I think the fourth woman in the group had planned before the trip to defect at a convenient point. You know I'm talking about Sandy Miller. She mulled everything over carefully, of course, while working at the gas station. A marvelous idea. If somebody gets lost in the wilderness, people will eventually think the person's dead. Sandy's no longer alive. That's how a person can disappear and acquire a new identity."

She doesn't look at me. She doesn't move. Just a flutter of eyelashes.

"Fiona went abroad after the trial and her acquittal and returned to Canada as Sandrine. She had a new name and wanted to be near her sister. She worshipped her sister, who had done so much for her. But then she learned Joe Salomon's family were still pursuing her. They even put a private detective on her. She had to disappear again. But this time she did it so that she couldn't be traced. She had to disappear in the wilds of Labrador. She knew about the Remote Point Lodge through her sister."

She sneezes all of a sudden. It sounds like an explosion.

It's really ice-cold in the car. But I've almost finished my narrative.

"You disappeared from the group, and somebody must have helped you escape. You had your face surgically altered later. Then you found a new life in St. Anthony. Near your sister. But not so close that it might attract attention."

Now my nose starts running. I wipe it with a tissue. Our breath fogs up the windshield.

"Your plan nearly succeeded. You were even able to fool Vyann Kippen. Hats off! But something caught my attention. A detail. You and your sister have the same artificial eyebrows. Microblading it's called, isn't it? The shape of your eyebrows is identical. A thing like that stands out in St. Anthony. That was the clue for me. And the names. Ina from Fiona, who then is Sandy, the abbreviation of Sandrine, and then Trina from Sandrine. Ann Price turns into Kellyann Mercer."

I open the door.

"As I said, I'm the only one who knows for the moment that you are Fiona. I'm not going to do anything. All the best."

As I get out, Trina Modeste still hasn't uttered a word.

It doesn't surprise me. Just one word would have been risky for her. I walk back to my car and start up the motor and the heater.

Trina, alias Sandrine, who calls herself Sandy, alias Ina, alias Fiona, will be looking to begin a new life again somewhere. Maybe under a new name. She'll always be on the run. But she also knows I'm giving her time, or else I'd have outed her long ago.

Martha Calambaro seems to be concentrating now entirely on the RCMP and their problem with Frank Delgado and

Austin Sullivan. That seems to be of more interest to her employers than a twelve-year-old case that was already decided in court. She'll let Inspector Allen know she doesn't appreciate being summarily fobbed off the way she was. Mick Hudson will be useful to her there. Because if news is published in Toronto, he's free to make it public in Happy Valley-Goose Bay.

I go past the stationhouse, leave St. Anthony, and approach the deserted campground where my home is. No media in sight—that's good. They're probably all in Happy Valley-Goose Bay. I quickly take refuge inside. In the warmth, I begin to shiver. As if my body has waited until now to be responsive.

I walk into the kitchen. Something hot will do me good. A chocolate drink. I heat some milk in the steamer until it foams.

Am I no longer a good policewoman? Am I operating in a gray area? Have I crossed a boundary and cannot go back? Has my grief over Gerald changed me so much that I haven't got a handle on myself?

I stir powdered chocolate into the hot milk.

I don't know what happened in Fiona Gelp's house twelve years ago. She was acquitted at trial. She can't be tried for the same crime twice. I know just as little about what happened among the four women in Labrador. Why should I judge Trina Modeste?

I move to the living room with my steaming mug and my cell phone.

I enter the number that I keep secret.

My informant in Vancouver answers. That means the coast is clear.

"I was about to call you," she says. "Things are happening. Caesar and Pontius are leaving. Against their will, so I hear."

That *is* a surprise.

"How'd it come to that?"

"I don't know, but it's about time those people were thrown out."

Caesar and Pontius aren't their real names; my informant

and I are extremely careful when talking to each other. Those two officials stirred up opinion against me in the Vancouver RCMP and did far worse than that.

"It's got something to do with the goings-on where you are," she says.

I had clued her in about Delgado and Sullivan during my Caribbean vacation. The shooting incident rapidly filtered up to RCMP headquarters in Vancouver. But we didn't talk about Gerald. My informant knows when to hold back. A lot has to happen before people like Pontius and Caesar quit unwillingly. Fred's remark comes to mind: *Maybe the special investigators discovered things we haven't got a clue about. On Delgado's smartphone, for instance.*

"Did the special investigators find something on Delgado's phone?" I ask. "Evidence pointing to Caesar and Pontius?"

"You don't have this from me," she replies. "Delgado secretly shadowed you in St. Anthony and reported to certain people."

Wow! In St. Anthony. An RCMP man. And I didn't suspect a thing.

"That's outrageous!" I say. "And the public will probably never hear about it—that's the way it always works with things like this. It will definitely be swept under the rug."

The pressure inside me builds up more and more; my anger too.

A pause at the other end.

"Caesar and Pontius simply believed they were untouchable," she says. "Sometimes it's better not to feel too safe."

"I haven't felt safe for a considerable time now," I say angrily. "It may sound strange, but it toughens me up."

"We're rid of those two," my informer says. "Now it's time for the next ones."

But who are these enemies? The question's hanging there unanswered.

We end the call with no formalities.

I reach for the hot chocolate. Maybe I'll burn my tongue.

So what.

There's a number on my cell phone. It's the number of the highest RCMP official in the country. She's right at the top. When Commissioner Jill Perrier took office, she promised to promote and support women in their ranks. We were given this number as a direct line to her.

I enter it.

An assistant answers.

"Detective Sergeant Calista Gates here. I'd like to speak to Commissioner Perrier. It's urgent."

"What is it about?"

"Threats and violence against RCMP women like me from within our own ranks."

"Commissioner Perrier is in a meeting at the moment. I shall let her know."

Of course. The usual excuse. They'll appease me; they'll refer me to someone who'll palm me off with platitudes.

I'm sitting on the sofa with the chocolate that's as hot as the fire inside me. There should be clouds of smoke coming out of my head like the steam from the cup. It's easier to feel my rage than my pain about Gerald.

Not five minutes go by when my cell phone twitters like a bird.

"Detective Sergeant Gates. Commissioner Perrier here. What can I do for you?"

It's her. *It actually* is *her!*

My surprise is great, but my fury is greater.

I nevertheless choose my words deliberately.

"Commissioner, I am turning to you because I am unprotected in my current posting to such an extent that it cannot go on like this. There are forces within the RCMP who are trying by all available means to get rid of successful policewomen. There is a covert intrigue against me, a regular witch hunt. If these forces succeed, it will discourage capable women from choosing this profession. I must come to a decision."

"It's good that you've called me about this, Sergeant Gates," the commissioner says. "I've been informed about the events in Newfoundland and Labrador. Sergeant, I've been following your career. To my mind, the time actually *is* ripe to make a decision. I have an interesting proposition for you . . ."

EPILOGUE

The snow cover glares in the sunlight.

The dogs are flying weightlessly over the plain.

Tiffany keeps one eye on her team and one eye on the sled.

A lady sits beneath the pelts, the owner of a travel company. She wants to send more tourists to Tulliq.

She couldn't have come on a better day.

This light. This sky.

Almost unearthly.

Relief flows through Tiffany.

The whole thing almost blew up.

"The lady has heard that your last client lost his life at Crater Lake," the hotel manager informed her. "Gerald Hynes. Now she's hesitant about choosing you."

Instant apprehension seized her. Will that haunt her from now on? Will it wreck the reputation and the business she's built?

Then a thought struck her.

She raised her chin.

"Not true. My last assignment was the police chief in St. Anthony. She was very satisfied."

"Calista Gates? Okay," the manager replied. "I'll tell the lady."

Whatever took place, an hour later the trip with her team was firmly booked.

The dogs are running in unison as if gliding on rails.

The white hills on the horizon shine like a promise.

She rejoices.

Things are moving ahead for you, Tiff. By leaps and bounds.

AFTERWORD

One of my most memorable trips took me to the legendary crater lake in the Pingualuit National Park in the Canadian province of Québec. Like Crater Lake in this book, it was created by a meteorite crashing to earth over a million years ago, and the lake is almost perfectly round. You can even see it from space. Unlike the crater in *Cold Dread*, it is not in Labrador but in the northern part of Québec in the Inuit territory of Nunavik. Pingualuit National Park is administered by Inuit, more precisely, by the Katavik Regional Government. Inuit women and men guided me to the crater lake and on hikes in the area. The landscape is characterized by an almost mystical, spare beauty that stayed with me after the trip.

I drew my inspiration for this novel from that stay in Pingualuit National Park. However, people and events in *Cold Dread* are completely fictitious; they have nothing to do with my experiences in Nunavik. I enjoyed wonderful, impressive days there that I recall time and again, filled with amazement and delight. Here's a link to the national park website for those who want to know more about it:

https://www.nunavikparks.ca/fr/parcs/pingualuit

In Labrador, you can find smaller crater lakes such as the

circular Mistastin Lake Impact Crater, which was also formed by a meteorite.

I mention in *Cold Dread* the Nunatsiavut Regional Government that administers the imaginary Ilungilak crater in the northeast of Labrador. This existing Inuit government was created in 2005; the administration is located in Nain but has nothing at all to do with the fictitious events in this novel.

Port Brendan, Ilungilak, Tulliq, Alliarkuk, Sivinganik, Camp Pinnacle, and Poqii Lake, are invented places, even if many of them were inspired by real localities. Tulliq is based on the Inuit settlement of Nain but very loosely. On the other hand, Goose Cove, St. Anthony, St. Anthony Bight, St. Carol's, Roddickton, Englee, Corner Brook, Main Brook, Happy Valley-Goose Bay and St. John's actually exist; they are situated in Newfoundland, except for Happy Valley-Goose Bay, which is on the east coast of Labrador.

I came across a rather old newspaper article in the *Vancouver Sun* about the phenomenon of fumaroles. It describes holes in the ground in northern British Columbia through which volcanic fumes exit and where bear bones were found, among other things. It immediately captured my imagination, and I researched it some more. The picture of a gigantic ice pillar that formed from rising steam on the volcanic Mount Erebus in the Antarctic has stayed in my head ever since. A human figure looks like an ant beside it. As far as I know there are no fumaroles in the Labrador subarctic because there's no volcanic activity. I've taken poetic license to transplant fumaroles into northern Labrador. But please don't expect to find fumaroles or those ice pillars there.

ACKNOWLEDGMENTS

It is always a great relief to be able to ask questions of experts who know their field inside out. Garry Rodgers—a former RCMP homicide detective and coroner, now retired—enlightened me about many aspects of police investigating and patiently replied to my emails. He's also an internationally successful crime writer and has an interesting blog https://dyingwords.net.

Boris Kutzer, in Ingenried, Bavaria, gave me valuable information on snowmobiles, particularly about the tracks skis leave in snow (his website: www.motor-schlitten.de).

I took vitally important information on sled dogs from two books, among others: Blair Braverman's *Welcome to the Goddamn Ice Cube: Chasing Fear and Finding Home in the Great White North* and *Mit meinen Hunden: 6000 Kilometer durch Sibirien, China und die Mongolei* (*With My Dogs: 6000 Kilometers through Siberia, China, and Mongolia*) by Nicolas Vanier.

Over the past twenty years I've visited settlements and destinations in Inuit territories and come in contact with the people there. I don't pretend to understand Inuit and their culture thoroughly. But I have tried to depict them as authentically as possible, neither inflating nor trivializing them, nor portraying them as one-dimensional or naïve. I hope I've achieved that respectfully.

When I finish writing and hand the manuscript over to other hands for the first time, I feel rather vulnerable. But it's infinitely important to have an outside critical opinion. I place this confidence in my beta readers, and every time I'm dazzled by how well they master the assignment. Filled with admiration, I thank Irene Zortea, Helen Radu, Hans Kurth, Karl Uhr, Beny Affolter, Susanne Keller, Ruth Omlin, Klaus Uhr, Gisela Dalvit, and Koni Frehner for their effort and engagement.

Readers who have long known my books are aware that I've worked for years with the editor Gisa Marehn because her skills are impressive. With every book, I look forward to her returning my manuscript because I know it's become so much better. Many heartfelt thanks, Gisa Marehn.

My translator, Gerald Chapple, has again given me the gift of gifts and delivered a beautiful, highly accomplished version of the original novel. It is such a joy to see that nothing was "lost in translation"; on the contrary, it has gained a shiny, new luster. Thank you, Jerry!

Many thanks to my proficient copy-editor Lindsey Alexander who did a marvelous job making this text smooth as a pearl in a mussel shell.

A shout-out to my proofreaders Michele Hodder, Maureen Matteson, Paula Dunn and Cheryl Shoji. You did an excellent job which means so much to me.

My thanks also go out to Tatiana Vila for cover design and Inca Vogt for book interior design. Inca is very versatile and writes suspenseful thrillers www.inca-vogt-autorin.com.

I consider myself lucky that my mystery thrillers have found fantastic readers. Many of you write to me or publish reviews; you read and respond to *Bernadette's Letter* or chat with me on social media. I've so much to thank you for, you're a steady source of delight, stimulation, and amazement.

When I begin my next new story, you will be with me in the room.

Bernadette Calonego
Newfoundland, November 2024

P.S. If you enjoyed *Cold Dread*, then I'd be hugely thrilled by a review/rating on Amazon or another platform like LovelyBooks, Facebook, Instagram, GoodReads, or TikTok. That support would be invaluable to me. Your feedback doesn't have to be a long essay; a short, spontaneous, quite personal evaluation can have a great effect.

I am active on social media (Facebook, Instagram, TikTok). I also write a blog on my website and send *Bernadette's Letter* bimonthly to those who sign up for it on my homepage (www.bernadettecalonego.com/eng). In my newsletter you will learn a lot about life in Canada, my experiences in Newfoundland and Labrador, and about books and movies and interesting facts I've tracked down in my reading.

Do follow me on Amazon as well by clicking on the *Follow* button on my author page.

You can also reach me by email:

info@bernadettecalonego.com. I will write back quickly.

No matter how you stay in contact with me—by reading, writing, clicking, or reviewing—I appreciate any and all interaction!

Greetings from Newfoundland and many good wishes to you.

Yours,
Bernadette Calonego

ABOUT THE AUTHOR

Bernadette Calonego has published thirteen German books, eleven of them crime novels that almost all take place in Canada; ten have been translated into English. Originally from Switzerland, she has lived for more than twenty years in Canada, splitting her time between the Vancouver area and Newfoundland; she now lives in northern Newfoundland where her bestseller *Stormy Cove* and most volumes of the Detective Calista Gates series are set. Her nonfiction book *Oh, wie schön ist Kanada!* found a spot on the *Spiegel* bestseller charts while her Calista Gates thrillers appeared on the German BILD most-bought books list. Recently, Bernadette Calonego published a travel guide to the Canadian province of Newfoundland and Labrador. She made a name for herself as a foreign correspondent for many well-known newspapers, such as the *Süddeutsche Zeitung* in Munich, *Der Standard* in Vienna, and *Tages-Anzeiger* in Zurich. She has earned a reputation as an author of mystery thrillers inspired by the Canadian wilderness and her adventures in the untamed North of her adopted homeland Canada.

More about Bernadette Calonego can be found at:

facebook.com/Bernadettecalonego.Author

instagram.com/bernadettecalonegoauthor

tiktok.com/@bernadettecalonegoauthor

ABOUT THE TRANSLATOR

Gerald Chapple is an award-winning translator of German literature. He received his doctorate from Harvard and went on to teach German and comparative literature at McMaster University in Hamilton, Ontario. He has been translating contemporary German-language authors for fifty years. His prose translations include Michael Mitterauer's history of Europe from 600 to 1600, *Why Europe? Medieval Origins of Its Special Path*, and Anita Albus's *On Rare Birds*. He has translated nine of Bernadette Calonego's novels. The most recent, *Cold Dread*, appeared in 2024 as the fifth novel in her series featuring Detective Sergeant Calista Gates. The poems of Günter Kunert have been the focus of his many poetry translations. He lives in Rhinebeck, New York, with his wife, Nina, an architectural historian, his children, and grandchildren. When not translating, he can usually be found studying birds, butterflies, and dragonflies or reading, wrestling with a garden, and listening to classical music.

BOOKS

BY BERNADETTE CALONEGO

The Zurich Conspiracy

Under Dark Waters

Stormy Cove

The Stranger on the Ice

Murderous Morning

Cries from the Cold

A Dark Chill

Bay of Evil

Missing in the Dark

Cold Dread

Made in the USA
Las Vegas, NV
12 April 2025

20866350R00256